THE VISCOUNT
ST ALBANS

THE VISCOUNT ST ALBANS

LOVE IN NETHERFORD VOLUME II

NATANIA BARRON

SOLARIS

First published 2025 by Solaris
an imprint of Rebellion Publishing Ltd,
Riverside House, Osney Mead,
Oxford, OX2 0ES, UK

www.solarisbooks.com

ISBN: 978-1-83786-445-4

A CIP catalogue record for this book is available
from the British Library.

Designed & typeset by Rebellion Publishing

To those who fight for love against impossible odds.
Spoiler: Love wins.

CHAPTER ONE
THE VISCOUNT IN THE SOUTH WING

WHEN SILAS DRAKE, Viscount St. Albans, inherited his title, he had not anticipated managing an outbreak of vampires as part of his daily duties. Nor that he would have one within the walls of his home, the newly renovated and much coveted Burkley House. Nestled in the middle of eighty acres of quaint woodlands bursting with game and flora, the great house was the largest and most modern for miles around, and certainly the talk of most of nearby Netherford. No detail had been overlooked, no expense spared, and it stood like a sprawling Hellenistic monument in its warm, marble glory.

This was his inheritance, his legacy, a vision spanning generations.

In his mind, Silas had traced his future with the firm and confident hand of a storied poet—which he was—moving swiftly toward the culmination of his greatest composition.

He ought to have been writing the sequel to *The Lady of the Lost Kingdom*, his novel series about the daring and beautiful Lady Sibylle Voltairis, which he published under the *nom de plume* of D. B. Mansfield. His editor, Thomas Winmore of Hecate Press on Leadenhall Street in London, had already written twice in the last week alone to inquire about the next edition. Yet, his manuscript remained slim and avoided. Only Mr. Winmore, his closest friend and cousin Roland de Grateloup, and his valet Fintan knew of his alternate identity. If his great aunt ever discovered he had built the family fortune back with a career as quotidian as novel-writing, she would disinherit him forthwith. She believed that, after gentlewitches and preternaturals in general, novels were the harbinger of the end of polite noble society.

And indeed, the further irony of his life remained the stark contrast between his fortunate, celebrated existence, and the half-mad vampire living under his roof. As if that scribe of fate had simply forgotten to let the ink dry on the last few lines and smudged the end to incomprehensible gibberish.

She was not just *any* vampire, of course. She was Viola Brightwell. And Silas had once been hopelessly in love with her.

He was fairly certain that remained the case, but she did not want anything to do with him. She also screamed, tore at the walls and curtains, tried to eat his aunt's cat, and moaned through most evenings in a most unladylike way that was both terrifying and, if Silas was honest, sometimes strangely arousing.

Ophelia Byrne, a rather scandalous vampire herself, had been in and out of Burkley House to assist with Viola's transformation as much as she could manage. She, along with Petronilla Rookwood-Nourse—a gentlewitch of American persuasion related to the Gentlewitch of Netherford, Liege Edith Rookwood—provided protection when needed.

However, it had been three months since Viola's transformation, and she was still no more manageable than she had been when she'd left.

It was all quite untenable.

Silas sat at his desk, unable to focus on any of the mountain of correspondence before him, when he heard a soft knock on the door.

Fintan opened the door. Though he was older even than Silas's father, Silas's valet cut an impressive figure in his pristine black suit and red satin sash. Once, Silas's mother had commented that Fintan may have had a streak of the fae in him, given his perpetual youthfulness. Indeed, though his hair was a moonlight silver hue, his noble, elegant face had remained little changed in all the years Silas had known him.

"My lord, Liege Edith Rookwood and her companion, Miss Brightwell, are here to see you," Fintan said. He narrowed his haunting, violet eyes just slightly. "They are half an hour early."

Silas stood, wiping his fingers on a handkerchief. He did not worry overmuch when it came to appearances and Liege Rookwood. Although she came from an old house, she and her companion were far from formal. Indeed, they had the comfortable ease of friends, now, drawn together by their love of Viola Brightwell.

"Please, show them to the receiving room. I will be there presently."

Fintan nodded and slipped away, leaving Silas to gather himself. The thick, relentless heat of August meant that even a short jaunt to the receiving room left him rather sweaty, and in his haste, he forgot he was carrying an ink-stained handkerchief.

He'd wiped his brow with it.

This, he did not realise, until his aunt, the Dowager Viscountess St. Albans—who was not expected in the receiving room—let out a choked noise and gestured to his face.

Fintan came scrambling to the rescue, and Silas had to swat him away to get through to his guests.

"Welcome to Burkley House, Liege Rookwood," Silas said, bowing low. "As always."

Liege Rookwood rose from the green velvet chair she'd been sitting upon and bowed in turn. She was a tall, pale, freckled woman, favouring masculine fashion and frippery, with short, russet hair, and clever, dark blue eyes. Her companion, wearing a profusion of muslin in a lemon-yellow hue that contrasted beautifully with her warm brown skin, was more diminutive, composed of a pleasing plumpness. Miss Brightwell wore her tight curls up in an elegant bun, though errant wisps tried their best to escape it. Like her sister, Viola, Poppy had deep brown eyes and black hair. But where Poppy was rounded, Viola was lean and lithe. They shared the same full mouth and high brow.

Silas could not help but push down that ever-present wave of longing inside of him, seeing these two together. They had such a comfortable, loving connection, even through their recent trials.

"St. Albans," said Liege Rookwood, "I appreciate you seeing us on such short notice."

"Short notice, indeed. You weren't due for another half hour. But Molineaux here did not mind the company," the dowager viscountess said, arranging the yellow-eyed tabby on her lap.

"My pleasure, to be sure," Silas said, taking Miss Brightwell's hand and kissing it gently. She smelled of jasmine and sunshine. "I suppose you are here to discuss Miss Brightwell—Viola, I mean."

"In a sense," said Poppy Brightwell, resuming her seat and taking her companion's hand. "We have decided to spend the rest of the Season in London. Given we have had such little progress with Viola, I hoped to find someone there who might offer us additional assistance whilst Edith is attending to gentlewitch business."

"London?" Silas asked. "I suppose that is the most expected course of action. You may find some people willing to come to our aid, or at least get a bit of a respite. Especially you, Miss Brightwell."

Liege Rookwood went very still, as she sometimes did, as if her whole body had to remain unmoving for her thoughts to properly align themselves. And perhaps they did. "Yes, well, it is for that very reason we have chosen to go. Though it makes Poppy anxious to leave Netherford Hall. I have made her a necklace with a bit of the glass from the house, and this seems to keep her settled when we're at a long distance, which is a good beginning. But Viola's state has weighed too heavily on us, and London, and its fashion and frenzy, will be good for us."

Poppy gazed adoringly at her companion, fingering the aforementioned necklace. "It has taken some convincing, but it is for the best."

"Of course," Silas agreed. He hadn't thought of it that way, but then again, he rather disliked the company of people in the city these days. It was here, in the country, where he preferred his solitude. After a decade in Paris, he felt as if he had flushed city life from his mind almost entirely. A shame, though, that it could not last.

"Though the whole idea of leaving Viola here makes me ill," Miss Brightwell said, glancing toward the main entry as if her sister might appear at any moment's time. "Mama is not too keen on it either, but even she admits there's little we can do to help."

Only Poppy remained brave enough to visit Viola. Silas was beginning to think the family might be giving up on her.

"Well, she cannot stay here indefinitely," the dowager viscountess said, more to the cat than to anyone else. "We do have a life to lead, and the viscount must marry soon, and wisely. Having someone in such a condition in the house will only be a detriment to our standing in society."

Silas recoiled inwardly at his aunt's tone. Ever since Viola's transformation, the mere idea of marrying anyone else made him feel nauseated. As if the house itself was no longer built upon solid ground, the windows made of candy floss and everything poised to come tumbling down around him. It was not a sensation he was accustomed to in the least.

"Our standing in society can take a few more blows, Aunt May," Silas said as smoothly as he could, though he was concerned he might have to choke back his own bile. "Remember, Viola did spend years tending to you when you were ill. We can at least commit to keeping her until the end of autumn."

"That is quite kind of you, my lord," said Miss Brightwell, unable to keep the tears from her eyes. "I am indebted to you, indeed. My greatest hope is that we shall find some answers, and then we will not have to presume upon your kindness any longer."

Liege Rookwood continued when her companion's voice faltered. "One of our Warders, Basil, has told us of an apothecary in London known to attend to some of the more curious ailments among our kind, in Spitalfields."

"Ah, you must mean Culpeper's," Silas said, quicker than he ought to have. He really needed more sleep.

"Culpeper's," the dowager countess snorted. "No society-conscious individual in their right mind would consider darkening *that* doorstep."

Poppy Brightwell straightened her spine and looked down her nose at the old woman. "Which is why *I* will be attending, and not the gentlewitch. Unlike my companion, I have no marital or family ties to the city. And Molly Hode will accompany us. Basil can stay behind and tend to the needs of the house while we're gone."

"I will also be consulting with the staff at De Laune's, the apothecary in Blackfriar's with whom you are no doubt familiar," said Liege Rookwood. "Or so, at least, they have indicated a comfortable knowledge of Burkely House in their letters to me."

The dowager viscountess said nothing at that, turning her lace-strewn head away from the tide of the conversation as if she hadn't heard a thing.

"It's been some time now since apothecaries have risen in the world, you know," Silas said. "Though there are plenty of charlatans, still. Either way, I do wish you the best of luck. Would that I could accompany you both, but I fear my duties here at Burkley House preclude me from London adventures at present."

Silas knew a great deal about apothecaries, in truth, through his best friend and cousin, Roland de Grateloup. But his knowledge mostly extended to Paris, of course, given all his years spent there at school and in other pursuits best left undiscussed in present company.

"I've contemplated visiting Viola again. Before we leave," Poppy said, wringing her hands nervously. "But given how our last meeting went, I think it best to wait until we have a way to calm her more reliably."

The gentlewitch took her companion's fretful hands and, in an unusual show of outward affection, kissed her fingers. Indeed, if one looked closely, the bruises from Viola's last attack upon her sister were still visible about her neck. Of all her visitors, Poppy agitated Viola the most. Much to Poppy's distress.

Strangely, Viola had never attacked Silas directly. Sometimes, she fell asleep in his presence after hissing and screaming, which Ophelia told him was a most curious circumstance; she attributed it to a sense of trust, buried among Viola's violent distress.

"Miss Byrne believes Viola's greatest chance is in finally accepting her fate," Silas reminded them. "I don't know if any poultice or brew would assist in that, but for now we will continue to help her toward her future fate. I am uncertain as to how long this state will continue—not just for her benefit, but for those of us awaiting her decision."

"She is lucky to have a guardian in you," Miss Brightwell said softly. "Vampires are relatively rare, and sadly there is little literature of medicine to rely on. But if I can find anything, I will."

Silas did truly admire Miss Brightwell. He found himself swallowing on an unexpectedly thick throat as she proclaimed her intent for her sister. "I have no doubt about that," he said. "And, on my oath, I will keep her in as much comfort and peace as I can."

NEITHER COMFORT NOR peace were on the docket for that evening, alas. Like so many days before, Viola remained in a deathlike slumber until just after tea. The moaning began first, then the shrieking. Ophelia was late, and Petronilla was away on family business, so Silas was left to reinforce the doors to Viola's quarters with the help of the staff while they waited. He had already needed to replace the thick, oaken doors twice; this third, iron-fortified door would be far more at home in a medieval dungeon than a modern manse like Burkley.

Once, he had tried visiting Viola alone, and for that he now boasted a scar down the length of his right forearm where she had raked him with her long, silver nails. If Petronilla hadn't arrived when she did, prepared with both spells and other repelling techniques, Silas might not have made it out alive.

Yet, he could have sworn Viola recognised him in that moment. That was just before she tried to flay his skin, of course. But given all the blood and his own screaming, he hadn't had time to reflect or respond appropriately.

When Ophelia Byrne finally arrived, she came with an unexpected guest: her brother Laertes. Since the incident with the Boagane, the other Byrne sibling had been conspicuously absent. Which was curious. Of the two vampires, he was the outgoing one, prone to gossip and dramatics.

"I apologise for my tardiness, but I finally coerced Laertes out of Howarth Castle. And for good reason. I think I may have puzzled out a mystery at last," Ophelia said, her deep blue velvet dress catching the candlelight as she strode toward Silas.

Silas could not linger long on Ophelia's form, for though she was always striking, it was Laertes who caught his attention for the sheer shock of his presentation. The vampire was thin and wan, his already pallid skin waxy and grey. His hair, that vampire black so dark it did not reflect light, was unkempt and bedraggled. And his waistcoat wasn't even buttoned correctly.

Ophelia's nostrils flared slightly as she beheld her brother. "As you can see, my lord, Laertes is not well."

"Is it—catching?" Silas knew the question was ridiculous, but then he knew of some diseases passed from werewolves to humans, and he didn't think Viola could endure another inconvenience.

"Alas, no," Laertes croaked, his clear and musical voice barely recognisable. "It seems unique to me."

Ophelia did not withhold the look of disgust on her face as she beheld her brother. Clearly there was more to their dispute than this mere difficulty with Viola. "Laertes took some of Viola's blood before she was turned. This, he did not inform me of until very recently. After months of trying to understand why my own spawn would not bend to my commands or react to my presence, it just now occurred to him that his actions might have impacted us—only when his health began to deteriorate as a result."

Laertes sniffed, petulant as a school child. "My sister speaks as if she is well-versed in the art and study of turning vampires, but she is not. Neither of us are. Indeed, despite our centuries-long existence, we have never even contemplated expanding our family."

Silas's patience was wearing thin. And as ridiculous as the Byrne siblings seemed, he knew well enough not to allow them to lull him into a state of comfort. They were still predators. Idiotic predators, but predators nonetheless. Given Laertes had tried, unsuccessfully, to feed off Poppy just before the fight with the Boagane, he worried Viola might have been taken advantage of.

"I apologise, but I require a little more clarity on the matter," Silas said. "If you drank from Viola without her consent…"

"I most certainly did not," Laertes said crossly. He had to steady himself against the door, shuddering as a wave of discomfort went through him. "But she demanded I take her back to Netherford Hall in the midst of that most tumultuous evening. I had no strength in me to do so and was without a supplier. Viola agreed, and then later, drank from Ophelia in the fracas."

"This is all very untoward," Silas muttered, wishing he could escape this most scandalous conversation.

Ophelia shrugged her round, lace-covered shoulders. "Well, it is simple vampire biology, my lord. If Laertes had been clear with me on the matter, I would have been able to determine the issue far earlier. For it seems, as strange as it may be, that Viola is a spawn to us both. I turned her, but she and Laertes were bonded in blood at her time of mortal death. That means we are equally responsible for her care and, as you can see, equally subject to the consequences of neglecting it."

"So, you believe Laertes is ill because Viola is also his spawn," Silas said.

"Well, I do. My theory is quite sound. But we shall know within moments. He has been falling more and more ill since the incident, and I thought it was merely depression or a reaction to finding a new food supply."

"I hate drinking sheep," Laertes moaned, leaning his clammy head on the door jamb. "They leave such an unpleasant aftertaste."

CHAPTER TWO
THE VAMPIRE IN THE NORTH WING

VIOLA HAD BEEN breathing ash and fire for so long that when she caught a gasp of cool, fresh air, for a moment she thought death might have finally claimed her. Stars knew she had prayed for it, willed herself into an oblivion of melancholic surrender if only to free herself of the clutches of this abominable pain.

She remembered glimpses of faces, now and again, especially the vampire woman—Ophelia?—and the witch whose aura was a conflagration. The rest was rage. Such complete, unadulterated rage, she forgot ever feeling anything else. The rage was pain, and the pain was rage, and all she wished was an end to it all. For what point was there living—if this was living at all—if the only sensation she knew was the burning, aching, endless agony?

To say nothing of how it felt to see the other woman, the one with a face she knew and yet could do nothing but hate, and mourn, and scream at.

And the tall man.

But she did not want to think about that man.

Flinching, Viola felt a cool hand on her brow and, despite herself, leaned into it. The pressure of a gentle hand on her shoulder followed, along with a slow, steady lessening of pain, and the murky film over her eyes lifted, strand by strand, until she could see clearly.

All but the colour she remembered in the world. Gone were blues and yellows and greens. All that remained was grey, with shades of red.

"Viola, do you know me?"

The man's voice was low, tinged with a brogue, but the effect was soothing. Viola turned to face him and, to her surprise, recognition registered deep in the abyss of her mind.

Laertes Byrne. A vampire. Handsome, but even paler than a vampire ought to be.

"I do," Viola said, her voice dry and cracked. The effort alone caused her to cough painfully. Laertes provided a blackwork patterned handkerchief, and Viola took it gratefully.

Her hands were clawed: silver talons curved from the tips of her once-delicate fingers. The realisation sent a pang of terror through her body, and she curled in on herself beneath the damp sheets, closing her eyes shut—as if not seeing what she had become would somehow undo it.

"Yes, you are a vampire," said the other person in the room. Ophelia. "Just like Laertes, just like me. The claws on your fingers can be managed with time and effort, but the important thing is for you to focus on *us* now, darling."

"I am a monster," Viola rasped, peeking through her snarled hair.

"And so are we." Ophelia reached over to tidy Viola's shift, the motion surprisingly comforting. "I couldn't figure out what was holding you back until I went back over what happened again and again. Now I understand."

"What happened?" Viola asked, looking around the room. It was the most beautiful room she had ever seen, new and clean and gleaming. She only wished she could see the other hues. The sun peeking through the thick curtains made her eyes water and she had to look away.

"What is the last thing you remember?" Ophelia asked.

Viola pressed her hands to her chest. She could feel her bones beneath. She couldn't remember the last time she ate food, and yet the mere thought of bread or cheese made her stomach turn.

"I remember convincing Mr. Byrne to take me to Netherford," Viola said, after a moment.

"And he drank your blood in return," Ophelia said, not hiding the disdain in her voice.

Viola looked at Laertes, taking in his handsome features one by one. She felt something stir inside her when she did, a kind of kindling connection. It was not love or attraction that she could tell; rather, it was a recognition from soul to soul. If such a thing still existed inside of her.

"I offered," Viola replied, reaching for Laertes' hand. Without hesitation, he gave it to her, as if compelled to do so beyond his own desire. "He was very tired and did not think he could make the flight without it. My sister had drained him, earlier." She gasped, memories cutting through her. "Poppy—where is she?"

Before she could ask, Laertes assured her, "Your sister is alive and well, living at Netherford Hall with the gentlewitch."

"Though she's since gone to London," Ophelia added.

"I should have died there," Viola said, knowing it was true. "I did *die* there. The beast—the Boagane—it threw me against the wall and I died."

"You drank my blood," Ophelia said. "So it wasn't as easy as that. You were so brave, and we could not leave you."

"We would have had to kill you if we didn't turn you," Laertes said, rubbing the back of Viola's hand as if she were a precious, delicate jewel. As if he cherished her. "And that would have been a horror neither of us could have endured."

Viola pulled her hand back, not unkindly, but firmly. "I hardly knew you. My death would have been no pain."

Ophelia glanced toward the door a moment, but Viola could not see anyone lingering there, though she had thought she felt a presence. Then the vampire sat down on the edge of Viola's large bed, smoothing the intricate brocade coverlet with her small, delicate hands.

"We are taught that when a person dies with vampire blood in their body, they do not truly expire. Their soul is extinguished, leaving behind a shade in its place—a sort of impression of a soul. Like a shadow before a windowpane." Ophelia spoke slowly, carefully, measuring Viola with her arresting stare. "In that state, there are two options. One, to become a revenant, untethered to the true soul and bent upon death and destruction. A true monster with no reason, no mind beyond the gathering of food, and no capacity to love. Second: to become our spawn."

A revenant! Viola had heard stories before but had no idea that was how they were made. During the Coven Wars, when vampires revolted against the Empire in France, revenants had run wild through the English army, destroying battalions with astonishing strength. Some of the vampire lords were accused of raising revenant armies to terrify the enemies on the front. Rumour had it they fed on the dead and tortured their captives before doing unspeakable things to their bodies.

Laertes nibbled on his lower lip like a concerned child, then he shuddered. "Becoming a revenant would have put this whole town at risk, and certainly the viscount and everyone involved. Having to kill you would have also caused us each great pain, for though revenants are not full vampires, they are still part of us."

"I have been so hungry here, in the dark," Viola whispered. "Was I becoming a revenant?"

"No," Ophelia replied sweetly. "No, my darling, you were not. You were simply going through the pains Laertes spoke of, but due to the fact you have a full set of vampire parents, as it were. Laertes drank your blood, so when you were separated from your soul, he cleaved to it still; then, when I fed you again, which I pray you never remember, you became bonded to me. Laertes was suffering as well, and I did not think to consider it was related until just recently."

So, Viola had two vampire parents. What on earth would Mama say? "I feel so much more clear-headed. Hungry, still, but... I believe I may have lost myself for a time."

"You may yet. Becoming a vampire is a complex business." Ophelia produced a small book from her velvet pockets, bound in gold and embossed red leather. It shone to Viola's eyes like a great, rubied wonder. "Ours was a time far less civilised than now. We were born to vampires, not made, or so we were told. And our family, our ancestors, are all gone. So, I'm afraid we will have to walk side by side together."

"You were born?" Viola could scarcely believe the words. "Born of vampires?"

Ophelia nodded, turning the book over in her hands. "It does not happen any longer, or rarely. Our numbers were reduced so drastically over the last three centuries, most new vampires were created for ill-conceived purposes, or else out of malice. Strictly speaking, your existence is... well, *illegal*."

It was enough to push her off the edge of emotion. Viola buried her head in the pillows, breathing in the soft rose-petal sweetness as tears filled her eyes and flowed. Someone rubbed her back as she wept, but she still felt terribly alone. She understood why they kept her alive, and the risk they were taking to keep her as their spawn. Her parents had taught her well to be grateful for such unexpected kindnesses. And yet she could not help but feel overwhelming grief. This was not the life she had planned for.

At least Poppy was alive. At least she was happy. That would have to be enough for now.

When Viola sat back up, she looked down at her pillow to see she had shed tears of blood.

Two DAYS PASSED, and although she had moments of disconnected despondency, Viola was improving. Though she did not remember, she had been drinking a large amount of sheep's blood, and it was not so terrible as she might have imagined. More than anything, it made her feel better, sharper, more like herself. The Byrnes insisted that feeding on blood was the way to connect her soul across the planes, to keep her human aspects within close reach. And, indeed, the more she drank blood, the less she experienced bouts of that oppressive madness.

But she did not *want* to be a vampire. The best she could do was try and pretend she could still be Viola Brightwell.

She had dressed and washed with Ophelia's help and agreed to go sit in one of the parlours in the north wing of Burkley House, though not after some considerable convincing. Viola was terrified to see the viscount again, feeling increasingly guilty for upending his life so terribly. The Byrnes had invited her back to Howarth Castle, which was built for vampire comforts: thick drapes, fresh blood, and the best wallpaper money could buy. But it was some distance from Netherford, and she liked the idea of being close to her family should she regain her composure long enough.

Petronilla Rookwood-Nourse, it turned out, was Viola's first visitor besides the vampire siblings. The witch no longer looked as if she was crowned in flame, now that Viola's eyes had cleared, and was instead again a small, birdlike woman with austere curls and a fine nose.

Viola was terribly embarrassed how little she could remember of one of the people responsible for keeping her alive during her most turbulent days.

"I'm glad we can finally meet," Petronilla said, sitting across from Viola. She smelled of woodsmoke and flux.

"You have my profound thanks," Viola said, trying to still her trembling hands. Despite all her changes as a fledgling vampire, calming her nerves still seemed as difficult as it ever was. Perhaps even more so. "I am afraid I do not recall much of our exchanges, but you had little reason to offer me such kindness and guidance."

Petronilla smiled, her eyes softening at Viola's admission. "My dear, there are few as experienced in the ways of vampires as I am. And my magical predilections make me particularly suited to work with you."

"I do not wish to hurt anyone," Viola said. "And you have given up so much of your time assisting me—but I am uncertain I am yet safe to be around."

"Oh, nonsense. I have worked with vampires for decades, now. When I lived in America, I worked closely with the local families to pass laws providing them protection and rights whenever possible. As you know by now, there are few left in the world, and those who remain are often the target of considerable alienation, not to say the most heinous crimes."

If Viola had blood to spare, she might have flushed in response. Instead, she only felt the gnawing bite of unease in her stomach. "I was not aware of such happenings in America."

"People think it's limited to the smaller towns out west. But, in Massachusetts, the great coven capital, that's where some of the most egregious injustices have happened. And there is a long, shameful history my ancestors were in no small part responsible for."

"Lady Rookwood-Nourse has a remarkable history of fighting for those less fortunate than herself," came a man's voice from the enormous doors leading to the hall.

Silas Drake, Viscount St. Albans, stood there, his strong frame silhouetted in sunlight, the carefully arranged tight curls atop his head flashing almost red to Viola's gaze.

Her heart, which once beat so furiously, now pounded steadily and loud, and she staggered most inelegantly to her feet. It was the kind of motion she would have once chided Poppy for, but given her audience, Viola could not keep her wits or actions about her.

"My lord," she said, averting her eyes. She hadn't had the heart to ask what state he had last seen her in, but she knew she had been indisposed.

He was still so very handsome, just as much as upon their first meeting at the Holly and Sickle. His hazel eyes, though, beneath his beautiful brow, looked older than she remembered, possessed of a sadness that stole her breath.

"Miss Brightwell." He took a step closer and then stopped, his hand balling into a fist momentarily. "I regret I did not see you earlier, but I admit you look quite refreshed."

"I am changed," she said. "But I am not dead, and I have you and Miss Rookwood-Nourse to thank. Along with the Byrnes, of course."

"I assure you, I need no thanks. The unfortunate circumstances of your situation were quite beyond any of us. And given all you did for my aunt for so many years—this house is more familiar to you than it is to me, I suppose," Silas said.

Viola looked around for a sign of the Byrnes as a chill crept over her, a deep, unrelenting self-consciousness. She wanted to hide, to get as far away from Silas as she could. How could he even *look* at her in this condition? How could he say a single word of kindness when she was such a wretch? He was so poised. Acting so maddeningly normal.

"I'm afraid I have imposed on your kindness for far too long, my lord. I have spoken with the Byrnes, and they've told me Howarth Castle is far more amenable to those in my condition. I would not be indebted to you any longer," she said. For reasons she could not fathom, her lips were throbbing. But not in time to her own heartbeat.

Silas looked troubled at her words, and shifted from one foot to another as if his posture might lighten his mood. His look of concern was devastating. "Howarth Castle is quite a ride away from Harrow House, and your family is anxious to see you. Here at Burkley, you need only cross the field and go through the hedges to Netherford Hall."

The viscount took a few steps closer to her, and she could smell his fragrant cologne, that deep, vanilla spice she recalled from their moments together before she'd been turned. It addled her head, pulling an emotion both hungry and full of lust from her body.

Viola knew, in that moment, she was not ready for polite company. For while sorrow welled up inside of her—and undoubtedly her eyes had begun bleeding as she struggled to keep back her tears—she was suddenly possessed of a mad desire to throw herself upon Silas and touch his body, his skin, his hair, any part of him he would allow. The urge was unbearable, to the point of pain, and her breathing started coming in anxious, panting gasps.

And her head! The pain was insistent, a vice squeezing at her temples and twisting down the column of her neck. Her flesh quivered in places she ought not consider in polite company and Miss Rookwood-Nourse was trying, in vain, to keep her calm.

By the stars, she was going to ruin her family's name even further!

"Laertes!" She hadn't even thought about who to call,

and yet the vampire sire had been the first upon her lips.

With a flash, Laertes appeared before them all as if stepping through a shadowed curtain of gauze. His expression stricken, he looked madly around the room for the source of Viola's distress.

In a moment, his arms were around her, and the fury simmered to a manageable degree.

"Do take our sincere apologies, my lord," Laertes said.

A cold, calming darkness claimed her as the vampire swept Viola off to her rooms.

LAERTES BYRNE WAS ill-equipped to be a sire to a spawn, and yet he was incapable of ignoring the constant paternal affection he felt for Viola Brightwell. Oh, he had felt lust and desire for hundreds, if not thousands, of people before. And, in his way, he felt affection for his sister—though it was most often tinged with annoyance.

With Viola, however, he had no point of comparison. He adored her. He could not stop looking at her. He was proud of her. Yet he had no desire to touch her or seduce her. All he wanted to do was protect her, to nurture her, to prevent her from feeling even a mote of pain.

He felt like a mother hen keeping watch over her brood. What absurdity!

"I doubt she'll wake for at least an hour," Ophelia said, glancing up at Laertes over her copy of *Grando's Guide*, which they had both been studying to better acquaint themselves with the expectations of raising spawn. The details were painfully sparse, but it was all they had. Laertes had never collected books on the subject. Until Viola happened, he'd never even considered siring. "The mix of comfrey and rose petals seems particularly good at keeping her subdued for the time being."

Laertes pulled his gaze from Viola's placid face, wincing as she spasmed in her sleep. "Are we certain it isn't harming her?"

"No," Ophelia said. "But we can't have her eviscerating the Viscount St. Albans, now, can we?"

"I don't think she was trying to eviscerate him," Laertes said, taking Viola's hand and squeezing it gently. It made him feel strange to hold her. Complete in a way that terrified him. "I believe she was drawn to him. Physically."

Ophelia put her book down, blinking in response to Laertes' observation. "Why, of course she was. Brother, half the time I forget you have a brain between your ears. But you are proving a most intuitive sire. I had not been thinking of lust; I had been thinking of violence."

"I sensed it. Her lust. You did not?" he asked her.

Pursing her lips, Ophelia shook her head. "I'm afraid I mostly only sense Viola when she is hungry. I feel echoes of it, particularly in my fangs." She opened her mouth to display her long, ivory canines. "And her fear. I can feel that, too. But it's in my knees. An ache, as if I want to run away."

Yes, that was all quite familiar to Laertes. "I wonder if, when you turned her, something in my blood changed—as if her blood called to me, somehow."

"Or it is simply the way a sire feels for his spawn. We cannot know, really. Not even Grando explains what his *feelings* were, only what one must do to keep spawn safe." She sighed, pinching her nose with her fingers. "I fear I may have to go to Bath to speak with Maurice."

Laertes sneered. He detested Maurice on principal. "He's a pompous ass who makes my narcissism appear measured."

"You just don't like him because he lavishes all his attentions on me when we're there," Ophelia said.

"I'd rather eat nails than endure time with him," Laertes said.

"Which is why I think you should stay here with Viola while I speak to Maurice on the matter. He's the oldest among us; and though, yes, his personality is grating and exhausting, I am far less bothered by his foibles than you. He may have a copy of Parvus, which is the foremost authority on siring."

"You and your books," he sneered. "I think we are far more likely to find answers in our own intuition than among ancient medieval tomes. Besides, you'd get sick being away from Viola. And you are a miserable soul when you're feeling ill."

Ophelia stood, picking up her velvet skirts, and came to sit beside Laertes. "Whatever has befallen us, I do not believe the burden has fallen equally. It is as if we have split the symptoms of spawning in twain. You are clearly her protector in the flesh—I must be her protector in mind and spirit."

"You sound quite brave, sister," Laertes said. "But I think your connection with her will mature in time."

"I only know that when she was in her greatest moment of desperation, when her very soul began fraying with the pain and horror, she called your name. Not mine."

Laertes almost wouldn't have believed the note of sadness in his sister's voice if he hadn't felt so changed himself. Ophelia was always the vain, practical one, prone to aloofness. She was a serial lover, trained in the ways of seduction as few before her could ever claim. Now and again through the centuries, Laertes had glimpsed longing or a sense of loss from her, but it always faded.

Now, gazing at her face, he wondered if they were ever going to go back to the way they were. Should Viola go through her transformation fully, she would be a vampire for decades—centuries, even. It would be their job to keep her and teach her, protect her, and even love her.

An unwelcome wave of emotions caught in Laertes' throat, and he started when he felt Viola squeeze his hand back.

She was awake, and seeing her flash of recognition, and disappointment, cut through to the heart of him. Would she always resent him? He wouldn't blame her. The weeks he spent away from her, before he truly understood the cause for his affliction, were some of the worst he had ever endured. Reuniting with her had healed a wound he thought might never mend. Now, she would never live as a mortal again, and he and his sister were the vehicles of that agony.

"I would say all is well, yet I do not think you would see it that way," Laertes said. "Not yet, anyway."

Viola did not let go of Laertes' hand. Instead, she drew it a little closer. "It does feel better, when I'm here, with you both." She turned her luminous, dark eyes toward Ophelia. "I can see the beauty in you both, the power. Part of me yearns for it, as if I might reach out and touch it."

"It is here, waiting, for when you are ready," Laertes said.

"Well, there is a *small* matter of timeliness," Ophelia said.

"There is?" Laertes asked.

"Yes," said his sister. "We never made a choice to be what we are, Viola. We are simply as we were made. Although the worst of the danger has passed for you, the time between being turned and becoming a vampire, there are allusions in the works I've been reading that imply the threat is not entirely gone."

Viola's grip tightened, and Laertes put his other hand atop hers. "I did not handle myself very well with the viscount. Or with the witch, for that matter. Does it have to do with that?"

"I don't yet know. I suspect it might. I think you are not fully accepting the change. Or your soul has somehow not properly reconnected. It appears, from my reading, that it is customary for a new thrall to drink of a mortal's blood within a fortnight of their change. It cannot be animal blood, nor can it be collected blood. It must be taken, in good or ill intent, to fortify that connection," Ophelia explained.

As children, Laertes and Ophelia had fed upon their father, first, and then the house thralls, when they were older. It was as natural as drinking water.

In other circumstances, Laertes would have been angry at his sister for divulging such information without discussing with him, first. But he somehow felt it best he learn these matters along with Viola, and that Ophelia continued as their stalwart scholar. He doubted he could stomach reading stories of spawn turning to revenants; just the idea of it alone made him want to weep.

"I should leave Burkley House first thing," Viola said. "You offered Howarth Castle."

Ophelia frowned, pulling her shawl tighter around her shoulders. "We thought so. But I believe being in closer proximity to your family will help keep you stable and mitigate the risk of your becoming a revenant. It will remind you of them and give you a reason to remain."

"It will make me miserable," Viola whispered, her voice breaking with tears. "And the viscount... Silas... I..."

She loved him. And he loved her. And, by the shroud, Laertes wished he could save them both from the heartache coming. Some impossibilities were too great, even—and especially—in love.

"It is not safe for you to be anywhere else, especially given that Miss Rookwood-Nourse is here," Laertes said. "The viscount has offered you space here for as long as you need, and he's even written to a friend in London about more tonics to see if they might help."

"And the gentlewitch is in London as well, attending to some important business with the Coven. She has also promised to help," Ophelia added.

Laertes wiped a bloody tear from Viola's cheek. "I don't know if this helps, but I am—we are—sorry for all this. It is a heavy burden to bear, but you are not alone."

Viola considered him for a moment, then nodded and turned away.

CHAPTER THREE
THE GENTLEWITCH IN LONDON

EDITH ROOKWOOD HAD made many wrong assumptions about her companion, Poppy, since they began their relationship, but never more so than how she'd expected her to react to London. Having grown up in the crowds, noise and bustle of the city, Edith believed Poppy would struggle. She was such a wild creature, so at home in the fields and the dales, that the mere idea of her among the dingy, soot-stained buildings of London felt entirely alien.

Yet from the moment Poppy set eyes on the glimmering bend of the Thames, she was *enchanted*.

She pressed to the window of their carriage, hands gripping the leather handle, her mouth constantly agape at every new wonder.

Edith loved watching Poppy at any time, but she felt a special kind of joy when she didn't realise she was doing so. Poppy's beauty was apparent to just about everyone who met her, but *they* did not see the private moments, when the young woman truly shone. When Poppy was so engaged in the world around her that she stilled, and the chaos that so often followed in her wake seemed to pause. Her cheek, her curved neck, the fall of her curls following the line of her bonnet. Ah, but Edith loved her beyond words.

"I truly did not believe you'd find London so charming,

33

my love," Edith said, taking Poppy's hand gently. Her gloves were soft and warm.

Poppy reluctantly tore her attention away. "We must go for as many walks as possible. Oh, Edith. You told me the buildings were tall, but I truly had no idea they were so beautiful."

"They are quite covered in soot and grime," Edith said.

"That hardly detracts from their appeal. Look at how the sooty stones atop that building bring out the marble sculptures in such relief," Poppy explained.

Edith craned her head to see. They were approaching Piccadilly, so they would be arriving at Hyde Lodge soon enough. Given she no longer had a home in London, Edith had decided to stay with Stafford Vale, an illegitimate but very wealthy son of the Duke of Buckingham. Hyde Lodge was Vale's home, a sprawling Palladian manse not far from her favourite pub, St. Catherine's Inn. There was little better escape in London than a good house and a dark pub.

"I see what you mean," Edith said, although she really didn't. There was plenty of relief already in the friezes and statues. They just looked rather dirty.

"And you never mentioned all the flowers," Poppy scolded. "They're practically growing out of the walls! I've never seen half of them. They must come all the way from Spain."

Spain, in Poppy's mind, was the most far-off and exotic land she could think of. It was terribly endearing. She had read many books on travel, but she was always most enthralled of Spain. Edith would have to introduce her to some of the diplomats she knew, if they had time enough.

Vale met them at the front of the house, a small fleet of servants in his wake. He was of middling height, a little round about the middle, with long, chestnut brown hair kissed with white at the temples. At the moment, he wore a brocaded purple dressing gown and matching velvet slippers. His hands were outstretched in welcome.

"Liege Edith!" Vale embraced Edith, kissing her on the cheek before swirling away and capturing Poppy in a similar manner. "And your companion, Persephone Brightwell. My stars, Edith, she's even more lovely than your letter indicated."

Edith felt consternation rise in her chest. She most certainly had not written a single word about Poppy's beauty.

"Poppy, if you please, Lord Vale," Poppy said.

"Just Vale, if you please, Poppy," Vale replied with a wink. "Now! We must give you a tour and get you settled into your rooms. Bernice! Hopkins!"

Two servants broke ranks behind them—a frosty-looking old woman and a young man with flax-coloured hair. They all wore similar robes of pale damask, cornflower blue, with a light floral spray.

"Bernice here will show you to your rooms," Vale continued, gesturing to the old woman. "And Hopkins will lead you to the parlour once you've had a chance to refresh. It is such a dreadfully long trip from Netherford, though! And I hear the roads in Kent are miserable this time of year."

"I'm afraid they're miserable all times of the year," Edith said, proffering her elbow to her companion. "But I will be writing a letter to Lord Gibson on the matter. It seems to me with the recent challenges with the pub portals, we may all be in need of such travel sooner rather than later."

"This is why I never leave London," Vale said, shaking his head as they walked up the marble steps. "Such a rugged, unpredictable landscape out there. I prefer the music of commerce to the howling of wolves."

* * *

THEIR ROOMS (FOR they were given the use of an entire suite) faced west, and had a lovely view of Hyde Park and the Serpentine. The park had a most excessive proliferation of flowers this time of year, and with it, all the insects and birds one might expect. Unlike her companion, Edith was not a person much interested in flora and fauna, finding the encroachment of bees and other crawling creatures most unwelcome. For Poppy's sake, Edith refrained from murdering the little pests—at least in her presence.

In terms of decor, Edith had forgotten just how eccentric Vale was. As a world traveller, a scholar of magic and ritual, he had collected thousands of relics, books, paintings, sculptures, and pieces of furniture. Often, the furniture had no distinguishing use other than looking interesting. There was nothing uniting the collection but disunity itself: buteh swirls beside plaids, velvets pulled over sheers, gilded gold frames next to silver. The entirety of the enormous home was more like a cluttered shop of curiosities than a gentleman's lodgings.

Of course, Poppy *adored* it.

"I have never been so inspired," Poppy declared, resting her hand on a stuffed tiger carrying a silver tray. The poor taxidermied fellow was not in the best shape at present, one of his eyes appearing to melt into the puckered stripes on his chin, and at least three teeth gone missing. "Edith, have you ever seen such a feast for the eyes?"

Edith had, and she was staring straight at her. "I have visited Vale many times, indeed. And he has since acquired even more clutter. I pity the staff for having to keep everything dusted."

Poppy was well-acquainted with Edith's sidelong answers to avoid the painful discomfort of opposing opinions and saw through the evasion easily. "I know this is not your idea of beauty, my love."

"My idea of beauty is any room in which you are standing," Edith said. She watched as Poppy softened her stance and strode over to her.

"Edith…" Poppy murmured softly.

Reaching up to touch Poppy's face, Edith felt an instant welling of passion and desire. Both were ever-present when Poppy was near; but touching her skin… Stars and the speckled firmament! It awakened her magic. "Persephone…"

The moment their lips connected the world dissipated around them. Joy flickered and kindled in Edith's chest, opening and unfurling as their bodies drew closer, the rustle of cloth punctuating their ragged breathing. Ah, she could live inside the sensation, her magic alive and her heart full of long-awaited comfort!

Edith kissed Poppy's neck, brushing her lips across the tender skin, smiling when her companion let out a moan of desire. She slipped her hand over Poppy's shoulder, then down to cup her full breast, revelling in the way pressure pushed her cleavage up, straining at her stays. She wanted nothing more than to push Poppy onto the horrendous display of brocades upon the bed and make her writhe until she could no longer speak coherently.

Alas, a knock on the door left them both trembling and reassembling their clothing. Poppy giggled, then bit Edith's finger when she tried to shush her.

"Later," Edith said, her voice low with the weight of wanting. "We must be guests, first."

"Hmm, must we?" Poppy asked with a coquettish sway of her hips. "It was such a very long carriage ride, and all that *jostling*…"

Edith had to will every mote of her body away from Poppy, giving her a warning look as she opened the door, pausing momentarily to smooth the curls at her brow.

Bernice stood at the door, a tray of food in one hand and a letter in the other. "Excuse my interruption, my liege," she said smoothly. "But there is an urgent letter for you. And the master insisted I bring nourishment post haste."

Well, she supposed food was necessary. The letter, however, was far more intriguing. Very few people knew she was in London, and even fewer where she was staying. Vale was loved for his wealth, but not his status—in fact, many resented his residence in Mayfair. It should, to their minds, be reserved for the acknowledged scions of gentry, not their bastards. Edith always thought such notions outdated and, truthfully, rather bigoted. The Coven Council had tried, without success, to eliminate the strictures on succession, but to no avail.

And indeed, bastards were, apparently, at the fore of Edith's current circumstances. For she immediately recognised the seal upon the letter: Roland de Grateloup, the bastard child of an unknown lord and the High Witch herself. His existence had nearly cost her the seat of High Witch, in fact. To this day, few knew how she managed to win over the more conservative voices among the Council to her side.

Shutting the door, Edith broke the seal, which was charmed. And inside, she recognised the ink as bloodbark, another sign its contents were unusual—perhaps dangerous—to read.

Her neck prickled with an unwelcome presentiment. She was due to speak to the High Witch in two days, just before the next Coven Council gathering, ahead of the start of the parliamentary session.

My dearest Edith.

I write in haste and with great concern, for it appears my mother, the High Witch, has gone missing.

At first, I was certain she was simply away on one of her adventures, given her habit of wandering—a proclivity, of course, which we share.

For all her wandering ways, she never misses a payment to me, nor does she miss our visits. She has now missed both. I was in Paris, but am no longer welcome there, and since I cannot be in London long without attracting most unwelcome attention, I must ask you meet me to discuss the matter as soon as possible. I will be at the Tippling Philosopher for three nights before absconding elsewhere, likely to visit my cousin, your neighbour, Silas Drake, viscount etc.

I am concerned for my safety, and that of any of Mother's friends. There are few in London I trust.

All best,

R de G

"What is it?" Poppy's expression, so bright and glowing moments ago, had gone serious, her dark brows heavy over her eyes. "Edith, you're pale as milk."

Indeed, Edith felt rather faint. "I'm afraid we must change our plans for the evening slightly, my love. The High Witch is missing. And her son is in dire trouble."

"Should we tell Vale?" Poppy asked.

Edith closed her eyes, sending out quiet, prying tendrils of her magic. Her powers were not great compared with many other witches of her age, but her skills were unique. Like the High Witch, Edith could command liminal magic. These tendrils, she found, worked like extensions of her own intuition.

Technically, she had told Poppy she wasn't studying liminal magic any longer, since it had nearly caused the wholesale destruction of their homes, families, and relationship. But she was working directly under the High Witch, and, she reasoned, Poppy didn't need to know *everything*. Especially around gentlewitch magic. Especially when it could hold the key to fixing the pub portals, and secure the future of the Rookwood legacy.

With this magic, Edith could feel the mood of a place, sense the residual energy left by those within. She had not considered doing so with Vale, for he was always far removed from such concerns.

But was he?

Her magic returned with a sense of unease, remnants of distraction, anger, even violence, after a moment's concentration. Warning.

"We must be very careful," Edith said. "I have half a mind to send you back to Netherford Hall."

"Oh, I wouldn't go even if you told me to."

Edith had to chuckle. "Of course you wouldn't. Alas, even if I did send you back, it would raise alarm. We are already enough of a spectacle. I wouldn't want the Ton to think they'd scared us away."

"I'm very hard to frighten," Poppy said. And it was true. She was the bravest person Edith knew, and, if she was honest, far too good for her.

"So, we must act as if nothing unusual has happened at all. I will make my excuses tonight, and we will go and see Roland. He's St. Albans' cousin, and the son of the High Witch. As her son, I trust him. He is even more disdainful of polite society than I am, and I'm certain he wouldn't have reached out to me without due cause. If the Coven or Parliament knew the High Witch was missing, there would be headlines on every paper from here to John O'Groats. As it is, if people know, they are keeping very quiet about it."

Poppy took a deep breath. "Well, the good news is you are taking me on an adventure, my love. The bad news is that I have no idea who any of these people are. Roland? Is that a name I should know?"

"Trust me, you will wish you'd never heard it soon enough."

THE TIPPLING PHILOSOPHER was a small public house, crammed between a brick-fronted tenement and the remains of what might once have been a printing shop. By the time they arrived, Poppy's head was pounding from having to navigate in the dark, and her feet ached from even a short time on the cobblestones. Halfway over from Hyde House, Edith declared the streets too crowded for a carriage and decided to go it on foot. At first, Poppy had been delighted. But then she'd realised just how filthy the streets were.

Edith was sincerely bothered by what she had read in the letter from Roland, and Poppy wished she had more experience to help her. Though visiting London had so far proven a thrilling experience, seeing the lines of beggars and gin-tipplers along the way had sobered her significantly. They had dressed in large, billowing cloaks, to better cover their faces, but no matter how close Edith was, Poppy felt far from safe.

As if anticipating her question, Edith turned to Poppy and said, "I've hired two guards. They're not far. They are discreet. And Molly Hode is overseeing them, so if they are in any way untrustworthy, they will have to deal with her wrath. Remember, here in London, there are thousands of Warder families."

"Oh," Poppy said, trying not to stare around her like the country mouse she was. The Tippling Philosopher was only marginally safer looking from this angle, thanks to the golden light from within and the hint of red velvet curtains and stained glass. "I'm sorry—I don't mean to seem so out of my depth."

"My darling, you *are* out of your depth. But, if there's anything I've learned about you, it's that you would never allow that to fluster you." She kissed Poppy on the cheek and then opened the door for her into the pub. "In fact, I would go so far as to say you thrive in the chaos."

That did make Poppy feel better. And she was somewhat relieved to be visiting a humble pub rather than a formal meal with Vale. Eccentric though he was, she was unused to the kind of decorum that landed and Coven-born families performed on a daily basis. Poppy had a difficult enough time managing the kind of grace Viola seemed so naturally predisposed to.

Viola.

Every time Poppy thought about Viola, holed up in Burkley House like some monster, she felt as if she were dying a little. Her vision prickled, her head swam, and she had to steady herself on the banister just inside the pub. Hadn't Viola first met Lord St. Albans at a pub?

Edith usually noticed Poppy's lapses of panic and sudden melancholy, but she was too focused on finding her acquaintance now. Poppy had to centre herself, using the techniques Edith had shown her: focus on what she could feel. What she could see. What she could smell.

Overwhelming malt, sawdust, onions, and smoke. Enough to make her eyes water and obscure her vision in the already dimly lit space. Whoever had decorated the place was quite fond of portraits, for they festooned every wall. Some looked rather ancient, judging by the patina and frame designs, while others must have been painted recently, given the subjects' clothing. There were far more men in the pictures than she would expect, too.

Poppy did not enjoy the feeling of all those eyes on her. Even if the patrons did not notice her presence, the portraits followed her every move.

Stopping to ask a passing barman a question too low for Poppy to hear, Edith then directed her through the pub and down the stairs to the basement. She must have squeezed Edith's hand a little too hard, for the gentlewitch paused and gave her a look of reassurance and comfort.

And lo, below the Tippling Philosopher stood another pub space altogether. This one was accessed through three different heavy curtains, each more opulent than the other, some tied with golden cords. Poppy blinked in the brighter light, provided by dozens of colourful lanterns in the Persian fashion: they shone like caged jewels, hanging from posts and nestled in corners. The furniture followed suit in its design, scrolled wood embellishments and a dizzying array of inlay designs. The room's overpowering scent was a heady mix of ancient ingredients: oud, labdanum, opium, and sandalwood.

No one looked up at them as they passed through, for every booth or table hid behind more drapes and screens of varying opacity. Poppy thought she glimpsed shadows moving in a most provocative way behind one of them, and stood, fascinated, until Edith ushered her toward an enclosure marked by a ruby-hued lantern and deep green damask.

Edith made a motion with her hands Poppy had since learned was a kind of magical signature to detect charms, and in a moment, they had crossed into the small space together.

Another lantern lit it from within, not with firelight but witchlight, pale green tinged with sapphire blue. Which all seemed set up precisely to emphasise the beauty and elegance of the man waiting for them inside.

Roland de Grateloup was the most striking man Poppy had ever seen. Immediately, she recognised the features of Virginia Cawley, the High Witch, in her son: the pale, moonlight hair so blond it was nearly white; the bright, intense gaze; the strong brow and aquiline nose. But where the High Witch was tall and lithe, willowy and elegant, Roland was powerfully built, muscles moving beneath his clothing as he stood to greet them. And he was even taller than Lord St. Albans, if that could be believed. He wore figured silks tailored into the latest French fashions, his collar frothing over with Brussels lace. Shockingly, he wore an earring in his left ear, studded with an enormous diamond.

If he was looking to blend in, he certainly wasn't doing a very good job of it.

"Roland," Edith said, clasping his hand in hers. She had to look up to meet his gaze.

"Liege Edith," Roland said, his voice low and his accent polished, bowing to Edith and then taking Poppy's hand and delicately kissing it "And this must be your stunning companion, of whom I have heard such praise from my cousin."

Poppy's cheeks burned with his words and, stars, she could listen to him speak forever. His voice, low and musical, begged for attention.

"May I present Persephone Brightwell of Netherford Hall," Edith said, a rare smile turning her lips up.

"Just Poppy is fine," Poppy said.

Roland grinned at them, his gaze flitting from face to face. "What a remarkable match. You will need to tell me more details of your courtship when we are less pressed for time. Alas, circumstances being as they are, I must 'cut to the chase,' as they say."

Every inch the gentleman, Roland waited until both Edith and Poppy were seated comfortably before speaking. He poured a glass of wine for each of them, expertly, going on a moment about the vintage before examining his own glass.

"I'm afraid the streets will be running red with blood before this is all over," he said dramatically. "We haven't much time to act, and I am relying on you, Edith."

CHAPTER FOUR
𝒯HE 𝒫ROMISES 𝒷EST 𝒦EPT 𝒰NSAID

FROM BEHIND MOUNTAINS of papers, Silas Drake scribbled out doggerel poetry. He hoped, perhaps, that attention to his art form—regardless of its quality—might distract him from the ever-growing hole of dread yawning inside him. If he could manage a few poems, perhaps he could return to Sibylle's adventures in the Caribbean.

No. It just made it worse. He could not shake the searing jealousy coursing through him every time he thought of Laertes Byrne. Laertes, the foppish Scottish vampire who, until now, had been nothing more than a local nuisance, someone to be tolerated for the sake of tradition.

Had Laertes always been so handsome? He supposed so. Vampires were, overall, uncomfortably attractive. Not Viola, though. There was naught uncomfortable about her. Her beauty had always stopped his heart; now, though, it was like dying a little every time he saw her. Her beauty sharpened every day. And now that she had shown signs of improvement, his mind whirled with improper considerations.

Fintan knocked softly and let himself in. "The Dowager Viscountess St. Albans, my lord," he said.

Silas hardly had time to slide the poetry under a book before his great aunt shuffled in, supported by the young Miss Kesby, Viola's replacement since the accident. Miss

Kesby was from a local family, but of slightly higher rank than the Brightwells, her father the third son of a baronet. Silas ought to have remembered more details, but she had the sort of personality one immediately forgot upon meeting. Oh, she was lovely enough, and well-mannered. It was only that when she spoke and responded, it might as well have been from a script in a play than any spontaneous conversation between like-minded souls.

Aunt May, no doubt, thought Silas would take to her as a replacement in his heart, as well.

Thankfully, Miss Kesby did not remain. Once Aunt May was situated with the cat, she excused herself immediately, following Fintan out into the hallway.

"Given you have not brought tea, I believe we are in for a serious discussion," Silas said from across his desk.

The old woman pursed her lips sourly, as if she had sipped wine turned to vinegar. "You are a very clever man, Silas. Fate has smiled upon you in a dozen ways. Your father sent you to the very best schools, you spent a decade in Paris living as a man of your station ought. We, your family, have laid success out before you in ways few in the realm can boast."

Growing embarrassment crept down Silas's spine. These scoldings were regular, but usually she warmed up to them, rather than going straight into the lambasting.

"And I am very grateful, Aunt May. You know I am," Silas said.

"Grateful? How are you to know my mind?"

"I didn't mean to presume—"

"There is a vampire in Burkley House, Silas. Who apparently lives here. And now, after you promised me she would be gone, there are two more flitting in and out of this great house. A house your great-grandfather Malachi Drake began, from the very roots of its foundations."

47

Few people took such a tone with Silas, and though he would have stood his ground with anyone else, being in the dowager viscountess's presence cowed him. As the only living heir to the St. Albans name, he had a duty. An unavoidable duty. Though he wished for any other circumstance many times over, he could not escape it.

Besides, without her approval—as the official elder of his family—he could accomplish very little with his title. She held the key to his influence and his career. Silas stilled, taking hold of his quill firmly. As dowager viscountess she had very little power, save one: as the living wife of the previous Viscount St. Albans, she could contest Silas's right to a seat in Parliament if she believed he no longer upheld the family name befitting the Crown and Realm.

"She does not have anywhere else to go safely," Silas said. "I had hoped Howarth Castle was a viable solution, but I'm told it is not advisable given her current state. Her turning was unconventional. And she dedicated years of her life to Burkley House, even before I arrived."

Aunt May frowned even more deeply, flexing her lace gloved hands. Her expression softened then, and she petted the cat on her lap as if only he understood the agony she endured. "Everything about this circumstance is unconventional. I know you had the illusion of affection for young Miss Brightwell, but it was doomed even before she was turned monstrous."

"Aunt May, I will not allow her to be taken from the house until she is deemed safe," Silas said. "And she is *not* a monster."

"You poor boy," she said, half to the cat. "I didn't expect you'd come to your senses on your own, of course. Men rarely do, even in the direst circumstances, when bewitched by love. But your time of dalliances are over. You must have known this day would come. It is your responsibility to make an advantageous marriage. Even if Miss Brightwell were to manage in polite company, by some miracle, she is a *vampire*."

"What if there is a cure?" Silas tried. He wished he'd asked Fintan for wine before he'd left.

"Even then, her pedigree is severely lacking. I pray you come to reason soon enough. In the meantime, I am giving you an ultimatum."

That overwhelming sense of nausea swept over Silas again, and he swallowed on a dry throat. "What is your proposition?"

"It is to preserve your legacy, boy. One cannot escape their legacy, no matter how hard they try. And you, until recently, have been a most fine representative of that line." She adjusted in her chair. "It has been brought to my attention that aiding and abetting in vampire spawning is considered a criminal act."

Sila scoffed. "That legislature is ancient. It also forbids witches from walking through gardens and the use of magic to enhance one's appearance," he said pointedly.

"Perhaps. But it is still a consideration. Vampires are not as civilised or trustworthy as witches are—and even witches always put their own desire far above ours."

It was an outdated and rather bigoted view, but Silas let it stand. "I will do everything in my power to help Viola. You know that."

"Even if it comes at the cost of your seat in Parliament? You know how hard your father worked to ensure you had a place among your peers, but it will not last should you squander it away cavorting with such unsavoury individuals."

Aunt May knew, he supposed, first-hand, of how fragile one's reputation could be. He always pitied the dowager viscountess; as she had aged and withered, her sister remained young and powerful, having a child well into her sixties. Theirs was not a noble family, but one blessed with magic, save that Aunt May had none at all. And no tolerance for it. She'd married into her station. Virginia Cawley was the first gentlewitch in generations in the Cawley line, so remarkably talented she had been given the highest status on pure merit. It was not surprising the dowager viscountess resented such power.

But she was quite mistaken about Titus Drake and his dreams for Silas. Silas's father had run the family fortune into the ground, along with their reputation. Since Edward, Aunt May's beloved son, had died in his forties with no heir and no spouse, the title had gone to Titus, who had done nearly everything in his power to drink and gamble away every last penny. Silas hated to admit it, but his father's death had been something of a relief to him. They'd never been close, and Silas had always had to act as the responsible party when he was home. Fintan had been more of a father to him, by a long measure. Silas's dreams of taking up the place in Parliament once occupied by Malachi Drake were his own, not his father's.

None of these things would be appropriate to reveal before the ailing dowager countess. Which meant Silas had to retreat into a visage of propriety and gratitude. "Very well. And what else?"

She pursed her lips, considering her next words, before continuing. "I will allow Miss Brightwell and her growing cadre of miscreants to remain here so long as you entertain at least one prospective bride per week. I have already drawn up a list. I am expecting reports on each of them, written, delivered regularly. I do not suppose you will find any one of them to your liking, so, once I have presented you with enough candidates, if you do not pick one, I shall select for you. Then you can get to work making an heir and, perhaps, once that is done, you may live out the rest of your life as you please once I am dead and in the ground at last."

Silas could have said a number of things to his aunt. In fact, he often rehearsed them when he was feeling particularly frustrated. This was not the first time she had been so direct with him—nor would it be the last, he suspected. In his mind, he was always sterner than in reality, sensitive to her loneliness and limited time here on earth.

Had he the courage, he would have told her that living in his grandfather's shadow and enduring the pressure of her expectations made him feel like a snail shoved into a shell three times too small. And that shell was of her own making: namely, Burkley House.

He'd have told her she was a bitter old woman whose clawlike grip on the past and on tradition had alienated her from her entire family to the point their few relatives purposefully avoided visiting to spare themselves the trouble.

For good measure, he might have added that, should he feel the need, he could contest her involvement in the estate and would likely win given he was tied to the family by blood, whereas she was by marriage only.

Were he petty, he would also point out that her jealousy over her sister's power and status made her appear resentful and bigoted.

Then, once he was done, he'd chastise her for her terrible treatment of Viola Brightwell, who had been her stalwart companion for years only to fall out of favour the moment she needed help the most.

But he said none of those things. The all-encompassing sense of responsibility weighed heavily upon him. This was one of the reasons he and Leige Rookwood had become friends in their short acquaintance. Though more tragedy scarred her family than his, she too understood the profound stress of being a young, lone heir to a powerful dynasty. The expectations, both in London and in the country, were substantial.

Perhaps Aunt May was right. If he were to marry right, he would have the support he needed at the house. Though he had some distant cousins, none of them had any interest in the title or the holdings. He was the last St. Albans, given a powerful position with a great burden. As much as his fondness for Viola drove him, he could not expect her to move comfortably in polite society. Especially now.

He wished Roland were here. He wished he had more time. But wishes, his grandfather was fond of saying, were merely echoes of ambition, built for the weak of spirit and those lacking in skill.

"Yes, Aunt May. I will abide by your wisdom."

"Good lad. Now, help me up. It's time for my nap."

Aunt May allowed Silas to help her stand, though the cat was indignant at being removed from the warm lap.

Just before he closed the door, the dowager viscountess added: "And you will need to figure out what to do with Miss Brightwell. I am not aware of marriage laws around vampires, but certainly she will need someone to take care of her. Those Byrnes are ill-suited to the task, and someone must contain her before she is irreparably ruined."

VAMPIRES WERE NOT invisible in mirrors, exactly, but the image was never quite clear. Just as light flitted from their hair, so, too, it bent and refracted in unpredictable ways. Viola stood by the tall mirror in her room, and she could see her dress and her gloves, the shape of her body beneath, but whenever she tried to glimpse the detail of her face, the impression was like looking through a greased window.

Somehow, it was worse than not being able to see her face at all.

Ophelia was gone, and Laertes had arranged dinner with the viscount for the evening. Two days had passed by uneventfully, and with a more regular dosage of hawthorn, considerable sleep, and a steady diet of sheep's blood—she had to agree with Laertes, it left a persistent offal taste in her mouth—she was finally ready to meet the viscount again. And, hopefully, soon to entertain her family. They had written her letters, but she could not reply in kind for the splattering blood on the paper from her tears.

Laertes met her outside her rooms, dressed in scarlet satin embroidered with thistles. Just seeing him set her at ease. Indeed, as Ophelia had posited, she had bonded to him in a far more direct way than with his sister. To his credit, he had been nothing but filial with her. And, indeed, since spending more time together, he looked more youthful and brighter with each passing day.

As a matter of self-preservation, Viola had done her very best to avoid Lord St. Albans. She was mortified over her behaviour in the parlour, but Laertes insisted it was entirely their fault for pushing her too far, too fast. Besides, he had still offered her use of the north wing, and she couldn't hide away in the shadows forever. It was her duty to do well by her family and her guardians, now.

She'd not had the occasion to visit the dining hall since the fateful night the Boagane nearly killed her and her sister. Well, technically it *had* killed her. Since that evening, the decor returned to everyday elegance, which was, to be certain, far beyond what Viola experienced in her life at Harrow House. She had worked with the dowager viscountess at length, picking the patterns on the drapes to compliment the plate designs, along with the varnish on the parquet flooring, in the months leading up to Silas's return. Yet, even in the short time she'd been absent from the house, she noticed embellishments she could only ascribe to the viscount's own desires: bronze statues, crystal candelabras, and marble busts of varying number throughout the hallway and into the dining hall.

Lord St. Albans stood at the head of the table, his beautiful hazel eyes shadowed in the candlelight. He'd ordered the drapes drawn to accommodate Viola's light sensitivity, a struggle Laertes assured her would dissipate with time. For now, though, it caused her to tear up, and that just meant more blood stains. To ensure no sartorial embarrassments would occur, she'd chosen a dress of dark blue velvet limned with silver embroidery for dinner. Dark velvet was so very forgiving when it came to blood stains.

Petronilla Rookwood-Nourse was also in attendance, seated to the viscount's left. She looked lovely in pale grey, her pearl earrings big as grapes dangling from her ears. When Viola entered, the gentlewitch gave her a kind smile.

"Good evening, Miss Brightwell, Mr. Byrne," Silas said, inclining his head to each of his guests.

Fintan helped Viola to her seat, and she fell into the familiar pace of preparing for dinner. Unlike the Byrnes, however, Viola remembered the taste of food, and longing settled into her bones again. She had tried to eat food, but the results were catastrophic: crying blood is one thing, vomiting it up another, unforgivable trespass.

Laertes, bless him, worked directly with the viscount to proffer the best blood they could find, cleverly put into wine bottles, along with golden goblets, for each vampire guest.

"Thank you for your continued generosity and patience, Lord St. Albans," Viola said, just as the staff presented the viscount with his first course. He was sitting far enough away that Viola could not see the soup, but it smelled horrendous. Laertes had warned her about that, too, and so she wore a sprig of lavender stitched into her cuff to ward off the encroaching odour.

Lord St. Albans paused mid-spoonful, placing his utensil back beside the bowl. "Miss Brightwell, as I have said before, it is the very least I can do."

"I fear I have been a great inconvenience upon you and your household," Viola said, unable to keep the words from flowing freely. She was both relieved and hurt that the dowager viscountess, a woman she once counted as her friend, was not in attendance. Since her turning, Lady St. Albans had avoided Viola. Laertes suggested she did not find vampires tasteful, especially in the same household as the viscount.

"My dear," Laertes intoned from across the table, "we have all lost considerable time and pride in the last few months, but none so much as you."

"Mr. Byrne is right," Lord St. Albans said. "Of us all, you have endured pains and changes more significant than any of us. Netherford—indeed, all of England—is indebted to your bravery against the Boagane. That sort of evil has not roamed our realm in generations, and you threw yourself into the thick of fighting without a thought for yourself."

Viola had never been called brave in all her life. She blinked back tears, focusing on her meal swirling in the goblet. Her life had been so ordered, so perfectly organised. Now, she was a ruin of emotions and monstrousness. "My sister was in peril, my lord. We are a close family, and she has always been especially precious to me. I cannot imagine my life without her."

"Nor she, you," Lady Rookwood-Nourse said. "I'm certain the Byrnes told you how many times she visited you during the most turbulent parts of your convalescence. She was certain she was capable of waking you from whatever power kept you so indisposed."

The gentlewitch had such a way of speaking around delicate matters. Viola scarcely had time to feel embarrassed. "She deserves as much time in London as possible, then, to recuperate. I imagine she is charmed and terrified by the city."

"Have you been to London, Miss Brightwell?" Laertes asked her.

Viola smiled, glad of the conversation and its comforts. "I have, yes, but only once. Poppy wasn't allowed to come, for she was still ill for a few years after her accident. I was twelve or thirteen, and I accompanied Mama and Heath to an exhibition at the British Museum."

"My goodness, you say you are from middling stock, but I'm afraid I've never managed an invitation to the museum in all my years. Theirs is a very exclusive circle," Lord St. Albans said.

"Well, Mama was a tutor for some years, and one of her students was a courtier to King George—she is an expert in history and languages—and in thanks for her assistance, he arranged an appointment. This was just after the presentation of the Rosetta Stone, I'm told," Viola explained. "However, being so young, I was mostly fascinated with the antiquities of Egypt there. So macabre and beautiful."

"'Macabre and beautiful' is a most apt description for vampirekind," Laertes said. "Perhaps Isis herself called to you then. Perhaps she knew your future."

The idea of a goddess of any sort having an inkling of Viola's most terrible circumstance seemed unlikely, but she did not wish to offend Laertes. She could not tell if he enjoyed being a vampire or if he simply knew no other way, but she was courteous enough to nod kindly.

"Will you be going to London soon, my lord?" Viola asked, very much wanting to change the subject.

"I must, at some point," replied Silas, "though I admit I keep delaying my plans. I spent so many years dreaming of finally coming to Burkely House, now that I am here, I am loath to leave it again. Besides, I have some things I must attend to in the coming weeks."

The doors leading to the sitting room opened with a great creak, and the dowager viscountess emerged, grasping her assistant's hand. She was looking frailer by the day, and Viola worried after her, even if she cared nothing for her in return.

So, Viola was not surprised when the dowager countess sniffed the air and said, "Yes indeed, Silas. You will be quite occupied for the next few weeks."

"Is it a secret?" Laertes asked with hint of offense. "I wasn't aware."

"It has only just been decided," the dowager countess continued. "The viscount will be entertaining potential brides every week in the house until the autumn equinox. At the end of that time, he will select an eligible candidate."

Viola did not move. She did not breathe. She allowed the words to wash over her, locking each one into her heart—or what remained of it—and closed the door. Of all her vampiric powers—keener senses, remarkable strength, and glorious speed—this was the most useful. She could cool her emotions and lock them away. This was no mere impulse, as she had been struggling to contain the last few days. No, this was a devastation of the heart. And using every scrap of her own power to push away her feelings at this news was paramount to her survival.

There was considerably more conversation after that point, Lady Rookwood-Nourse suggesting a few prospects and Laertes looking stricken, for some reason. But Viola could not find it in herself to be angry. She felt, instead, adrift on a cold sea, numb and distant. She was sated from her meal, comfortable in her chair, and starting to see an end to her time here at Burkley House.

If she had a heart, perhaps it was broken. She could not say. People often said vampires were heartless, but from her experience it felt just the opposite: they felt too much in extremes, too easily, and too deeply—or not at all. She had loved Silas Drake. She had dreamed of their marriage, their life together. And even though she was a stranger unto herself, now, she realized she had held out a thin shred of hope he would fight for her, that they could make Burkley House truly their home.

But, as Viola had learned recently in her vicious turn of fate, becoming monstrous meant being reborn. And not everyone followed you into the next chapter of your life.

Of course, she did not dare to catch the viscount's eye, though she could feel him looking at her, daring her to. Their love had been doomed even before she was turned; it was time for her to move past it, past those girlish dreams, and into whatever future she could muster.

SLEEP CAME FITFULLY that night. Silas could only see the look on Viola's face, so cold and remote and deadly, as his aunt announced their upcoming plans. She had gone still as a statue, her unmoving lips pressed just so, her hand clasped around the stem of the goblet. The goblet filled with blood. Because she was a vampire.

In his logical mind, Silas knew she was a monster. He had seen it in her face tonight. The face of a predator. But also, the face of a woman breaking on the inside. He would get Heath to come visit, if he could. Perhaps Mrs. Brightwell would even venture over, now that the risk was so much lessened. Even if the thought of her, bloodthirsty and hungering for him, made a thrill of desire twist down his stomach and further down.

A cold, delicate hand suddenly closed over his mouth. "Shh. No screaming. Not yet."

Silas almost didn't recognise the voice, but then he saw the curve of her neck in the moonlight, the tumble of black curls, and he knew: Viola. Her skin glowed, just faintly, the whites of her eyes faintly blue. She wore nothing but a shift, the lines of her body visible as she settled upon Silas's bed.

She hadn't made even a whisper of a sound on the carpets.

Silas nodded slowly and she gently let go of his mouth.

He didn't dare breathe. She was so close, and his whole body responded to her, the scent of roses enveloping him in a mist of wanting.

"Is this a dream?" he asked.

Viola tilted her head, the vague impression of her lips turning downward as she gazed at him. "I might be dreaming. You are not." She paused, her fingers lingering just above his collarbone, moving as if she played an invisible piano forte.

"How did you get here?" Silas dared not catch her hand in his, though every mote of his being screamed for that touch. His heart beat helplessly in his chest, his ribs aching with restraint.

"I was thinking of you. And then, in a moment, I was here, in the room, watching you try to sleep. I should care, but at the moment, I do not." There was no mirth in her tone, and yet Viola's wonder was apparent. "Perhaps I am capable of things at night I would not be otherwise."

"Viola," he said, swallowing before he could finish his plea. What was he asking for? "Your reputation might not recover from this sort of behaviour."

"What sort of behaviour is that, exactly?" She shrugged one shoulder, teasing.

"You know I must soon find a wife," Silas said, finally

taking her hand in his. It was no longer cold, and the skin was so soft it made him shiver.

"Silas."

His reply was automatic, a reflex. "Yes, love."

"Would you let me touch you?" Her voice had dropped to a near whisper.

He wanted nothing more. "Please," he said. If he sounded like he was begging, he cared not.

Viola ran her fingers down the side of Silas's face, her captivating eyes tracing the lines of motion as she did so. His body erupted into gooseflesh the moment she raked her nails across the hair above his ears, cut so short she easily met his scalp.

"When you lived in France, you were with many women," Viola said, her hands splaying now, meeting the skin of his chest beneath his loose-necked chemise.

"I was."

"Did you enjoy your fancies?" Again, her tone was dreamlike, nearly without any detectable emotion. Just a hint of curiosity.

He exhaled sharply as Viola made her way to the planes of his stomach, her thumb gently swiping across his navel. If he had been concerned she would see his passion rising before, he had no doubt of it now, for she approached the apex of his thighs.

"I can stop."

"I won't ask you to," he said, then hissed as she grasped him fully in her hand, his back bowing with the sudden, blessed contact.

Viola breathed out slowly. "Those dalliances. Did you love them?"

"I was never in love in France. But I took pleasure and— Brimstone, Viola!" Silas cursed as she began further ministrations upon the front of his chemise, her eyes dancing with irresistible mischief. He had no doubt she knew what she was doing, or else was a born pleasurer.

Or, perhaps, a reborn vampire.

He stopped, taking her wrist in hand and sitting up slowly. She was so beautiful he couldn't breathe, and he had never wanted anyone as desperately as he did in that moment. Yet Viola was new to her life as a vampire. He trusted her, but he did not want to dishonour her.

"Have you ever been in love?" she asked, allowing him to take up her hands and kiss them.

She pulled truth from him as easily as a child freeing a dandelion of its fluff.

"You know I have."

Viola leaned forward, her forehead resting on Silas's chest, their hands still intertwined. "You will soon be wedded," she said. "To a woman with a fine yearly sum and a fertile womb."

Now came the sorrow, thick and impenetrable. The whole room felt heavy with it. "I am shackled by duty."

"And I, by my monstrousness."

"If the gentlewitch and your sister find a cure, there may be yet a chance of you leading the life you had imagined," Silas said. It was not enough.

She tilted her head up and gave him a soft, sweet kiss upon the lips. "I will never be enough."

"Viola, please..."

The room shuddered with sudden static, and Laertes appeared a few feet away from the bed, glowing with an even brighter intensity than his spawn. He did not have anger or blame in his expression, but rather, a deep, abiding pity.

"My dears," he said, hand to his heart. "Please, do not take my appearance for disapproval. I wish nothing more than for you two to commune together. But Fintan approaches, and I should speak with you both if there is to be any further congregation."

Viola evaporated away before Silas could respond, all trace of her dissipating into shadows, leaving only a small indentation in the bed linens. He pulled the blankets up over himself to cover what was painfully obvious.

"Mr. Byrne—where did she go?"

Laertes rubbed the back of his head. "You and I must speak tomorrow afternoon, my lord. I must visit Viola now."

"I don't want—I do not go into this marriage circumstance with any hope for myself. You and she are welcome here as long as you are able. But I do not wish to cause her any undue stress. Nor do I wish to take advantage of her situation."

"My lord, Viola is changing, yes. But she is still Viola. I believe when she died, she was in love with you. There is a chance that has shaped her, now, and has left her confused and in a deep melancholy after tonight's discussions."

Silas's head ached, spun, and he looked up to see Laertes so much closer than before.

"I truly am sorry," the vampire said, touching Silas's cheek. He was such a handsome creature.

The viscount's vision went dark, just as he was about to say something, and he fell into a soft shadow of sleep.

With a start, Silas woke from beneath his bedsheets, sweat clinging to his skin, utterly alone. A dream. He had dreamed it. Or that was what he told himself to assuage his mind of guilt.

He almost would have believed it if not for the lingering scent of roses.

CHAPTER FIVE
A WOLF IN GENTLEMAN'S CLOTHING

THE ODOUR OF true desperation clung to Roland de Grateloup like gin on a sailor's breath. Here he sat, the son of Virginia Cawley, nursing a bottle of wine as his stomach twisted in agony and hunger, begging for help from a middling ginger gentlewitch and her common companion.

Stars and devils, he really had sunk beyond redemption, hadn't he?

Two weeks before the bloody incident, Roland was the talk of Paris, celebrated and lauded, enjoying a constant rotating schedule of lovers and scholars—sometimes both at the same time. Granted, it was never as fun as the years when Silas was involved, but the viscount had the kind of family connections that only allowed for a short detachment from one's responsibilities.

One of the few joys of being a bastard was the complete lack of responsibility. Indeed, responsibility was actively discouraged.

Now, he sat, crammed into a dark hole of a pub, across the table from his last hope.

"Streets running with blood?" Liege Rookwood asked. "That seems a bit apocalyptic."

"Positively cataclysmic," her companion agreed, grabbing the gentlewitch by the arm. They were a pretty pair, though contrasting in almost every way.

"It's all happened rather quickly," Roland said, measuring his words and the tone of his voice as best he could. Though he'd taken a lion's dose of his tonics, he knew keeping his temper in check was paramount at this time of the month. Being this far underground helped, too. "And it began with me waking up in a pool of blood."

"You seem to run into pools of blood quite regularly, sir," Liege Rookwood said. "Were you not the High Witch's son, I might ask you to excuse us from any further implications."

"I think he was being dramatic, my love," Miss Brightwell said, but then laid her gaze directly on Roland. She had the most enchanting black eyes, full of mischief and cleverness.

Roland sighed, then quaffed the remainder of his third glass of wine. His nose tingled a bit with the continued administration of alcohol; a sign he would sleep well tonight, should he find a suitable place to do so.

"Alas, I am not aiming for theatrics, Miss Brightwell. My tale is a frightful one, and I have not the time to do it justice," he admitted.

"Do try," the gentlewitch said drily.

IT WAS NOT the first time Roland de Grateloup had awoken in a puddle of blood, but it was the stickiest. As he slowly came to, his mouth a ruin of halitosis and the remnants of his last meal—mussels with too much sage—he noticed how tacky the sheets were, and how crusted the side of his face had become. Initially, he thought perhaps last evening's libations had ended up spilled in bed, or perhaps some melted chocolate.

But then he caught the scent, previously masked by the heavy opium and perfume dimming his mind and his senses.

Blood.

And a body. Throat slit. Pale eyes open. Limbs askew. Skin wan and waxy.

He knew he hadn't killed this person. Given his condition, he had no need of blades. His nature prohibited it, to some extent. Why reach for a dagger when one's body was made to kill? And to kill elegantly.

Not that he had killed anyone recently.

Blood caked the side of his body that had rested next to the corpse. Roland did not want to look, did not want to see who it was, but he could not prevent himself. Someone had set him up, there was little doubt to that cause—and with reason. For every dalliance and patron in Paris, he had twelve enemies ready to see him fall. Being a matchmaker was a delightful business, until you matched the wrong people—or rather, the right people, but in the process, upset richer, more influential, more terrible people.

Hands trembling, bile rising, he touched the delicate shoulder and turned the corpse over.

Henri de Roquelaure, scholar and politician's son. One of Roland's conquests, but a cheerful fellow with a penchant for ropes during their congresses.

Someone had carved runes into his chest, but they clearly had no knowledge of the occult. It read, *My feather is your grave*, which, he supposed, was a bad attempt at the famous last words of one of the Poisoned Mages of 1696, who had said, "My vengeance is your death." Unfortunately, the characters for *feather* and *vengeance* were quite close.

What could Henri have ever done to deserve such a fate?

Gods, and bebothering devils! Henri's father was part of the Parliament of Rouen, but one of the more progressive members, believed to be part of Les Chevaliers d'Uriel, an ancient band of witch protectors. Politics, Roland was certain, had everything to do with the situation. No one knew of Roland's particular circumstances, aside from his connections at the apothecary. But surely...

He needed his mother. He needed her *now*.

"Monsieur de Grateloup, vous êtes en état d'arrestation pour meurtre. Ne résistez pas, ou nous devrons recourir à la force!" They were going to come into his room whether he liked it or not. The sound of a club rapping on the door shocked him to action.

Quietly as he could, Roland reached for the amulet around his neck and crushed the glass. Shards pierced his hand, taking their toll in blood, and he waited for the wash of magic to transport him to the safe house his mother had established for him years ago. He'd only used it once, and it was a costly gift, but one he knew he could rely on.

Until now, it seemed.

No tide of magic reached him, no comforting, familiar signature of the High Witch's protection. Just more blood, coursing down his arm and dripping to the floor.

The police began beating upon the door, hard enough to shake the gilding off on the other side. Golden flakes rained down as Roland stared, his hope draining from him as surely as the life had left Henri's body.

They could not find him here; he would surely be accused of the murder. But he could not escape with his mother's power, and that boded even worse; for if her magic was not working, the only explanation was her own peril.

Roland was not a man of heroics, nor was he a man of action. But, as a famed lover and courtier, he did know how to escape a room, and quickly. Abandoning all but his small pack of tonics, he leapt out of a window into the Paris night, skittering across the rooftops, beneath the full moon.

"AND HOW DID you get to London?" the gentlewitch asked after Roland's description of his escape.

He was uncertain how much he could trust Liege Rookwood at the precise moment, but he was tired of second-guessing every word and every relationship. That she had found her way to London at this precise moment was a miracle in and of itself; or else, some distant machination of his mother.

"I have some connections, still. And other, less obvious skills," Roland said. He did not yet trust them with the details of his affliction, but he suspected they would both put the pieces together sooner rather than later. One cannot easily leap from rooftop to rooftop as a simple mortal, after all. "That part does not matter so much as what I uncovered when I at last made my way to the safe house. It was ransacked. There were signs of struggle—burn marks on the walls—and the scent of brimstone in the air."

"Brimstone?" Miss Brightwell asked, looking to her companion for explanation.

"It's a common misconception that witches leave a signature of brimstone—sulphur—when they practise corrupt magic," Liege Rookwood said, a wrinkle forming between her brows as she contemplated on the matter. "Though it was used to imprison, kill, and injure many a witch in the years before the Peace. It is, however, powerful in counteracting many witch powers, or at least weakening them."

Poppy frowned. "Well, that's quite convenient, isn't it?"

"I can't imagine the amount of brimstone required to weaken someone like the High Witch," Miss Brightwell said. "And you believe she is in danger, Monsieur de Grateloup?"

Miss Brightwell's pronunciation was so charming, Roland did not dare correct her. "I have asked around London, to the best of my limited abilities, and there are at least twelve different accounts of the High Witch's whereabouts. Summer is typically her escape, when she goes to the safe house to rest and recuperate—she would not be due back at the Coven Hall for another three weeks. But I have heard whispers of sightings along bridges, in mirrors, and attending a number of high-profile dinners."

"Mirrors?" Liege Rookwood perked up at this mention, leaning forward closer. "How curious."

"My mother is possessed of strange and complicated magics, as you well know. However, fraught as our relationship has been, the fact she did not come to my call, and that her talisman did not work, is the greatest proof I have. She has protected me all these long years, and I am afraid I must beg protection from you, her acolyte."

Miss Brightwell looked surprised indeed at this revelation and turned to her companion. "Acolyte?"

Liege Rookwood coughed into her handkerchief. Clearly, Roland had exposed a secret unknowingly. He was, unfortunately, rather good at that. No matter. Every good relationship needed a little deceit in it now and again. He had no doubt they would find their way back to one another. Woefully, these two were perfectly matched.

"Yes, Poppy. We will speak of those details later," Liege Rookwood said dismissively. Judging by the jut of Miss Brightwell's chin, this matter would follow them immediately after this meeting. To Roland, she asked, "And you have no family to go to? No other supports?"

Roland laughed bitterly, wishing he could shield his contempt for his father's family. "Alas, my birth is, in itself, a heresy. My father, wherever he may be, does not acknowledge my existence, nor my validity as a human being. He is much too occupied with his own children to ever bother with me. So, I come to you. I am told, Liege Rookwood, you have a unique set of skills that might aid me in remaining out of sight for a while."

She would say no. She would refuse him. Why should she help him, anyway? It wasn't as if Roland had any social capital, save for his charm, a terrible reputation, and mountains of money. Money he couldn't access without his mother's magic.

Gods and monsters, he was tired. The burden of the last few weeks fell upon him without warning, his pleasant alcoholic shimmer now turning sharply toward melancholy. Well, if they refused to help, he'd just transform and eat them, right here for everyone to witness the carnage. There were worse ways to die than with a belly full of witch. The Brightwell woman would be quite delicious; there was something unusual about her, and he did enjoy exotic delights.

What *was* he thinking? Brimstone, his tonic was wearing off.

"Did you hear what I said, Monsieur de Grateloup?"

He absolutely had not heard a word she said. He was thinking about what the flesh of her companion might taste like.

"Beg pardon, my liege," he said, graciously as he could as he fumbled for more wine. "I think I need another glass of wine."

Liege Rookwood put her hand upon the smooth-necked bottle and levelled Roland with a dark stare as piercing and knowing as his mother's. The Witch's Eye, they called it.

"I said, I am willing to help you on one condition," said the young gentlewitch, in the tone of a rather severe schoolmistress.

"Anything within my means," Roland blurted, attempting to wrest the wine bottle from Liege Rookwood. It would not move beneath her grip, far stronger than one might expect of a woman her size.

"Darling," Miss Brightwell said, concern in her voice, as she drew the curtains tighter around them. "What is going on?"

A laconic smile crept its way across Edith Rookwood's face as she beheld Roland, as if for the first time. His mother had mentioned, on more than one occasion, how smart this gentlewitch was. But, like most estranged bastard sons, he had not truly heeded her warning.

"Monsieur de Grateloup is more than what he appears," the gentlewitch said.

"My liege, I would appreciate if you moved your hand. I am in dire need of a drink," Roland asserted, his voice a near-whine.

The gentlewitch leaned forward, eyes glinting in merriment. "Tell my lovely Poppy here why you can't move your hand."

Confounded woman. He would have bitten her if he had the energy. But, alas, he wanted the drink more than he wanted blood, if only because it reminded him of who he truly was.

"Because she is wearing a ring of witch silver," Roland gritted out.

"What is witch silver?" Miss Brightwell asked, her pretty lips pursing at the end of her question.

Thankfully, Liege Edith replied. "It is a carefully crafted alloy which allows us protection against certain, potentially dangerous preternaturals. Particularly, it works to repel vampires, revenants…"

She let go of the bottle, and Roland hissed at her, despite his attempts at civility. When he said, "and *werewolves*," he looked every bit the monster he feared he'd become.

Miss Brightwell did not start or shout, she merely blinked a few times, as if she'd simply had a confusing thought rather than learned Roland's deepest, darkest secret. "You're a werewolf?" she whispered.

Ah, but he hated the word. He hated the way people looked at him. Hated the way he felt when he watched people come to terms with the monstrosity before them.

No amount of good breeding, fine clothing, or manners could ever change the terrible truth of it.

"I am cursed to *live* as a werewolf," Roland corrected, gulping deeply. The wine was rich, sweet, and burned away the worst of his shame. "But I am *not* a werewolf, not by nature."

"I'm certain that is quite the tale," Miss Brightwell said, obnoxiously sincere.

Roland sniffed back drunken tears. "It happened when I was a child. My mother, already established in politics and the Coven, bore me in secret. I grew up in the South of France, in the town of Grateloup. One autumn, our house came under attack. I was separated from my protectors, and the ensuing attack left me as one of them. My mother arrived in time to kill the pack's leaders, but not in time to prevent me from becoming cursed. We have tried, in vain, for more than twenty years to find a cure."

Before he could argue, Miss Brightwell had thrown her arms around him in a fierce, protective embrace, regardless of the gentlewitch's protestations. Roland looked helplessly at Liege Edith, who just shook her head and took her chair, pouring her own glass of wine.

When Miss Brightwell pulled away, tears streaked her face. "Oh, fate has drawn us together, Monsieur. For we also seek a cure, though to vampirism rather than lycanthropy."

He blinked. He was drunk, but certainly not drunk enough to have missed them both being vampires.

"Poppy's sister," the gentlewitch clarified. "It's one of the reasons we're here in London. Poppy was hoping to visit Culpepper's, or any other establishment that might assist us in keeping Viola from herself."

They had hope in their eyes, both of them. Painful, exasperating hope, pulling at Roland's heartstrings like a toddler at the harp. Culpepper was naught but a charlatan, and an overpriced one at that. If there was one condition for which they were even more unlikely to find a cure than his own, it was vampirism. For once, Roland felt as if perhaps he were not the most cursed man in England.

And a better man might have given in to that hope. But he was not a better man. "I will arrange a meeting with Culpepper, if you would like," Roland said. "Provided you promise me sanctuary in the coming weeks."

"Of course," Edith Rookwood said. "I can arrange for your travel from here to Netherford and will give you a letter of introduction for my majordomo, Auden Garcliffe."

Oh, indeed. Roland had met Auden Garcliffe on more than one occasion. He'd forgotten the fellow was part of the Rookwood clan. That would do quite well.

"And I'll be safe?" Roland asked.

"As safe as I can make you. We plan to return to Netherford in a week's time, and you may accompany us. Once there, I can perform the proper spells to conceal you from even the most prying eyes," the gentlewitch said. In another witch, the claim might have come across as a boast. But Edith Rookwood had an odd, matter-of-fact way about her that left little doubt of her skill.

Miss Brightwell finished wiping her eyes on her cloak, before turning to Roland. "Do you have somewhere to stay in the meantime? I can't imagine the Tippling Philosopher is terribly comfortable or safe."

"I can abide a few more days. But not much longer. I am unsure of whom I should trust in this town, and although I once counted Stafford Vale among my friends, he was one of the last people to see my mother. So perhaps the two of you can do some of your own sleuthing while I tie up loose ends," Roland suggested.

After an appraising look that went on slightly too long, Edith Rookwood nodded her head. She took off the witch silver ring and offered her hand. He shook it, mustering a toothy smile he hoped looked less predatory than he felt.

POPPY WISHED SHE could find her way to Lord Vale's house alone, for she did not want to speak to Edith if she could help it. Her companion had lied to her. For months! Edith had looked Poppy straight in the eyes and promised she would not practice liminal magic, the very power that had attracted the Boagane to them and cost Viola, well, *everything*. But she still had. It didn't matter that it had been done under the High Witch's tutelage, she had kept it from Poppy. Like so many other things. Of *course* she didn't know about witch silver, how could she? Poppy was just a simpleton, after all, incapable of understanding all of Edith's *terribly* important witch business.

She was so angry she couldn't form coherent thoughts, let alone words.

"Poppy, look at me," Edith said from across the way.

Poppy just shook her head stubbornly. She knew the moment she opened her mouth she would burst into tears.

Edith sighed, full of weariness and regret. "I know better than to try and explain it to you. You know I had my reasons. But you are well within your rights to be angry at me. I lied."

"That isn't even a proper apology," Poppy said, anger now searing past her tears. "'Well within my rights'? Edith, you *promised* me."

"I shouldn't have done that. But I was afraid you'd try and stop me," Edith said.

That was worse than remorse. Poppy's heart broke as the realisation crystalised in her mind: Edith loved magic more than she would ever love Poppy. And either she would have to learn to live with that or live without Edith.

CHAPTER SIX
ᴹISSING ᴾERSONS ᴬND ᴾERSONIFICATIONS

"MY LORD!"

Silas, busy working, glanced up from his desk. The voice came from outside, not within, and he strode to the open window to find Petronilla Rookwood-Nourse standing just outside the grasp of the rose garden, blooms flushed red in the dusk glow. Had so much time passed since he'd sat down to his correspondence?

Devils, he was going to be late for his appointment with Miss Eliza Atwater.

Except: there was a most alarming tone to the young witch's voice.

"Miss Rookwood-Nourse," Silas said, gathering what remained of his wits. Most of them had been lost to the ledger for the day, he feared. "May I assist you with something?"

Miss Rookwood-Nourse gave an exasperated sigh, blowing a lock of hair from her forehead in the process. "Two matters of interest to you, my lord. One, Miss Atwater's carriage approaches with haste."

"Good, good," Silas said, reaching for the shutter to close the window.

"I said *two* matters." Miss Rookwood-Nourse looked perturbed. Silas could not recall her ever projecting anything other than absolute composure.

"My sincere apologies," Silas replied.

"Miss Brightwell is missing, Silas."

"Miss... Brightwell?"

Oh, stars. Stars and the speckled firmament, *no*.

AN EVENING DINNER had sounded ideal when Fintan suggested it, and Miss Atwater was quite amenable. From his few interactions with her previously, that was not surprising: Eliza Atwater was known for her general agreeableness in almost every situation. She was pretty, but not too pretty; she was tall, but not overly so; she had a significant sum a year, but not enough to compete with the viscount's own reputation. In education, she excelled, for Eliza was the fourth child and only girl among the Atwaters of Golford, renowned for their ties to the Pirate Wars.

Miss Atwater arrived with her chaperone, her elder brother George, who may well have been her twin save that Silas knew they were a few years apart. They were of a height, both slight and slim, with long, aristocratic noses, and fair, flaxen hair. Miss Atwater wore the latest fashions, a coral-hued taffeta gown with a spray of interlocking branch embroidery upon the hem.

Once, during dinner, Silas thought he heard a thumping noise above but was not interrupted further. Although they had not yet located Viola, he was certain the staff could manage. Besides, Laertes was her sire, and aware of the importance of the week's dinner. Last he had seen, Laertes was searching the lower gardens for Viola, and believed he was close on her trail.

To call the dinner dull would have done a disservice to dullards. This was not Miss Atwater's fault; her brother spoke over her at every chance he got, regaling Silas with stories of their enchanted childhood—which sounded rather plain and unremarkable to him—or else reminding everyone gathered just how much a year he was worth. Apparently, he'd recently been betrothed to the daughter of a baronet and would become even richer in the New Year.

Given the small group, Silas had aperitifs served in the drawing room. In regular circumstances, he and Mr. Atwater would have separated from Miss Atwater to discuss details of Miss Atwater's dowry, or else other manly matters, but as the dowager viscountess was indisposed, that would have left Miss Atwater without a chaperone. That, and the idea of having to spend *any* amount of time with Mr. Atwater alone, made Silas cringe.

"This is very good," Mr. Atwater said from the velvet green couch he'd settled into, raising the brandy Fintan had poured him. It was not the best of the house, but passable in good company. "Did you bring this back with you from France, my lord?"

Silas, who drank slowly and deliberately to keep a clear mind, nodded. "Yes, indeed. I arranged for a small import, myself, of a variety of labels."

"Ah, I remember the years of the blockade," Mr. Atwater said, putting his nose into the brandy class and sniffing. "It's a good thing the witches had their way with Napoleon, or we'd still be without this marvellous stuff. Did you fight, my lord? Or were you a sympathiser?"

Perhaps Silas ought to have imbibed much faster. "I am no soldier, Mr. Atwater, nor was I a French sympathiser. I remained in Paris for my education and at my father's request, under the protection of the Coven Consulate there. It is a lucky thing we have witches to serve and protect the Crown and its people, for even in times of war we are able to build bridges."

"I might go to France next year," Miss Atwater said. "Well, providing the travel restrictions are lifted for those of us without coven connections."

"Ah, indeed. And what do you plan to do there?" Silas asked Miss Atwater, hoping the vein of conversation might lead him to somewhere he wouldn't have to fight the pull of sleep so relentlessly.

Miss Atwater tilted her head in confusion, as if the question was an odd one. "I—well, shopping, I suppose." She paused again. "Did you hear something, my lord?"

A prickle of knowing shivered down Silas's spine, the lingering scent of roses wafting toward him. "This part of the house is new. It's still settling."

"And a magnificent home it is," Mr. Atwater said, just as his sister opened her mouth to speak. "I say, the rumour in town is that this was the most expensive undertaking in Kent's history, or at least since records began."

The man truly was shameless. "Rumours fly throughout the county, and though I can attest to its significant cost, 'tis nothing in comparison to some," Silas said. "The original structure was still in good shape, but we had a mind to expand considerably upon the vision."

There. A sound. A high, keening wail, followed by a scrabbling sound like claws across brickwork.

Silas cleared his throat, hoping the guests did not hear, but now Miss Atwater's gaze darted around the room.

"Is *that* just the house settling?" she asked.

"Ah, no. I believe that might be bats. We've had issues with them from since before the renovation, and I think they may be angry at us for upending their lives," Silas said.

"I hear nothing," Mr. Atwater said, sneering over his snifter to his sister. "Eliza has such a vivid imagination, Lord St. Albans. You will have to excuse her anxieties. But, as with so many of her most unfortunate sex, she was not blessed with a strong constitution."

"Miss Atwater, tell me, do you read?" Silas asked her, trying not to let his expression drop when Fintan entered the room, his violet eyes practically vibrating with concern.

"She reads enough to keep house," Mr. Atwater said.

"I did ask Miss Atwater directly, sir," Silas said, his temper getting the better of him. Raised by strong women, and in proximity to the most powerful witches of their age, he had little time for men who built up their own egos by tearing down those of the women around them. The Coven Council may be praised and lauded, but there were still plenty of men prepared to stoke the fires again should the mood change. He had no doubt Mr. Atwater would be among the first with the torch.

Miss Atwater flushed pink, blotches spreading down the front of her gown as she tried to find the appropriate words in response. "I—my lord. I am certain I would read whatever you would like me to read."

It was the singular worst answer Silas ever could have asked for. It was bad enough that Miss Atwater lived in the shadow of her brother, that he clearly thought she and all women were inferior, and that they both were obsessed with money. But to have *no* intellectual curiosity? To act as if Silas were the sort of man who would want a woman to read only because it pleased him? He felt nauseated.

"My lord," Fintan said, coming up to him, "a word, if you please."

"Of course," Silas said, taking the moment to wipe the anxious sweat from his brow.

Another sound, like someone moving a garderobe across wood floors, sounded above, followed by an unmistakable cacophony of shattered glass.

"We have located Miss Brightwell," Fintan said quietly. "She is currently confined to the master's suite upstairs."

Silas's bedroom? Visions of his recent dream came flooding back to him, and he finished his cognac in one gulp. Part of his soul ached to be with her, to help her, but he knew it was likely his doom. Having to endure the Atwaters had put him in a morose mood as it was.

"Has Mr. Byrne been apprised of the situation?" Silas asked.

"He has. And he and Miss Rookwood-Nourse are doing all they can, but..." Fintan shivered as a low moan, close and terrifying, echoed down the hall.

Silas, fear coursing through his veins, called for some of his footmen immediately. To his guests, he said, "I'm terribly sorry, but there is a matter I must attend to. It is best if you make your way into town for the evening. It appears we have a—a structural matter on the first floor that has just come to my attention."

Mr. Atwater stared, aghast, but Silas could not mistake the look of relief on Miss Atwater's face. Perhaps the discussion was as painful for her as it had been for him. There was some measure of comfort in that.

There would be other women, he supposed.

"Where shall we go?" Mr. Atwater asked as Fintan took him by the elbow and began escorting him out of the Drawing Room.

"Fintan will arrange for you to stay at the Locke and Key. It's just a mile down the road. Very lovely. Mrs. Grigsby makes some of the most delicious pies you will ever taste," Silas said quickly. "I appreciate your visit. I'm certain we're bound to see each other again at a fete or two in the autumn."

It was possible Mr. Atwater said some words before he was entirely ushered away from the viscount, but Silas was not interested in hearing them.

"She needs human blood."

The words rang in Silas's head with crystalline clarity.

Laertes Byrne, always the pinnacle of composure, looked shaken, ill, and certainly terrified.

"I'm sorry, could you please clarify?" Silas asked.

They both stood outside Silas's own bedroom which, judging by the sound, was now scarcely more than a shell of its former glory. Inside, he was told, Miss Rookwood-Nourse had Viola in a kind of holding spell, but it wouldn't last too much longer.

"Ophelia wrote me from Bath," Laertes said, wiping a bloody tear from his cheek. "She warned that Viola's emotional state could worsen, perhaps even speeding her change to a revenant if she was still rejecting the bond. I thought, briefly, this might not be a concern, as she seemed calmer the last few days. Then she had a difficult night and has not recovered since."

"You say human blood. I presume you know how to get some?" Silas asked.

Laertes raised a single, black brow at the viscount, as if he had asked the daftest question this side of the English Channel. "I tried to give her some of my own. It was enough to lure her back, but now she is even more upset, and I am significantly weakened. She took more blood than I was anticipating."

"Surely there are blood banks. I recall you once received regular deliveries," Silas said, knowing he had once paid Viola's own father for his blood.

The vampire bared his teeth in pain, clutching at his chest. "If Viola transforms into a revenant, she may take me with her. My powers are muted, now, utterly useless. The bond is strong if accepted, but if not, it can be parasitic. Silas, she needs the blood of the living."

The blood of the living. The mere idea of her feasting upon someone else made Silas irrationally angry, and not for reasons a logical man might cite. It felt an intrusion on his deepest desires. Bad enough Laertes had done it, and their connection was familial; paternal, almost.

"Whose blood?" Silas managed to say through clenched teeth.

Laertes blew out a long breath, shaking his head. "It's a significant responsibility, my lad. A moment generally revered among our people. But mark my words, it will help keep her from turning into a revenant."

"And will the volunteer be susceptible to vampirism after?"

"Not at all. She is not a complete vampire, so she is incapable of spawning another. The only symptoms, after the feed, would be fatigue and soreness as their body replenishes its stores."

"I will do it."

Silas couldn't consider it any longer. Oh, he was quite aware this was a terrible decision, potentially catastrophic. But as wretched as it was to offer himself as a thrall to Viola, it was even more impossible to contemplate her taking someone else.

The vampire steadied himself on the door as another rattle shook it to its latches. "Certainly, you have staff for this sort of thing, my lord," he said. "You are much loved; I doubt anyone would think twice about assisting in this situation."

"Absolutely not. I am responsible for Viola. I have promised her parents. I have promised myself."

"This is a highly concerning situation," Laertes moaned. "I do not see how it plays out well for either of you. No matter the outcome, it will make your subsequent marriages that much more difficult. It is a sacred process, you understand. It could bond you together even more than you already are."

"And you would have her feed from a stranger?" asked the viscount.

"I see your point. Regretfully," Laertes admitted. "Very well. I will go with you, for in her state, she might need assistance."

"No." Silas put his hand on the doorknob and looked Laertes straight in the eye, steeling himself for the scene in his bedroom. "Only if I call for you."

"My lord—"

"This is not a request, Mr. Byrne."

And with that, Silas entered into the chaos.

Hunger ate at her mind, gnawed on her bones, and nothing would sate it. Let the fire witch kill her, let the magic burn through her body so Viola could be free. Death was the only answer to the ever-present ache inside of her, that she would not allow herself to recognise. The beast within her. The monster. The red-eyed fiend who longed for violence and possession, seduction and indulgence. It could not be her; she could not accept it. She was a burden to her family, a drain on her keeper in this gilded cage. Death, perhaps, was too kind an answer.

All at once, after she raged and raged, the bars of her fiery cave released, smoke filling her vision. She screamed and hissed, clawing at the drapes and ripping across the coverlet on the bed. A flurry of feathers cascaded around her, infuriating her even more.

Then, that smell. Sandalwood and vanilla. A shape moved by the door, eclipsed for a brief moment by the shape of the fire witch. Tall, broad, elegant, the man who haunted her dreams.

"You know, Viola, I have tried putting this all down in words," he said, calm and polite as their first meeting. If Viola didn't smell his fear, she would have never known.

Her chemise hung in shreds from her body, her stays

loosened, baring her breasts. A small part of her, the part that faded by the day, felt a twinge of embarrassment at that, but then she defied that feeling, drawing up to her full height and jutting out her chin with all the pride of a born royal.

"You are food," she said—or else the monster did.

She stalked closer to him, her feet so quiet it made her a bit giddy. Hunting would be a delight, wouldn't it? Perhaps she should chase the man into the woods and make him think he had half a chance. She could listen to his heartbeat rise to a crescendo, and then drain him until it stopped.

And it would be glorious.

"Perhaps more than food," the man said. He had a very nice voice. "I have never told anyone this, outside of my cousin Roland, but I am a writer. An author, I should say. Quite popular in France, as well, to the point that I helped fund a good portion of this house's renovations. My father was beyond terrible with finances. He'd never have approved of my artistic life, but as it is, people enjoy stories of the arcane and strange. I've never written about vampires, though," he continued, even when Viola came up to him and hissed in his face.

She knew he could not see well in the dark, but Viola could measure every line of his face, see the pity and the fear in his eyes. His heart, his blood, were so close she could feel them, *taste* them.

"I will kill you," she whispered, not interested in his words or his confessions. "I can't stop."

"I won't ask you to," the man said. "The point is, as meandering as I have made it, that I have wondered, time and again, how I would write our story. I remember seeing you for the first time so clearly, your face and your voice etched indelibly into my memory. My whole being felt changed on the deepest level, as if every mote of my soul knew yours."

Viola could, she knew, kill the man that very moment. He was practically begging her to. Except she remembered his name: Silas Drake. And she remembered him the night she became the monster.

Viola. Violence. *Vampire.*

"Then you were taken from me, and all I could think was that I hadn't fought hard enough. I hadn't asked you to dance. I hadn't kissed you properly. I hadn't told you any of it, for fear my reputation might be ruined. I could have managed marrying a woman of lower rank, but I was afraid of denying my great aunt, afraid of the spectre of my parents, perhaps. I was a coward, then. Even though that life for us may be gone, I do not wish to languish in cowardice now."

The essence of herself, of Viola Brightwell, rose to the fore as Silas took her hand and kissed it, the monster quietened.

"Fight for me now," she whispered, tasting the blood of her tears.

Silas pulled her forward, his hand so firm about her waist it made her hitch in a breath of air. He smoothed back her filthy hair as if each tangle was precious. Then, he picked her up and put her upon the one chair that remained upright in the room.

Her whole body tingled with anticipation, no longer burning with agony and fury, but something slower, headier, and more delicious.

"You are sick, and I hold a cure. So, willingly, I give you my blood, in hopes that, in time, we can perhaps write the end of our tale. Even if it does not mean we find our way back to one another—if only to give you a chance at finding a whisper of happiness." Silas tilted his head to the side, loosening his pristine white cravat.

Viola understood. The monster understood. That balance was sweet, saccharine joy.

Gently, reverently, Viola touched the viscount's neck, feeling the shift of smooth skin to rough at his jawline. Did he remember the visit the night before? Or had that been a dream, too? It was getting so terribly difficult to tell one way or another.

Here, though, here Silas felt real.

"Maybe you should let me go," she said, her thumb brushing across his bottom lip. He let out a moan that sent shivers to her core. "I am dangerous."

"I am finding I like your danger."

"I cannot ask this of you."

Silas covered her hand with his, pressing it against his cheek to turn his head even more, to bare his neck in full. "Which is why I give it. Choose what is freely given, Viola, in hopes we can keep you long enough to find a cure, or a way forward."

HE THOUGHT, FOR a dizzy moment, she would refuse him, and he would have to either kill her or run from the room in shame. Or die in her clutches. His body came alive with giddy fear as she moved—so suddenly he did not have time to cry out—and he felt the sting of her teeth sinking into his neck.

The pain spread from his neck into his jaw and ear, radiating out and down his arm. Silas's vision exploded in blossoms of red, like melting roses, as her soft lips pulled upon his skin, slowly at first, and then building in intensity. Her hands trembled, one on his chest and the other cradling his cheek, as a frisson of passion coursed through him, arousal and terror twisted together in an ecstatic combination.

His body came alive as his lifeblood drained, a magnificent contrast of sensations clouding his brain. To keep himself grounded, to focus on the moment, he reached up to hold her back, feeling the delicate muscles and bones of her body rise and fall with each new draught of his blood. Her legs held him tight, pressing in upon his waist, throbbing in time with her feeding. He imagined what it would be like to hold her similarly, their bodies joined elsewhere, skin slick and face flushed.

Silas felt the edges of his consciousness slipping sooner than he'd hoped, an inexorable tide pulling him into a blessed, cold emptiness.

"Viola," he whispered.

She did not stop. She only drank more fiercely, her fingertips now fully clawed, digging into his shoulders.

"Please, you must stop."

A song began then, inside of him, a mournful melody he had never heard, resounding in his brain. He had never heard the song before, and yet it filled him with longing and sadness, like a fleeting memory the moment before sleep overtakes the mind.

Some sort of presence flitted across his consciousness, yanking him out of his near slumber, and when he said, "Enough," the room went perfectly still, as did Viola.

She froze and slowly unlatched her teeth from his neck, wiping her chin with the back of her hand. Lids heavy, he slumped back on the floor, barely catching himself. She followed him, slinking her body up his, and tenderly brushed over his brow with her fingers.

Then she kissed him, brazen and shameless, and he returned the favour, just before falling into a deep, dreamless slumber.

CHAPTER SEVEN
ON THE PROWL

POPPY MUST BE beyond furious, for although she joined Edith in bed, she refused any further conversation or attention of any sort. Given all they had learned, the gentlewitch knew how much of a strain it had to be remaining silent and still for her companion. And yet, Poppy fell asleep quicker than usual, her breathing even and sweet beneath the ostentatious coverlet in Vale's guest room.

Guilt was a strange emotion for Edith, in both senses: unfamiliar and mercurial. Poppy had every right to be angry with her, but didn't Edith also have a right to keep some parts of her life secret? They were not wedded in any legal capacity, for their bond was far beyond such concepts. That, and Poppy was absolutely against the idea. Edith supposed it made her anxious, or unsettled, to be bound to another for all time.

In the moment, keeping Poppy from knowing her studies with Virginia Cawley had felt like a matter of Coven privacy. Not even the rest of the Council was aware, for liminal magic was so very rare. Some believed it a myth, or else a lost art entirely. Poppy was afraid of liminal magic because she did not understand it and, in her experience, only bad had come of it. Except liminal magic was no more 'good' or 'evil' than any other kind of power, and Edith couldn't very well forget all she had learned. She and Virginia had agreed it was better to find out more—and master it—than fall prey to it once again.

Not for the last time, Edith realised just how removed Poppy was from her life as a gentlewitch. It had not seemed to matter before, when they were in the first throes of love. Now Edith worried Poppy might never be truly happy living on the edges of the magical world, the politics of the Coven Council, and all that came with being the companion of a gentlewitch.

She turned to watch Poppy's face in the last of the candlelight, her heart constricting at the strange irony of her lying so near yet feeling so far away. Loving a person was certainly the most difficult thing she had ever done.

Knowing sleep would not claim her yet for a long while, Edith rose and went downstairs. She had planned on going straight to the library, but she noticed the warm glow of firelight down in the drawing room. She was caught between propriety and her own curiosity—Vale was a known eccentric, so there was nothing surprising about him being up at such a late hour. Still, Edith remained cautious. Roland's words had discomfited her.

When a servant passed her with a tray laden with hot chocolate, however, Edith's resolve crumbled. Normally, she did not enjoy company, but even if Vale was part of the larger conspiracy against the High Witch, he was still among one of the most learned scholars and travellers in the realm.

Once inside the foyer, Edith found Vale in a high-backed chintz chair with an enormous tome on his lap. He dressed for the evening, velvet slippers matching the chartreuse hue of his voluminous banyan. She could not quite make out the pattern from where she stood, what with the bright firelight.

"Well, I was hoping someone might join me after all," Vale said, gesturing to a matching chintz-upholstered chair across from him. "Call it intuition."

"Thank you, Vale," Edith said, tightening her own banyan and taking the proffered seat. Her travelling nightclothes were nowhere near as soft as the ones she wore at home, and she had a sudden longing for Netherford and its dependable routines. "It's been a rather long evening."

"I hope all is well." Vale set his book down on a small side-table and took his hot chocolate in both of his hands. He drank from an ostentatious enamelled goblet, two-handled, the pattern depicting dual dragons entwined. "I was disappointed you and your companion could not stay for dinner, but given your long visit, I am certain we will find another opportunity."

Edith was glad of the perfectly uninteresting teacup in her hand, Derby by the looks of it, with a gold and rose pattern design. It glinted in the firelight as she raised it to her mouth to sip. Having been once poisoned, she had learned a simple and nearly undetectable charm to detect unnatural ingredients. This, she was certain, was just chocolate.

"Indeed," she said. "And my apologies. It appears London had plans for us even before we were able to make our own."

Vale pursed his lips, looking at Edith appraisingly. "I understand it is quite late, and you are already quite taxed, so you may of course reject my offer, but I would like the opportunity to speak frankly, my liege."

"Of course," Edith said automatically. "I hope we have not offended you beyond repair. Tell me how I may remedy matters if that is the case."

"Oh, nonsense. I am one of the most difficult human beings to offend this side of the Thames, which is no mean feat," Vale said with a light laugh. "No, it is only regarding the company you kept tonight."

Molly had assured her no one had followed them, but that didn't rule out tampering with Roland's letter on the way in. "I wasn't aware my goings-on were yours to mark," she said.

Vale sighed, deep and sorrowful. "You are a guest in my home, and had you come to me first, we might have had this conversation in more comfort. As it is, I imagine Monsieur de Grateloup has rallied you to his side and told you a story worthy of the greatest authors of our age. But I pray you listen to what I have to say—even if you disregard it—for it may serve you in the future."

"I did not take you for a political creature, Vale," Edith said. The chocolate was very good, but difficult to enjoy given the turn of conversation.

"I am not. You know I have always eschewed the ridiculous bureaucracy and restrictive rules of our class. I have moved in circles both profane and praised and learned a great many truths from them all. And although I once counted Roland de Grateloup as a friend, I am concerned for him, especially the most recent accusations against his person."

"Please, do explain."

Leaning forward, Vale clasped his hands together. "I fear Roland has been doomed from the beginning. He has known this, of course, and it is likely you know of his afflictions."

Edith nodded, "Yes. Lycanthropy."

"Indeed. The rumour is he contracted it some years into his childhood, assaulted where his mother was not able to protect him. It is a fiercely guarded secret, known only to a handful of those closest to him and to the High Witch. But I have gathered—from a direct account, no less—that it is not true."

"Why would he lie about being a werewolf?" Edith asked.

"No, no. He is most certainly a werewolf. But I do not believe he was *turned* into a werewolf at all. I have it on good authority that his mother, Virginia Cawley, entered into a tryst, knowingly, with a member of the Grey Moon Brotherhood."

"That's preposterous," Edith said, repulsed by the very idea. The Grey Moon Brotherhood were an ancient and secretive witch-hunting society of monster-hunters and lycanthropes, officially outlawed but still tolerated in both England and the Continent. Their history was sordid, but their recent reforms claimed they had changed their ways and now focused primarily on education and supporting the poor. Any witch worth her salt knew better, of course, and every few months rumours of their attempts to infiltrate local politics grew.

"The High Witch would never do such a thing. To lie to her own son? To involve herself with such miscreants? It does not sound like the woman I know."

The scholar stared into the fires. "I would not believe it save that I know the heart is a fickle thing. When presented with this intelligence, I, too, struggled to find reason in it. I threw myself into my studies, travelling as far as the Belarusian Governorate. That is a tale for another day, for it nearly led to my own early demise. That said, I was able to confirm what I had begun to suspect: though werewolves, and their political allies, have insisted from time out of mind that they can produce other werewolves through bites, it is not true. Their bloodline is built solely on inheritance by direct progeny."

Somehow, this was worse than what Edith had expected. "Accusing the High Witch of what, exactly?"

"I cannot imagine any scenario in the world in which the High Witch would have done anything against her will, given her power and proclivities. But I understand why she might have told Roland he was turned, for children are valuable among the werewolves. Theirs is not, as some assume, a patrilineal society. They have a king and a queen, measured equally together, with great power between them. Their hatred for witches has nothing to do with the women involved, simply a blood feud that goes back almost a millennium."

"If Roland does not know this, then what harm is he? He would be even more innocent."

Vale gave a sympathetic nod of agreement. "In some ways, yes. But his nature, my dear. He has ever been coddled and spoiled, likely out of guilt. It is not, in any way, surprising his behaviour may have turned murderous."

"And what makes you say that?"

"There are rumours. From Paris. The whispers tell me he may have been involved in a most grisly murder."

"He hardly seemed the sort to me," Edith said, defensively. She very much disliked misjudging people. Roland was a challenging individual, yes, but his story, and his remorse and panic, seemed very honest. He was desperate, yes. But she didn't want to reveal all she knew, either. It seemed unlikely to her that Virginia Cawley's son, no matter how spoiled and French he was, would resort to cold-blooded murder.

"He has been suppressing his power for years, now. I know this because we have often been lovers. There is scarcely an apothecary from Dublin to Mumbai who hasn't worked with him. And I fear there is only so much that tonics and tinctures can do. Not to mention, there are consequences of not expressing one's true nature. Violent ones."

"You do not think the Grey Moon Brotherhood framed him?" Edith asked. "It seems far more plausible. He does not strike me as the sort of man willing to do the dirty work himself."

Vale sighed, gazing into his drink. "If his nature is as I suspect…"

"Is it so hopeless for those unwillingly turned?" Edith asked. She felt so weary. "Poppy's sister, as I wrote, was turned by a vampire. She is resisting. And she is not well. I had hoped there would be someone in London capable of helping her. I have done all the research I can, and it is old, impenetrable magic."

The fire crackled and popped as Vale considered Edith's words, casting little shadows through the grate that danced like grasping hands.

"You have full access to my library and any contact that might be helpful," he said at last. "I do not want to say hope is futile, but I do believe hope in traditional methods is. And whether or not Roland de Grateloup will help or hinder, I do not know. Both he and the High Witch have accumulated many enemies in the last few years and knowing the Grey Moon Brotherhood is involved does not bode well. Hopefully, in a week, when the Coven Council returns into session, Virginia Cawley will set all concerns to rest. But meanwhile, I warn you against attracting attention unless you are confident of your own skills in battle."

THOUGH NEARLY EVERYONE thought her a country mouse, Poppy was not without friends in London. No, indeed, one of her dearest friends, Miss Rawlings-Vijay of Netherford, had a brother named Nathaniel who worked for one of the most prestigious tailors in Witch's Row, the aptly named Last Stitch. Poppy knew the establishment was held in the highest regard, and she had long desired to peruse their embroiderer's hall, where some of the most talented stitchers worked on their craft.

Poppy had many hobbies, but embroidery was her most beloved. Having the chance to spend an afternoon amidst the floss and needles seemed like a wonderful use of her time.

Especially since she was avoiding Edith as much as possible. She wanted her anger to cool before they had a more serious discussion, and few things in life distracted Poppy as well as beautiful embroidery and passementerie.

Alas, she could not venture out alone. Molly Hode accompanied her; given the number of Warders in London, it would be easy for Edith to find a temporary substitute. Poppy doubted Edith would leave the library, anyway, so she did not argue when the gentlewitch insisted Molly go with her.

"You're sulking," Molly said, not ten minutes into their ride to Finsbury.

"I am not *sulking*. I am ruminating," Poppy asserted, even though Molly was right.

"We just passed Somerset House and you barely even looked at it. The Brightwell lass I know would be demanding we stop at every turn."

Molly wore her crimson braids tucked smartly into a twist at the base of her neck, and she wore the new livery Edith had commissioned, every button gleaming. On a regular day, without the impending heartbreak and difficulties facing her, she'd have certainly said something complimentary.

Molly, who had grown up in Netherford and had known Poppy since she was scarcely seven years old, was absolutely right. The Warder, and her twin brother, had a most annoying habit of having the right of things.

Poppy frowned into her collar. She'd opted for a sheer muslin fichu that was somewhat old-fashioned, but made of the most darling lace. The frills at the top made her almost smile. "Did you know Edith was studying liminal magic?"

Molly just pursed her lips.

"Oh, of course you did. You're her chief Warder," Poppy said with a huff. "I think I'm the only person in all of Netherford who truly had no idea. She promised me, Molly. She *promised* she wouldn't."

"Promises of a gentlewitch are fickle at best. Have you spoken to her about it?"

"Not at length. I discovered it when we met Monsieur le Gardeloup, who was aware. Or at least, worked it out."

"I do not think Edith lied to spite you, if that's what you're worried about," Molly said, adjusting in the seat. She was a large woman, powerfully built, and such contraptions were not made for her. "I think she likely did it to protect you. At least, that's what she told me. She knew you'd be upset if you knew."

"Of course I'd be upset!" Poppy said hotly. "Molly, it was liminal magic that lured the Boagane to us. It was liminal magic, ultimately, that killed my sister and gave her this half-life as a vampire." She felt the prickling of tears and blinked them away angrily.

Molly took Poppy's hand, the caring touch of a friend. "Precisely. Poppy, think on this: you cannot put magic like that back. Once it's out, that's it. Edith is very good at it. From what I have heard, she's struggled most of her life to find a magical discipline she could depend on. If she does not learn to control it, she could put us all in danger."

"But what if that's what happened to the High Witch? What if her toying with liminal magic took her life?" Poppy asked desperately. All this emotion was making her heart and head ache.

The carriage came to a stop by the glittering sign of the Last Stitch, a veritable parade of admirers peering in the gilt-framed windows, pointing at the stacks of silk velvets and pastel muslins. Poppy's mood darkened further, wondering how on earth she would ever manage to get an audience with Mr. Rawlings-Vijay through such an enthusiastic clientele. She did not enjoy large crowds at the best of times and was suddenly acutely aware of her old-fashioned lace and last season's muslin.

"Perhaps we should come another time. I thought being here early enough would avoid the crowds," Poppy said, settling back into the chair.

"No need, we're not stopping here exactly," Molly said, grinning widely. "I sent word ahead, and there's a secondary entrance behind the building. Mr. Rawlings-Vijay will meet us there."

Relief flooded Poppy's heart, and she just barely contained herself from flinging her arms around Molly in thanks.

The carriage jolted to a start, and in a few moments, they had pulled past a small gate and into a little courtyard limned in pink wisteria and the most exuberant dahlias she'd ever seen. There was hardly time to admire them, however, for just as she'd begun examining a lovely foxglove, she heard her name.

"If it isn't Persephone Brightwell," said a cheerful voice.

Poppy turned to see Nathaniel Rawlings-Vijay standing at the threshold of a lacquered wooden door, head rakishly tilted, and a bright smile upon his face. She had not seen him in over a decade, as he'd been sent to London long ago. Although Jamini, his sister, had never had a love of London, he'd worked his way up the ranks at an impressive rate. He'd been a rather thin fellow before, still lanky with the awkwardness of his young years. Now, at nearly thirty, he was roguishly handsome, his deep brown skin glowing against the lavender hue of his frock coat.

Like most tailors, he had a very ostentatious style, often preferring an adapted Court style dress instead of the more sober designs more popular among menfolk these days.

They embraced as old friends and, in a flurry of movement and chatter, Poppy was pulled into the most beautiful rooms she had ever seen.

The building itself was vaguely Tudor in its design—many floors connected by immense, deep wooden staircases—

and ornate stained glass upon every window. Each floor had a speciality, ranging from printed cottons of every design and weight, to the finest mulberry silks, to the most delicate embroidery floss Poppy had ever encountered. The latter took up an entire side room, the spools lined up in a dizzying array of colours.

Nathaniel narrated constantly as he ushered her through it all, an endless font of knowledge as to the history of the building and its importance in London and Coven history:

"We are the only establishment contracted to develop Coven's robes, the dyes we use are from an ancient Burgundian recipe believed to have been inspired by Hildegard of Bignen... We dye all the material here at the facility, whether it's the warm-weather cottons of the summer or the velvets of the cooler climes... If I could show you that area, I would, but I fear it is a most exclusive spot; even I have only managed my way there a few times..."

"My goodness, how incredible," Poppy said, truly swept away in the majesty of the place. "It must be a wonder to come to work here every day."

Nathaniel laughed merrily as they came to the top floor, which held both the notions and passementerie departments. It was a bustle of workers moving between baskets and shelves full to bursting with goods, counting, examining, and sorting them as necessary, or else comparing them to samples of cloth.

"Well," said the tailor, "it is work. And although the *building* is enchanting, I assure you that not all our *clientele* are. We have some remarkably exacting customers, many of whom pay more than my own salary a year in single costumes. Especially with the harvest season coming on soon, and all the celebrations that will entail. Every year they all strive to be more elaborately and memorably dressed than the others."

"Oh, what a wonder it must be to dress folk for such festivities, though!" cried Poppy. "Do you have a witch on staff? I've seen some truly wonderful ensorcelled headpieces. The cost must be unfathomable, though, on top of everything you do here."

"Indeed, we do. Miss Poppinstock is our resident witch. We call her a *panimancer*—a cloth conjurer—but truly she's an illusionist with a keen eye for colour and design," he said. "You'd like her. She is passionate about her work, and a charming conversationalist."

After the tour, Nathaniel brought Poppy back to the embroidery hall, where she observed a magnificent team hard at work embellishing an enormous tapestry. It was, Nathaniel informed her, a commission from the Queen herself, a depiction of the Battle of Hastings when Adela of France—a witch of great renown and mother-in-law to William the Conqueror—directed the arrow that slew Harold of England, therefore beginning the First Great Peace.

Poppy knew well the story was far more complicated than that, given the later rise in anti-witch sentiment and the eventual and systematic murder of witches across England and the Continent, but it was a symbolic moment in the establishment of what some considered the beginnings of the Empire.

The depiction was rendered in silk and silver to an astonishing vision, Adela at the centre with her son-in-law William guarding her from the ground, and her daughter Maude holding a flaming sword aloft. Their features reminded Poppy of faces from Greek and Roman sculptures, their bodies muscled and draped in medieval robes that shone in the light. The embroiderers were adding gemstone beads, sequins, and even little mirrors to the final product, making the characters shimmer and reflect the light as Poppy walked down the long corridor. Their chatter kindled a warm sensation inside of her and she wondered what it would have been like to live in London and work at such an auspicious establishment.

Nathaniel leaned over to Poppy. "I know it looks ostentatious, but I'm told there is a much deeper story behind it," he murmured. "From what we've gathered, the Queen is concerned about the Prince Regent and the influence of his mistress, given his estrangement from the Princess of Wales."

Princess Caroline was a staunch supporter of the Coven Council, and indeed her candidacy as the Prince Regent's companion had been championed by the High Witch herself. The Prince Regent generally kept out of politics himself, preferring to carouse about town and drain the royal coffers. It was said that although he had no discretion with other women, he had grown closer to his first wife— now mistress—and her closest advisors. Meanwhile, all eyes were upon Charlotte, the sole heir to the throne. Despite their efforts extramaritally, only Charlotte was a legitimate heir.

The tailor's words made Poppy's skin prickle. "The Crown has ever been on the side of the gentlewitch class; it is difficult to imagine an England without it."

Nathaniel sighed. "Not if you hear the merchants go on about it. They claim the Coven Council is passing legislation to limit profits. They see many opportunities to make more money outside the Council's restrictions. And there are more nefarious mutterings, reminding many of us of the past ills, musings if perhaps witches were better off, well, you know."

"Liege Edith says there will always be such ugliness, but that we mustn't give it credence. Not—an—inch. If it wasn't for what the witches did, who knows what could've happened to this country? It's far from perfect now, but at least it isn't the vision that the previous parliament had. Before they started listening to the witches."

"When profits are concerned, and thirst for more, one can never predict." The tailor picked up a spool of embroidery thread in deepest scarlet and thoughtfully brushed his fingertips across it. "Which reminds me. You haven't heard aught about the whereabouts of the High Witch, perchance, have you?"

Poppy tried to look appropriately surprised. "Not recently. Why?"

"She was due this morning for a fitting for her Coven robe, and didn't show up. She's usually incredibly punctual, and it isn't the kind of thing I'd expect from her. She almost always sends word ahead, given that she is so conscious of our busy schedule. But she often speaks of your Liege Edith, so I was curious."

"Time must've gotten away from her. I suppose, with all of her responsibilities, and everything going on, it must've just slipped her mind." Did everyone in London know of Edith's work with the High Witch except for Poppy? It really was the most terrible feeling, living in the dark.

As HE WATCHED Poppy Brightwell and Nathaniel Rawlings-Vijay leave the Last Stitch, Roland de Grateloup felt an immense ache of longing. Not for them—his few friends were of a much higher standing than either of them—but to be inside the Last Stitch himself. He was a man of taste and style, and he'd had to slip into offensively simple clothing to find his way around town. The linen was hardly broken in, the cotton lining banal, and the tailoring a true travesty.

No, it was not wise being out in the open. Especially in an area dense with the kind of people who knew his mother and, likely, knew of the accusations against him. Still, he had an impressive aptitude for passing unnoticed, one of the few effects of his condition he actually appreciated. When he wanted, slipping into the shadows was painfully easy, and his footfalls hardly made a sound.

As he immediately backed into a wall of a human being.

Roland wheeled around to come face to face with a towering, red-haired woman, standing with her arms crossed and a smug look on her freckled face. Judging by the hideous assortment of buttons on her equally offensive ensemble, she was a Warder.

"Really, Monsieur de Grateloup," she said, her voice just low enough so he could hear. "For someone wanted for murder, you'd think you'd exercise *some* degree of caution."

"And who are you?" he asked in the haughtiest tone he could muster.

"Molly Hode. Liege Edith Rookwood's personal Warder."

"What a quaint accent," he said, trying to take a step back, hindered by the actual brick wall to his left. She'd penned him in.

"Netherford's in the heart of Kent, and most of us who grew up there prefer to chew our Rs rather than omit them." Molly grinned, picking a stray leaf off Roland's shoulder.

Roland tried not to flinch, but he was late on his afternoon tonic dose. His nerves always frayed if he left it too long between draughts, and alas, 'too long' seemed to grow shorter every day.

"I have no plans on hurting Miss Brightwell, so you've no need to flex your brawn at me, Miss Hode," he said.

The Warder looked wholly unimpressed, blinking slowly, her broad face slack. "You're a wanted man and a werewolf. I'd not be doing my job if I hadn't taken notice of you skulking about. The last thing she needs right now is the likes of you haunting her shadow like some wretched stray."

The gall of this woman!

"I am doing no such thing. I'm merely curious," Roland explained, his patience thinning. "I need to find my mother, and since she and Liege Rookwood were among the last people known to have spent time with her, I wanted to mark their movement in case she came back around—or in the event they'd been withholding evidence from me."

"Why would they do that?" Molly asked, taking an apple from her satchel and examining it. She gave it a good scrub on her jacket before taking a big bite. Roland hated the smell of apples, he always had, and it just made his distaste for the Warder that much sharper.

"Because people are terrible on the whole, with a few minor exceptions. And even most of those are intolerable without the application of either alcohol or delusion."

Molly laughed through her nose and Roland was far too pleased with himself for the feat. She actually had quite a pleasant face, when she wasn't scowling. "I would have to agree with you there, save for the fact that Liege Rookwood and Miss Brightwell are both among the very best people I know. I'll admit, I had my reservations about them initially, but now, I'm only grateful I get to protect them and help keep the Rookwood legacy alive." She took another bite of the apple, juice dribbling down her chin before she wiped it away with the back of her hand. "And that means ensuring their safety from, among other things, werewolves."

Roland sighed in resignation. "I suppose that is within your rights. But I am merely a wisp of my former glory."

"Walk with me," Molly said, taking his arm and not giving him much of a chance to argue one way or another. She was terribly pushy. "I have an ulterior motive in speaking to you, but Miss Brightwell is visiting some of the nearby shops and I need to keep my eyes on her."

A feeling almost like hope, or belonging, kindled within

Roland's breast. He liked the idea of helping. He was a helper, after all. A celebrated one, at that. It was just so very difficult to help people when they thought he'd violently dismembered and murdered a young lordling.

"Look natural," she said, shoving him gently. "You're shaking like a leaf."

Was he? By the comet's tail, he was a wretched creature. "It's got nothing to do with you," he said, pulling his hat down over his eyes as best he could whilst maintaining enough of a view to see where they were walking. "No doubt you're aware my condition requires certain tinctures and potions to keep it suppressed. Previously, I'd relied on my mother's network to get my supplies, but since leaving France—"

"You have a strange definition of 'leaving.' You say that as if you were gently ushered to the door."

Roland opened his mouth, then closed it. He couldn't tell if he adored this woman for her brash and direct observations, or detested her. Perhaps it was a measure of both. "I have had to resort to second-rate alchemists, the sort of folk who won't ask questions. This requires a bit of grit on my part, and a great deal of trust in what I am fairly certain are mostly charlatans."

"But you have figured out which ones are not," Molly said.

"I suppose you are asking on behalf of Miss Brightwell's sister," he said, dimly recalling the conversation they'd had below the Tippling Philosopher.

"Indeed. My brother Basil, who is also a Warder, pointed me in the direction of a few establishments, but I'm not as learned in the way of herbs as he is. I'm not without some skill, but he's always had a keener understanding of them than I have."

"Rather aptly named then, isn't he?"

Molly rolled her eyes. "How very clever. I'm sure I have never heard that comment before in all my life."

"So, you'd like me to risk my tenuous anonymity to assist you in your search?" Roland asked, perking up at the prospect of securing some advantage. He would bend the situation to his benefit if he had to. What else did he have to lose?

"Yes. And I'll pay for your next round of potions," Molly said, tossing him a small coin purse, heavier than it looked. The bright tinkling of the metal within sent his heart soaring.

"I can't stay in London long," Roland confessed, feeling the ever-present anxiety crawling down his spine. Were people looking at him, or at Molly? "But I will help as I can."

"As Liege Edith said, we will take you to Netherford, if we can trust you," Molly said, stopping as they came to a narrow alley lined with apothecary shops. Roland had observed Miss Brightwell and Mr. Rawlings-Vijay enter one of the weaving houses just behind them. The dyers and the apothecaries tended to cluster together in big cities like London, as their raw materials often overlapped.

"Why, whatever reason could you have not to trust me?" Roland asked, giving Molly the most innocent expression he had on offer.

"Everything." She jutted out a hand toward the row of apothecaries. "Which one's best?"

"I don't think you'll find a cure to vampirism," Roland explained, rolling the leather coin purse in the palm of his hand, feeling the calm that came before his potions settling upon his shoulders as he contemplated his next move. "But, if anyone knows anything about suppressing the worst of it, it would be Madinia Dee's, third door down—the one with the goat for a handle."

Molly headed that way, not looking back.

He scurried after her. "What am I to do?"

"Come, go, I don't care," Molly said. "Just don't give me any reason to mistrust you, and I'll make sure you stay alive."

That, Roland decided, was as good an offer as he could ask for.

CHAPTER EIGHT
DECEPTIONS AND DEVASTATIONS

"My lord?"

Fintan's voice cut through Silas's feverish thoughts of Viola Brightwell feeding from his neck.

"My apologies, Fintan. I was elsewhere."

The butler cleared his throat pointedly. "I was asking about the cravat for today. There is the lavender just come from Miss Rawlings-Vijay, or the crimson paisley."

Reflexively, Silas's hand went to his neck. They were still deciding on his day's attire, and Fintan had not yet seen the marks of Viola's ministrations the night before. The feeding left him somewhat dazed, and a little giddy. He'd been late to rise for the first time in months.

"The crimson, but—"

Silas tried to protest, but Fintan had already seen. The man had the keenest eyes Silas knew. A great help while birding, quite a catastrophe when trying to hide the very obvious puncture marks on his neck from the vampire woman he certainly could not be in love with.

Brimstone and pestilence, he needed to be more careful.

"I don't want to hear it from you. The last thing I need is yet another lecture on my responsibility and reputation to uphold the St. Albans name. Trust me, I am quite aware." Silas couldn't even bear to look at the man.

Who was strangely silent.

Fintan was not a man of many words, but given the circumstances, he ought to have at least a mild retort.

Silas turned to face him.

The valet's face was a most perplexing shade of puce. The viscount's immediate reaction was to see if the man was choking, so distressed did he look. When he was certain he was breathing, he relaxed, but only a measure; for Fintan was struck clearly by some ailment.

Moving to the door, Silas opened it to the hall and tried to call out for anyone nearby. But he was a long way from any assistance, given how far the vampires were staying—all on his aunt's insistence. He didn't suppose he could call out for Laertes and have him magically appear.

"Miss Rookwood-Nourse?" he tried, but to no avail.

Then, just as he was about to run to find one of the other footmen, a flash of white and grey flew into the room and across the plush woven carpets, moving at a pace he was certain was preternatural.

Molineaux.

Before he could grab the dratted creature, Molineaux jumped up and bit Fintan on the arm. Horrified, Silas attempted to remove the feral cat, but Fintan stopped him with a strong hand, knuckles white with the effort of restraint.

The valet gasped, then cried out: "No, he knows what he's doing!"

"He is a cat!" Silas said.

"And what difference would that make?"

Silas wondered how he could sound so collected given the most bizarre situation unfolding before them.

But Fintan was right. The shock of the cat bite had, somehow, freed the valet from his fit. A moment later, Molineaux disengaged and then curled up in Fintan's lap while he breathed deeply, calming himself.

"You deserve an explanation, my lord," Fintan said, looking sheepish for the first time Silas could ever recall. "And I regret, I cannot give you one."

Silas's heart still beat a furious tattoo in his chest; he had never considered Fintan's mortality before. The man—if he was a man at all, and Silas had his doubts—seemed eternal, immovable. He'd tended Silas's father for decades, and helped raise the children, back before Sylvie...

"Please do try," Silas said. "At very least, inform me how to avoid doing it again."

Finan closed his deep violet eyes, methodically petting Molineaux with one hand and placing the other on his heart.

"It is a *geas*."

"Whatever for?" blurted Silas, rubbing the sides of his face. He just wanted to get his day moving—there was so much to do! And Viola. Demons below, what was he going to do about Viola?

Fintan winced, the muscles at his neck twisting in response. "You see," he said, teeth clenched, "it prevents me from even getting near the subject. Understand only this: I am pledged to your family's safety, and to you in particular." He paused, as if waiting for another punishing spasm, but none came. "Your life is of utmost importance to me."

"Miss Brightwell wouldn't hurt me," Silas said, though he was far from certain on that count. "You mustn't worry."

The valet blanched again, the apple at his throat working up and down.

"I'm sorry—understood," Silas said. He sat down across from Fintan, looking him in the eyes. "I will refrain from that line of discussion. I can see why, if you've sworn to ensure my safety, my indiscretions with a vampire might be of some concern to you."

Molineux's eyes, green as grass, turned to Silas and then, finding him wanting, closed as he leaned into Fintan's touch.

Fintan nodded weakly. "It is a difficult situation. You know I am—" He gasped again, his fingers trembling with the effort against the pain. "There are things. You must— careful."

Silas would have to speak to someone about this. Fintan was his valet, yes, but he had been more of a father to him than anyone else had. There was nothing in the world he wouldn't trust him with, and yet, as he observed the pale-haired man before him, he wondered just how much he knew about Fintan in return. Nearly nothing. Just propriety and kindness and stalwart loyalty to the St. Albans family. That and his penchant for not aging.

Surely, there must be information in his father's letters and notebooks. He would have to try.

"Well, it's lucky for us that silly cat came by when he did," Silas said, trying to add a bit levity to the situation. "I swear I don't recall him being in the house until a few weeks ago."

Fintan's smile was almost sad. Then he said, "The feline persuasion sees through mortal guises."

PERHAPS VIOLA BRIGHTWELL ought to have felt embarrassed by her behaviour the night before, but she could not find it in herself to. She felt revived, no longer prone to fits of emotion and, well, *violence*. As shocking as drinking Silas's blood had been to them both, and everyone involved, it had invigorated her beyond belief. So much so she was planning a walk through the gardens at Burkley.

How strange it hadn't occurred to her before, to check in on her handiwork, given how much work she had put into its renovation and planning. Their father had once said Viola's soul expressed itself best in florals, and he was not wrong. She loved blooming plants, vines, trees, and bulbs. And here, at Burkely House, she'd worked with the dowager viscountess to create a solace, and a piece of living art. Of all the projects she'd assisted with, it was the garden she felt most proud of, and most at home in.

Her colour vision had not entirely returned after the feeding, but it heartened her to see a range of reds and purples, and hints of green, all along the pathway to the central fountain and mosaic. Late-blooming alliums bent their heads as she passed, swaying in the wind, while phlox released their soft scents into the air. The larger trees toward the periphery rustled in the breeze, and with her new hearing, she could almost distinguish each leaf from the next.

A sense of hope, of a life after this agony, unfurled deep in her heart—or what remained of it; Laertes had offered a course on vampire biology, but she was not willing to hear the details of what living as an undead might ensue.

She wished Poppy were here to see her. Although Heath and Oliver weren't far, she couldn't imagine seeing them yet. They'd ever lived a life apart from the Brightwell girls, even if their father was entangled in it, in his own strange way. Heath would be preparing to go back to Cambridge, she realised, and Oliver alone at home.

The sound of gentle footfalls caught Viola's attention, and she saw the fire witch, Petronilla, emerging from one of the hedges, brushing leaves from the hem of her gown. The ash trees were already beginning to shed their first leaves.

Petronilla looked up and smiled, seeing Viola standing still among the swaying flower globes. "Viola. What a joy it is to see you out in the garden."

"It is a joy, indeed," confessed Viola. "Thank you for all your patience with me these weeks and months. You have been a guardian spirit, of sorts; even in my most monstrous moments, I remember you like a great pillar of fire, powerful and stalwart, keeping me grounded."

It could have been a trick of the light, but Viola thought she caught a sheen of tears in Petronilla's eyes.

The gentlewitch inclined her head. "It felt like my duty, Viola. That is all I can say to explain it. Though I am a powerful witch, I am not talented in the broad sense. Fire is what I command, and fire alone. And, as I learned, it is a very useful skill in the presence of vampires—not just as a tactic for frightening them, but to help them. It was a strange thing to discover."

"Much of this new life is strange," Viola admitted with a sigh. She brushed her hand gently across the dahlia to her left, its soft petals cool against her palm. "I am feeling far better than I have in ages, yet I fear it is not a sustainable situation." She gestured to the garden at large, the house, the sky. "Here at Burkley House, I mean. Not with all the viscount's impending responsibilities."

Petronilla came up beside Viola and linked her arm in hers, as comfortable as a childhood friend. It felt natural, and Viola found she had no desire to drink the gentlewitch's blood. In fact, any sense of discomfort or hunger was conspicuously absent.

"I don't think the viscount would like to see you leave," Petronilla said softly, gently squeezing Viola's arm.

"Ophelia will be back soon, and hopefully I'll be strong enough to continue without…"

"I think you know that your relationship with the viscount is only complicating things," Petronilla said. "But I do not blame you for wanting distance, either. I suspect the viscount's rather pallid appearance today is connected to your current strength."

Viola nodded, fighting back a shiver. "The Byrnes have

thralls at Howarth Castle," Viola said. "Given my reaction to my most recent feed, it's possible I will transition more comfortably."

"And how do you feel about feeding upon someone who is not Silas Drake?" Petronilla looked pointedly at Viola, her eyes searching and a faint crease appearing between her eyebrows.

"How did you know?" Viola asked.

Petronilla's gaze was pointed but kind. "It seemed inevitable to those of us with eyes."

"What does it matter?" Viola half-whispered the words. She did not want to weep again. "He must marry well and soon, and I am but a distraction."

"Did he say as much?"

"No, of course not. He is kind, and attentive, and generous. He would never say such a thing to me—I know the dowager viscountess has no love for me and prefers I leave soon, but he has fought for me still."

Petronilla went quiet, her gaze fixed upon the house rising in the distance as they made their way across the lawn, their dresses swishing with every step. Viola wondered what she was thinking. She was a strong, beautiful gentlewitch in the prime of her life. But she was also still new to England, far from the country she called home. Viola could not imagine what that must feel like—she had only lived in England, and only truly knew Netherford.

"I used to believe in love," Petronilla finally said. "Now, I am not so certain. But when I see the way the viscount looks at you, when I saw what he endured after we thought you were dead... Why, it makes me wonder if I have just grown too cynical in my long years."

Though she wished it was not so, Viola's stomach turned a little cartwheel when Petronilla described the look on Silas's face. And, indeed, the very centre of her warmed with the thought of being close to him again, hearing the sounds he made when experiencing the pleasure of her bite.

"Were you in love before?" Viola asked. Now she felt embarrassed. She was rarely so forward, especially in matters of love—where she was not concerned. Though she did, once, fancy herself a bit of a matchmaker. It seemed a lifetime ago.

"Perhaps." Petronilla gave Viola a knowing look. "At the time, I would have said 'yes.' with absolute certainty. My brother Giles certainly thought so."

"I would never have spoken of such things with my brother. But you did? With Giles?"

"In this case, it was necessary. The subject of my affection was a friend of his from his years at Harvard. I don't know what would have happened if the stars had aligned correctly, but instead it was a great deal of heartbreak and inconvenience all around."

"Did he declare his affections?" Viola found herself very intrigued in the turn of conversation. Thinking about someone else's doomed love life made her blissfully distracted from her own.

Petronilla's look was sad, deeply, for one heartbeat, but then made of steel the next. "Not to the correct persons involved. I'm afraid he was not willing to summon up the courage to do so. His family was... politically involved, one might say, and aligning with the Rookwood-Nourses was not considered a sound decision. Though we had money, we had the wrong connections. Alas, sometimes love has naught to do with it, I'm afraid."

It sounded so practical the way Petronilla said it, as if marriage and courtship were no different from purchasing a home or deciding which college to attend. She supposed, for some sorts of people, it wasn't. Being from a family of meagre means, she had never considered such things.

Her dowry was nearly laughable, and she had never truly desired marriage until she met Silas. Viola had thought she would spend her days taking care of her parents and the dowager viscountess, and if her brothers decided to have children, perhaps assist them.

And now, well, she was a vampire. Finding love and security in a marriage was a relatively easy matter before, though not her most pressing preoccupation. Not that she was opposed to marriage like Poppy was. On the contrary. She had just never found a person with whom she could even imagine spending a lifetime with. What 'a lifetime' had meant a few months ago, however, was significantly shorter than it meant now.

"I do not know if what I felt for the viscount was love," Viola said, at last. "Or what he felt for me. All I know is the woman I was is changed; I am an entirely new being, and although his kindness here has given me a glimmer of hope in a sea of uncertainty, I will not linger long where I am not wanted."

"Well, I quite enjoy your company. And as I am a witch of significant means, even the dowager viscountess must suffer me. *And* my friends," Petronilla said.

And though she did not say it, Viola felt a stirring of real affection for her new friend. She squeezed her arm gently, and they made their way back to the house in comfortable silence.

LATER THAT EVENING, after she had rested and refreshed herself with a meal of swine blood—which she found more tolerable than mutton—Viola dressed for dinner on her own. Silas had tried to send a maid to assist her, but Viola insisted she not put the poor girl in danger.

As she left the room to walk down the hall, Viola felt a

familiar prickling sensation under her skin, and she knew immediately Ophelia was near. The smell of old roses and fresh paper flitted across her senses, then was gone, and without questioning where her feet took her, she progressed down the great staircase to see Ophelia Byrne shaking rain from her cloak while two servants attempted to help her. They were clearly still frightened of vampires.

"Ophelia!" Viola said, with heartfelt relief. "You've returned to us."

Ophelia was just as beautiful as Viola remembered, resplendent in a deep maroon gown of taffeta, trimmed with green fringe. She met Viola's eye with unmistakable solicitude.

"My goodness, you look quite refreshed," Ophelia said, going to Viola and taking her face in her hands, examining her like a concerned mother. "Did you fully accept the bond? I have to admit, I would have thought I'd sense something even from a distance, but—"

"No, no. I don't think so. Oh, I've so much to tell you," Viola looked around, not wanting to frighten the servants, and motioned Ophelia to walk with her. "Shall we walk to dinner together?"

"I'm afraid I do not have the patience tonight for a mortal dinner, but I will walk you there," Ophelia said. "And after you have explained your adventures, I will tell you mine."

Once well out of earshot, Viola described in broad strokes what had occurred between her and Silas the night before. She had expected Ophelia to be elated at the news, but she was quite sober about it.

"Did I do something wrong?" Viola asked when Ophelia fell silent, her dark eyes growing unfocused as they walked through the gallery.

Ophelia shook her head, pressing a hand to her cheek. "No, of course you didn't. I am glad you have found some comfort and, I suppose, a willing offering. But after speaking with Maurice, there are new concerns about your turning to consider. Not to mention why it hasn't settled yet."

Fear drove itself between Viola's ribs. She had been feeling so encouraged of late; now it slipped from her like melting ice.

Before she could say anything else, Viola turned her attention toward the sensation of Laertes—the scent of fresh pine and old leather—just as he emerged from a side door nearby. He wore a rich brown frock coat over a cream silk waistcoat, and for the first time in an age Viola thought he looked rested.

He did not embrace his sister but nodded in welcome. "Ophelia. You weren't expected for another three days."

"No, indeed. But what I learned in Bath had to be relayed in person. There are strange goings-on afoot in the county and beyond. Pray, let us all meet this evening after you have dined with the viscount, and I will share all the knowledge I have," Ophelia said.

Laertes looked at her quizzically. "I would press more, but I know you well enough to know better." He inclined his head at Viola. "My sister always has her reasons."

Viola was not convinced. There was an odd scent about Ophelia, a foreign smell that made her nose tickle. She could not place it, not in her vampire mind nor in the remnants of her human one, but she was certain it was dangerous.

When Ophelia was gone, and far from earshot, Viola asked, "This Maurice. Is there perhaps some history regarding the two of them? I seem to recall mention."

"Everyone has history with Maurice," Laertes said. "At least, those of us in England. He's one of the oldest vampires we have on record. He predates our line by about a few hundred years. We call him Maurice now, but only because most folk can't pronounce his Irish name: Muirgheas." It sounded like *m'wear-geese*.

"I can understand the difficulty," Viola said, though she found the way Laertes said the name quite lovely. "And it sounds like an old name, indeed."

"Old as the Pact itself. According to Maurice, his father was Toirdhealbhach, once High King of Ireland. He reigned in the twelfth century."

"That's quite an impressive pedigree," Viola said softly, thinking of her own most humble origins.

Laertes gave her shoulder a gentle squeeze. "Ah, well, I shall tell you about your own now, for vampires need not trace their lines through womb birth, but through blood birth. And you, my dear, come from a line most noble indeed."

OPHELIA COULD NOT banish the thought of her visit to Maurice from her mind. Though she wanted to tell Laertes and Viola all she knew—indeed, *had* to tell them, as soon as possible—she needed time to put the facts together.

She should have been better prepared. But that was the difficulty with being the most powerful vampire in the nearest environs: complacence was easy. She was so very used to getting her way, to seducing and conniving through any problem, that when she was at last confronted with one with more power than she, it caught her completely off guard.

Which was particularly embarrassing given that her last interaction with Maurice had gone precisely the same way. Ophelia was merely delusional.

It was a disaster from the start. The moment she set foot upon the grounds of Combe Park, Maurice's manor house overlooking Bath itself, she felt the lure of his power. The air itself became thicker, somehow, redolent of gardenias just past their fullest bloom. Walking the winding pathway up to the main house left her cold and exhausted.

She had barely touched the door handle when she was magicked inside, blinking straight to the receiving room.

Maurice dangled lazily off an intricately carved rosewood chair. It looked more like a throne, really, and completely in harmony with the deep purples, crimsons, and gold strewn about the massive room. Ophelia felt transported back in time, as if she were at Hampton Palace attending Queen Anne once again.

And Maurice had been there, too. He'd served King Henry VIII before his early and untimely death, acting as the court historian and advisor to the crown. When he wasn't tangled with Ophelia, of course, which was, indeed, a most routine occurrence.

"Ophelia Byrne," said Maurice, his voice as deep and resonant as she recalled. His long, black hair was combed back, tied neatly with a red satin ribbon, his arched brows rising just slightly. She'd kissed that brow a thousand times over the centuries, enjoying her place as his favourite and most cherished of lovers.

The scent of turning gardenias intensified, making her stomach turn. Too much gardenia began to smell like rotting, she found.

"Maurice," she said, with a short curtsey. He was no king—as vampires held no such notions—but he deserved the proper greeting as one of the eldest among them. Even if Ophelia detested him.

And she always had. Therein lay the rub.

There was somewhat amiss inside Miss Byrne's mind, as she had often observed: it was most difficult for her to separate a sense of dislike from a sense of attraction. Indeed, when it came to prospective lovers, the more she detested them, the more likely she wanted to relieve them of their garments. No worse than in present company.

Maurice did not rise, at least not physically that she could yet detect, but his sinful lips curved into a knowing grin. "And here I thought I'd never see you again after our last altercation. You were very adamant about it. What were your words? Ah, yes, the curse of a near flawless memory— and I quote: *The next time I set eyes upon your face it will be through a wall of flame on your funeral pyre.*"

She would not take this carefully placed bait. Ophelia reminded herself she was a lady of standing, that she had worked decades to move up the ranks in society after nearly losing it all, and that she did not need to respond to accusations regarding her previous behaviour, even if they were entirely true.

"I promise you, I wouldn't be here were it not a necessity," Ophelia said, as curtly as she could manage. To say keeping her composure was a challenge was an understatement. Maurice was her superior, and his very presence addled her brain.

Not as much as it once had, thankfully, but enough to ensure she keep her guard up as much as possible.

"Your beauty never ceases to take my breath, Miss Byrne," he said. His words were full of honey, but his face remained, as always, near inscrutable. "And you have grown even more devastatingly lovely in the years since our last entanglement."

"I am not here for flattery, Maurice," she said. "I assure you, I have plenty of that in Kent."

"No doubt. You were always my most talented protégée." He stood, the powerful aura of his magic roiling across the floor like an unfurled cloak of velvet. "I do not see your ever-loyal brother about. I hope he is not your source of distress?"

"Not directly, no."

Maurice rolled his neck like a fighter preparing himself in the ring, his lean muscles straining against his silk waistcoat. Again, his magic pressed in upon Ophelia's every pore. "As always, I am willing to assist you in whatever matters concern you—for a price."

Damn her heart, or what remained of it: it thumped in response to his allure. Indeed, his power—and hers—was known as that: the Allure. Only the most powerful vampires could use it upon their own kind. Laertes could Allure humans and some minor magical folk, but he was always her lesser.

She should leave. She should throw herself into more books, more libraries, anything but involve herself with Maurice. But hadn't she always found her way back to him? Hadn't she needed that edge of hatred and obsession again and again? Ophelia was so tired of fighting for everything: the castle, her thralls, her brother, and now Viola. Once, she'd had a dream of civilised living among mortals, noble vampires reformed and respected. She'd wanted nothing more than to lose herself in the finery and frippery of those short-burning lives, to live and love upon the moors like the popular novels always portrayed.

His hands were in her hair before she could fight it. And, stars, her whole body sang in reply at that tender touch. A need she knew only he could satisfy rang out from the deepest hollows of her soul.

"You always come back," Maurice whispered as he traced a line down her neck to her rising breasts, making her back arch. Heat, life, desire, and savage wanting roared to life inside of her despite herself.

"You ruined me for other creatures," she whispered to him, her voice low. "You vile monster."

The vampire bared his teeth, drawing Ophelia closer—

so close she could feel his arousal through her skirts. If there had been any resolve left in her, it melted as swiftly as honeycomb in the flame. "You poisonous rose," Maurice said. "I should leave you to your sorry state, so piteously enflamed and wanting."

"But you won't," Ophelia breathed, breaking open his waistcoat with such force the ivory buttons clattered upon the parquet flooring by the hearth. His body was not warm as her human conquests were, but cool and familiar—the skin so smooth beneath her touch, as if carved in marble. She shivered. "You like the taste of my poison."

For all her detestation and protestation, she knew Maurice was as lost to her wiles as she was to his. There was some comfort in that.

Maurice tensed for just a moment, a brief slip of his composure, then he said: "May I?"

Ophelia answered him with a biting kiss, fierce and claiming. He tightened his grip on her even more as a sweet, sultry drip of blood entered her mouth from his.

Her whole being sang to life, and as she felt that welcome intrusion of his body into hers, she realised why she so craved his attentions. For all the lovers she had taken, in as many ways as she could endure, none of them came close to the glory of being taken by Maurice. When their bodies mingled, when all that was left to their senses remained in touch and pleasure and movement... she actually felt alive.

REGRET DID NOT descend as immediately as Ophelia expected. They had made their way upstairs after making a frightful mess of the receiving room, breaking both a table and a chair—nearly lighting the carpet on fire at one point. In their headier, more reckless days, they would have drained a thrall or two. Once, they'd left a corpse, though the man had died of a heart attack, and not the vampires' ministrations; for a vampire's most basic need is to keep their prey alive. Drinking from the mortal dead was forbidden.

Everything about Maurice was fine: his clothes, the linens, his skin, his way of speaking. If he had a chink in his armour, she had never found it, and if she couldn't find it, surely no one could. He had genuine affection for her, knotted though it was with resentment.

They did not hold one another, but lay breathing in the incense-riddled air of his grand boudoir, face to face.

"You could have been a queen among the vampires," Maurice said, his deep blue eyes—like shadowed sapphires—searching her face. "But instead, you chose a life of manners and local politics."

He had asked her to marry him. But then, he had wanted to ally with the French vampires and overthrow the royals in the great rebellion. He wanted to leverage the chaos to take back what was once theirs: the ability to control and feed upon humankind as they pleased.

Ophelia had many faults: vanity, vainglory, and viciousness. But she had little taste for violence, and no particular need to assert herself queen of anything. Maurice imagined a new kingdom, the two of them side by side, channelling enough power to turn the tide in a war, and in all of history to come.

Of course, the rebellion had not lasted. The vampires did not win. And Maurice had returned to Bath and a life of quiet indulgence while the world moved on.

"I chose freedom," Ophelia corrected, stifling the urge to kiss him again. He would be ready and willing, she knew. But she had come here with a purpose. "For with power comes responsibility, and I would prefer to flit around this sphere without the shackles of debt and duty."

"And yet you have a spawn, now," Maurice said.

"How...?"

The vampire kissed her forehead. "I am an ancient being; our blood has comingled. I knew the moment she was made, Ophelia. It is so rare, this gift, but I admit I never expected it of you."

"It was unintended," Ophelia said.

"It is hard for me to imagine anything you do as unintentional," Maurice observed. And he was right, of course.

So, Ophelia explained, as vaguely as she could, the circumstances around Viola's turning. To his credit, he listened to fully half of the story before tiring of it, slipping his hand between her legs and watching her crest the mount of passion once again. That great climax left her breathless, calling out his name, and trembling in the wake.

"After all this time, I can still make you sing," he said, a wicked gleam in his eye.

"I should have just written you a letter," Ophelia said, moving to the edge of the bed and taking a drink of blood from the goblet he'd set aside for her. "Less hazardous."

"Oh, but my darling, you always run headlong into danger, those sumptuous curls bobbing along behind you and your bosom heaving."

"Less discussion of my bosom and more of the spawn, if you please?" She was finally getting irritated enough to banish the haze of desire.

Still completely naked, Maurice turned onto his back and rested his hands behind his head. His black hair fell down one side of his shoulder, stark against the alabaster hue of his skin. Not a single strand of grey in eight hundred years. She could stare at him for hours and still find his form a wonder.

"Very well. You are concerned, I can see, that your new spawn may become a revenant, since she is rejecting the vampire change," Maurice repeated. "And, as a born vampire, and given the limited research on the subject— thanks to the campaigns of our oppressors—you would like access to my library, or my opinion on the matter, or both."

"That is the gist," she replied.

Maurice went very still and very silent, closing his eyes as if to sift through his own knowledge and memories. Or to be dramatic. Or, more likely, both. Ophelia wrapped a nightgown around her body while he filled up the silence with his pretentiousness.

"As for books, I have none. After the debacle in France, I returned to find my most coveted titles stolen or burned. I suspect the wolves of it, but then, I suspect them of almost everything these days. My spies tell me they may have been looking for an answer to their own dwindling problems— for they are only born, not made."

"I'm not here to discuss werewolves, Maurice."

"Indeed, you are not. But you are lucky that I am old and learned, for the lore of our kind exists not just in tomes and scrolls, but also in my mind. So, I will tell you what I can. But in exchange, I require some information as well."

Of course, a part of her had thought the price for the information might have been the toll on her body, but that was never the case with Maurice.

"I will share as I must," Ophelia said.

"Well, then, in that case, we absolutely *must* discuss werewolves."

CHAPTER NINE
AN IMP OF FAME

ONCE, SILAS RECALLED, he had actually enjoyed afternoon hot chocolate with the dowager viscountess. She had not always been so irascible and pushy, instead doting on him and showering him with the affection he simply did not receive at home. He believed it was due to her, in no small part, that he had escaped the terrible fate of his own father: a life of violence and drinking that had alienated him from nearly everyone.

Yet, as the years progressed, and Silas never married, nor showed even the slightest interest in producing an heir, she'd become single-minded. Well, of *two* minds: that he would marry, and that he would take up his place in Parliament, as his grandfather had before him. Titus Drake had not just brought the St. Albans family to the brink of financial ruin but had nearly destroyed their good name as well. And that was, frankly, all the woman had.

"You need to consider the family legacy," the dowager viscountess said, tutting over tea.

It was a rainy afternoon the day after Viola and Silas had… Well, best not to think about such things while he was in the presence of his aunt. Which simply made Silas think about the situation even more, and in greater detail.

"I assure you, Aunt May, I *am* considering the family legacy," Silas insisted as Fintan brought about a small dish of biscuits, the ones stamped with the wandering witch; he so enjoyed eating them along with chocolate.

The dowager viscountess pursed her lips in disdain. She clearly did not find him convincing in the least and, truthfully, he was only considering the family legacy when he wasn't trying to figure out what to do about Viola Brightwell or maintain the estate, and that took up most of his time. He hadn't even had a moment for his writing in weeks.

"Your first few meetings with prospective brides have been disastrous."

"The Atwaters were awful enough. But that wasn't entirely my doing, nor Viola's. I do appreciate your research on these young women, but Miss Atwater was simply not the kind of woman I could see myself settling for."

"She has *ten thousand a year*, Silas," the dowager huffed, retreating into her fichu like a disgruntled tortoise. "Surely you could settle for that."

"I would prefer not to 'settle,' if it can be helped. It's only been a few days."

"And already, the situation in the north wing is becoming untenable." She pulled out a small sheet of paper from her pocket, smoothing out the wrinkles with her plump and veined hand. "So, here is my new list."

"Your new list?"

"I have started with the greater families in Netherford and the surrounds."

Silas took the paper and glanced down at the names, at least fifty in total. The local families, naturally: Greenstreets, Durlings, Finches, and Wayfairs. They all had daughters of marriageable age, though a few on the younger side—and they came from considerable wealth and reputation. Next the peerage: he was not surprised to see the de Greys—headed by Marchioness Audalie de Grey—along with the Countess of

Darlington, who he had known in his London days. Oh, how Roland would laugh to see her listed, given their combined history. Then came the newer money, including both the Bahadur dynasty and the Nakai family. On and on the list went, and heavier fell the shroud of his duty.

"This is quite a selection," Silas said, handing the paper back to his aunt. "I will need months to get through them all."

"Precisely. So, I have found you a solution."

Silas did not like the sound of that. Fintan did not either, for Silas noted how the butler straightened his spine.

"Do tell."

He was so warm. Why was he so warm? The cocoa was nearly tepid with all the cream he'd added.

"Well, you might as well know, since the invitations have already gone out…"

"Invitations?" How had she had time for all these details? Perhaps she kept an entirely different staff he wasn't aware of. Confound the woman.

The dowager viscountess smiled, the lines on her face deepening like a wizened cat. "Well, we're to have a ball, of course. And you, like Prince Charming of old, shall select the one most suited to you."

Silas stared, sweat slipping down his back. The mere idea of parading about like some petty prince made him feel ill. He did not altogether dislike festive engagements, but preferred smaller, more intimate occasions over balls.

"A ball? Why, aunt, I was expecting we'd host something for the winter holidays, but such things need time."

His aunt shook her laced head. "Precisely. You have little time, and I have plenty to spare. Since it is such an imposition to sit and entertain each prospective bride individually, we shall make better use of you, and this household. That gives you ample space to finish your letters to Parliament, arrange to have Miss Brightwell committed—or carted off, or paid off, I do not care—and we can settle the family name and legacy at last."

Silas was well and truly caught. Helpless to deny her, lest he upset her more than he already had. Though they shared no blood, he still was responsible for her health and her comfort, even if she was a busybody with a penchant for gossip and general distaste for anyone who did not meet her standards of propriety.

"Very well," Silas said. "I suppose there is nothing I can do to sway you."

"No. Nothing you can do at all." She leaned forward, taking his hand in hers. "Silas, my dear, I know this seems quite overwhelming at the moment, but I promise you, in the future—once all this vampire madness is behind you, and you are standing tall in London—you will thank me."

Rising, Silas kissed his aunt on the cheek, and then started toward the doors to lose himself once again in his work, except he heard a clatter coming from down toward the kitchens.

The dowager viscountess clearly heard nothing, having already returned to her reading.

Curious, Silas made his way toward the sound, down the long corridor off the foyer. Someone was shouting, ordering and commanding.

Then, a flash of white hair and the glimmer of gold silk caught his attention as Fintan slid out from the library and into Silas's path. There was blood on his face.

"Miss Brightwell, is she—?"

Fintan cringed, grunting, as he tried to say something but was prevented by the *geas*. He caught his breath, shaking his head as if it might help dispel the magic. "The vampires are all fine," he said. "It's the werewolf we must worry about."

"Werewolf?" What now? Stars, Silas was just beginning

to think there might be some semblance of normalcy in his future.

But he had scarcely repeated the word before he caught himself. Only one werewolf would ever dare to show their face in Burkley House.

Fintan seemed to catch Silas's realisation. He nodded slightly.

"Oh, no. What has Roland done now?"

IF EDITH HAD to mark the moment their day truly took a turn for the worse—an ever-increasing spiral of misfortune—it began with fish dinner at the Countess Rocksavage's home, during what was supposed to be an intimate affair. She had told the countess not to bother with a large list for dinner, that she and Poppy had had enough conversation and excitement already, but she either did not hear her or simply did not care. Of course, Stafford Vale was invited; it would have been an insult to do so otherwise.

As Edith made her way to the parlour, Poppy some steps behind her and still sulking, she was shocked to see at least twenty people gathered, already dining on canapes and sipping cordials. Vale, clothed in an expertly embroidered suit, looked positively thrilled with himself, preening as he spoke to a woman with black hair in a cornflower blue gown.

That was the Countess Rocksavage, of course, who hailed from Cheshire but stayed frequently in Portman Square on lease. She was in the House of Lords, and was one of the High Witch's staunchest supporters. Without her, very little would have been accomplished between Lords and the Council.

Behind the countess sat Lady Claudia Cowes and Lady Anne Redfern, current co-generals of the Coven Council, from Bury St. Edmunds and Old Sarum respectively.

Across from Edith stood the trio of Lord Thynne of Bath, Viscountess Milton of Yorkshire, and Lady Andalusia Rose-Zannat of Yorkshire. Even Blackwell Sipher was there, the recently elected Guildmaster General.

Edith's jaw tensed with the sudden onset of anxiety. These were the very people she wished to someday work alongside, who were tied to the future of 'the Crown and the Crescent,' as the alliance between England and her gentlewitches was known. Why, just yesterday, Edith had been going over one of Lady Redfern's brilliant papers on the need to include hedge witchery in the Coven Council, much in the way the House of Commons functioned in contrast to the House of Lords. She argued that with a fifth arm—alongside the Coven Circles, Guildmoot, House of Commons, and House of Lords—there would be balance, and finally, a better representation of all minds in the country. Some, like the Countess Rocksavage, would go even further to insist they should also consider other preternaturals. This, of course, was often implied, but rarely spoken out loud. And even Edith, for all her progressive thinking, struggled with the idea of welcoming those of fae and fiendish provenance to law.

"There she is, the gentlewitch of the hour!" Vale said, clapping his hands three times. Everyone turned their heads to Edith, who in absence of anything else to do, bowed awkwardly.

Where was Poppy? She'd been behind her just a moment ago. A shiver went down her arms, that very rare but clear sign of prophecy. Oh, she never could prognosticate the future or anything of great importance: but she often knew when someone was about to enter a room, or sense what they were going to say, before they were going to say it. The High Witch said it was related to her proclivities with liminal magic, explaining it was tied to the threads between liminalities. Which Edith was still trying to figure out.

The clatter of falling silverware heralded Poppy's arrival into the parlour room, as she had miscalculated her steps—likely assuming the room was going to be half empty—and knocked into one of the footmen, scattering a variety of spoons upon the floor.

What brief attention they had given Edith was immediately shifted to Poppy. She was wearing one of her old dinner gowns, which her sister had helped her remake from Mrs. Brightwell's frocks. Yellow, lightweight silk, with delicate stripes and floral motif. Beautiful, of course, on Poppy's warm brown skin, but far from the current fashion. It was even, if Edith were honest to herself, a bit too comfortable for the gathered company. Next time they were to visit guests of privilege, she would have to help Poppy pack.

Now, though, a thorn of shame twisted in her chest. If they had known half of Parliament was joining them for dinner, Edith would have insisted on custom clothing for both of them.

"Liege Edith!" It was Blackwell Sipher, coming to her rescue, the only truly common person in the entire assemblage. "I take it, by the look on your face, that Vale has, once again, brought us together without informing our most honoured guest."

Guest, not *guests*. Not Poppy.

There was no time to run to her aid, for the first course was already being set, and whether Edith liked it or not, Blackwell Sipher was showing her through the parlour and down the hall to the dining room.

Sipher escorted her to her seat, some distance from Poppy, and the service began in earnest.

Edith hardly managed a sip of the clear soup before it grew cold, amidst all the conversation around her. She never did like loud places, nor being in the middle of conflicting discussions. It made it ever so difficult to understand which to follow, leaving her overwhelmed and feeling inadequate. She tried to catch Vale's attention and express her frustration, but the man was not having any of it. He, most likely, saw this as a great entertainment. Edith detested surprises, especially when it changed the course of her plans.

Poppy was seated down and to Edith's right, between a young man with tight curls and a purple cravat whom she did not know, and the Viscountess Milton. Neither was including Poppy in their conversations, sometimes even speaking over her to converse with one another.

For her part, Poppy kept very quiet and focused on her meal.

Just as the fish course was laid out—a spicy, curried whitefish with a bright chutney—Vale began his introductions and welcomes. He went around the table, citing everyone's pedigree and function, and referred to Poppy as "Miss Persephone Brightwell, companion of the Gentlewitch of Netherford." Which was not wrong in any sense but lacked the flair and enthusiasm of all the other introductions.

"Oh, Liege Rookwood," said Lord Thynne, "I was just regaling our host with the story of your first visit to Parliament. Never shall I forget your most rousing discussion of late seventeenth century law and its connection to expunging the Hunt at last. Your insight into the Witchfinder trials was most thought provoking."

"Indeed, indeed," agreed the Viscountess Milton. "You couldn't have been more than eighteen at the time, if I'm not mistaken. And you came with such passion and determination. It was so refreshing to see the future of Parliament standing right there before us."

Edith remembered the day well, and many times wished she hadn't been so forward about her study. She was too young to understand what such an appearance might mean for her own life, nor how it would impact her mother—a longtime critic of the entire Parliament for over a century—and their relationship. When she'd come home from the presentation, her mother Georgina wouldn't even speak to her. Aunt Cassandra had at least explained why, as she always did; ever the peacemaker.

"I was a very enthusiastic young witch at the time," Edith said. She did not much like the fish and was glad for a moment's distraction. "And I have done far more research on the subject since then. I'll admit, my initial insights were rather superficial."

Lady Redferne giggled. "My dear, nothing you have ever done in your life is superficial. You have always shone remarkably. Your cleverness is truly impressive."

The Coven was proud of her. How strange. It had never been brought up before. Not that they *didn't* have a good relationship, only that she had always thought them rather indifferent.

"In fact, we were all quite surprised when we didn't see your name in circulation during the primary gathering," Lord Thynne said, leaning back to allow the footman to fill his sherry glass. His mustaches fluttered out like wispy feathers. "I realise you've been quite occupied in Netherford, but we were all hoping, with the backing of both the Coven Circle and the Guildmoot, that you might consider a formal petition."

Edith's nose tickled, as if she were going to sneeze. Or weep. She disliked doing either of those things. What she wanted was to be done with this whole room and Vale's scheming, wrap Poppy in her arms, and take her far away.

Except that wasn't entirely the whole truth. No, a few months ago, should this same situation have arisen, it might have been counted among the best days of her life.

"You understand, given everything that has occurred in the Rookwood family in the last year, that such a consideration was quite beyond my ability," Edith said slowly, not wanting to touch too much upon a sore subject.

The Countess Rocksavage grinned widely, shaking her shoulders as if delighted with herself. "But you are not *opposed* to the idea."

"I..." Edith looked over at Poppy, but her companion was focused on a small boule of bread. "I would have to consider. I admit, I am somewhat surprised to find such a tide of support among you all. There have been few missives from London since my retirement to the country and given everything that conspired with the Boagane and the High Witch, I was beginning to think you were all quite done with the Rookwoods."

"Oh, never!"

"The very thought!"

"Fiddle faddle!"

The whole table, save Poppy, erupted in protestations of their innocence. Edith was not fooled, nor was she swayed to their machinations—for that is what they were. She may not have agreed with her mother's politics, but she was still her daughter. Those with power will always flatter and fawn, Edith knew. Vanity was weakness.

Then again, she was one of the closest gentlewitches to Virginia Cawley. It was likely that word had spread to each of them, and common decorum forbade anyone from speaking of it. With the Prince Regent continually signalling less patience and more intolerance, and the King ill, eyes were everywhere, waiting for all gentlewitches and anyone associated with them to make mistakes, no matter how grievous or pithy.

It was difficult to recall exactly what happened after that. Edith could have refused the wine and the attention, but her vanity got the better of her in the end as she regaled the table with her own knowledge of parliamentary law, in what she was sure was dazzling detail. It was easy to disseminate the information: her mind was like a library, volumes of knowledge ever at her beck and call. When someone asked a question, she only had to reach to grab the book from her intellectual archive and bring forth the facts.

They complimented her, they doted on her, and though she was quite aware in the back of her mind that she was being used, she was also very tired. Tired of having to put her dreams and ambitions to the side to do the responsible thing every time. And joining Parliament *would* be responsible, wouldn't it? There would be significantly more income, and although it meant time away from Netherford, she would have a hand in far more matters of importance. People would remember her, not as the odd daughter of Georgina Rookwood, the talented and polarising gentlewitch of Hatchney House who had died in a horrific fire, but as Liege Edith Rookwood, on her own merit.

"My goodness, I haven't seen that particular pattern in some time," said the woman to Poppy's right, commenting on her dress. She was a viscountess, or some such, but Poppy had not been given the time or the freedom to learn any of their names. No introductions.

Poppy was supposed to know all of them. This was Edith's world, and understanding it was as easy as breathing for her, but Poppy did not care a whit. Not for lack of wanting to. She loved Edith—at least, she used to be certain of that—and she wanted to share the things she loved. But Parliament and politics quite literally made her fall asleep. She was far more interested in categorising herbs, learning new embroidery techniques, and taking up any new hobby that allowed her to capture the world around her in colour and sound and language.

Still, experienced or not, Poppy knew a veiled insult when she heard one. Just because she was country born and raised, middle class and rough around the edges, did not mean she was that naïve. She'd survived Antonella Greenstreet's cadre of vicious, rich, and entitled young women in Netherford, and these people were no different. London was just a bigger city.

One tack was to feign ignorance, let them think her a country mouse with no real education. Another was to tell the truth: that she and Edith had been hoodwinked into coming tonight and were unprepared for such a large meeting. Neither of those could end well, she thought. Upset as she was at her companion, she did not wish to ruin the evening for her. She wanted to support her as long as possible, even if she was beginning to truly believe their pairing may be doomed after all.

So, Poppy did as she often did when in the presence of people she did not know: she gave herself a new personality. It was not entirely unlike her, for she would need to consider maintaining it for a significant time. She was never comfortable with lying outright—mostly because it was difficult for her to recall which lies she'd told whom—but she could absolutely twist the story.

"Oh, yes, well," Poppy said, smoothing the front of her fichu. It was old lace, from her mother's mother, refashioned many times over. Precious, though. And it made her feel beautiful, even if it had yellowed a little with time. "The pattern is repurposed from my mother's gown, a voluminous thing she wore just after she married my father."

"How sweet of you to honour your mother in that way," the viscountess of wherever said in her condescending way, dismissing her.

But Poppy would not let it go.

"Oh, but it is not to honour my mother," Poppy said, adding a coy smile.

Reluctantly the viscountess turned her head, brows furrowing at the impertinent continuation of the conversation. Poppy knew they had already trespassed upon Edith's time and expectation: arriving without announcement like this was surely as bad as walking outside in one's shift before worship on Sunday.

"No?" The viscountess was not interested in the conversation at all, but Poppy did not care.

"Indeed not. You see, you may have heard our family had some dealings with a most hideous hedge witch in our past. It's a watered ducapes, you know, this particular weave. But it's said that the water used was from the tears of the hedge witch herself."

Poppy would remember this story, mostly for the look in the viscountess's pale blue eyes. Her expression warred between absolute confusion, disgust, and the need to keep herself composed. Ducapes was not watered with any sort of fluid, Poppy knew, but rather rolled to achieve its texture. But certainly this noble woman had no idea.

Thankfully, after that, the viscountess left Poppy alone. And although she was certainly pleased with herself for a few minutes, she noticed the sideways stares and the way people angled themselves from her when she moved from the dining area into the music room.

One of the other gentlewitches sat at the pianoforte and played a warbling rendition of a vaguely familiar song. Poppy didn't think she was very good, but it might have also been her own mood. She often found when she was angry or irritated, her view of the world was coloured with it. It did not help that Edith made absolutely no effort to pay her mind. Every time Poppy thought her companion might have a moment to speak with her, she was pulled away off in another direction.

She wanted to be done with London, this city of sprawling homes and new silks, full of people who had no idea what it took to build or to weave. Certainly, there were far worse people in the city than these gathered—and perhaps there were few better—but she still would never be accepted among them, and nor would she seek it.

When Blackwell Sipher, one of the few who had introduced himself to her, sat at the pianoforte, she slipped away silently in the direction of the stables. She could find her own way back, and the servants had been nice enough to her earlier.

She'd scarcely made it to the foyer when she felt a hand on her shoulder.

"Poppy. Where are you going?"

It was Edith. The woman had a most vexing ability to sneak up behind her, like some ghost of old.

The gentlewitch smelled of cherry cordial and bright sweat, and her eyes were tired but still glistening with just enough merriment to irritate Poppy.

"Why, my liege, it is clear the current company has no need of someone of my most quotidian nature," Poppy said, inclining her chin with as much poise as she could muster in the moment.

"There is nothing quotidian about you, my love," Edith said, taking her hand gently, almost asking permission with her hesitancy.

Poppy, who had avoided speaking to Edith entirely during their carriage ride to Countess Rocksavage's, relented so much more quickly than she ought have.

That was the problem with loving someone. Even if part of you knew you should let them go, they were so threaded into your mind it was painful to fight against it all the time.

"I will never be a part of this life of yours, Edith," Poppy whispered, tears springing up before she could choke them down. Her chin wobbled, lips trembling. "I can bring you no status, no power, no strength in a room full of people like that."

Edith's answering embrace was more comforting than warm chocolate by the fire, wrapped in perfect mulberry silk velvet. Every inch of Poppy's skin seemed to rejoice in the comfort, even if she fought against it still, internally. The spark between them was ever-present, and she suspected it always would be.

The gentlewitch kissed Poppy's forehead. "Do you truly believe I would take these scoundrels over you?"

"You didn't speak with me. They were terrible to me."

Edith's answering sigh was tinged with regret. "I know. I was cross with you, still. And confused. But I saw you speaking with the Viscountess Milton, and it was as if my whole world tilted. You carry yourself like a queen, you met her gaze for gaze, without knowing quite how much influence she has. You are so brave, my love. So brave, and so beautiful. And I would truly be a churl were I to squander it."

"You lied to me. And then Vale lied to us. I cannot live in a world so rife with deceit. It is not in my nature. I will be gobbled up."

"I will not let you be so consumed. At least, not by anyone who isn't me," Edith pulled away to give Poppy a look of most scandalous desire. And oh, how her body tingled in response to it! "I could not stop staring at you tonight. Surely you noticed that."

"I figured you felt guilty over your behaviour."

"I was. I am. But I was also bewitched. You may not possess the power of sorcery in your veins, but you are made of powerful stuff, Poppy. And I am more the fool for ever doubting you could handle all the truth of me. I'm afraid I may make decisions at times which may run counter to your wishes, but I hope we can come to agreements—that you and I can find balance in each other's hopes and aspirations. I was wrong to put mine ahead of you."

Poppy sniffled, as Edith presented her with a lilac-scented handkerchief. It was not just any handkerchief, but one of the many she'd embroidered for the gentlewitch: her initials and Poppy's, intertwined with a crocus and a bee flower orchid.

"I want to go home," Poppy said, for it was the truest of all the many feelings bandying about in her heart.

"Then home we shall go."

POPPY'S DISCOMFORT WAS mostly gone as they walked hand-in-hand toward the carriages and waited for their coachman to arrive. It was quite likely the gathering would go on for hours more, late into the night, and no doubt she and the gentlewitch would be the most central topic of conversation. But that was fine with her. Let them talk.

It was not until the carriage lurched away, gravel crunching under the wheels, that Poppy realised someone else was in the carriage with them.

No matter. Edith had a knife to their throat and a spell across their chest, readied for blood, before they even uttered a word.

ON SECOND THOUGHT, it might not have been the best idea to hide in Liege Edith's carriage, sulking in the shadows until he fell asleep. But Roland de Grateloup was never terribly good at planning: he felt it diluted the possibility of surprise; and without surprise he rarely felt excitement. How some people moved about the world with lists and tomes, following their instructions to the letter, he simply could not comprehend. What a waste of a one's existance, really.

Though, given his lack of preparation had led him to this moment—a gentlewitch of surprising capabilities holding both a dagger and a spell to his person with absolute murderous malice—he decided a cursory attempt at planning might have saved him the concern of wetting his pantaloons.

"No, Edith! That's Roland!" Poppy Brightwell pulled back on her companion's arm, though the viciousness in her gaze did not abate one whit. "Oh, for the star's sakes, release him."

Slowly, Edith Rookwood removed the encircling spell and the buzzing pressure around Roland's chest at last relented. She was supposed to be a middling gentlewitch, but demon's balls, that hurt. If his mother were in any way accessible, he'd have to ask for more details about that kind of power. Not that she was likely to give them to him, but knowing he had the ability to run to his mother always gave him a sense of control, however unmerited.

"I have no malicious intent, I swear!" Roland protested. "I needed a safe place, and as of late that precludes just about every place in London that isn't this specific location."

"That is debatable," the gentlewitch said, her voice still tinged with fury. "Quickly. Explain yourself."

Roland rubbed ruefully at his sore ribs. "I distracted your Warder. And then slipped in."

"I think my liege means, what led up to your entering our carriage?" Poppy offered gently. "Are you running from someone?"

"I…" Roland tried and failed to think of the words he'd use to describe what happened. But he wasn't entirely sure himself. "I am being hunted."

"By whom?" Liege Edith asked.

"I am not certain," Roland replied.

The gentlewitch flattened her lips in a look of searing consternation. "I'm not in a mood to play games, de Grateloup."

"I know. You never have struck me as a person of trifling matters, but my memory on the matter remains fuzzy at best."

"Molly told me you were following Poppy earlier," Liege Edith said. "Badly, at that. For someone supposedly of a lycanthropic heritage, you are about as conspicuous as a child drooling at a sweet shop window."

Poppy gasped. "You were following me?"

Roland groaned. There was no time for these inconsequential details.

"Yes, and now the Grey Moon is following me. Which is a much more pressing matter than your current, and obvious, annoyance," Roland said.

"And you've put it upon yourself to endanger us," said Liege Rookwood. He could feel her magic prickling his senses, pressing down upon his every pore. It was similar to, but not precisely like, the way he felt his mother's magic: insistent, threatening, and yet almost exhilarating. As if he was about to experience an event most never managed in their lifetimes. He loathed it.

"I am *desperate*," Roland said. "My face is plastered on half the billboards in town, the police and the witch-patrol are around every corner. I am an innocent man, but I understand their enthusiasm all the same. It does seem quite likely I did the deed, especially given my mother's continued absence."

"I should dump you on the side of the next crossroads," Liege Rookwood muttered, finally settling back into the carriage cushions.

"But we won't," Poppy said, with less enthusiasm than Roland would have liked.

"I ask a simple boon," Roland said, hand on his heart. "My mother trusted you with my secrets, with my care, but there is another who can offer me protection, and distance. Deliver me to his home, and I will darken your doorstep no longer. Unless..."

He did love dangling secrets before people. The drama of it. His mother said, on more than one occasion, that he had missed his calling in the theatre. The trouble with theatre, however was one was forced to endure *actors*. If there were one group of people in the world truly more insufferable and narcissistic than Roland, it was them. At least he came up with his own verbal ripostes. They had to rely on playwrights.

"Roland, I do think the gentlewitch is losing her patience," Poppy said, stilling her companion with an outstretched hand. "It is best for everyone if you clearly state what you might know. We have just endured a most exhausting dinner party and are no closer to knowing the fate of your mother."

"Ah, well, I don't expect that lot to know anything," Roland said, gesturing vaguely toward where Countess Rocksavage's townhouse had been. "The moment they smell weakness, they start sniffing about like hounds on the trail. My guess is they are trying to woo you to their cause."

Liege Edith flinched, clearly shocked by Roland's intuitive deduction. "I hadn't counted you for a political creature, de Grateloup."

He laughed, mirthless and cold. "Alas, for years growing up, the only way to tell what my mother was doing and where she was, was following her political exploits in the papers. I suppose I learned much by accident. And that was *one* of her inner circles; she has a few. Those are, unsurprisingly, the ones who sought out a replacement rather than involving themselves with the current situation."

"Explain. Now," said Liege Edith.

Roland took a deep breath, reached into his breast pocket, and handed a letter to the gentlewitch. Dark though it was, even the most basic hedge witch could cast an illuminating ink charm, and she did so without so much as a twitch of her finger.

The ink's eerie glow cast her face into strange contrast, and Roland was reminded, not for the first time, of his general discomfort around gentlewitches. They always seemed to yearn for more power, even when they already had it in spades. His mother always couched her desires in terms of the betterment of Crown and Coven, but he knew, deep inside, her ambition was an ever-burning need, pushing her ever onwards. He was an inconvenient mistake.

"The Grey Moon Brotherhood is claiming they have Virginia Cawley," the gentlewitch said, glancing up just a fraction of a moment before reading the missive again. "And they say they have already reached out to Parliament with an ultimatum but have been unsuccessful in reaching an agreement."

"That is preposterous," Poppy said.

"How did you get this?" Liege Edith asked. "It isn't addressed to you. It's meant for the Prime Minister, Perceval."

Roland did not want to waste time on the details. "I came across it by some considerable, though admittedly rather underhanded, pains. But that, unfortunately, led the Grey Moon straight to me. I gave them the slip, fortunately, and now I must at last bid adieu to London."

"We are not a carriage service, sir," Liege Edith said. "What do you take us for?"

"I take you for a liminal witch, my liege," Roland said, firmly and without more flattery than it required. "I know you use a Janus wardrobe, and that you have, indeed, expanded their craft and use. Given the state of Pub travel, it would be a most welcome advantage." When Liege Edith didn't reply, he continued coolly: "My mother speaks very little of her world, but when she does it's in regard to the things of which she is most proud."

They all fell silent, the carriage jostling.

"And where, pray, shall you be going once you have access to my Janus key?" Liege Edith asked.

"To visit my cousin. By marriage, technically, but still blood in my heart. You might know him: he's the new Viscount St. Albans. But I know him as Silas Drake."

Roland prepared for the response from the two women, but none came.

"This carriage is heavily warded. How did you get through?" Liege Rookwood asked.

"Son of a witch. You don't grow up in the shadow of Virgina Cawley without learning a few tricks," Roland said proudly.

Was the carriage going more quickly than expected? No, must just be the stress and his overactive imagination.

"And did you repair it on the way? Or did you leave a gaping hole in our defences, essentially trumpeting our presence to the entire city?"

Oh, dear. He truly had proved himself a fool, hadn't he? "Repair?"

Before he could confess to his thoughtlessness, the carriage shuddered as though hit by a great force, the curtains obscuring his view a moment while Edith let out a very un-gentlewitch-like curse.

Poppy pulled open the window, falling back immediately, shock across her features.

"Wolves. Immense wolves," she breathed. "I've never seen anything of the like."

Roland did not need to look to know their form and features: massive, shaggy, grey-pelted beasts with lines of silver down their back hackles. Werewolves. Now that the wind changed, he could smell them, both unpleasant and familiar.

He felt the bubbling response of his body, static and insistent, the need to join them. He'd been cutting back on his potion, straining his will to make up for the lack to avoid shifting. Not a very good idea, he decided, given the present situation. But the Grey Moon Brotherhood wasn't supposed to have their werewolves in London—they were supposed to stay in Paris.

"I'll go fight them, but I might never return," he volunteered, only because the words were gallant. It seemed the appropriate response given the situation. "Or..."

"Speak quickly or taste death," the gentlewitch warned.

"Do you have a Janus key with you?"

Edith hesitated for a quick moment, but Roland already knew he'd convinced her.

THE MOMENT ROLAND flashed out of existence, vanishing out the carriage door, one of the werewolves came careening into their carriage, tearing and snarling, sending the horses into a frenzy. There were not many werewolves in Netherford, but Poppy was certain none were this big nor this ugly. Unlike wild wolves, these werewolves were bare about the snout, and they produced a most unwelcome amount of saliva, which frothed up into their noses and down their necks.

They also spoke, which was unsettling.

"Come out, come out, little birdies," one of them sang, just as the carriage jolted again. "You've got nowhere to run."

And indeed, they were now heading along the empty stretch beside the Serpentine as the pack pursued them.

"The coachman!" Poppy said, as the carriage came to a stop.

Edith lurched forward and captured Poppy's mouth in a searing, perfect kiss. The kind that made the soles of her feet curl in anticipation. Though fear certainly tinged that desperate kiss, Poppy felt emboldened amidst it all.

"Stay inside the coach," Edith said, whispering against Poppy's ear so her whole body shivered in response.

"There are werewolves out there," Poppy said, grasping Edith's coat lapel. She still smelled of wine and tasted of the last sugared cake they'd been served at Countess Rocksavage's.

"They won't attack me," Edith said, then stopped herself. "Well, they shouldn't. If they do, you will have to report it to Parliament yourself."

"Edith!"

Edith cupped Poppy's face in her hand. "Trust me."

Snarling rose outside and Poppy felt helpless as Edith threw open the door of the coach. The waning moonlight reflected on the water behind them, making it difficult to distinguish the werewolves, their hulking shapes seeming to suck what light was there into their pelts.

The gentlewitch landed on the gravel pathway, her arm going wide in an arc. Thousands of small baubles of light rose across the trajectory, a warning flare, spinning up into the night sky.

"You won't have long," Edith said to the frontmost werewolf. He had a missing ear, Poppy observed. "Say your piece or wreak your havoc, but you will not go down without a fight."

Poppy counted three total werewolves, and they began pacing, hackles rising, but not approaching yet. They were sizing them up. The horses screamed, the coachman struggling to keep them from hurting themselves.

"What did you do with the foundling pup?" the frontmost werewolf asked, his voice surprisingly human, coming through such terrible teeth.

"I've sent him to safety. I've been charged with his protection," Edith said coolly, as if she were discussing parliamentary politics and not the remarkable escape Roland had just made. "He is not affiliated with you, or your clan, so there should be no concern."

"He is a murderer," said a second werewolf, a smooth woman's voice, surprisingly refined. "We are doing you a service. Protecting him will only bring doom to your demesne, witch of Netherford."

Poppy did not like the sound of that. She wanted to help Roland. For all his bloviating and puffed-up nonsense, he was rather charming. And she didn't think he was capable of orchestrating such a sloppy murder.

Edith threw open her cloak and pulled out a sword, long, silver, and wicked looking. Poppy could not imagine where she got it from, for she certainly had not gone armed into the presence of Countess Rocksavage. She'd not even seen such a weapon among their things at Netherford Hall.

Though, concern aside, she was quite glad Edith had thought ahead.

"If you threaten Netherford, or anyone under my protection, one more time," Edith said, her voice low and resonant in a way Poppy had never quite heard before, "you will come to regret it."

The coachman was whimpering, having given up with the horses and, instead, cowering on the other side of the coach.

"Shhh, quiet now," said the first werewolf. "We bring no threats. Just messages. Roland de Grateloup is ours by right and by blood. Long have we waited for him to escape his mother's clutches. Law gives us the right to claim him."

Poppy, incapable of holding back, leaned out the window to address the werewolves. "You may have the right to claim him, but he clearly doesn't want anything to do with you. He's nothing like you."

The first werewolf laughed, raspy and low, like the sound of grinding rock. "He is more like us than he has any idea. He has one week to come to us; if he does not, we will hunt him down. And there will be more than three of us between you and your precious human companion."

Edith's sword sizzled to life, the hilt blossoming upward until the whole of the blade was engulfed in blue tendrils of light.

"Looks like someone needs to know how serious we are," said the third werewolf who hadn't spoken until now. Their voice was younger than Poppy would have thought, and that broke her heart.

The werewolves twitched their ears in unison, and then the third sprang—not at Edith—but the coachman.

Edith twisted, her sword just barely missing the creature as it snapped at the air, the coachman shrieking. Poppy shrank down into the coach. She flinched at the horrible sounds from the horses as the werewolves made quick work of the terrified animals.

The scent of blood filled her nose, and Poppy willed herself to look at the scene again. She could not quite make out what was happening, but judging by the wavering lights, Edith was trying to fight off the werewolves singlehandedly.

"Edith!" Poppy screamed.

Just then, she heard a sound like thunder—or rather, she felt it. Wards, she realised, snapping into place, just like at home in Netherford. And with them, Molly Hode, an axe in both hands, running into the fray.

CHAPTER TEN
OF CLOUDLESS CLIMES AND STARRY SKIES

ROLAND DE GRATELOUP, natural nephew of Dowager Viscountess St. Albans and cousin by marriage to Silas himself, lay face down, completely naked, half protruding out of the fountain at the centre of Burkley House's front grounds. It was unclear as to whether he had run straight in, or was deposited there, but given his unconscious state, Silas could not say. Had the fellow been awake, there was no doubt he would have provided every detail of whatever adventure brought him to that most unfortunate position.

Fintan was at the forefront of the excavation attempt, thankfully having the sense to grab woollen blankets on their way out the door to conceal the worst of what was so unceremoniously visible of Roland's person.

Silas's first thought was how thin and pale his cousin looked. Granted, the overcast day did little to help, but it hurt his heart to see him so drastically changed. Theirs was a most congenial friendship, even if Roland was intolerable at times with his narcissistic tendencies and tedious attempts at procuring love matches.

He was just about to help Fintan roll Roland upon the blankets, when they all heard someone approaching the house. Two figures emerged from the direction of Netherford Hall through the narrow path between the hedges, both gasping and red-faced: Auden Garcliffe, the gentlewitch's uncle and majordomo; and Basil Hode, her second Warder. They looked rather frantic, and Basil was holding a bottle in his hands, proceeding toward them with care, so as not to agitate it.

"Wait! Be careful!" Mr. Garcliffe shouted. "Don't approach the man!"

Silas and Fintan both hesitated at the urgency in the Warder's voice.

Mr. Hode, as delicate of nature as his twin sister Molly was sturdy, was terribly winded by the time he got close.

"Missive from... Liege Rookwood..." he gasped, bending over and clutching his side with his free hand. "Werewolf!"

Auden, no less winded, spotted Roland's form in the fountain and took a step back. "Heavens. Perhaps there was less cause for alarm than we initially assumed."

"I know," Silas said, trying not to show his increasing frustration. "Roland is my cousin." He could see Laertes Byrne peeking out his window at the goings on. They did not need to draw attention from anyone, let alone the vampires. "Roland has long been afflicted, and I'm quite aware of his situation, and have been since we were children. I would not have approached him if I believed him a threat."

Mr. Garcliffe raised a brow, scrubbing at his beard a moment. "Well, it seems we did not need to run so fast then, Mr. Hode," he said. "Though we bring tinctures for him, which should help further. The gentlewitch was very clear in her instructions."

"Very well." Silas gestured to Roland's prostrate form. "For now, I could use every hand we can get. And I am glad you are here, Mr. Hode. For I was wondering what kind of physic I ought to call given the present situation, without raising alarm. Vampires are one thing, but werewolves are their own kind of trouble."

* * *

ONCE THEY WERE safely ensconced in the east wing, they warmed and dressed Roland and stoked a fire. Fintan did the majority of the work before excusing himself to tend to his duties, but Silas lent a hand now and then, feeling that the work kept his mind from spiralling in directions he'd rather not contemplate. They'd chosen the east wing strategically, as it was the farthest possible direction from the dowager viscountess, who haunted the west wing like a fitful ghost. She doted upon Roland, but only because he was his mother's greatest shame. And she had no concept of his predilections. Or that he was a werewolf.

Mr. Hode walked around Roland, hesitant at first, but with building confidence as the werewolf remained dormant. He placed two long fingers upon Roland's pulse points, scribbled some notes in his little leather journal, and then went to his satchel.

"How did you get word so fast?" Silas asked. "Has the gentlewitch returned?"

Mr. Hode looked up, a kind and patient expression on his face. "Oh, no. Alas. Tomorrow, perhaps. I received word from my sister. It's a somewhat unusual phenomenon, but we have always been able to communicate via Warding lines. As far away as London 'tis not as reliable as from town, but she still managed to communicate the details, if haltingly. It's a bit like listening to a distant song."

"I can't imagine he walked this way," Silas said.

Mr. Hode tried to hide his embarrassment at Silas's uneducated question but managed a kind reply. "No. He has remnants of liminal magic upon his person, and I found this clasped within his hand."

Mr. Hode pulled a small iron key from his pocket, shaped like a twisting octopus.

"That's a curious key," Silas said, although he could have sworn he'd seen one before.

"It's a Janus key. The gentlewitch is one of a few of her kind capable of making them. They can turn any door into a portal, much like our pubs. Though it appears this one ended up miscalculating. Or else Mr. de Grateloup ran and fell."

"It seems unlikely," Silas said. "He has ever been a most perplexing individual, built for romance and debauchery, but not for adventure. I don't think he would run anywhere on purpose, save perhaps to preserve his life."

"Well, about that…" Mr. Auden said from the window, where he had been surveying the sloping green grounds. "I suppose you may not have read the papers of late."

Silas breathed out. He hated the papers. They had dragged his mother's family through the mud when she'd married his father, and then him after his birth. There were many reasons he left for France, and the news was one of the most significant. He only read the papers when Parliament was in session, and then with all the other parts excised by Fintan's scissors. He found a great deal of pleasure knowing the shreds were used to light the furnace.

"Fintan gives me an overview, but I'm certain if he'd seen something pertinent, he'd let me know," Silas said, not a little defensively. Fintan, for his part, was oddly absent from the room, likely making tea or up to something far more useful.

Mr. Garcliffe gave Mr. Hode a significant look, and Silas prepared for the blow. Perhaps he should have taken a more serious approach to the papers, if only for his own good.

"It appears Mr. de Grateloup is wanted for murder," Mr. Garcliffe said, wincing as he explained. "In Paris. A diplomat's son."

Silas felt the blood in his body run cold, icy tendrils shivering down his neck and back. "Roland would never… I mean, he has some strange tendencies, but I lived with him for nearly a decade. He is not the sort of person to bow to his baser nature." Well, at least not homicide.

"Perhaps not," Mr. Garcliffe said, gentle and infuriatingly calm. Silas supposed it came from practice, having to deliver such news to a gentlewitch regularly. "The gentlewitch does not seem to think so. You see, she wrote me about Mr. de Grateloup, warning me not to heed the news. The letter just came today. You can imagine my surprise when Mr. Hode came to me with word of your cousin's most imminent arrival."

"I cannot see how he'd be any safer here than with Liege Rookwood," said Silas, pacing the length of the room and back. He pinched at the bridge of his nose, feeling more than a little dizzy.

"The wards," said Mr. Hode, now finished with his examination. "You're aware the gentlewitch has been protecting this building since Miss Brightwell's unfortunate accident, aren't you?"

No, he most certainly was not. "I did not realise her wards—your wards—extended beyond the property of Netherford Hall."

Mr. Hode did not look concerned at the glimmer of anger coming from Silas. In fact, the man shrugged. "Well, after all that occurred here, and given Miss Viola Brightwell's residence, it should not surprise you that the gentlewitch was persuaded to extend extra protection to you. Persephone Brightwell is a very convincing individual."

"That she is," said Silas. "Still, it would have been far more acceptable if they had informed me ahead of time. I do not wish to burden the gentlewitch with additional work."

"Regardless, Mr. de Grateloup will be safe here." Mr. Garcliffe put a comforting hand on Silas's shoulder.

"Or at least, safe from any outside threat," Mr. Hode said.

* * *

ROLAND DE GRATELOUP had innumerable weaknesses, but specifically one for delicate men with red hair. As he came slowly, agonisingly, to his senses, he came face to face with the most handsome man he had ever seen of that precise description. His eyes were between yellow and green, his skin smooth and without blemish, his features fine and nearly aristocratic. Though the moustache was ill-placed.

Shame he was scowling so terribly. And he smelled of lavender, and Roland detested the stuff.

"Drink this. Now." The man held out a small bottle of iridescent green glass. "Please."

"Good morning to you as well, darling," Roland said, reaching for the bottle. Memories of his flight from the werewolf pack prickled at the back of his mind, but he did not have the energy to consider the implications. He knew he was at Burkley House, which was all that mattered.

"Drink," insisted the beautiful man. "We can't risk a moment more."

Clearly Silas had alerted his staff to his condition, or at least this man. Handsome though he was, his clothing was a peculiar mix of last century's fabrics with military garb. He'd never seen anything quite like it. And so many buttons. Not that he minded buttons aesthetically, but they did slow down disrobing significantly.

One sniff and Roland quaffed the tonic. He wasn't feeling particularly wolfish, but that was likely due to his exhaustion. And it was true, he had been stretching out his doses, given he had next to no money and was wanted for murder. Even the seedier establishments in London were hesitant, given his reputation.

It tasted far worse than even the most noxious tonics he'd managed in the last few weeks: sour, bitter, and burning all at the same time. And, stars above, it had lavender in it. The cloying, horrid flavour made him gag. But, sure enough, he immediately felt the soothing effects of the tonic coursing through his body.

"If you end up actually being a murderer, I'll be the first to poison you," said the man, his tone as bitter as the brew. His Kentish brogue was positively charming, though, in that rustic, chewy way.

"That is a rather dramatic introduction. I suppose you know me, then?" Roland asked. For once he wished his reputation had not proceeded with him. The man had such perfectly sensual lips.

The man appeared to soften slightly at the break in decorum. "I am Basil Hode. Warder to the Gentlewitch of Netherford."

Hode. Hode? Where had he heard that name? And recently… "Oh! You must be a relation to Molly Hode!" Roland was quite pleased with himself for remembering. Sometimes it was difficult to access memories after unconsciousness.

"She is my sister," said Mr. Hode, hesitating. "Twin sister."

"How delightful. Yes. She and I met in London. She's very good at her job."

"Found you skulking, did she?"

Roland opened his mouth, then shut it. "As I said, she is very good."

Mr. Hode rose and placed a few items into his leather satchel. "I am a passing Warder, but a very good apothecary. You will need tinctures every two nights, as I do not have the quantities or the brewing methods accessible in London at present. It is an expensive and laborious process, and the viscount has been kind enough to pay for your treatment."

"You don't suppose I need a more thorough investigation, do you?" Roland asked, waiting to see Mr. Hode's reaction.

There was a brief moment when he thought perhaps Mr. Hode hadn't heard him. But then, delightfully, the Warder's cheeks flushed a most remarkable shade of crimson. If his life ever returned to some version of normalcy, he would have to see just how much he could get the fellow to flush.

"I have duties at Netherford Hall," said Mr. Hode, all brusqueness. "I will return tomorrow to see your progress, but I am quite confident in this recipe. Should there be any issue, Fintan will alert me."

And with that, the angelic, ornery creature left Roland to his very detailed thoughts.

WHETHER AS A function of his nature, his parentage, or both, Roland was generally a very quick healer. That he had been unconscious for so long after he'd used the Janus key was something of a concern, but once the tonic did its work he was up and about. Fintan himself came in to help with Roland's bath—although he was quite clean from the dousing in the fountain, as he'd learned—and had a most splendid change of clothing. Though Silas was a bit slimmer than he, the viscount always kept some of Roland's things for him. He had his own room at Gorham Manor, where Silas had grown up, and from what Fintan implied, the entire west wing was his to use.

Silas was a constant in Roland's life and had been since their youth. Never quite as wild or unmoored as he, no matter the situation he always provided Roland with a soft place to land. It did not hurt that Roland was related to the dowager viscountess, of course, but he liked to think his friendship with Silas went beyond familial ties.

However, the longer it took for Silas to meet with Roland, the more he began to doubt that affection.

True, Roland was generally not the sort of man to worry

himself with perceptions. He'd lived on the margins of society long enough to know it afforded him a great deal of freedom. However, of late, without his mother's protection, fine cracks in his façade had begun letting in traces of doubt and, shockingly, self-consciousness.

Roland lasted approximately three hours before he left his room and went looking for Silas, or Fintan, or anyone who might give him some answers. Or at least some wine. Silas could certainly afford it.

He'd scarcely made it to the foyer when he felt a cold kenning at his back, the sense someone was watching him.

Turning slowly, shoving away the werewolf senses starting to rise in him, he saw a woman standing on the other side of the glass by the promenade. She was a petite creature, lovely in a small, feminine way, wearing a green gown embroidered with a boteh motif about the cuffs and hem.

She stood remarkably still, staring at him with dark eyes, unafraid. When she turned her head, Roland understood: her hair did not catch the light. It absorbed it, making it both heartbreakingly lovely and terrifying. Spidersilk hair. *Vampire* hair.

That was when he noticed the similarity: it had to be Miss Viola Brightwell, Poppy's sister.

"I won't hurt you," he said through the small opening in the glass between them. The promenade connected the gardens to the west wing and allowed a view into the lovely hallways strewn with sculptures and paintings worth more than Roland's own life.

"I wasn't concerned on that count," said the vampire woman. Ah, she was just the sort Silas preferred, and that explained some things. Hadn't Silas written to Roland months ago about a pretty country girl he had found himself enchanted by? Yes, no doubt her becoming a vampire complicated his plans even more.

Roland bowed, scenting her at last: dust and roses—no, violets, too. "Roland de Grateloup, at your service. I had the distinct pleasure of meeting your sister Persephone in London. She is charming and…" He tried to find the right word to describe the enthusiastic woman. "Ebullient."

"She is both those things. Yes, I am Viola Brightwell, of Harrow House but lately Burkley. I admit I am a bit jealous you've spoken with Poppy. I fear when she left, I was not in the most agreeable of moods."

Roland was surprised to find himself feeling a twinge of empathy, unwelcome and strange. "She mentioned. I know she was searching for a cure for you, and I am afraid I could not offer her much hope at present, given my own current circumstances. I suppose you know of my affliction."

"You did make rather a spectacular entrance," she said, her lovely voice a little hushed, but with merriment in her eyes. Yes, he knew precisely why Silas was so enchanted. A woman this lovely *and* with vampire appetites. It was almost enough for him to consider wooing the fairer sex. "I don't suppose we'll be likely to forget it any time soon."

No doubt they would have continued having a most pleasant conversation, had the great oak doors to the hall not opened and Silas appeared, flanked by Fintan.

"Roland! You're awake, thank the stars!"

"Much to my bitter disappointment. I was having such delightful dreams. And none of them included being framed for a murder," Roland said, embracing his cousin. Silas gripped a bit harder than usual, and Roland caught the look of longing and wariness in Violet's expression as she backed away from the window.

"Miss Brightwell," Silas said, seeing her. "You look lovely this afternoon."

Roland caught the hitch in Silas's voice, noted the way his whole body adjusted, his breathing changed. He didn't just find this woman a passing fancy—no, Silas was absolutely besotted with her. And yet he was keeping his distance. Silas's restraint was infamous, but Roland could always help push him over the precipice.

Perhaps that's just what he needed right now. Perhaps that is why the stars brought him back. Love matching was his most revered pastime, and if Silas was already this taken with her he would just require gentle goading to spiral toward true love.

True love. It was for everyone else, but not for Roland. At times, he felt the irony. Yet he could not stop himself from exerting his matchmaking skills upon anyone even vaguely receptive.

"My lord," Miss Brightwell said, dropping into a gentle curtsey. Through the glass she looked ephemeral, her marvellous eyes glittering with just a hint of tears. Or, blood, most likely. Vampires were a most peculiar biological puzzle.

Roland could feel the tension between the two of them, taut as a bowstring, and yet they both pulled away. Didn't they understand that the more a person denies their body and base desires, the more they rise to the forefront? Or maybe that was their game.

Silas cleared his throat. "Well, it's good that I see you now. I've just gotten word that the gentlewitch and your sister are to arrive this evening back at Netherford Hall. We've all been invited to meet with them."

"You must excuse me, both, then," Miss Brightwell said quickly, her hands trembling as she adjusted her gloves. "I must prepare for Poppy's arrival. We have much to speak of."

"You let her drink your blood?"

Roland and Silas had endured many a night of debauchery, but it typically ended with the werewolf on the far sultrier side. Not that Silas didn't have appetites, they were just nowhere near as varied or open to interpretation as Roland's.

Now, listening to the young viscount detail his tawdry affair with Viola Brightwell—which sadly, had yet to end in any clear consummation or profession of love!—was enough to keep Roland giddy for weeks. With this whole being-wanted-for-murder business, he had started to wonder if he would ever get back to his favourite pastime.

Silas, who had caught on to Roland's schemes, leaned back in his chair and took another sip of brandy. "I will share more details if you tell me a bit more about your circumstance. And Aunt Virginia."

They'd gathered in Silas's study while catching each other up. As yet, Roland had not shared much, mostly out of embarrassment.

"You absolute tease," Roland pouted. Brandy made his head ache, so he was making his way steadily through a bottle of finest claret. "There really is little to tell, other than my absolute innocence in this matter. I was framed in France, I barely escaped to London—your Aunt Virginia is apparently missing, and has entirely abandoned me, and werewolves are stalking me."

"I'm beginning to think I'll need to employ some Warders of my own," Silas mused, shaking his head. He looked so very tired.

"Well, the gentlewitch has a spare. Lovely to look at, but the sourest personality I've ever seen," Roland offered.

Silas laughed shortly. "Basil? Oh, he's a good chap. But it is possible your reputation proceeded you. Not to mention your proclivities. Mr. Hode has many responsibilities, and though I am paying him well, he'll be making the trek from Netherford to Burkley far more often than he'd like, I suppose."

"My reputation? Do you speak of me so often?" Roland teased.

"No, but perhaps I ought to have. Not to mention spending more time reading the papers."

"I cannot blame you for your distraction. Miss Brightwell is clearly a woman of quality."

The viscount dropped his head at the mention of Miss Brightwell again, staring into the contents of his brandy snifter. "She is a vampire."

"And I am a werewolf. What difference does that make? If she makes you happy, you ought to stand up to our irascible old aunt at last and be done with it." Roland barely got the words out before he saw the answer in Silas's expression. "Ah, yes. Of course. *Your* reputation."

"I've been invited to London, to meet with the Lords," said Silas. "My father burned so many bridges, and now they are reaching out to me. Years of my work, finally paying off. Could you imagine what would happen if they discovered I was pursuing not only a woman of low status, but a vampire at that?"

Roland truly loved his cousin, more than anyone in the world, really, other than himself. But his confounded sense of honour and loyalty was exhausting. Even now, poised on the edge of possible happiness for the rest of his life, he found a way to make himself utterly miserable.

But Roland was not without his own charms. He knew any pressure to pursue Miss Brightwell would end in Silas resorting to drastic measures to keep away from her. Clever though he was, the viscount's practicality was one of his least appealing character traits. But he was, at the heart, a hopeless romantic.

So, Roland would simply resort to gentle orchestrations. Not today, however.

"You're right, I suppose," Roland said, at last, feigning a

yawn. "And I must apologise again for trespassing on your beautiful home."

"You always have a place here, Roland. At any home of mine."

The sincerity was enough to render Roland mute.

Sensing the unwelcome presence of emotion, Silas continued quickly: "Fintan is already finding the best barrister in the county, and we will slowly find our way back into the good graces of London culture."

"Oh, brimstone, I certainly hope not," Roland said.

This, at last, elicited a laugh from Silas. "Before we do, we shall meet tonight at Netherford Hall and learn what the gentlewitch has discovered in London, and what we might be able to do to assist."

CHAPTER ELEVEN
FAIR AS A STAR

POPPY WAITED ANXIOUSLY in the withdrawing room, smoothing her skirts, as their guests arrived. In the last turn of the sun, she had watched her companion nearly murder a werewolf, escape a whole pack of them, and then cast a spell so beautiful and horrific, she was left blinking in awe.

And now her sister Viola was returning to them at last.

Yes, she had always longed for a more exciting life, but she had to admit even she had her limitations.

Poppy glanced over at Molly, trying to reconcile the picture of the Warder, gleefully slaughtering two of the werewolves, with the woman who stood guard now beside her brother Basil. The Warders both seemed even more sombre than usual. Molly had a healing cut across her cheek, and Basil looked as if he hadn't slept in days.

Edith, seated next to Poppy, leaned over. "My darling, it's getting quite cold in here, and our guests will be here any moment. There's only so much we can do when…"

When Poppy was anxious, the house had a habit of cooling. Half of Poppy's soul resided in the building, and this was a somewhat inconvenient side-effect. Indeed, when Poppy blinked over at her companion, she noticed her nose had gone red.

Deep breathing helped, as did the gentle pressure of Edith's hand around hers.

"You'll have to forgive me, but just last night you were fending off a pack of werewolves, and now my sister is returned—with a werewolf. And two more vampires," Poppy said. "I must say, but if there was ever a moment to be anxious, it would be right at this moment."

There was no more time to discuss the nuances of her temperament, for the immense doors to the withdrawing room opened, and then there was Viola, flanked by Lacrtes Byrne and Roland de Grateloup.

Propriety and decorum be damned. Poppy shot from her seat and ran into her sister's arms, weeping and muttering what must have been entirely incomprehensible. Viola, for her part, tolerated the attention while the gentlewitch and Auden scurried about the room trying to get everyone comfortable.

But they were altogether invisible to Poppy. She kept looking at Viola, words utterly beyond her. Indeed, the whole withdrawing room slowly bloomed, hyacinths dangling from the ceiling and rose hedges growing up around the borders, pulling furniture toward the walls in its enthusiasm. If Poppy could stop it, she would, but she could not. She was the house, and her joy was flowers.

She looked like Viola. A bit peaky, perhaps, and dressed in far darker hues than she'd ever been before. There was the hair, of course, void of all its sheen and remarkably soft-looking. Her eyes, though…

"I know I've changed a little," Viola said, searching her sister's face. "I am so terribly sorry for how I behaved before."

"Don't you even begin," Poppy said, taking her sister in for another embrace. She smelled so different. Floral, but dusty. A bit like old incense. "You're here, that's all that matters. And you can do nothing to charm me, for I am impervious to vampire Allures. This ridiculousness is all entirely my own."

Mr. Byrne stood protectively by Viola, putting a gloved hand on her shoulder. Poppy still did not like the vampire, given their previous interactions, but she knew he had stuck by Viola in the direst of circumstances, and on days when Poppy simply could not manage. Nor their family. Did Viola recall any of that?

"My sister sends her regrets," Mr. Byrne said to the gentlewitch. "I'm afraid she is a bit overwhelmed by the last few days' proceedings."

"Thank you all for coming," Edith said, standing a little stiffly. "Especially our esteemed Viscount St. Albans."

Poppy knew Edith didn't enjoy large groups of company over at the house, and after the last few days' constant nonsense, she worried her companion might lose her temper. It happened often enough Poppy had learned when to expect it and how, when possible, to ease the gentlewitch through it. But some days, like this one, were beyond planning.

And Viola was *here*. Truly here. Poppy kept sneaking glances at her sister, refusing to let go of her hand, fighting back tears every time she let the realisation wash over her. Confound her feelings, it was so overwhelming. She loved her sister so much it hurt, sometimes. Not being able to help her in the last weeks had been almost more than she could bear.

"There are a number of matters which require our gathering, but first I must report on our attack last night," Edith said. She lifted up her sleeve, showing some of the gashes she received in the tussle. None as serious as what Molly endured, but still shocking to see upon the person of a gentlewitch.

The group gasped and Roland had the decency to look embarrassed, at least. Then, Edith went into a straightforward account of the attack and the evening before. They'd decided before the meeting on Edith's leadership in the conversation, given Poppy's less than reliable narration. It was not that she miscounted things, only that it was difficult to separate the important details from the ones best left in her mind.

Regardless, the circumstances were dire.

"There hasn't been a werewolf attack on a gentlewitch in years," the viscount said.

"Not since 1767," Edith chimed in, ever the expert. "And that was a lone actor, at that point, ravaging the countryside. Not a measured, coordinated pack attack. For anything akin to this, we would have to go back at least another hundred years."

"They're not afraid of the Coven," Roland said, pinching his nose. "Clearly. My mother is conspicuously absent, whether the Grey Moon had anything to do with it or not. As it stands, they have little to fear, it seems."

"The Coven Council is fragmented, but it's politics as usual," Edith said, pacing back across the carpet and pouring herself a bit of brandy. "But one thing is clear: the Cawley family is in danger. Mr. de Grateloup is in danger. The Grey Moon, presumably, was behind our attack, and they wanted to send a clear message: they're coming for you, Mr. de Grateloup."

Roland sank down into his chair, real fear in his vibrant eyes. "I have no desire to number among their ranks, nor any others. I'd sooner throw myself into the Thames than be affiliated with the Grey Moon."

"From what I know, the Grey Moon itself is fractured," said Basil, timidly at first. When Edith gave him a nod to continue, he stepped forward and away from his post. "Warders, as a rule, need to be apprised of as many factions as we can. And gentlewitches are not the only ones to employ us these days—Warders and wolves have a long history of collaboration. Though werewolves are, of course, quite capable of protecting themselves, they're often vulnerable during the full moon, when in their baser state."

Roland snorted, glaring at Basil. "That is a common misconception, Mr. Hode. Werewolves are no less capable during the full moon—in fact, quite the opposite. Our powers are at their height. And as such, our energy signals are incredibly strong, especially when gathered. That is why Warders are needed: to dampen the impact and keep the pack hidden."

"Be that as it may," Basil said, turning his back on Roland in a way that left no question to his opinion of the werewolf, "Molly had other business in London, and accidentally discovered another terrible piece of this puzzle."

"Werewolves," Laertes said, throwing up his hands. "Warders. And people say vampires are complicated."

Molly sighed in annoyance but continued. "None of the papers have reported it, but Osmund de Hetrus is dead."

"Osmund de Hetrus?" Poppy asked. The name was vaguely familiar, but she could not place it.

Roland blanched two shades paler. "Osmund... He was my mother's Warder."

"Why hasn't it been reported?" the viscount demanded. "The de Hetrus family must know immediately."

"The manner of death was nearly identical to the murder Roland was framed for," Molly said. The tone of her voice indicated she was clearly not yet convinced of the werewolf's innocence. "Except for one small detail."

Basil indicated his neck, putting two fingers upon the delicate arteries there. "In addition to the gruesome dagger marks, someone had fed upon the Warder. Not before the murder... but after."

Mr. Byrne grasped the edges of his seat, Viola pursing her lips as if she felt his emotions in tandem. Perhaps they did. There was so much about being a vampire Poppy had to learn if Viola was willing to tell her.

"I do not like the sound of that," Mr. Byrne said. "If that

is true, I can think of only a handful of reasons, and none of them give me much hope."

"And how did you get such a close look at the body?" Roland asked. "Are we to assume this is all just masterful coincidence?"

The viscount gave his cousin a measuring, slightly warning, glance. "This is a family matter, but a complicated one. I would appreciate your focus in this, Roland. I am certain Miss Hode will provide details in due time." He turned to Mr. Byrne. "I'm afraid I am not as learned as I ought be in regards to the preternatural—do you mind telling us what this means?"

Mr. Byrne looked at Viola again, sharing some kind of unseen communication. Poppy felt an unwelcome welling of jealousy rise in her chest, hot and sharp. It had only been a few months. How could they have become so close? Viola caught her eye then, her brows up, and then her expression softening as if she understood. The language of sisters endured beyond the death of the soul, it seemed. They would speak of it later.

"This is far more my sister's area of expertise, but drinking from the bodies of the slain—for a vampire—is an act most profane. Though we are death-like, we seek life to bring the balance. Drinking the blood of the dead causes madness, but provides power," Mr. Byrne explained, his expression grave. "It is forbidden and has been for centuries. You understand, vampires are a dying species— yes, I know that is an ironic turn of phrase, but it is true."

Basil spoke next, to Poppy's surprise. "I think it is even more insidious than that. At first, I thought it absolute conjecture—the wanderings of my sometimes ridiculous mind. I have the brain of an apothecary, so I am always thinking of mixtures and tinctures, both new and old. It was Fintan who reminded me."

"*Azothine*," Roland said. "A potion made from the distilled blood of a werewolf who has fed upon a vampire, cursed by the blood of the dead. It is a cycle of life and dying, and negative space of power, wherein even the most remarkable witch would not be able to fight back. In some books, witch blood is also included, making it even more powerful. It would be fatal to any mortal, but a strong enough vampire or werewolf—disgusting as the idea would be—could survive it. It is said that was how the werewolves were so strong during the war."

Edith stood stock still as she listened, brows down tight in concern. They all looked to her, for of the three preternaturals, witches always had the highest standing in such matters. "Witch, werewolf, and vampire," Edith said. "The three most powerful preternaturals. It is said, once, there were dreams of uniting us all. Instead, as witches grew in power—and then became woven into society itself—the more bestial were pushed to the edges. I suppose it is terribly naïve of me to think we could go on as we were forever, that they wouldn't fight back."

"The Coven Council needs to be alerted," the viscount said. "And Parliament—at least, those who we can trust."

"And who, pray, can we trust?" Edith asked the viscount directly. "I have just returned from London, as you well know, and I must say the casual lack of concern about the High Witch's disappearance makes me think the rot goes far deeper than we can imagine. My lord, you must keep Mr. Hode with you at least, for protection, here at Burkley. Though I know the dowager viscountess is no friend to witches, she is still Virginia Cawley's sister. Roland has already been targeted, and it won't take much to deduce his whereabouts."

"We're to have a ball," the viscount said, exasperated. "It is perhaps the worst possible time for such a thing."

"Perhaps not," Roland said. "For we would not want anyone to know what we suppose. I saw the guest list, you see—"

The viscount gave a rough laugh. "Of course you did."

"It was scattered about, just waiting for the right pair of eyes. Well, if half the folk invited show up, we'll indeed have a most delightful cross-section of local and London personalities. Cleverly, cautiously, we can gather information without raising suspicion."

"What if the Grey Moon, or whatever horror this death-drinking vampire is, attack the guests?" Poppy asked. Sometimes she felt it was up to her to have a voice for the humans.

"Poppy is right," Edith said, shaking her head so her curls danced just enough to catch the light. "I would advise against it, St. Albans."

Roland shrugged. "It is highly unlikely they would do anything. No matter how bold, werewolves are covert creatures. Besides, the viscount can employ more Warders, and we can put together other precautionary measures. Like your ring, my liege."

Edith looked down at her ring, thoughtfully. "I will have to consider it."

"You also have three vampires, pledged to your safety, my liege," Mr. Byrne said. He put his hand on his chest, bowing slightly. "That is no small thing."

"So long as you promise not to sip from the guests," Roland intoned.

Viola's scowl was a beautiful thing. "We *are* civilised, Mr. de Grateloup."

For all the excitement, Poppy's flowers began to droop. More and more she felt as if she was being pushed to the margins of a grand adventure full of preternatural power. And that seemed terribly unfair.

* * *

THE WALK BACK to Burkely Hall was quiet, the crisp autumn night refreshing on Viola's face. Yet she did not feel cold, for she was always cold. Always a vampire. And that would not change.

Before they left, she had promised to speak with Poppy the following day. She could see just how desperate her sister was to catch up with her, and she truly did want to take the time to meet again with her family... Yet so much of her had changed, every mote of her shifting, that she worried she might disappoint them. It was not that she no longer felt affection for them, it was only that her new life was so different, so altered. Recalling her time living at Harrow House was like glimpsing someone else's existence through a frosted glass.

Deep in her thoughts, she had not noticed that the viscount had drawn up beside her. She smelled him first, which was something she was getting used to, and then there he was: a little breathless, and so very beautiful.

Laertes and Roland remained some paces behind them, their voices a little too low for her to hear.

Looking over at Silas, her chest ached with need. Drinking from him had saved her, perhaps, but it had done nothing to mitigate her affection for him. It had only intensified it to the point of constant aching, hunger, and want.

When he spoke no words, she said, "I did not know there was to be a ball at the house. I am still used to being part of such things, but I suppose I must learn to detach myself from those expectations."

"Oh, Miss Brightwell," Silas said. "I am afraid I have been terribly inhospitable. Were it my decision..."

"But your aunt," Viola said. Yes. The dowager viscountess. "Your aunt, who I stayed with and entertained, who I cared for and assisted in every detail of the house and its grand reveal. I understand people have prejudices, of course I do. But before, I had the spirit, but not the money; now I have the money, but not the spirit."

She had been thinking that phrase during much of the evening's earlier proceedings.

Silas fell silent. They had once had such easy conversations, so natural and comfortable. Viola had never known connection on such a level. There always existed a palpable tension between them, but the sort best resolved with kissing. Now, so much else lay between them.

"Should you require any additional assistance, while you are here, please know I am happy to provide," Silas said softly.

Viola felt her soul stir at that, the deeper, wilder hunger awakening. "I would not presume upon your kindness any further, my lord. Already I am clearly an inconvenience."

"Well, my aunt be damned. You are invited to the ball, Viola," Silas said, stopping just by the edge of the little tributary that marked the boundary between Netherford and Burkley's House's sprawling land. "I say so."

"Silas, I cannot disobey the dowager viscountess," Viola said. "This is not only her house, this is her ball."

She hoped he would deny it, stand up for her, declare that she ought to come. But he did not. "I am so sorry," he said, looking away from her.

"Do not pity me," Viola said, that urgent flame of anger back again, flitting around in her ribs. It made her want to bite him even more. "I have two families, now. This time, next week, I shall be at Howarth Castle, where I belong."

He did not touch her, but in her vampire vision she could see the wanting in his eyes, the desperation. "Come visit me tonight," he said. "Come. And let me grant you what strength I may while we still have time."

The practical, logical part of Viola knew this was a most terrible idea. Understood that her affections for Silas Drake, Viscount St. Albans, should not be encouraged. He had made it abundantly clear he could not pursue her in a proper way.

And yet...

She had long put other people's wants and desires over her own. She could ascribe this feeling, perhaps, to her new powers as a preternatural—except it felt more of a personal revealing. Deep inside of her soul, there had always lived a creature of desire and need, she had only caged it for so long, always playing the most responsible of all her siblings, always carrying burdens far beyond her own.

Well, her own family was frightened of her, now. Poppy wasn't, but then again, Poppy feared nothing. Except, perhaps, losing those she loved. And she *had* lost Viola already. But Mama had not visited, Heath had only written once, and Oliver hadn't left Harrow House in weeks. Papa was the only one who wrote regularly, but he acted as if nothing had changed at all, and Viola was tired of weeping blood all over the papers over a woman she was no longer.

So why *shouldn't* Viola have what she wanted? Whom she wanted? Right now? If she truly accepted this change, stopped resisting it, she would live for centuries. Silas would become just a footnote in her history, so it didn't matter ultimately.

The idea broke her heart.

"I shouldn't have spoken so," Silas said, taking a step away from her. "I have shamed you."

"No, Silas, please," she said, relishing the sound of his name on her lips. A whisper, a forbidden thing. *Her* Silas.

She watched him swallow, struggling with words. He bowed his head and said: "I would like nothing more in all the world."

Stars and the speckled firmament, his eyes dazzled. Were they not in the presence of Laertes and Roland, she might have done something rather rash. As it was, her body thrilled with the impending connection.

She leaned over to him and whispered: "Then come and find me."

SILAS WANDERED THE dark hallways of Burkely House, quiet as he could, the floors in the old wing creaking around him. Though much of it was a new construction, some of it still held the shape of the previous home. He could swear they had their own feeling, too, the older places. As if they remembered their old arrangement, remembered Silas as a boy traipsing through the dark passageways and sneaking under tapestries.

Tonight, though, he sought a different distraction: Viola Brightwell.

Then come and find me.

That challenge had lit his blood afire, the promise and the seduction in it. They could not be together, not for long, but he would reach out and take what he could, while he could, and while she offered. And in response, he would give all he had.

Viola was not in her rooms, but Silas found Laertes at the piano forte, plucking out a sad, Gaelic tune, the intervals familiar and distant to him at the same time.

The vampire looked up at him, eyes mournful a moment before resuming their hard cleverness. "She is not here, my lord," said Laertes, still gently playing the tune.

"I was just checking to see…" Silas tried to say, but the words were unconvincing. "I'm sorry." He rubbed at the bridge of his nose.

"Why are you apologising to me?" Laertes asked. The

song picked up in its tempo, a melancholy rise followed by a marvellous crescendo.

"I should keep my distance, and yet I feel I cannot," Silas confessed. "Is this some power she has over me?"

"Viola is a vampire, but she does not yet know how to Allure. What she feels for you is natural, and one of the few remnants of her life before she was turned."

Silas felt embarrassingly relieved at that. "She tells me you plan to return to Howarth Castle after the ball. You know, of course, that you are always welcome here at Burkley House. I hope I have not made you feel otherwise."

Laertes rocked side to side, the silvery stamped buttons on his banyan flashing in the candlelight. "We are vampires, viscount. Being welcomed into a mortal's home, as you have done, is the greatest compliment you could ever give us. I mean it when I say you are the best among men. But we draw strength from our own homes, our 'hives,' as they are so oft derogatorily called. I believe Viola is close to accepting the change, but staying here is not wise. We agree that once she has the opportunity to reconcile with her family, we will take the winter at Howarth. She will learn all there is to learn, and Ophelia and I will take good care of her."

"I have no doubt of that. I apologise if I ever implied otherwise," Silas said. In his anger, especially in the early days of Viola's illness, he had exchanged many ugly words with Ophelia. But then, he had wondered if Viola had been broken irrevocably in some way, gone beyond the capacity of reason.

A life without Viola's wit and grace...

Laertes closed his eyes, lost in the sound of music. "There is no shame in wanting her still, my lord. I know, as a mortal, you are not often allowed to express your passions. I cannot imagine existing in such a way. Exhausting, truly."

He paused in his playing, a sustained note unresolved in the air. "For those who live such short lives, I cannot imagine the point of such denial. But, I suppose, I am not, nor have I ever been mortal."

Silas swallowed, sighing as Laertes finally resolved the chord. The last notes resounded deep in his bones. "Fear drives us, Mr. Byrne. And freezes us. To make no mention of duty. For short as our lives are, we live to create a better, brighter future for those who come after us."

"Ah, yes. The dratted legacy," Laertes said. He turned on the bench, clicking his heels together with all the elegance of a polished concert pianist. "But what price legacy, if you leave nothing for yourself?"

SILAS FOUND VIOLA on the roof. He'd nearly given up, especially given the sombre conversation with Mr. Byrne. Then he heard a skittering sound, not the clawed menace of foxes or the impish patter of squirrels, but the briefest movement. A foot across the slate.

Indeed, there was a balcony off of the observatory on the second story, built to have better access to the dome for cleaning. Only someone with an intimate knowledge of the house would even know of the small iron lattice, hidden as it was behind a trellis. And few in all the county knew Burkley better than Viola Brightwell.

Initially, he had dismissed the idea she was outside, for it was raining and thinking such behaviour would be far more expected of the other Brightwell sister. But no: there she was, face upturned to the starry sky, her arms wrapped around her knees. Viola wore nothing but a pale shift, which clung to her legs, dragging down the fabric at her shoulder to show an expanse of her smooth skin. She'd undone her hair, and her curls sprang to life with the moisture. Though as Silas drew closer, he noticed some of the locks had plastered to the side of her face.

"The night is damp, Miss Brightwell," Silas said, shielding his eyes from the downpour. His banyan whipped about his legs as he got his bearings, the figured silk stained almost black with the moisture. "But I have found you, nonetheless."

"I never liked the rain before," Viola said, dreamily. She did not look at him. "And yet I find myself drawn to it, now, as if each little drop awakens my skin, reminding me of who I used to be and whispering of what I am becoming."

"I hope I can remind you, a little, of both worlds," Silas said, slowly taking a seat next to her. His heart pounded in his chest, rattling against his ribcage like a frightened animal. Except he was not frightened. He was excited to feel her again, to hold her again, if she would permit him. "I'm still here."

"I know." Viola turned at last, her head tilting in that new way, that measuring way. "You remind me of innocence. But I do not think you innocent, my lord. Roland tells me your adventures in France would bring a blush to even a storied courtesan."

Such a curious woman. And such a bold question. The Viola Brightwell he knew would never have broached such a subject, not so directly. But then, he doubted that Viola Brightwell would have climbed to the roof on a rainy night, either. Though he missed that old version of her, he was growing more and more infatuated with her as she was now.

"I have had many lovers, yes, if that is what you are asking," Silas said, finding the truth far easier to speak than he imagined.

"And are you a good lover, my lord?"

He laughed, and it felt like sunshine blooming in his chest. "I have not had many complaints. I have enjoyed the act of love, and I take care to ensure the women who lie with me find their own pleasure, as well."

"And of those women you so generously pleasured—did you love any of them?" There was no judgement in her voice, no pressure. The question was posited almost clinically.

Love. He had wished for love; and some of the women he'd lain with were bold and beautiful, clever and kind, wicked and winsome. And yet, he did not find love in them, did not sense a kindred soul. There had been moments of giddiness, and in some cases, even weeks of jollity. It never lasted, though. And, at times, he wondered if he was merely not meant for such feelings.

Then he saw Viola Brightwell in the Holly and Sickle, and he believed in love.

She deserved a direct answer, though, and he said: "Love is a complicated emotion, you know. I did not strictly seek out companionship in most of those women, but rather a person of like-mindedness, a willingness for adventure, and perhaps good conversation. Our goal was mutual passion, but for me that begins in the mind. Is that what you seek, Viola? Passion for passion's sake, or to connect?"

At the casual use of her name, he caught a flicker of a smile. "I have always hungered for your mind and for your body," she said simply.

That comment went straight to his groin, and despite all the rain, Silas found his mouth rather dry.

"Then we are both aligned," he said, softly as he could, his heart beginning to beat with anticipation.

"You have not asked after my conquests, my lord."

"I do not care," he said. "You could have bedded a thousand and one, or one alone, and it would not matter to me."

"And what if there were no others?"

Her question felt like an ice arrow to his chest. Viola was in her early twenties, at the most, and while it wasn't unusual to be chaste, he had never considered a woman of her beauty and poise to have remained so. Again, the distance between their experiences yawned wide between them.

"Viola," he said, moving closer to her. "Are you saying you have never taken your passion with another before?"

She remained very silent, looking up again at the rain, breathing in the cold without concern. Silas wondered if her vampire form meant she was not bothered by such fluctuations in temperature, for he was beginning to shiver as the wind rose around them.

"Would it matter?" she asked.

Silas felt the shame of not having answered her question. "It would only matter in the sense of it being your choosing, for whatever this is between us, this fickle and short glimmer we have. Long have I yearned for your touch, for the bewitchment of your gaze—long before you ever died and were remade. I had thought that would change, given what you are now, and yet I am more drawn to you than ever." He took her hand, drawing cold fingers to his mouth and kissing them, eliciting a gentle gasp from Viola. "My intentions are to love you, body and soul, while I still may. There is little courage in it, I know, but tomorrow is never promised. And I would regret a thousand lifetimes if I did not confess that every dream, and every waking thought, I desire you. All of you."

Faster than Silas could track with his eyes, Viola was upon his lap, her legs straddling his hips, rooted against the angle of the roof. The strength in her—brimstone!—his whole body rose to meet hers, his spine arching with her touch, with the connection, his blood thundering in his ears.

Viola took both sides of his face in her hands, stroking his cheeks with her thumbs, as she gazed into his eyes. The very marrow in his bones replied, aching desire pulling him to attention, lost in that dark gaze. Perhaps she was weeping, but the rain washed away all the blood before it could show. Somehow, he knew she was, but that the tears were not of sorrow, but of a kind of release. A surrendering. The answer to a call long drawn out between them.

The feel of her body filled his head as his hands found her skin, taut under the sodden cloth of her shift. He pulled aside the garment, making room to trace a line across her ribs and over her back, noting every indentation and curve of her. Silas felt her trembling response, could tell she was holding back.

"No one can hear us," he said, leaning up to whisper in her ear. "But I do want to hear you say it."

"Please," Viola said, grasping him back, fists full of damp velvet. In the distance, lightning illuminated the sky, followed by a low rumbling of thunder. "Take me."

He buried his smile as he took her lips in his, sighing as she opened her mouth in response. Viola moaned, the sound only stoking the pull of his own desire, as if she were already connected to him. As he turned his head, he felt the brush of her sharp teeth against his tongue and, stars, he would die happily here, her hands on his chest, her body pressing down into his.

Gently, he found the place where they met, rewarded with a breathless *yes* as he stroked lovingly at that marvellous pearl at the apex of her sex. He found no resistance as he sank a finger into her, barely able to contain himself as she let out a cry of pure, unrefined passion. Almost laughing, wondering if he would spill himself before they had even managed a proper coupling, he added another finger, using his thumb to delicately roll her pearl. Her mewling reply was an ample reward.

In and out, he pulled pleasure for her until she froze,

tilting her glorious head back to the sky, her peaked breasts angled to where he could feast upon them. Then Viola cried out, her release resounding through her whole body. Never, in all his life, had he seen such a beautiful sight, nor imagined his heart could sustain joy of this magnitude.

"Stars, Silas," she said, as she settled back on his lap, eyes still hungry.

Water ran in rivulets down her chest, and he greedily lapped up the water, the smoky taste of her mingling with the tang of fresh rainfall. He could stop now, he could die happy, if this was enough.

"I love you, Viola," he said, before he could stop himself.

Viola stiffened for just the briefest of moments, but then her hands found the rise of his pleasure, and he stirred in response, no longer a master of his own thoughts. If he spoke, the words made no sense to his ears for the fluttering of his heart; if he cried out, it was swallowed in the thunder rolling across the landscape.

Viola rose up, glancing at his neck for a moment. He nodded, then squeezed her hips, so slender in his grasp and yet so powerful in her magic. He wanted this; he wanted her. All of her. Whatever she would give him.

This time, Viola did not bite him right away. She licked at the spot first, her breath hot against his skin, as she positioned herself above his cock. The space between them was so slight, and yet he felt a fullness in their connection even before they came together.

The whole world held its breath. And he knew, even before her teeth sank into his neck, that he would forever be changed. He would forever be lost to Viola Brightwell. And he did not care. Not for his seat or for his legacy or even for his damned great aunt.

The sting of her bite turned to the most honeyed sweetness, for she lowered herself upon him at the very same moment.

Her body arced, and voiceless, Silas soared to the heavens and back until her glorious pressure surrounded him fully. There was no comparison to this pleasure, this ecstasy, not in all the world or all of his experiences.

Their joining was a rhapsody, charged with lightning and thunder, slick with rain and blood: Viola pulled life from him as she drew out his pleasure. The weight of her, the grasping of her body around his, it changed him in that moment. He became something else, someone else, and it was a blessed, beautiful escape from reality.

Viola pulled back from the bite, fresh rain cleaning the wound, and with what strength he still had, Silas turned her around to sink again into her awaiting depths.

Face to face, brow to brow, they took their pleasure together under the stormy skies.

CHAPTER TWELVE
AMONG THE UNTRODDEN WAYS

EDITH ROOKWOOD COULD not sleep, nor had she even attempted to make her way toward bed. Every time she closed her eyes, all she could see was the look on Poppy's face when she realised they might die. Fearless, brave Poppy had kissed her so fiercely it had left a brand on Edith's soul, no doubt to her companion's love for her—even though they had been in a difficult phase as of late.

She fingered the Janus key in her waistcoat pocket, turning over the iron octopus shape over and over again, waiting for the metal to warm against her fingers. Staring into the fire in her office, she knew it was better to abandon sleep at this point. So, she sent a note to Molly Hode to alert her to Poppy's movements, even though the Warder likely knew without the courtesy of communication.

Janus keys were rare, precious items, and Edith's own pair were the fruit of years of research and work on the High Witch's part. The Janus wardrobe of Netherford Hall was a rare item, indeed, but it only worked inside the house. The Janus *keys* could be spelled to turn any door into a portal. She still wasn't certain how or why Roland had not arrived at the Holly and Sickle—as that was the key's intent—but now she used it for that very cause.

On nights like this, which happened more frequently these days, Edith would take the key and go to the Holly and Sickle to tinker with the witch portal there. Ever since her arrival in town last year, the portal had not behaved well—it seemed to her a harbinger of problems with the larger witch portal network. She hoped working on it here in Netherford might give her more insight into how they functioned, and how the High Witch had orchestrated their spellwork.

As per usual, Edith was greeted by the new innkeeper, Sophronia Pemble. She was a hedge witch, the daughter of Salvinia Pemble who worked upstairs. Theirs was a tenuous peace, considering the challenges between gentlewitches and hedge witches, but Sophronia had proven to be a stalwart and reliable replacement once the Hodes were installed at Netherford Hall.

Sophronia was a small, pale woman, with fierce black eyebrows and a penchant for wearing elaborately embroidered overcoats. She had a lovely voice, and could play a large assortment of musical instruments, so for the first time in centuries, the Holly and Sickle hosted performances.

Judging by the state of the pub—the chairs still pushed aside, the piles of pottery stacked on the bar, and the lingering smell of sweat and ale—they had danced late into the night. Only a few patrons remained, including Captain Evans, who sat reading by the hearth.

"Good evening, my liege," Sophronia said. Her voice, surprisingly low and raspy for a singer, was even more rough than usual. No doubt she had spent hours singing and entertaining the crowds. "Can I get you some claret, perhaps?"

"Not tonight, thank you, Miss Pemble," Edith said. "Have there been any changes to the witch portal today?"

"Nothing unusual. Quiet as a mouse, I'd say. Except for when that storm came through an hour ago. I'd swear I could hear the portal cracking. But then, I was in the throes of music, so it might have been my imagination." Sophronia shook her head, looking disdainfully in the direction of the arch built into the side of the pub's walls.

To a general passerby, the witch portal looked rather uninteresting, more like an old threshold that had been covered up with wattle and daub. But etched into the frame were witch marks and a quatrefoil, and the moment Edith approached it, it began glowing a faint blue hue.

And indeed, it didn't take long for Edith to spot the cracks in the mortar and little splinters all along the frame. She reached up to touch the wood and had to pull back when a painful spark flashed between her and the portal.

"That's never happened before," Edith muttered, sucking on the offended digit.

"You don't suppose the weather did that?" Sophronia asked. She came up to stand beside Edith, wiping her hands on an old towel at her waist.

"I wouldn't rule anything out, but it wasn't an unusually fierce storm," Edith said. She leaned forward to look again at the portal, this time careful not to touch it.

"Sometimes, I've learned, the things that seem the most usual hold mysteries we can only begin to fathom," Sophronia said. "But then, I'm just a hedge witch who runs an inn."

With that cryptic comment, Sophronia went over to speak with Captain Evans by the fireplace.

Edith took out the implements—an array of weights, tuners, stones, and feathers—she used to read the signature of the portal. Every time she came to the Holly and Sickle, she would take the measurements, write them in her journal, and then compare them against the previous points. In the brief times she had been able to repair the portal, the only consistency was that when she balanced the fluorite beads and the Whitby jet cross, they made a high-pitched whine.

She took her readings, and everything was as expected at first. Until the Whitby jet cross flew across the room and embedded in the hearth just a hand span from Captain Evans.

"My apologies, Captain," Edith said. "That was highly irregular."

Captain Evans was an admirable fellow, and Edith counted him among her friends. So she was not surprised to hear him say, "I have dodged worse, but perhaps the measurements should wait until there are fewer soft bodies within throwing distance."

"That is a good measure of advice," Edith said, and she put her hand up to examine the area she had been observing.

Only to fall through the portal.

EDITH WAS FAMILIAR by now with liminal magic, so she did not react with fear upon moving into the new space. She did, however, wonder at the power at work. Liminal magic, and liminal places, had a distinctive magical signature both in smell—like slightly burned raspberries—and in texture—like the air after a summer storm.

Here, another magical signature met her, twining in the darkness between. It smelled of freshly tilled earth and cloves, tinged with just a hint of freshness—coriander, perhaps?

A flicker of hope coursed through Edith as she got her bearings, wondering if at last she would have answers about the High Witch's whereabouts. Could Virginia have at last found a way to communicate to her? It would make sense it was the portals. They were built by her hand, after all, woven with her magic over the decades.

As usual, there was no ground, no light, at least not directly. It was up to Edith to provide illumination, and she did so easily. Light, of all the elements, was the easiest for her to conjure, though nothing so artful as the luminomancers who commanded exorbitant prices for their work in the great cities of the world. Baubles, as she called them, rose from her hands and danced around her head like a crown of planets in orbit.

Just as she finished positioning the baubles, Edith's feet touched the ground. She'd never touched the ground before in a liminality. She could conjure an impression of it, and indeed such bearings were important when using the space to prevent motion sickness and stability. Not doing so resulted in monstrous headaches and often prodigious vomit.

Her own weight came back to her as she looked around, her eyes adjusting. At first, she had the terrible thought that she had been swallowed by some celestial whale, for what looked like immense ribs rose all around her, pale and ghostly.

The scent of earth intensified, making her think both of Netherford Hall during the spring thaw and of the freshly turned soil of graveyards.

Someone was watching her.

Never the most talented witch, at least by the measure of the great gentlewitch trials, Edith had learned how to feel magic when she could not produce it. And a gaze, even from a mortal, could hold power whether they knew it or not.

This gaze, well... it was unlike any she had ever felt before.

"I know you're out there," Edith said. She moved her baubles, so they swirled around her hands. Though they posed no danger directly, she could hope she looked somewhat threatening in that moment if her pursuer sought to harm her. "Show yourself."

A laugh, low and feminine, made Edith's hair rise. Then,

a voice, full of whispers said: "A little witchling, so far from home. Tell me, where did you come from?"

Edith did not see any harm in answering this question. "I come from Netherford. I am its gentlewitch."

She thought she caught the hint of a figure, flowing white hair fanning out from behind it, but then it was gone. Virginia Cawley had such hair, but no such voice. And she would have known Edith, wouldn't she?

"Netherford. What strange words you use for your places," said the voice.

A rattling sound, like seeds in a wooden box, followed when a warm wind whirled about Edith. She had the odd sensation that the wind was, somehow, at the beck and call of this person who spoke to her.

"Do you intend to cause me harm?" Edith asked, turning around slowly. She kept seeing the figure out of the corner of her eye, a female form draped in moonlight and cobwebs. Maddening business. "For some have sought Netherford with such ill intent, and we have sent them back to the Abyss."

Laughter, again. Delighted laughter.

"So, you are the one who destroyed the Boagane. I thought you might be. Let me take a good look at you."

Before Edith could argue, the creature swirled into place before her, her body forming from the very air itself. Her eyes were green, large and flecked with gold. Edith had been right about the hair: it was bone white, straight, and long, moving about the creature's head as if alive. When the creature turned her head, Edith noted the unusual ears: twice peaked, two sharp points at the very tips. And those tips rose high and were pierced with gold hoops.

Edith was relatively tall for a woman, and yet this creature looked down upon her, those strange, enormous eyes set like jewels in her angular face.

"Ah, I see now," said the creature. "You are like the other one. But I do not think you came here a'purpose. There is too much lost in your eyes."

"I came through a witch portal. I was trying to fix it, not travel."

Wrinkling her nose, the creature shook her head. "You should not try to fix it. It is a misery for us. Every time. This is the trouble with witchlings: they have access to the power, and they use what they don't understand. That is how you get Boaganes."

"You seem to know a surprising amount about me and my kind, but I do not know who—or what—*you* are," Edith said.

She tried to sound diplomatic, but the words were harsher than she meant. The Boagane had nearly cost Edith everything, and she did not like the implication of the creature's words. Even if it was partially true. At least, that was what Virginia Cawley had led her to believe.

That laughter again. "My name is Tailte, if that helps you. And I am one of the fae, as you call us. And you are in my realm."

Edith's face blanched, and she looked around wildly as if this new knowledge might give her more clarity to her surroundings. "Is this a wood? In Faerie?"

"A realm of it, yes." Tailte leaned forward, reaching toward Edith's hair and taking a short curl between her two fingers. "It is a beautiful colour. Did you know none of us are so blessed by fire? Only silver, now."

Gently, Edith pushed the fae woman away. She did not like people touching her hair, other than Persephone Brightwell. "I did not mean to trespass here, Tailte. I assure you. If you show me the way, I will leave immediately."

"Walk with me, witchling," Tailte said. She raised her arm and, in a grand gesture, parted the trees before them—

or else, they simply bent to her whims. "And then I will show you home."

As the trees opened, Edith saw the glint of moonlight on a great lake. Stars swirled overhead, comets and falling stars of every colour imaginable. Great clouds of blue-green swirled overhead, and at the edges of the lake Edith saw the outline of trees higher than Parliament Spire reaching toward the heavens as if in worship, or recognition.

They walked together between the trees, and Edith felt drowsy and almost a little drunk as a rich perfume of jasmine and ripe melon enticed her senses. The world came to life as they passed through the threshold, and Edith heard the cries of birds in the distance—birds she could not recognise by voice alone—and the riotous gurgling of a rushing river. Reedy grasses swayed in the wind, their heads making hollow sounds as they knocked together now and again like curious wind chimes.

If Edith had wanted to refuse the fae woman, she could not have. Not only was she bewitching, but she had a sad kind of wisdom Edith found irresistible. She knew she would regret not following Tailte for the rest of her life if she refused.

"The wind knows your name, Edith Rookwood," Tailte said after a moment. "And now, so do I."

Some witches could divine names, it was true, and yet it seemed this connection was far deeper. As if here, in Faerie, all of the greatest witches and preternaturals of the mortal world were but flecks of mica in comparison to the Great Shah's jewels.

Tailte took Edith to a bench at the lake's edge, carved from a single piece of marble. Even in the dim moonlight, Edith caught veins of gold and silver running through it. It was warm to the touch, as if it had been sitting in the sun for hours.

Arranging her flowing robes, Tailte looked out across the water. "This is all I have left, the only place where we can cross to the mortal realm. Once, our people lived side-by-side, and we built a world of beauty, knowledge, and truth. Until mortals became jealous of fae power and took it for their own."

Edith had heard stories of the fae, but never quite from such an angle. "The story we are told is a different one: that the fae sought to imprison and control humankind, and so a great witch, by the name of Rosmerta, devised a way to separate Faerie from us forever."

Tailte tilted her head this way and that, as if measuring that information for the first time. "I remember Rosmerta. She had hair like yours."

"You knew Rosmerta?" Edith asked.

"She attended Queen Damona, and she ate of the apples of the divine orchard. Then Rosmerta and her lover—Damona's favourite fae consort, Moritasgus—burned the orchard to the ground, escaping to the mortal lands. Damona cursed Rosemerta and Moritasgus, that though their offspring would be fae, they could never return to Faerie. Worse even, they would seek the blood of humankind, always living as pariahs."

Vampires. Tailte meant *vampires*. "I suppose that explains some things," Edith said. "But what of witches? If Rosmerta and Moritasgus's children became monsters, as you say, then how did we come to be by your reckoning?"

Tailte took a deep breath, for a moment seeming frustrated by Edith's questions. It was difficult enough for Edith to understand human expressions, let alone those of a fae woman with eyes the size of skipping stones.

"Moritasgus grew bitter and corrupt and left Rosmerta to brood with his children and their spawn; Rosmerta, who long sought a cure for their children, eventually fell in love with a mortal. She had eaten of the orchard, so she lived a long life, and her veins ran with magic. Rosmerta's first daughter with her mortal lover was named Navia, and she was the first witch. She was a shape-changer, as well, and in her wolf form, she lay with the King of Wolves, and begat a litter of the first werewolves. For centuries, witches in the mortal lands rode great were-beasts to battle under her banners."

Edith could see, in her mind, every detail as Tailte described the stories. Though it was difficult to imagine gentlewitches astride werewolves, or living peacefully alongside them at all. "That is quite different from what our books say."

"Of course it is." Tailte laughed again, splashing her toes in the lake water, as carefree as a child. "Consistency makes for boring stories. Conflict makes mortal hearts beat harder."

"So, by your account, Rosmerta was not responsible for bringing down the boundaries between fae and the mortal realm," Edith said.

Tailte held up her palm, moonlight kissing it like silver gilt. "We brought the boundary down, but in doing so, trapped some of the fae on the other side. With you. They still live among you. They still intermingle. But, as you can see, there are holes between us, Edith Rookwood. Holes in the boundary. Your High Witch visited me often, and said she and I had a strained relationship."

Edith's face flushed hot with a mix of shame and fear. "Virginia Cawley is missing. Are you behind that? Did you capture her? Is she here?"

"The High Witch was warned that her portals and her trespasses would raise our ire. But she did not believe it. She was too proud, too confident in her power. And now the wolves and the bloodthirsty children have discovered that magic and will use her to make it their own."

The bloodthirsty children. The vampires. It was hard to imagine people like Laertes or Ophelia capable of executing any scheme requiring the level of skill needed to imprison the High Witch.

"She is my mentor, my friend," Edith said. "I don't understand why you would tell me this."

"Because my son lives in the mortal realm, Edith Rookwood. And I have never sensed his presence until now."

"Your son? I'm afraid I do not know of any fae, Tailte."

"He is near you. He is among you. But he, too, is cursed, and I cannot see him, cannot reach him. But you can. You are that rare witch with the ability to find the in-between places, to lead those who would follow you across the threshold."

"Then liminal magic is from the fae?" Edith asked.

"Liminal magic is the fae itself. It is the very pattern of our worlds, the space between the warp and the weft." She smiled sadly, long hair flowing in the wind. "If you bring me my son, I will help you find Virginia Cawley."

Edith had no idea who the fae woman's son could be. "I will do what I can, but I do not know where to look."

"He would be a changeling child, unaware, but powerful. A creature of song and joy."

That hardly narrowed things down. "Do you have his name?"

"One cannot utter the name of a changeling in Faerie. Not even me."

Edith wasn't certain what that meant, but she understood the complex rules of magic, nonetheless. "And what of the witch portals? You said not to fix them."

Tailte looked wistful again, lowering her chin and turning her eyes toward the moon. "The portals are breaking Faerie, making our own world unpredictable. It is why the Boagane escaped—and there are more like it. We have the tools to fight these monsters, but you do not."

"That sounds to me like a promise of a bargain," Edith said. "I know better, you know."

"Time is slipping, Edith Rookwood. I gave you a sword once, I can give you one again."

So *that* explained the sword she'd used to fend off the werewolves. Edith had, admittedly, gone to reach for her chatelaine—hoping a pinch of salt or a charm might help—and found the cold hilt of a sword. In her pride, she had assumed it some gift on behalf of Virginia Cawley or else from the in-between place itself. She had found many curious items in her travels, lingering there. Though none had been glowing swords.

She hated feeling helpless to protect Poppy. It gnawed at her when she couldn't sleep, followed her around like some hound of anxiety. There was so much about Poppy that she couldn't control, and so much she did not and could not understand. The idea she could have an edge to keep her safe took the last shred of her resolve.

"How do I find your son?" Edith asked.

"THE WEREWOLF STENCH is terribly distracting," Ophelia Byrne said, batting at her nose with her linen handkerchief.

Viola watched the vampire delay, yet again, sharing news from Maurice. The first time, she had claimed a mysterious vampire ailment having to do with being too close to chickens. The second, she said she had important correspondence.

Finally, Laertes had cornered her in the little den they'd been using as a sitting room, and told her, in no uncertain terms, that she was being a mercurial little vole.

"We will manage the werewolf later," Laertes said. He looked very smart in an aubergine-hued woollen overcoat, a profusion of yellow silk at his throat. "Sister, I know you are often out of sorts after a visit with Maurice, and I have some measure of sympathy, but I am beginning to dread what you're going to say."

Cowed, Ophelia settled her shoulders. "It is not good news. I wanted to do some more reading, to verify what Maurice said, and I have confirmed every word."

Viola did not like the sound of that. "But I have been feeling quite splendid," she said, by way of explanation. Especially after last evening. Stars, she was surprised she wasn't glowing. "Perhaps this Maurice misunderstood the situation."

Ophelia kept silent until Laertes gently kicked her shin. Sometimes they were like precocious children together. Playful, ancient, blood-sucking children. But it gave no doubt as to their relationship. Still, Viola thought the set of Laertes' jaw meant he was more than merely flustered. No, she could *feel* it from him.

"We should have gone to Maurice weeks and weeks ago," said Ophelia at last. "And I feel sick over it."

"What is so terrible you are incapable of saying it aloud?" Viola said. Sharp, brutal anger, that unfamiliar and unwelcome sensation since her change, flared up inside her breast. "I am not a child. I am capable of making my own decisions, but I require information in order to do that."

"You are a vampire child, and that is what makes this all so much more terrible," Ophelia said. "I fear you have only yet begun to live, and it must soon come to an end."

Laertes shot to his feet, his hands balled into fists. His fury was palpable now, a static sensation that made Viola's teeth ache. Especially her fangs.

"Come to an end?" Viola asked. "What are you saying?"

Ophelia reached across to take Viola's hand, and her bloody tears pattered upon her skin. "If I had known, I would have warned you about taking a thrall. It's the viscount—your feeding. He willingly gave you his blood?"

"Of course," Viola said.

"How often?" Ophelia asked.

"I… twice, now. Mind, I never would have taken without asking." Though, if she thought about it, it was certainly far more than a simple exchange. There was a seed of joy in it, of connection. Of hope. And so much passion she shivered recalling their rooftop escapades.

"Your instinct brought you two together, but we never could have known," said Ophelia. From the folds of her gown, she withdrew a small bound book, not unlike the editions she had been reading a week before. "I have read this over and over, and it is very clear what happens to a vampire's first thrall."

"He isn't a thrall. He's the viscount, that's all. When I'm prepared, I will take a more formal volunteer," Viola said, although the thought of feeding from another made her feel squeamish.

"Be that as it may, he is a mortal thrall in biological fact." Ophelia cleared her throat and read from one of the pages she had marked with green ribbon. "'The initial thrall of a new vampire must be their first kill. It is preferable during the first feeding but can take no longer than one moon's cycle. This sates the power inside the vampire, possessing the life that will, in turn, live forever in their bodies.'"

Laertes began pacing, rubbing at his temples. "You mean Viola must kill the viscount."

"If she is to survive," said Ophelia, handing the book to Viola. "And I know she will do no such thing, nor can you or I ask her to."

The type inside the book was hand-written, tiny, and written in a red-brown ink. She continued to read: *Should the vampire not kill their first thrall, they will fall into a blood sickness and become revenant.*

One moon's cycle. Indeed, it had been a full moon the

night she had taken that perfect draught from Silas when she had been finally free of the noise and the fire in her veins. Last night, the moon was already a quarter waning.

"We were born into a den of vampires," said Ophelia. "I do not remember my first thrall, nor taking their life. I suppose it is as instinctual as a babe at their mother's breast. Though rather more brutal."

Viola knew she ought to feel something terrible, some dread and anxiety over her inevitable demise. Ophelia would not say it, of course, but they would have to kill her before she became revenant. And doing so would cause both her sires extreme pain. Yet, as she looked between them, sensing their affection for her, she felt rather lucky. Yes, she had a family at Harrow House, and she would need to say her farewells to them—but she had another family, now, and she felt grateful. Even in such a short time, she had realised she'd been granted a second chance at life, at love, and at family.

But perhaps her whole life *did* end at Netherford Hall when she entered into the Boagane's trap, hoping to save her sister.

"I am so terribly sorry, Viola," Ophelia said. "Maurice chastised us for being such civilised vampires, and perhaps he was right. Had we not eschewed our baser natures, we would have known this simple fact and prevented this end."

"End! End?" Laertes puffed up his chest, heels clicking as he came to a stuttering stop. He'd finally found his words. "What on earth do you mean, sister? You think some book from that lying, scheming old pile of ash will rewrite our fate? Viola is ours. *Ours*. I will not allow her to fall into the depths while I yet remain."

"Laertes," Viola said, rising and going to him. She put her hands gently on his shoulder. "Please. I am not afraid. I am not angry. My making was a mistake, and I have time—

three weeks—to make amends. So many are not given that gift."

Laertes gaped at her, lines of worry etched between his luminous eyes. "You are braver than I have ever been. But, my darling, I cannot harm you. To do so would mean breaking my own soul."

"We no longer have souls," Viola said softly. "Perhaps there is a way out of this, and I have no doubt we can keep looking. But I feel freer, somehow, knowing the hour of my end. I shall live as brightly as I can. You must teach me every joy of being a vampire in the meantime, and I shall write to my family."

Ophelia wiped at her tears again. "I will keep looking, if I must. Maurice implied there were other, older tomes, but most were destroyed in the wars."

"What will the viscount say?" Laertes asked. "Perhaps we ought to take you to Howarth Castle after all."

Well, the dowager viscountess had made absolutely certain that Viola knew she was not invited, sending a note to her reiterating the situation. And Silas certainly had capitulated quickly. But, now that death—true death—faced her just around the bend, she did not have so much to lose. It would be difficult not to tell Silas, or her family. Poppy would have the most challenging time, of course, given they had just begun to mend. Viola truly was doing so much better; it was a shame she would lose it all to malice and destruction before the first harvest. She did so love the way the trees looked in the autumn.

"Yes, I would like that. But not until after the ball," said Viola.

IF THE WORLD was fair, which Roland was positive it was not but often dreamed of, he would have been allowed to attend the ball. He felt a bit like the Cendrillon of old, relegated to the cleaning and cooking and toil while everyone else bathed in good champagne and flirting.

This was all made more intolerable by Silas's insistence that Roland remain out of sight in general. That meant no trips to the celebrated Madame Rawlings-Vijay, the town's *couturière*, sister to Nathaniel Rawlings-Vijay. He was in need of new rags. Silas had a good eye for materials, but he didn't care a whit about tailoring, and his taste in cravats was two summers out of style.

Mr. Hode was at the door. Even before the Warder knocked, Roland knew it was him, could smell that pervasive herbal odour. Time for the dratted potion again, already.

"Come in, Mr. Hode," Roland called from the divan. It was a lovely piece of furniture, one he knew well, as it was brought from the old house. He particularly liked the feeling of the satin stripes on his hands when he ran them over it. "I'm mostly decent."

Brimstone, he needed someone to smother. Nakedly.

Mr. Hode entered, the enormous yellow door swinging open on well-oiled hinges, his eyes fixed on the platter before him. Usually, he simply proffered a stoppered bottle, watched Roland drink it, took some notes, and left. Today, however, it appeared the confounded Warder had more concoctions and implements.

His long legs made quick work of the distance, and he settled the tray beside Roland, only glancing up for a moment when the werewolf made no motion to sit up from his most lackadaisical position. Roland was in a melancholy mood, and simply did not feel up to keeping up appearances.

"That looks different," Roland said, gesturing to the platter with his unshod foot. "Are you experimenting upon me now, Basil?"

Roland noticed how Mr. Hode winced at his informal address, but said nothing.

The Warder indicated the platter which, Roland now could see, housed two different draughts—one red as rowan berries—as well as a minty-smelling paste, a few bits of jet carved into half-moons, and a tray of lovely biscuits.

"The biscuits are for me," Mr. Hode said, taking one. "The rest are my attempts to make this potion last longer than a single day."

"They did not have such troubles in Paris or London. I could always go a few days between administrations," Roland said. "But yours also tastes far worse than theirs. Even that irascible street mage on Grey's Inn Road by the cemetery had a better knack for flavour. And I'm fairly sure his *monkey* made the preparations."

Mr. Hode gave Roland that placid, measured look again, which was both irritating and handsome. He really did have the loveliest cheekbones. Even if he never did make proper use of them smiling. "I am not a street mage, but if you prefer a simian make your potion, I can certainly arrange for that, Mr. de Grateloup."

"Roland, if you please. Are we not past such pleasantries, you and I?"

"We most certainly are not."

"May I call you Basil, then?"

The Warder blinked twice, then said: "If it means we can proceed more swiftly through this administration, then yes."

Roland stood up, bolstered by the light crack in the man's veneer. Basil simply was not about to engage himself in any flirtation from their current position, nor without more prodding. The man was a marble bastion but could not remain so forever. Perhaps he did not fully comprehend just how beautiful Roland was.

"Very well." Roland tossed his golden hair back over his shoulder—a trait his French paramours loved to coo over—and unbuttoned the first few buttons of his waistcoat. His chemise was already loosened, but he took a moment to pull his cravat, unwinding the long silken measure, so his neck might be exposed.

At first, Roland thought he might not have had any effect upon the Warder. Though he was rarely wrong about a man's inclinations, he had misjudged, now and then.

Then, just as Roland went to reach for a biscuit, he caught the flush on Basil's cheeks, crawling up from his collar.

His pulse quickened, the power of desire a heady liquor in his veins. Perhaps he and Basil could find common ground. And then, perhaps, a common bed. Or a chair, or a wall. He was not terribly discriminating in that sense.

"Mr. de Grateloup?"

Roland had been lost in Basil's eyes. Apparently the man had been speaking, which really ruined all of Roland's daydreaming.

"I apologise. This biscuit was so delicious I lost my concentration," Roland said. "And please, dispense with this formality. You said you'd call me Roland."

"No, I said you could call me Basil if it meant I didn't have to spend such an interminable amount of time in here," Basil said. The words were harsh, but Roland had to believe they were partially in jest. "So far, that promise is proving in bad faith."

"Then by all means, please instruct me in your ways so you may be rid of me at the nearest convenience," Roland replied, reaching for another biscuit.

Basil, shockingly, slapped his hand away. "I told you before, food after. Besides, those are *my* biscuits."

"But I am terribly hungry." Roland smirked, leaning just a little closer to Basil. "You wouldn't deny me, would you?"

"I most certainly would." Basil grabbed the pale red drink and hoisted it at Roland, practically creating a barrier between them. "Drink this first. Then drink the second. I've mixed it with some champagne, which should make it more palatable to your refined tastes."

Roland pursed his lips, blinking lazily at Basil, before taking the tonic and quaffing it in three gigantic sips. He made sure to spill a little down his chin so he could wipe it away with the back of his hand. It tasted like old stockings and rye.

When he went to speak, Basil held up a finger. "Ah, ah! Next."

Somehow, the champagne made the second tonic even worse than the first. Perhaps the introduction of bubbles only intensified the bitter, noxious flavour.

Nearly gagging, Roland took the kerchief Basil offered him, as he coughed and sputtered until his eyes were streaming with tears. No, there was no way to orchestrate a pleasing presentation of his person. He simply looked wretched.

Before he could reach for them, Basil handed Roland two biscuits. Ruefully, he ate them, staring down the Warder as his stomach settled. But immediately, his body relaxed, all the muscles he'd been clenching released from the tension of resisting his werewolf form. His heart rate slowed significantly, and relief coursed through him. Never would he admit such a thing, and least of all to Basil, but living in constant fear of losing one's faculties to a bestial rage wore a man down after a time.

"It's not supposed to taste good to you," Basil said. He picked up the two jet sickles, weighing them in his hands. "You understand that every part of this concoction is designed to suppress what your body is trying to express every waking moment?"

Roland drew back at that most offensive statement. "My body is not trying to express anything, sir. I was tainted with this affliction at a young age, against my will and my mother's knowledge."

"Tainted?" Basil looked confused at Roland's explanation. "You mean to tell me you *contracted* lycanthropy?"

"Of course. A being of my bearing and parentage would never be born to such circumstances."

"You are a bastard, are you not?"

Roland rolled his eyes and fell back upon the divan. "If you are being clinical about it, yes. But my mother is—"

"I know who your mother is, Mr. de Grateloup. Everyone does. You remind us, constantly."

"Then you'll understand that my circumstances are unique."

Basil nodded, but Roland could tell he was unconvinced. Fine, he could be the expert if it made him feel better.

"Very well," said the Warder. "It doesn't alter the fact that the herbs and elements within are contrary to the affliction inside of you."

"Well, it tastes worse than my previous regimen and doesn't work as well, so I'm not sure what that says about your skill," Roland quipped.

To his credit, Basil remained calm in the face of such insult. "I don't think it's the recipe, Mr. de Grateloup. I think it may be your exposure to the werewolf pack."

"That's nonsense."

"And you are the foremost expert on werewolves? You've already admitted to staying clear of them for your entire life. Their influence was strong enough to cause a disruption in the Janus key's trajectory, according to the gentlewitch. One could only deduce it would impact your inner workings as well. Or at least, allow for the possibility."

No. No, that could not be. Roland could not be getting

worse. Getting worse let in a flood of other terrible possibilities he did not want to even consider, especially not now while he was still under threat of arrest and only living on his friend's good graces.

"Well, thank you for your theories. Now, if you'll leave me alone, I have a ball to *not attend*, and I must practice my sulking," Roland said.

Basil did not rise immediately but took out his journal and scribbled his notes in silence while Roland closed his eyes and waited. Finally, the scratching ceased, the divan squeaked, and the door shut, leaving Roland alone in the dark.

WHEN POPPY AROSE the morning after the storm it was to a cold bed and a warm hearth. The house always stoked the fire first thing in the morning in the cold months, but the storm must have brought in enough cold air for it to make the change.

Still, it did not make up for the fact that Edith was not there. They hadn't precisely made up after their disagreements in London, but it was curious Edith hadn't come to bed at all. Poppy was used to her companion being gone at strange hours, as she'd never slept well to begin with, but it was unusual to wake up completely alone.

Going to her wardrobe, Poppy pulled on her favourite dressing gown—a dizzying chintz quilted affair in a hectic red hue—and made her way down the hall toward the breakfast room. She could smell Sims' breakfast rolls, their yeasty, sweet fragrance making her stomach rumble. So, she followed the call down to the kitchen.

Surprisingly, Edith was sitting at the table in the working kitchen, eyes tired and hair ruffled, nursing a mug of coffee and a platter of eggs and ham, garnished with chives.

Sims, the cook, looked up. She was a willowy woman with white hair and a smooth face, but remarkably quiet. It was quite a contrast from Mrs. Pratt who cooked at Harrow House: she was all doughy softness, charm, and chatter.

"There you are," Poppy said. "I was beginning to wonder if I should send the Warders out for you."

Edith gave Poppy a wan smile. "Come, love, and sit with me a while. It's been a very long night."

Before Poppy managed to take a seat beside Edith, Sims had already added an assortment of cheeses, jams, compotes, berry scones, numerous buns, and a pot of hot chocolate for her. Yes, the house was magical, but Sims had a magic of her own.

"Thank you, Sims," Poppy said, taking a buttered berry bun. "As ever, your confections are a marvel of beauty and taste."

Sims nodded, nonplussed as always, and then went to the pantry to begin her work for the rest of the day.

"It isn't a good idea to stay up all hours, Edith. You are a very clever, very talented gentlewitch, but you are still just a mortal," Poppy said. She took Edith's hand and squeezed gently. Her fingers were so cold.

"I went to work at the Holly and Sickle, to try and fix the witch portal. But I was waylaid."

"By whom? Was it Captain Evans again? He really ought to just court Sophronia by now. Everyone can tell they're made for one another," Poppy said.

Edith squinted down at her coffee. "No, not Horatio. Though I agree with your assessment."

Poppy knew down to her toes that Edith was delaying telling her something, avoiding gentlewitch matters. "Are you in danger, darling? Is this about that sword you pulled upon the werewolves? It really was a marvel to see, but I was quite worried you might injure yourself in the process."

The look Edith gave her was full of warmth, the slight wrinkles at the edges of her eyes crinkling as she smiled. Edith reached out to brush a flake of buttered berry bun from Poppy's lip.

"Yes, my love. It is precisely about that sword, where it came from, and the kind of magic I seem to have stumbled into. And Virgina Cawley."

The answers were coming too easily. "You didn't make any bargains with questionable magical beings again, did you?"

Edith opened her mouth and then shut it again. "Not—not in the way you're thinking. Not for power. It's more of a mutual favour than a bargain."

"Edith!" Just when Poppy thought her companion was learning contrition, she was back at it again.

"Poppy. Let me explain myself," Edith said firmly. She was getting angry, frustrated.

"Quickly, or I shall lock myself in the boudoir for a week," Poppy threatened. Truly, if she wanted, Poppy could prevent Edith from going anywhere in the house. For she *was* the house. The boudoir was her own space, though, and Edith could only be invited. It was an especially good spot for dramatic periods of melancholy.

Edith glanced around the kitchen, as if anyone would give a whit what she was going to say. They were all from Ash-touched families, bound to support the gentlewitch in all things. "I met a fae. I—I think I was in Faerie. Briefly."

Poppy forgot how to breathe. She spent much of her childhood engrossed in tales of the fae, cobbling together the myths and tales of their pasts, wishing she could find a way to them. Sometimes, she thought she might be a changeling child herself. "Truly?"

"Truly. And this fae woman, she said she can help me find the High Witch. But I must help her, first."

Questions bubbled out of Poppy, and she could not stop herself. "But how did you escape Faerie? What did she look like? Did she follow you here? You didn't eat anything, did you? Was she beautiful? Gracious, I thought the way between here and Faerie was closed forever."

"Forever to mortals, perhaps, but not to the fae. It seems my magic, liminal magic, has weakened that barrier. And the veil in Netherford is particularly thin."

"I knew it!" Poppy said triumphantly. She sobered at Edith's peculiar glance.

"The witch portals have been chipping away at the boundaries for decades now." Edith wiped her brow. "And the fae woman—she told me her son had been trapped here, and I knew him."

"Someone we know is fae? A changeling?" Poppy could scarcely believe it. "I would guess Basil."

Edith chuckled. "He does have a rather whimsical way about him. But I don't think it's him."

"Why not?"

Reaching into her waistcoat pocket, Edith withdrew a ring very similar to the one she wore, the one made of witch silver. This was finer, however, wrought most delicately, in a pattern of rowan leaves upon a darker patina.

"Well, Basil or no, I can use this to identify the man, and I suspect he will be among those gathered at the ball on Saturday. I'll only need to shake his hand, she said, and his eyes will flash violet. Once I know who it is, I can broker a meeting between them."

"Why didn't she just tell you his name?" Poppy asked.

"I don't think she can say it in Faerie. There are all sorts of rules there. And oaths. They call that sort of spell a *geas*."

Poppy tried to put all the details of the conversation together in her head, but her imagination was swimming.

Someone in Netherford was fae this whole time! What a remarkable thing.

"You said this was about a sword," Poppy said, following their conversation back to the beginning.

"Yes. It appears this fae woman—Tailte is her name—can send me weapons across the liminality. She sent me that sword. I had gone to grab something from my chatelaine, and there it was. When the fight was over, I could no longer summon it."

"This does make me feel better about the ball, knowing you'll have a fae godmother. Oh, Edith, you wonderfully lucky woman," Poppy breathed, leaning forward to kiss her companion on the cheek. Then on the nose. Then on the mouth.

Edith laughed, gently nipping at Poppy's bottom lip. "I *am* lucky, in that I get to kiss you whenever you'll have me."

Poppy giggled. "And we get to have a grand adventure! Oh, perhaps I'll have a glimpse of Faerie. You'll have to tell me all about it."

"Of course, love. Once I'm rested, I will give you every detail of what I saw." Gently pulling away, Edith smoothed Poppy's brow and kissed it. "But not a word of this to anyone. There is a chance this fae person does not wish to be found, and so I must be delicate. Once we know, we will have a clear line back to Virginia Cawley who has, I am chagrined to say, rather annoyed the whole of Faerie with her spells. I can't help but wonder if she knew, or thought herself safe. Either way, there will be many questions once I'm able to find her."

Most of Poppy was elated at all this news, but that last bit sent a little frisson of worry down her back. Virginia Cawley was a strange and powerful woman, but careless she was not. Poppy always had the sense the High Witch was working on machinations far above and beyond everyone else, dancing to a tune no one else could hear. As intoxicating as the idea of a fae godmother might be, Poppy allowed a little wariness in.

"Of course," she said. "And you rest. We have an appointment this afternoon with Madame Rawlings-Vijay, after all, and we cannot be late for that. With all the town and surrounds in a tizzy over this ball, it's a miracle we were able to secure her at all."

CHAPTER THIRTEEN
AN HOUR-GLASS ON THE RUN

HALF IN A dream, Silas let the tailor do his work while he watched their reflections in the mirror. Sometimes, when he caught sight of his face in the glass, he saw glimpses of his father's features: the wide nose, the strong jaw, the slope of his brow. He supposed the other parts of him looked like his mother, though he had no memory of her, and the only portraits of her were small and unremarkable. When she'd died of consumption, he was only three, and given their status, he was primarily raised by their governess, Miss Clare. Miss Clare was now Mrs. Stuart and was married and had six children. Sometimes she wrote to him about her quaint country life, and even visited on occasion. In his mind, his mother looked like she did, not the pale, hollow-eyed person in the portraits.

His father didn't speak often of his mother, and he never sensed they had much affection for one another. That was not unusual, given their status and need for a suitable match to placate their families. Titus Drake's elder brother Meriweather had already scandalised the world by marrying the decidedly unmagical May Cawley, but her proximity to Virginia had proven quite fortuitous in the long run. Louisa Montagu, Silas's mother, was the only child of Lord Glastonbury and his wife Magdalen; the girl came with a remarkably hefty dowry. Such a sizeable dowry that there were dozens of suitors lined up to pledge their lives and troth. Titus had won with his wit, but within a year of their marriage was already on the way to gambling those riches away.

Silas liked to think his mother would have approved of his writing career. Stalled as it was, inconstant as it was, he had built the family reputation back with clever investing and good connections. He had no desire to be known for this endeavour, for it did not suit a man of his standing to write such frothy, shallow adventures. But they brought him gladness.

She would not, however, approve of his growing obsession with Viola Brightwell. After their night on the roof, he wasn't certain he would ever be able to look at her again in good company without becoming embarrassingly, and obviously, aroused. The feel of her, the enthusiasm in her! Brimstone. Her body fit to his without so much as a question, and she pulled pleasure from him as surely as honey from the comb.

"My lord?"

Fintan's ghostly visage swam into view in the mirror, a crease of mild frustration on his face.

Silas cleared his throat as if Fintan could hear his most impure thoughts. "Yes. This looks quite fine."

"Sir, one of the pantaloons is missing," Fintan said flatly.

The tailor, one Mr. Donal, peered up through thick, orange brows, and sighed most dramatically.

Silas did not have time to feel embarrassed. All he wanted to do was see Viola again. Which he knew was nigh near impossible. If the dowager viscountess saw her at the ball, he might as well sign away Burkley House forever.

"So it is," said Silas, adjusting his cravat so Fintan could not see the puncture marks there. Though, he had a feeling it didn't matter and Fintan could sense it on a level that bordered on the preternatural. "My apologies."

"Are there any particular colours you are interested in accenting?" Mr. Donal asked. He took out one of his fabric sample books, long swaths of silk brocade flopping out of each side. "I have an extensive account of almost all the ladies in town and their particular gowns."

A pang, again, as Silas imagined how beautiful Viola would look. What colours would she wear? Once, she had been a springtime sort of woman, her dresses always flocked with flowers. Now, though, she seemed to prefer sumptuous jewel tones, and sturdier fabrics. More expensive ones, at that; and well within her means, for she was now part of the Byrne fortune.

If only Aunt May could accept having a vampire as an heir. She would be such a splendid viscountess.

"No thank you," Silas said. "We shall keep as straightforward as possible."

Mr. Donal looked disappointed. "You wouldn't *believe* the lots they're casting regarding the colour of your cravat."

Before Silas met Viola Brightwell, such a comment would have amused him and maybe even excited him. He did enjoy the company of women, even if it was tiresome at times to feel such attention. Women were beautiful and curious, clever and kind—some were priggish and rude, but he never spent much time around them if he didn't have to.

Except, now Silas had seen, and tasted, and loved Viola Brightwell. She was not at breakfast that morning, and he tried not to think it had anything to do with their recent moments together.

And he'd bought her a gift. It was a silly sort of present. A hairpin made of a single piece of perfect white jade, carved into the shape of a heron. According to the seller, it was imported all the way from the Qing states. The moment he saw it, all he could think of was how beautiful Viola would look wearing it in the raven depths of her hair.

Silas breathed out, pulling down on the edges of his waistcoat. It was a bit looser about his middle than it had been a few weeks ago. He supposed allowing a vampire to dine upon you might have such an impact.

"I believe it," Silas said at last. "But I'm afraid I can show no favouritism, lest I run the risk of infuriating all the droves."

"Well, my advice is to have a plan going in," said Mr. Donal. "I remember when the Duke of Trosingdale threw a similar soiree for his nephew. The event went well into the wee hours of the night, and there were still women waiting to meet him when the sun came up."

Silas vaguely remembered Trosingdale. He had a perpetually runny nose. "What happened to the nephew after that?"

"It took him three months to even finish sorting all the proposals, and then he got the croup and died," Mr. Donal said.

It was difficult not to laugh. "I will do my best to make a swift decision—I fear if I don't, my aunt will do it for me."

"Wise. I am told the Greenstreets will be in violet muslin," Mr. Donal said. "A gorgeous set of dresses. The threads so fine they shimmer in the candlelight. I saw the bolts at Madame Rawlings-Vijay's last week and I did manage a little of it…"

"No thank you," Fintan said, before Silas could manage. "The viscount has been quite clear about his sartorial intentions. No colour accents. Are we finished here, Mr. Donal?"

It was unlike Fintan to take such a tone, but Silas was relieved. No doubt the Greenstreets had lined Mr. Donal's pockets most generously.

*   *   *

IN ONE BRIEF stroke of kindness, Roland was allowed to spend the afternoon and evening leading up to the ball with Viola Brightwell. Silas, it seemed, had taken pity upon him, knowing just how much Roland adored balls and everything having to do with them. They had attended some of the most elaborate events in Paris together over the years, including one event at Rosalie's that left him sore for days.

It was unusual for werefolk and vampires to converse, yet whether by circumstance of her not-quite-awoken state, or just that she was a charming, thoughtful, and beautiful creature, Roland found he quite enjoyed his time with Miss Brightwell. They couldn't have been more different, the two of them, and yet they had a common circumstance between them: being turned into monsters against their will and trying to learn to make the best of it.

Well, that wasn't entirely the truth. Roland most certainly did not make the best of it. He avoided his powers, the pull of his magic, as much as humanly possible. To submit to his wolf side meant madness, weakness, and fleas.

A masterful player of the pianoforte, Roland spent an hour going through his repertoire while Viola read from a small book, sent a few notes of correspondence, and took a few turns about the room from time to time. He quite liked her dress—a high-cut summer muslin died berry purple—and the way she had styled her hair. Vampire hair was quite mesmerizing to look upon, as it soaked up the light entirely. All vampires had black hair, just as he'd heard fae all had white hair when they still walked the earth, but he thought Viola's thick, tightly curled hair rather perfected the form.

He'd just finished playing one of his own compositions, a rousing number that included lyrics wholly inappropriate for current company, when he noticed Viola was weeping.

"Oh, surely my playing isn't that terrible," Roland said. He did not yet go to her, as he was unsure what dangers a crying vampire might engender to his person. He was also wearing pale blue silk, the precise colour of forget-me-nots, and he was loathe to sully it with blood.

Viola hurriedly gathered her composure, blotting her eyes with a dark satin handkerchief. "No, the music was beautiful, Roland. You really are a most talented player. It is only I am realizing many things at once, and it makes me angry. And when I am angry, I tend to weep."

"Angry?" Roland finally rose, striding over to where she sat on the divan. "Darling girl, it's impossible to imagine you angry about anything."

"Clearly you haven't met many vampires," Viola said.

"*Au contraire*. There are few in France, but most of them live in Paris, and I have been fortunate enough to call a few of them friends. Which they found most amusing, considering the *loup-garou* like myself are their sworn enemies."

"I have only lived such a short time as a vampire; I'm afraid the only ones I know are Laertes and Ophelia," Viola said, wretchedly.

Roland knew the tones of a woman in love, and he was certain Viola loved Silas. The challenge was, something else bothered her besides. She looked wounded, somehow, which was strange considering he very well knew what she and the viscount had been up to on the roof the other night. Keen hearing was a feature he could not will away, no matter how hard he wished. At least someone was getting some friction these days.

"Yes, the Byrnes. Curious pair, but clearly devoted to you. It's not every day a spawn gets two sires, you know."

"Being spawned at all is terribly rare," Viola said. "And therein is the problem."

Trying to gauge Viola's emotional state was giving Roland a headache. "Is something the matter, pet? I do find it quite the insult to be left here, caged like misbehaving dogs, but I'm certain you and I can find all manner of entertaining things to occupy ourselves with."

Even as he said the words, Roland did not believe them. No, he wanted to be in the great hall, festooned with florals and crystals, bedecked with witch spells and illusions. He wanted to be among people, to watch them and observe them, to flirt and be flirted with. He might even flirt with Basil again if he were allowed. If what they were doing could even be considered flirting. Theirs was a chemistry between hate and attraction, and for reasons he could not fathom, it made him anxious to consider which direction it might fall.

"I'm going to die, Mr. de Grateloup," Viola said, her fair head dropping in utter despair, though her voice did not shake at the terrifying admission.

"What now?" Roland asked. "Die? But you've only just achieved immortality. Let's not do anything crass."

"It is not for my wanting it, not really. Even though, I must admit, when the change first happened, I didn't think I would ever want to see the sky again or speak to my family. I didn't want to live, not as this." She gestured to her beautiful self, as if any piece was offending in the least.

"What changed?" Roland asked, even if he knew.

"Everything." Viola looked toward the great windows, her eyes tracking the florist as she wheeled a massive arrangement across the lawn. "I drank Silas's blood because my heart told me to do it, because it felt like the most natural thing in the world—because he practically begged me to do it."

"If you think he's got any regrets, I can assure you he does not."

Viola sighed, settling back down into the divan. She smoothed the fabric with the palm of her hand, in the very same manner Roland liked. "The Byrnes did not know about the importance of the first draught. They were born into a vampire hive, you see. So, they do not remember. And with spawning nearly outlawed everywhere, and they not desiring to sire anyone, they did not comprehend the risk."

"The risk to you?"

"Have you heard of revenants, Mr. de Grateloup?"

"Horrid things," Roland said. He'd only ever seen one, and then only from a vast distance. It had set every hair on his head on end, made his skin crawl unceasingly, as it ransacked a mass grave.

She raised her chin, as if preparing herself for something. "You cannot speak a word of this to Silas."

"Not a word," Roland said. He wasn't the best person at keeping secrets, but he sensed Viola needed to hear the words, nonetheless. That, and often he found those who asked for secrecy most ardently truly wanted the opposite outcome.

"The matter is this: when a vampire is turned, they must not just take their first thrall, but take their life, in order to prevent turning into a revenant. Ophelia discovered this truth from one of the rare, elder vampires in England, and then confirmed it in her reading."

It took a moment for Roland to connect the points in his mind, but when he did, he felt the blow of her pain. "You mean Silas."

"I could no more kill Silas than I could stake my own sister through her heart. I have two more weeks—until the next full moon, a poetic turn I am certain you will appreciate—and then Ophelia and Laertes will do what they must, for I will no longer be myself."

Roland lost all restraint, his heart beating so furiously he felt a little dizzy. "No, it cannot be. You love Silas. He loves you."

"He does?" Viola's lips trembled. "He cannot. Not as I am now."

"Ah, you do not know him as I do, Viola. He will not be able to bear your loss."

"He never has to know. We have constructed a few stories for the departure. I will tell him our affections were merely a reflection of the vampire madness, that I never cared for him, and then I will say my farewells."

"This is horrible. Utterly horrible. I cannot believe that in all the time vampires have trod this earth they have had to abide by such a beastly code of law," Roland said. "Brimstone, if my mother was here, I know she would have an answer. She kept me from turning entirely, taught me the herbs to use. Certainly, there could be something similar for you."

"I appreciate your earnestness, Mr. de Grateloup, but I am making peace with it."

"And yet you remain here, obeying the dowager viscountess's bigoted orders," Roland said. "This could be your last ball, Viola."

"Of course," she said with a shrug of her delicate shoulder. "Silas wants me there. And I want to *be* there. That is why I'm planning on going. Not for him, exactly, but to show them all I am not afraid of the dowager viscountess, and that she does not rule me."

"I knew I adored you the moment I saw you," Roland said, clapping his hands in glee.

Unexpectedly, Roland felt the prickle of tears as Viola stood and went to the window. A brave, beautiful woman, full of poise and poetry in her every moment.

"Tonight will be my last evening in public before we leave for Howarth Castle," Viola said. "I wish you could be my escort. It would be such a shock seeing the dowager viscountess's face when the both of us arrive."

"Oh, darling, would that I could. Though my soul aches for the release of merriment and mingling, I'm afraid my face is too well known among those in attendance, and I do not wish to bring more danger to our dear Silas as it is," he admitted. It was mostly true. At least saying it out loud made him feel rather valiant in the moment.

"Surely you're cleverer than that," Viola teased. "If they know your face, they might be inclined to panic. Surely there are methods by which you can conceal yourself."

He'd be lying if he said he hadn't thought of the same. He'd be willing to bet Basil even had a potion or two that might help. He just needed to convince him, which was the challenge.

"Well, if you can be brave in the face of certain death, my darling, then I will be glad to accompany you. But first, I believe we must consider our entrances and exits. We cannot arrive too early, nor by the expected routes. That would require an official announcement. But there are so many other routes we can take... It shall simply require a small amount of orchestration on my part—"

He paused, stricken by a sudden realisation.

Viola went to him, noting the look on his face. "Roland, whatever is the matter?"

He placed a hand on her elbow, chaste and sweet. "I am afraid I haven't a thing to wear."

GIVEN THE CHOICE of attending a ball or tending to her mountains of correspondence, Edith never would have left her office. The only reason she had even a modicum of anticipation—for she could never call such a feeling *excitement*—was because she knew Poppy had been planning their ensembles all week.

They were invited for propriety's sake, and Edith was

relieved she would not be the centre of attention, as she had been a year ago at the Greenstreets' ball. That time, she'd been poisoned—by accident—by an ambitious young woman who, no doubt, thought a love potion would work upon a gentlewitch. It had, instead, made her vomit most hideously and then exit the event with haste.

Auden appeared at the door, his face flushed, carrying a beautiful bolt of silk in one hand and an array of feathers under his other arm. He looked, at first glance, quite a bit like a fussy bird.

"Uncle Auden," Edith said, rising from her desk. "How go the preparations?"

"Chaotically. All of this last-minute business is hard enough on you and me, let alone on Madame Rawlings-Vijay."

"She is your fiancée, you know. You can refer to her by her given name around me—she will be family, soon. I do not mind," Edith said with a laugh.

Auden shook his head. He was truly smitten with the lovely *couturière* and every time Edith mentioned her, he got a most wistful look upon his face.

"Jamini." Auden actually grinned, tired though his eyes were. "She's got two assistants now, you know, and *still* struggles to keep up with the demand."

"I'm quite glad Poppy's been doing most of the work herself, then. Though I know she has been consulting your fiancée now and again. We still have her to thank for much of the final product," Edith said.

Auden put down the pile of fabric and shut the door quietly behind him after checking down the hallway. Something was on his mind. And she had a feeling she knew exactly what it was.

"You don't need to worry about the ball tonight," she told her uncle, before he could open his mouth. "You know, we've brought in half a dozen Warders from London, all at the viscount's expense."

"It's just... well, *werewolves*. Are we even prepared for such a thing? When we lived in London all those years, I'd only come across a handful of them—after their role in the wars, they didn't dare rear their heads."

Edith understood his anxiety on the matter and had thought long and hard about the topic. "I've learned some information lately that has me thinking a bit differently about werewolves, vampires, and witches. And I do think, in the grand scheme of the magical world, we are actually best served when we work together."

"Together?" Auden said, eyes widening in shock. "Working *with* werewolves? On purpose?"

"Not immediately, no. But we have Roland, after all. And the Byrnes are as good allies as I ever could wish for. Viola is leaning into her powers, and perhaps we will be able to have our own force for good, here."

"You seem uncommonly optimistic about this. I would think for one who has studied so much parliamentary law and history, the idea of a simple transfer of peace would be beyond your even wildest hopes," Auden said gently.

Perhaps she did feel hope. Not that she was ever hopeless, but Edith did tend to lean toward the more practical side of things. She didn't like disappointment, so it was better to be pre-emptively cynical.

Except now she lived in a world where Faerie was opening up to her, where changeling children lived among her friends, and where Viola Brightwell could find love, perhaps, or at least acceptance. Yes, there would always be the difficulty of politics and the Coven Council; she was not naïve about these things. Yet hope still lingered, and she could not ignore it.

"I cannot bring you into every detail, uncle," Edith said,

putting a hand gently on his shoulder and squeezing. "But we cannot live in fear of these bullies for the rest of our lives, and I have reason to believe we're being protected in ways we do not know."

He sighed in that way that meant he did not approve, but was resigned, anyway. "I know you wouldn't put people into danger knowingly. I've just grown to love this ridiculous little town, and all the ridiculous people in it. Some more than others. And it would break my heart, I think, to see them terrorised again."

"Well, I can't promise eternal safety, but between all the gathered witches, the vampires, and the Warders, if anything comes through the grounds, we will deal with it—at a distance—and keep the ball safe for everyone else," Edith reassured him.

"Of course, my liege," Auden said, bowing neatly. "I will see you this evening at the ball. For now, I must deliver these myself to Madame Rawlings-Vijay."

The truth was, both Edith and Petronilla had worked tirelessly along with the Hodes to construct a series of magical boundaries throughout the entire grounds at Burkley House. Petronilla's fire magic was often showy and dangerous, but it could be subtle and lovely, too. Molly was the most talented of the Warders, and so they wound their spells together to produce Warding Flames around the property. Indeed, they had crafted specific candelabras inside the great hall itself to alert them of impending danger.

Edith took her leave of Auden just as Miss Knightley, the Head of House, came about to assist him with his fabric burden.

As usual, it took a little time to find Poppy. She had a habit of taking her sewing to a new place every time she sat down to do the work, and Edith knew her companion would be working right up until the last possible minute. Perhaps there was some magic in the pressure of time coming up against her talent, Edith did not know. But Poppy assured her she enjoyed the excitement of it all.

Eventually, Edith found Poppy in the second-floor foyer, tucked into the bench below the window, using the last of the light to finish off her work.

For a moment, Edith merely watched Poppy as she sewed: her lips pursed as she stitched, her brows knit over her marvellous eyes, her feet tucked up under her skirts. She'd already had her hair done, and it was twisted and curled up beautifully, a sable masterpiece studded with tiny silver flowers—those had been a gift from Edith, and it made her quite happy to see them.

"I know you're there, Edith," Poppy said, not looking up from her sewing. "And I'm almost done."

Edith tried not to laugh. She came to sit by Poppy, carefully avoiding interrupting her light. "I shall await patiently for the final reveal," the gentlewitch said.

A few more minutes passed, a beautiful silence expanding between them, and Poppy leaned back and relaxed. Without words—a rarity for the very chatty Brightwell woman—Poppy held up the garment. It was a cerulean blue tailcoat of watered silk, the lapel, cuffs, and tail embroidered with the young woman's remarkable hand. The pattern was done in a colour just slightly darker than the tailcoat, interlacing leaves and small rosettes, adding a perfect touch to an already stunning garment. The floss shone, too, looking almost as if it had been done in enamel.

"The trousers are rather plain, but a good sturdy wool with a subtle stripe. They're still up in the room, along with my dress," Poppy explained as Edith ran her fingers over the intricate needlework.

"You know," Edith said, glancing up at Poppy's expectant

face, "I do believe you may have invented a new form of magic, for this work is absolutely exquisite."

"I got the idea from a plate I saw at a shop in London," Poppy said with a laugh. "The colours, I mean. I do so enjoy embroidering in every colour under the sun—but I thought, what if I simply add dimension and texture to it? I did the same on my dress, but the blue is an accent rather than the whole colour. We shall be a lovely pair."

Edith kissed Poppy gently on the cheek. "Always."

"Perhaps tonight you shall follow me to bed and sleep," Poppy said, a coquettish glint in her eye. "No more wandering off to Faerie."

"Well, if I go, I will be sure to bring you along. Yet I fear they may mistake you for one of their kind."

"I would never go. My heart is here, at Netherford Hall. And in your hands, Edith."

They were so close, nose-to-nose, and though joy certainly coursed its way through Edith's veins, she also felt worry writhing its way in.

"Did you hear from your family?" Edith asked, pulling away to take a closer look at her new tailcoat. "I know we invited them, but there's been a bit of concern given everything with Viola."

Poppy smoothed her skirt and then began putting her embroidery implements back in the little wicker box Edith had purchased for her in the spring. "Well, Mama says she will attend with Heath. My elder brother has been difficult of late, even more so since Viola's unfortunate circumstances, so I do hope he behaves. Oliver is still too young for the ball, but he's agreed to spend some time with Viola soon. Father isn't well enough to come, but I've promised him I will visit with Viola later in the week, provided she remains as fit and bright as she has been. Though given the dowager viscountess has specifically dis-invited Viola, my family will no doubt be confused to not see her in attendance."

"I know it's been a burden to you. I wish we had a way to bring Viola back to what she was before," Edith said. "But it appears there are limitations to our magic."

Poppy took a deep breath. "I think Viola will leave us soon for Howarth Castle."

"Truly?" Edith asked.

"I can always tell when she's planning something. And Burkley House is lovely, but it isn't built for vampires. For all my difficulties with Laertes Byrne, and your storied past with Ophelia, they have been so very good to her. I can always write to her, but it will be the best thing, I think. She needs time to figure out who she is and who she wants to be without..."

Without Silas Drake, Viscount St. Albans.

"You know, Tailte told me a strange thing—that vampires are merely cursed fae, children born to a witch and a fae prince, doomed to walk the mortal lands with a thirst for blood. What do you suppose might happen if Viola were to get to Faerie herself?"

"I do wonder at that," said Poppy. "Perhaps if your fae queen comes again to you, you might ask her."

If all went to plan tonight, Edith might have a chance sooner than Poppy realised.

CHAPTER FOURTEEN
Some Shape of Beauty Moves

THE MUSICIANS WERE late.

Silas stood in the middle of the great hall, wondering what series of decisions had led to the garish orange decorations strewn about the room, just as his guests began arriving. Their last banquet had been orchestrated by Viola Brightwell, and though it had been nothing as elaborate as this, every flower, bauble, and drape had felt *right*. Now, as Silas stared at the strange amalgam of printed silks, lace coverlets, and inexplicably offensive floral arrangements, her absence was a palpable ache in his heart.

How would he write this story? His books were simple adventures, medieval courtly romances that, despite appearances, always resolved pleasantly. There might be ghosts or curses, errant knights, or mischievous hags, but ultimately good won over evil.

Yet, in his tales, good and evil were much more clearly delineated. Heroes did not fall in love with vampires, they killed them. It was far easier in fiction than in life, for he could use the broad strokes of tradition rather than the strange complications of his own reality. When he ran out of ideas, he plumbed the depths of history to glean what he could and reshape it into something new. Readers loved that sense of familiarity. And he was happy to provide it.

No matter his story now, though, he chided himself for

his lack of chivalry where Viola was concerned. He really ought to have fought harder to let her come—stars, even her brother and mother were invited. He couldn't very well *not* invite them. His head ached.

Aunt May was nowhere to be seen, of course. Likely she would make some grand entrance at an entirely unpredictable time, just so he could know how much of a leash she held around him.

Last night, in a desperate attempt to settle his mind about Viola, he'd gone through all the estate finances and declarations. Even though his income from writing was considerable, it was not enough to offset the rest of the trust—and, foolishly, he had invested most of his funds directly in that trust. That meant his fortune was inextricably tied to Burkley House, and their other residences. Aunt May, as the dowager viscountess, still had the right to disinherit Silas, and would for another seven years. The law had been passed to protect women who, outside of gentlewitch inheritance, stood to lose the most when titles were transferred.

No, marriage—to a woman of means and Aunt May's approval—was the only way forward. He would have to enjoy what moments he could with Viola and then try, somehow, to move on.

A shuffling bang resounded through the hall, followed by the twang and crash of a stringed instrument falling to the marble floor, startling Silas out of his ruminations. The musicians had arrived and now, under the direction of a very red-faced Fintan, were desperately trying to assemble in the corner by the table of grey-looking canapes. Was the lighting off? Or was his entire sense of vision clouded by the most recent events with Viola?

He stared at the great doors at the top of the grand staircase, shuffling his weight from foot to foot. They were already behind schedule, but he couldn't very well have his guests enter the hall without music. The staircase was built to produce dramatic introductions, allowing guests to descend into the hall a pair at a time.

With a huge sigh of relief, Silas noticed Lady Rookwood-Nourse emerging from one of the side entrances, carrying the guest list ledger. She looked lovely, her piquant features accentuated by a marvellous cascade of crimson ostrich feathers in her chestnut curls. Her dress was a brilliant coral hue, offset by pale cream-colored stripes down the back, and she wore a glittering necklace of natural pearl.

"My apologies, my lord," Lady Rookwood-Nourse said, breathless. "There was a bit of a mishap in the kitchen, and a small fire—but all is well."

"Oh. Just a small fire?" Silas asked weakly.

"All dealt with, my lord,"

"You are our saviour in all of this," Silas said. He gave her a kind smile, hoping she sensed just how grateful he was. "I do hope Aunt May hasn't been running you entirely ragged."

"Not at all. I am used to working under my mother's direction, which I promise is far more exacting. Although her off-colour commentary about gentlewitches does grate on a person after a time."

"I hope she wasn't too horrid," Silas said.

"I am made of stern stuff, my lord." The gentlewitch flipped open the ledger and removed the stylus from its sleeve on the side. "Now, it begins."

The musicians began their swelling introduction, and so Garner, the head footman, commenced the announcements.

"Lady Cornwallis, escorted by her father, Lord Cornwallis," Garner drawled, as the first guests emerged through the grand doors. Lady Cornwallis wore white silk netting shot with silver, her pale hair twisted and lacquered into place as to resemble some sort of baked good, Silas thought. She looked smug, but lovely—given her fortune, she certainly could afford it.

"Lady Bridgewater, escorted by her brother, Lord Bridgewater."

"Miss Bahadur, escorted by her father, Shah Bayqara Khan."

"The Honorable Mistress Justice Wallace and her escort, Lady Winterude."

On and on the list went. Silas greeted each and every guest in person, shaking hands and kissing cheeks. Even the Atwaters showed up, much to his surprise, though there was a distinct chill between them.

"That makes sixty-seven," Lady Rookwood-Nourse said, leaning over to Silas and crossing out the Atwaters' names. "I must say, I'm surprised they came. But the dowager viscountess said it was in best taste to at least make sure they were invited."

"Of course," Silas said. He did feel bad for the Atwater woman, though not enough to ever consider matrimony.

The majority of eligible women had been announced, so now a trickle of regular guests came in through the other doors. He found himself searching for Viola's face, and Roland's, knowing full well he'd see neither of them this night.

Then he saw the Brightwells emerge, dressed in their finest—which was better than it had once been, considering their daughter was now half heir to Netherford Hall—and his heart stuttered in his chest. Heath bore such a likeness to his sister it only enhanced her absence.

Judging by the way Mrs. Brightwell looked about, she was hoping to catch a glimpse of her daughters. Edith and Poppy had not arrived yet, however, and Silas still wasn't certain how he was going to manage to explain the situation to Viola's parents.

He didn't have the chance, for he was immediately beset by the Greenstreet girls, all curtseying and giggling, a flurry of fluttering fans glinting in the candlelight and witchlights.

As USUAL, BASIL was stationed inside the manor. It was no offence: he was better at casting and testing wards in smaller spaces, and Molly hated being inside for longer than a half hour if she could help it. He kept glancing back up at the witchlights around the periphery, the ones he and Edith had worked together on, ensuring that he could see the warding lines.

It was strange to him that average people couldn't see warding lines. He had to unfocus his eyes slightly to perceive them, but they were *everywhere*.

Except around Roland de Grateloup.

Which is what gave him away.

Basil had not told de Grateloup this fact, mostly because he loathed the werewolf, but also because he wanted to understand *why*. His first inclination was that it was due to his mother's protection—surely the High Witch would know a thing or two about wards. But that didn't make sense. Wards were helpful to witches, vampires, and werewolves alike, along with anyone else wishing for protection.

De Grateloup must think himself terribly clever, Basil decided, for he had darkened his hair with some sort of tincture, found a pair of spectacles, and was wearing a hideous ensemble of humble wool plaid. No one would ever notice him, and given his knowledge of the house and surrounds, the werewolf had used it all to his advantage.

Which meant that in all likelihood, Viola Brightwell was bound to come.

These people and their complicated trysts!

The werewolf was so busy trying to look normal he didn't even notice Basil had sidled up next to him.

"You might have fooled the staff and guests, but I'm afraid even the homely cologne you've got won't mask the scent of *loup-garou*," Basil said.

Unflappable as ever, de Grateloup adjusted his ridiculous glasses. "I've no idea what you're talking about."

"Are you trying to affect an Irish lilt?" Basil asked. It was a terrible attempt, but almost precious in its innocence.

Roland sniffed in offence. "No."

"Well, your loitering has not gone unnoticed."

"I am not loitering. And I am not bothering anyone," de Grateloup said.

"You're bothering *me*."

The werewolf flared his nostrils, losing some of the composure he'd had moments before. "Which is an easily surmountable difficulty. You need only leave me alone."

Speaking with this man always made Basil's head ache. There was no hope of a straightforward discussion and no moving de Grateloup once he had decided his course of action. Such behaviour came from a lifetime of indulgence, whether or not he saw it that way. Of course, living as a bastard brought its own difficulties, but it did not preclude de Grateloup from many of the nastier features common among the upper class.

Basil could tell de Grateloup had never truly fought for anything in his life. He'd lived out his existence with the knowledge his mother would sweep in and take care of him, so pervasive were her power and influence across the realm. Except now she could not. The one rule he had to follow was to remain inconspicuous, and he couldn't even manage that!

But for all of it, maddeningly, he was dashing and charming and Basil had to force himself not to think about the ways he'd like to entertain Roland if they were not at such odds. At least, he wouldn't think about it until he was alone, in his bed, in the dark.

"Where on earth did you find those clothes?" Basil asked. "They smell of mouldy wood."

De Grateloup sniffed his sleeve, then wrinkled his nose. "I suppose that is a fair assessment. I found them in a cedar chest. One of the old viscount's things, I believe, stuffed into one of the spare rooms."

"The breeches are remarkably short on you." It was difficult not to laugh. For someone with such a muscular physique—a fact Basil had, regrettably, recognised a number of times in their interactions—the werewolf had very delicate calves and ankles. "Almost scandalously so."

Of course, de Grateloup answered with a lupine grin. "How delightful of you to notice. It is one of the true tragedies of modern fashion, the abandonment of true breeches for pantaloons. Boots have their places, of course, but there is nothing quite like the stark lines of a man's frame rising above a pair of well-heeled *souliers*."

Stars help him, but Basil's whole body reacted when de Grateloup spoke French, as if that foreign tongue unlocked a part of him that resonated only to its words.

He really ought to leave.

"I do prefer the freedom of a low heel, but for my profession, a sturdy pair of top boots is not out of place even at a ball," Basil said. He was glad about that, in fact, as he preferred the protection and the look of his current pair. As he was not attending as a guest, he did not have to abide by the same laws of fashion.

Basil could feel de Grateloup's eyes on him. Calculating, measuring, devouring. He was not so dim as to have missed the werewolf's flirtations, but neither was he so naïve to believe such flattery was reserved for him alone. No, de

Grateloup was an expert beguiler. There was nothing special about their interactions.

De Grateloup wiggled his foot, the light catching the flash of satin damask. They most certainly had no symmetry with his ensemble, but with the brass flower buttons, they were perfect for the werewolf.

"Silas says to stay out of harm's way as much as possible," Basil finally said. This was the main reason for the conversation, he had to remind himself.

"Silas knows I'm here?"

It was hard not to let his annoyance show on his face, but Basil managed. "He knows *you*, de Grateloup, and suspected you'd find your way here once the opening began. Just do not draw attention to yourself or I will be forced to escort you to a room. A boring one. With no outside view."

"I might have to take you up on that," said de Grateloup.

Basil felt his cheeks flush and turned away, barely managing to say, "Keep out of the way."

"I will be as inconspicuous as a church mouse," de Grateloup said, placing his hand upon his breast as if he had an ounce of honour in him at all.

"Let us settle for an unremarkable portrait draped in the corner. Mice are a nuisance, and with the house on high alert, we must—"

A horn blared. An *actual* horn. Everyone's attention swung toward the grand staircase, the musicians halting in their entertainment in dissonant surprise.

"His Royal Highness, the Duke of Sussex," came a resounding announcement. "And his daughter, Miss Augusta d'Este."

By all the heavenly bodies, *Prince Augustus Frederick* had come to Burkley House? With his illegitimate daughter, nonetheless, who could be no more than thirteen or fourteen.

They cut a sharp pair—he in his full regalia as a Knight of the Garter, and she in a court-style gown.

"And I thought *I* knew how to make an entrance," de Grateloup said. "Were you not just boasting how your wards were foolproof?"

Gasps ricocheted around the room, followed by applause, fractured at first but then wildly enthusiastic. The Prince and his daughter took one step at a time, measured and regal, while their attendants trailed after.

Not just any attendants.

"Those are Warders of the Crown, de Grateloup," Basil said. "Not many on this earth could confound them, no matter their talent. Few people, save your mother, would have any idea how to even detect them."

"Does that make us *more* or *less* safe?" de Grateloup asked.

That was a surprisingly good question, but Basil did not want to indulge the man with anything that could be misconstrued as a compliment. "A little of both, I think," Basil said. "Prince Augustus Frederick is a friend to the gentlewitches, but as we all know, the Prince Regent is not. His first marriage was annulled, and rumours have run rampant that he's seeking to get Parliament's agreement to make Augusta and her brother full heirs."

"Ah, so this is a political appearance," de Grateloup said. He sounded quite thrilled at the prospect. "How delightful. I never imagined we might see court intrigue all the way out here in Netherford, but now I'm beginning to think I was wrong."

Whether or not that was a good thing, Basil could not say.

AUDEN GARCLIFFE WAS mid-sip of his champagne when the startling tattoo of royal horns inflicted such a shock to his system that he inhaled the contents into his lungs. He was glad of the applause, for it allowed him some time to capture his breath. But he must have looked terrible, for in a moment, Jamini was at his side.

She looked resplendent in a gown of Dhaka muslin, the sleeves set with red embroidery. Radiant. Down to every last pearl set in her thick, black hair.

"It's the Duke of Sussex," Jamini said, gently patting her fiancé's back. "Can you believe such a thing?"

"I wouldn't put anything past the dowager viscountess, but my heavens, Miss d'Este is far too young for this sort of sport," he replied. Auden disliked the entire idea of a ball full of prospective wives, let alone those of both high status and questionable parentage. Well, not in his eyes. He was the last person to criticise such a thing.

"I doubt it's a serious offer, but rather a symbolic one. Everything the Duke of Sussex does is layered in purpose," Jamini said. "That he would come all the way out here, with his treasured daughter in tow, to the house of an up-and-coming viscount with strong ties to the Coven Council, is no small thing."

Jamini had, by dint of her profession, an intimate understanding of politics. It was not, as she professed, of a personal interest to her, but her clients had a habit of talking freely around her while she went about her work.

"And I thought the dowager viscountess loathed preternatural folk," Auden observed.

"She hates the Regent more."

"Have you heard any rumours at the shop?"

"Not a one. And I'm always listening." Jamini sighed, taking a sip of her punch and wincing. "Oh, my, this tastes quite curious. I think I shall have the champagne next."

Auden held up his glass, sediment swirling among the profusion of bubbles. "I don't know that I would recommend the champagne either," he said.

In that moment, now that the applause had stopped and the guests were doing their best to act as if the most astonishing news of the last year hadn't just occurred, Edith and Poppy came swirling toward them.

Auden immediately fought back tears seeing Edith's beaming smile. Poppy had planned their ensembles showcasing her most remarkable embroidery talent, and he had been kept apprised of the situation given Jamini's collaboration on the garments. The result was a rendering of Edith and Poppy's love in thread and silk.

"Gracious, my liege," Jamini said, curtseying gracefully. "You look like a princeling of the fae come to stride among us mere mortals."

Edith's smile faltered at that comment, but she recovered quickly. Indeed, Auden's niece had mentioned something about the fae in the last day or two, and their connection with the High Witch. He really ought to be paying more attention.

"I think we would make even the most elegant fae jealous," Edith said at last.

"And you couldn't have picked a better night for it," Auden said, inclining his head toward where the Prince and his daughter stood speaking to the Viscount St. Albans. "Although you may be somewhat eclipsed by this most unusual circumstance, now that I think about it."

Poppy pulled her companion a little closer, their arms linked together. "We shall have to speak with the viscount as soon as we can. But I fear food is on the way, and then dancing. And given he is at the centre of this entire business, it may be some time before we truly understand."

"I haven't seen the dowager viscountess, but I suspect she is the grand orchestrator," Edith added.

Indeed, the dinner bell clanged, announcing food on the way. He only hoped the food was a bit more dependable than the drink.

*   *   *

FOR ONCE, LAERTES Byrne was glad he didn't eat mortal food. All three vampires on the premises had agreed to feed before the event, so as not to cause any disruption, but judging from the smells and the reactions of the guests, whatever had gone on in the kitchens had not been a great success.

Without the distraction of food, Laertes was able to watch the guests with his full vampire senses. One of the ladies—a marchioness, if he recalled correctly—used an excuse to check on her hem to dispose of the snails into her napkin. Why anyone would look at a snail and consider it ideal for consumption, he had no idea.

Ophelia, sitting across from him, looked despondent despite wearing the most glorious gown she'd ever graced— she looked like a queen of vampires in mulberry purple.

"It seems vulgar to celebrate mortal matrimony, or the promise of it, when we can do nothing to save our Viola," Ophelia said, glancing around the room again. "And the dowager viscountess is a monster to try and publicly shame us by not inviting our spawn."

"The vampire calls the crone a monster, and the whole world trembles," Laertes said, fiddling with the chain on his pocket watch; it was ancient as such mechanisms went, being a gift from a young paramour he'd known in Vienna ages before. Sadly, it was a terribly unreliable thing, truly more form than function, but it gave him something to do when he was feeling restless.

"I expected to see Viola by now," Ophelia said. "I sense a growing unease in her."

"Well, given her situation I hardly think that's surprising," Laertes retorted. Honestly, sometimes Ophelia said the most ridiculous things. "She's going to die, at our hands, and there's nothing to be done about it. I'd be uneasy, too."

Ophelia pouted. "I mean this *evening*. I was hoping she would make an appearance, but the last I spoke to her she was second-guessing herself. She does not wish to embarrass the viscount—which is asinine—or infuriate the dowager viscountess. But I suppose she is holding onto what shreds of her mortal life she had left."

"I don't suppose our parents ever had to consider such difficulties," Laertes said. "But then, I don't remember much of them before they were murdered. Perhaps they agonised over our first thrall and kill—or they might have been compassionate. Though, given most of our kin, I'd say it's far more likely they simply let nature take its course."

"Nature," Ophelia scoffed, flipping her hand so the sapphire on her finger glinted in the light. "What is natural about *any* of this? I have pored over every tome, debased myself by speaking with Maurice, and outside Faerie there is no chance of our helping Viola."

The way she said 'outside Faerie' made Laertes pause. He knew his sister was in one of her moods—and understandably so—but he could not let that morsel simply dangle before him untasted.

"Do you mean to imply there is a solution *inside* Faerie?"

Ophelia rolled her eyes as if Laertes was the single most thick-witted person she'd ever encountered. "Of course there's answers inside Faerie, my sweet brother. It is the very intersection of our myth and making. However, it is far beyond our reach."

"Is it, though?" Laertes asked, stroking his chin thoughtfully. For a moment, he did fancy himself quite the romantic hero. Imagine him, striding into Faerie, demanding a potion or tonic or cure for some great bargain, all for his beloved spawn. They would write great novels about him, he was quite certain.

"Have you suddenly discovered a heretofore unknown

passageway to the land our gentlewitches so very clearly cut off from our world?" Ophelia asked, sarcasm dripping from her lips like venom from a snake's fangs.

"That is an unnecessary tone. You're not the only scholar among us."

"And what great, ancient tomes have you read lately?"

"I haven't read any of them. But not all experience comes in the form of reading."

They fell silent as the next course rattled in toward the tables, some gelatinous concoction that might have once been fish. Laertes could understand some of the appeal of human food, but the idea anyone would ever want to put a *fish* anywhere near their mouths absolutely baffled him.

He liked prolonging responses with Ophelia, who was always so impatient. So he stared her down until she said: "Fine. Tell me about your very enlightening *experience*."

Grinning, Laertes leaned in. "Have you ever taken a close look at Fintan?"

THERE WAS NO time for blame or anger, even though Silas's heart blazed with it. The gall of his aunt to invite the Duke of Sussex—and the gall of the Prince to have accepted! What the devils was he supposed to do now? Entertaining a prince was an entirely different matter than the well-bred and well-funded ladies of Kent.

His whole body felt gauzy as he made his way toward the head table, Fintan and the staff scurrying around to readjust the seating. Countess Rocksavage had to be moved next to Lady Mary Dunbarton, and that was going to be a disaster in and of itself if someone didn't intervene before dessert.

Did the food taste especially bad tonight, or was Silas simply so overwhelmed with anxiety everything tasted like bitter ash?

No time. He was sitting directly next to the Duke of Sussex.

The Duke of Sussex was a tall man, nearly equal in height to Silas, with a pink complexion and piercing blue eyes. His hair was certainly thinning, frosting as his father George III's had. Indeed, their bearing was quite similar. Dressed in his knight's regalia, he drew every eye to his substantial person, and he commanded that power with ease and comfort. Kingly, one might even say.

"Quite the place you've got here, St. Albans," said the Duke of Sussex, eyes going to the soaring ceilings. "Modern, but with a touch of the rustic past. You've set a new standard, I'd say, in this structure. Half the ton will be asking you for your architect once you're back in London."

Back in London. *Back in London?*

Silas must have taken too long to answer, for the Duke of Sussex tilted his head and asked: "You *are* planning to return to London, are you not? I have it on good authority that there's a spot in Parliament waiting just for you."

"Oh, of course—yes." Silas's voice came out thin and strained. "I'd heard rumours, given some of the recent retirements, but I hadn't heard official word yet."

"Well, I believe all eyes are turned upon you for that," said the Prince. "For isn't that the message you're sending? Tonight, you shall select one among these many blooming flowers—I suspect you'll have just enough time for a hasty ceremony before you head back to the city. Clean up and be done with it, keep it expected and uninteresting, take it from me. Don't go for symbolic or brave. A safe marriage is a balm to the soul, and a tempestuous one is a lifelong plague."

Why did everything have to be so political? The thought that this act, orchestrated by his aunt, would be perceived as a signal to Parliament made Silas's skin feel oily. Had he been deluding himself into thinking he would be able to leave it behind? He supposed he had. Coming to Netherford and throwing himself into the restoration of Burkley House—and then into Viola's recovery—had merely delayed the inevitable.

He would live a long, unhappy life with a woman he did not love. All because he was too cowardly to write his own story, because he feared a life without the promise of money and the security and stability it afforded. He'd worked so hard to claw his family's fortunes back to where they were now—would he squander that all because of an alluring vampire woman?

"I suspect you're correct," Silas managed to say as a footman leaned over him to serve a cut of pork.

"But that is not the sole reason I am here," continued the Duke of Sussex. "You may have guessed by now, but I wanted this opportunity to show the world—or at least this corner of Kent—that I am not afraid or ashamed of my beautiful daughter."

Without looking at Lady d'Este, Silas said: "She is—well, visible." The words were forced and very quiet.

Silas was horrified at the potential implications. He would not marry a girl so young, no matter her pedigree. And her pedigree was a dubious one at that. The Duke of Sussex had been married to a certain Lady De Ameland of Scotland, but their marriage had never been recognised by the Crown, no matter how many times they had tried. Though Lady De Ameland had not been seen in public for some time, neither had the Prince made any indications he would remarry.

Those close to the couple said they still corresponded, and that the children—Augusta and Augustus—were shepherded back and forth between their parents' properties. Given how few heirs of the Duke of Sussex's many siblings remained, it meant his children, if legitimised, could very well rule England in time.

The Duke of Sussex chuckled as a large, but very pale piece of pork slithered its way around his plate. Even the server looked embarrassed. "Well, I am certainly not here for the food. I hope you don't take offense, St. Albans, but you might need to consider new staff."

"Of course, your grace," Silas said. "My apologies."

"None needed. In time, no one will remember the food. But they will recall you sat with the Duke of Sussex and spoke to him over dinner before dancing through the night with the future Viscountess St. Albans. And that is what I want Augusta to remember. You are likely aware of the rumours regarding His Majesty's continued lack of support for my wife and our children."

Silas cleared his throat, heat crawling up his neck. This was the most uncomfortable conversation he'd ever had, teetering on the edge of treason with a man who outranked him in every way possible. "I may have heard," was all he could manage.

"And *your* reputation leads me to believe you have considerably more liberal ideas regarding our relations with preternaturals than the usual stuffed shirts who held your seat before. You are close with the Byrnes, for instance, as well as Liege Edith Rookwood—all of whom are happily under your roof tonight."

"They have been steadfast friends."

Was he going to talk about Roland? Was this some great farce, and in moments, they'd all be arrested?

The Prince took Silas's shoulder in one of his large, well-manicured hands. "I simply want you to know, and to see, that I understand. And I support you. And I want London to know that. You see, my daughter is a gentlewitch, as is her mother. That is the reason my father refuses our match.

Not because of her breeding, but because of her powers. Officially, it's due to her grandfather's somewhat rebellious youth. But I know that my beloved brother—who has done everything in his power to push the limits of Parliamentary acceptance—is, at the heart, truly bigoted and afraid of all preternaturals."

Prince George's reputation was even more scandalous than Roland's had been, and that was saying something. But to hear the duke speak so openly on the matter was confusing, to say the least.

Silas would have paid half his fortune to get the Prince to stop speaking. "I did not know that."

"And you had best be careful. George will target you for all the reasons I am drawn to you. Your invitation was a good excuse for me to leave, but I will not always be so free. The Grey Moon Brotherhood roam London again and, indeed, I suspect they will course through all our counties soon enough if we do not separate our allies from our..." He did not say the word *enemies*, but it was clear he was near to.

Silas had never been so relieved to hear the announcement for dancing in all his life.

"We will discuss more later, I think," said the Prince, finally letting go of Silas's shoulder, then patting it as if in benediction. "You've a crowd to dazzle, I'm afraid."

JAMINI TRIED NOT to be sour about the décor, but it was truly abhorrent. What were they *thinking?* She knew dozens of florists between here and Canterbury with a better eye for colour. Heavens, a child picking daisies in the field had more talent than what she saw.

She tried to be glad of the honour of even being invited. As Auden's fiancée, she was one of the few common folk on the list, though truly she spent more of her time assisting various young women with their attire than enjoying any of the food or drink. Which was just as well, considering the only thing more nauseating than the colour combination on the florals and swags was the meal.

Seeing her gowns against the backdrop of orange flowers and pea green garlands of ribbon made her head swim. Never in all her life had she considered the necessary harmony between gown and hall, but now it was all she could think of.

Viscount St. Albans was on his second dance, this time with Miss Cordelia Fulke, who was decidedly *not* wearing one of Jamini's creations. She had gone to Hoyt's, instead, and though her ensemble was lovely in its composition— pale lavender with an interlocking tulip motif—the material was an absolute disaster. It wasn't that Jamini disliked moiré. Indeed, watered silks were excellent when done right. But in this case, the silk had been tailored in such a way that Miss Fulke appeared to have been sweating profusely down her back.

Poppy Brightwell, who had taken a break from dancing, found her way to Jamini and playfully winked at her friend. "You appear lost in the pageantry of it all, my dear. Tell me, what is your assessment of this ball's most fashionable guests?"

"Oh, Poppy, you know I shall never tell." She laughed, getting a better look at Poppy's ensemble. It truly was the most exquisite embroidery she'd seen all night, and she knew her friend had stayed up all hours to complete it, and the matching swaths on Liege Rookwood's tailcoat. "But you are a vision. Oh, that blue does exactly what you hoped it would."

Poppy swirled her dress as much as the narrow gown would allow, causing the embroidery to catch the light at her waist. "Blue with just a slight kiss of silver," she said with a smile. "And you should see the way it makes the gentlewitch's eyes sparkle."

Jamini laughed. "Oh, she is positively scintillating." She gestured toward the gentlewitch, who was discussing something with her cousin, Lady Rookwood-Nourse, and glancing back every now and again to see Poppy. "She cannot keep her eyes to herself."

"I do not think we imagined this sort of place for ourselves, Jamini," Poppy said dreamily. She gave the *couturière* a sweet smile. "And you are one to talk. Mr. Garcliffe has been making eyes at you all night long, when he isn't fretting about every last thing."

Auden did have a habit of fretting, didn't he? But that was part of his charm. Jamini was the gentle, constant stream to his rapids, and somehow that balanced them both. And he did look absolutely perfect this evening, in a marvellous cravat of palest ivory, his striped yellow waistcoat flashing in contrast to the deep green top coat. And his shoes! She was very glad to have found a fiancé who delighted in fashion; she did not think she could have managed, otherwise.

"I do wish I had a closer perspective on the Duke of Sussex, though," Jamini said after a moment. "My brother Nathaniel has had the opportunity to dress the royal family now and again, along with the Coven Council, of course—there's so many of them, it's hardly an uncommon experience. But the finery on the robes of the Garter, well, I might never have the chance to see them up close again."

"Well, we shall make it our duty this evening to get as close as we possibly can. So much lace! And the detail—even from here I can tell it's rather splendid."

"No, Poppy, your duty is to enjoy yourself. Dance with your companion! Go. I am happy to sit here and take notes in my head about future compositions," Jamini insisted—

and she meant it. She was no dancer, and Auden *had* asked numerous times.

Then the music shifted to a sudden, scandalous strain: the waltz!

PETRONILLA ROOKWOOD-NOURSE WAS a practical woman by both nature and upbringing. Her mother was powerful, rich, and demanding, insisting that she and her brother Giles excel in every single endeavour of their lives, no matter how trifling.

It was for that reason she was an excellent waltzing partner. And, as she would have it, she ended up partnering with the Viscount St. Albans. Her cheeks flushed when she realised, though in the dim candlelight it was doubtful anyone could see. Not to mention the viscount had a similar condition to many menfolk she knew: he missed details.

Such was the curse of falling in love with the man. And he, as ever, considered her a good friend, a confidante, but nothing more. Of course, she had never broached the subject; not here, in England. Had she been home in America, courting some New York lawyer, it wouldn't have been considered so terribly out of fashion to keep her thoughts to herself. A little distance was exciting, but she found suitors in America preferred a more direct approach than here.

Petronilla did have a plan, however. A purpose. Initially, her mother had set her up to the business, working closely with Viola through her transition in order to remain in proximity to the viscount. A marriage of that calibre would keep them afloat for life. Yet, despite her efforts, which were considerable, Petronilla remained strangely invisible to the man. Which made this unreflecting love, unanticipated as it was, even more painful.

Now, though, the pressure was mounting on him. With the benefit of living at Burkley House, Petronilla had learned much from overheard conversations and discussions with the staff.

"Lady Rookwood-Nourse," the viscount said, with evident relief. "It is such a joy to see someone familiar."

"Tonight has been a continual progression of rather formidable women," she observed. The closeness of the dance allowed them the pleasure of conversation, and as his hand tightened on her waist, Petronilla had to suppress the shiver that ran down her spine.

The viscount sighed, and she could tell he was exhausted. When he was tired, he gnawed on his bottom lip. She had stored away these little details for the inevitable time of heartbreak, memories she might hold onto once this conversation was over.

He was still searching for Viola's face in the crowd, after all.

"Somehow it is even less tolerable than I imagined," he said as they made a turn together.

Years of dancing instruction, including ballet, were imprinted upon her limbs and muscles. Even though he was not a good dancer by any measure, he fell into her expert rhythm. "I hope we are not *all* so intolerable."

The viscount turned his gaze back to her, smiling kindly. "No, *you* have been a constant to me, a North Star. I truly cannot imagine what the last few months would have been like if you hadn't given so much of your time and power to our most unusual situation."

Petronilla could feel eyes upon her, the strange power of attention. And she could sense every candle in the vast room, each flame like a living soul, waiting for her touch. She could snuff them all out if she wanted; she could set them all ablaze. Few gentlewitches had the degree of control she did, let alone the strength of connection. If she willed it, Petronilla could truly give them a night they would never forget.

No. That way lay destruction and madness. It was the same lessons she had been working through so thoroughly on her visits home to London with young Henry Garcliffe. It might be wise to heed her own warnings. It was just so difficult to think straight when she was this close to the viscount.

"It is my pleasure," she said. "Pardon my asking, but have you considered your selection tonight? The dowager viscountess made her entrance about ten minutes ago."

The viscount's expression flattened. "I hadn't noticed. It's been difficult to do anything, between surprise guests and the constant barrage of cloying women. I have never smelled so many kinds of perfume at once."

"As ever, evading the important questions," she teased. "But I do not envy you, my lord. Few would find your position ideal."

"I keep thinking I will see her," he admitted, dropping his voice even lower. "Even now. Is it a fool's hope I hold? Will I always feel this way?"

"I cannot answer that for you. But I find, when the pressure of the future rises to meet me, my fear is mitigated when I merely look more closely to what I *have*," she said, letting the music move through her as she stretched her neck elegantly as they twirled again.

"Indeed? As of yet, I feel no relief as I look around. Merely dread."

"Perhaps I can be of assistance." She really did have to write it out for him, with a diagramme.

He glanced at her again, and Petronilla smiled with all the charm she could endure. "What are you proposing?"

"The Rookwood-Nourses are exceptionally well off, my lord. We come with significant holdings both here and in the Americas. We have seven thousand a year, which is an appeal to many but not one often promoted," Petronilla said. She had rehearsed this part times over. "And, of course, given our proximity to the Rookwoods of Netherford, we are well-placed in society. I know your aunt's far from a supporter of preternaturals, but surely she would prefer a witch of good fortune, even if she is American-born."

"I cannot say I expected such a proposition from *you*, Lady Rookwood-Nourse," the viscount said. He did not sound angry or surprised. That was a start.

She took a deep breath, closing her eyes. Now came the most difficult part. "I am also in the unique position of being a very practical woman, my lord. I do not think you will ever stop loving Viola Brightwell, nor would I expect you to. In fact, I would not require affection beyond the duties of public presentation, and should an heir be required... There are protocols through spellwork I might employ."

"I am not certain what to say," the viscount replied after a significant pause.

"I know you have not considered me among the lists of your suitors, but I was invited specifically by the dowager viscountess, and her instructions were clear: any woman of birth would be considered a potential bride." Petronilla squeezed his elbow gently. "Silas. I can help you escape this, and I ask for nothing in return other than your title. To the world, outside of your house, you would live unremarkably. Plenty of lords have married gentlewitches, and I am not tied to a town and so have no responsibilities. And I could support your... other endeavours."

"Lady Rookwood-Nourse, your help, as I've said, has been most appreciated. I am certain I haven't said it enough. However, this proposition will require much thought and, to be blunt with you, I am a bit taken aback. It would have been well to approach me sooner," said the viscount, just a hint of anger in his voice.

Truly, this was the part of the conversation she dreaded the most. It had happened by accident, really—mixed parcels of mail after a rainstorm, and a confused postmaster. But she could not afford inaction. Her mother had always told her that secrets were a woman's best weapons. The waltz was nearly over. The window of opportunity closing.

Petronilla leaned forward and whispered: "D. B. Mansfield."

EDITH WAS BEGINNING to feel annoyed. Her instructions from Tailte had been fairly straightforward: the garnet-crusted ring she'd been given would point in the direction of the fae woman's child. Apparently, its magic could only be wielded by a mortal—and although witches were preternaturals, they did not live forever. Witches had even better results than those without magic.

All Edith had to do was shake hands with every possible young man at the event. And although there were dozens of eligible young women, most of them had come with their escorts. Tailte said even touching an article of clothing would be sufficient.

So far there had been no indication whatsoever of anything out of the ordinary. The ring was far too ostentatious for Edith's tastes, but no one had seemed to notice.

For her part, Poppy thought the whole situation was suspect, particularly the convenience of the ring. A fae bargain was a bad idea in the first place, she'd said, and one with such a simple solution even more concerning.

She was probably right. She usually was.

Edith had shaken more hands and touched more shoulders than she ever wanted to again in her life. Why were men's hands so rough and clammy? Why did they shake so hard?

She'd rarely attended such events as a guest, and in the past could generally avoid touching altogether.

The waltz came to an end and Edith leaned back against the far wall, exhaustion stealing over her. She closed her eyes for just a moment, sinking into the welcome darkness, when she heard a ripple of shock skitter across the gathered crowd.

Opening her eyes, Edith glanced about the room—a figure stood at the top of the grand staircase, willowy and lovely in a gown of sheer silver. Who she was remained a mystery, for she wore a mask and veil over her face, so not even her hair was in view. Indeed, her gloves covered every inch of her skin, and a fichu concealed her neck.

No one made a single announcement. There was no escort. The ethereal beauty walked down each step with the poise of a queen. On cue, the musicians began a lovely suite, enchanting and a little mysterious. If Edith didn't know better, she'd have thought the woman was straight from Faerie itself.

As if drawn by an invisible string, the Viscount St. Albans made his way to greet her at the bottom of the stair. He turned his face to her in adulation, an expression Edith had never seen on his countenance. The crowd muttered, but no one stopped him. Even in the country, people loved a spectacle.

Without a word, they danced. None dared join them on the dance floor, for they were so perfectly paired and so intense, the world itself seemed to hold its breath. Edith had never found men particularly interesting to look at, yet Silas positively glowed with intensity around this woman.

Just across the room, Edith saw Poppy. Her companion was weeping, holding Madame Rawlings-Vijay.

Viola. Of *course* it was Viola.

CHAPTER FIFTEEN
What a Tangled Web We Weave

Viola was in his arms. Silas would have known her anywhere, and though despair wracked his bones, in this moment, he would have given anything to stop time.

She did not speak. She did not need to. Their world narrowed to a single point in time, their bodies, their souls, twining together in ways he had never expected.

Perhaps Silas should have cared about the look on the dowager viscountess's face. He ought to have considered the Duke of Sussex and his future in Parliament. And of course, he should have been mulling over Lady Rookwood-Nourse's proposition and rather shocking knowledge of his identity as D. B. Mansfield.

But he did not care. He barely registered the duke's retinue departing, or the temperature, or the concerns that had all weighed so heavily upon him moments before. It didn't matter. He was ready, now, to let it all go.

For what use was all his wealth, all his renown, if he could not wake next to Viola Brightwell every morning? True, he would grow old and she would remain ageless, but if she loved him—and he thought, after tonight's grand entrance, she must—then he was willing to give whatever years he had to her, and her alone. He would devote himself to her, open himself to her, share her dreams and help her heal. He would even learn to love

Laertes and Ophelia, because Viola loved them.

Even if it was impossible. He let himself believe it, in this moment. Because to do otherwise would have broken him.

THIS WAS FAREWELL. Oh, Viola had paced her room dozens of times, fretting and trying to muster up the courage. She did not want to anger the dowager countess or jeopardise Silas's place in society. Yet, the idea of dying without ever having a dance, ever having a moment with him, terrified her more than her inevitable demise.

When Ophelia had arrived with the silver-shot gown, looking as fine as starlight itself, and a matching mask—oh, she had never felt so understood. Ophelia often claimed to not have as much of an emotional connection to her as Laertes, but that was not true. It simply grew at a different pace.

Now, she had no excuse.

All Viola's anxieties, however, flitted away when she saw Silas's face at the bottom of the grand staircase. She knew, beyond doubt, he had been waiting for her all night. Perhaps the rest of the guests would not recognise her, but given what they had shared together, theirs was a connection beyond measure.

Three dances passed and then, expertly, Silas steered them away to the balcony, closing the door behind them. Fintan drew the curtains for their privacy. No doubt the guests were truly perturbed.

The smell of sweet late summer rose around them, stars glittering overhead as they stood in silence, neither wishing to break the spell.

"I'm so glad you came," Silas said at last. His voice was so weary it broke Viola's heart.

"I nearly didn't. But I had some convincing. I needed to say goodbye, and I knew I would regret if I didn't."

He stiffened, shoulders going back as if preparing for a blow. "I should have fought harder to keep you, Viola. Perhaps you will have no regrets, but I believe I shall look back on these days and wish I could have found another solution."

"I cannot fault you for your choices, my lord," Viola said, trying to keep her voice from shaking. Her hunger was a dull echo in her body, stilled from the nourishment of Silas's blood, but she still had to restrain herself from falling into his arms. "You must protect what is yours, and I must protect what is mine."

What she had left, that was. Even if everything had gone to plan, even if vampirism's price hadn't asked for the impossible, how could they ever have found happiness and acceptance together?

"I don't think I shall ever love another as I have loved you," he said, and Viola could smell the tears on his face, that salt sweetness of his essence. "All of you; as you are now, and as you were."

She dared not touch him, not the way her body cried out for his. Out of the corner of her eye she could see shapes moving by the drapes, everyone trying to see what mystery lay behind them. There was no mystery here, only surrender.

"Love matters little in the face of our realities, Silas," she said softly.

"I can see you again—you will return, won't you?" The viscount's tone was almost angry, perhaps fuelled by fear. "Perhaps in the winter. I cannot imagine another season without seeing your face."

Viola pressed her gloved fingers to her lips, for she wanted to sob. "I am bound for Howarth Castle tomorrow morning. We've already packed all our things. I don't suspect I shall return. This arrangement of ours, whatever it is, could only cause us both harm in the long run. My family cannot even look at me for fear, though I will bid my farewells to them. You must understand that—we cannot bring anything but despair and destruction to each other."

"So, there is truly no hope for us?" Silas asked. He raised his hand as if to touch her, but seeing her face, dropped his hand.

The way he said it, the way his eyes danced across her face... It shattered something inside of her. Viola knew no matter how hard she tried, he would always pursue her if he believed there was hope. They had shared so much, entwined their souls. Her body had told him, again and again, how ardently and completely she adored him.

"You were a thrall when I needed one—my affections for you are clouded by what I have become." The words were bitter on her tongue, her stomach like knives with the taste of her lies: "I could never love you, Silas. Not as I am."

Agony. Total and overwhelming. She could not look at him again, could not endure the brokenness in him.

Laertes. Take me away from here.

Darkness enveloped her, the calming whisper of velvet and the sense of calm only her sire could bring. And soon, soon, to oblivion and numbness and the final reckoning.

SILAS STARED AT the space where Viola had been. He'd only managed a glimpse of Mr. Byrne before the vampire whisked her away. For a heartbeat, he'd considered fighting back, challenging him. But what would that have done? He had only rudimentary training in fencing, and that wouldn't bloody do him any good against a vampire.

He understood, now. Viola had never loved him. She didn't need him. He had been a convenient means to an end, and this was her attempt to placate him, to give him closure. So much cruelty in that kindness.

Unless she was simply saying that because... well, he couldn't think of a reason why. Denial just wedged itself thoroughly in his breast and he wanted answers, not this pit of despair.

The grand balcony overlooked a sprawling mosaic in the middle of the garden depicting gambolling satyrs and a centaur, the whites of their eyes just visible at this distance. Never in his life had he considered the likelihood of surviving a fall from this height. And yet, his heart pierced as it had been, the look of contempt in Viola's eyes lingering in his thoughts, it seemed a fitting escape given the shackles of his situation.

Fintan emerged moments later, closing the door behind him. For a mere heartbeat, the sounds and scents of the party invaded Silas's dark thoughts, pulling him away from the precipice.

What was the point of love if it was this fragile? He had gone most of his life without its barbs. Now Viola had both given him all and taken everything.

"My lord," Fintan said, his tone cautious. "The guests are wondering if you might have an announcement to make."

The guests. The party. His arrangement with his aunt. Thank every star the Duke of Sussex had already left, but...

No. He could not give up. There was more to his life than Viola Brightwell, and he had been living in a mire ever since he met her. He had been happy before her; he could be happy without her. Clearly, that was what she wanted.

Silas would do this for Fintan. For Roland. For Edith and Poppy and the rest of Netherford. He would shore up his defences, he would abandon whimsy, and he would remove himself from the equation of happiness. Surely he would find some shape of joy in London, among his peers in Parliament. Accomplishment, perhaps. Meaning.

"Yes." Silas's own voice felt oddly distant, his ears whining strangely, his face hot. "Please announce that I have chosen Lady Petronilla Rookwood-Nourse as my bride. Should she be amenable, the wedding will be two weeks hence." He twisted his father's crest ring from his hand and gave it to Fintan. "Give her this. I shall be in shortly."

After an unearthly long pause, Fintan said: "Yes, my lord."

Silas waited until he heard the doors click shut behind him. The music and chatter was so loud inside, it felt like a blow to his face.

Then he pulled off his gloves and threw them to the ground, tore off his tailcoat, and let out a long, wretched scream.

He never saw the figure, lingering behind him, until it was far too late.

IT HAD BEEN too long. Roland paced outside the balcony doors yet again, not wishing to disturb Silas.

What the devils was he thinking? No one looked more shocked than Petronilla Rookwood-Nourse at Fintan's announcement. The whole thing was crass, in Roland's most humble opinion. To make such a show, before dozens of people of status, after dancing with a woman from some ethereal dreamworld? What was he on about?

"Oh, stars and speckled firmament, it's *you*, isn't it?"

Roland swung around to see the freckled gentlewitch looking at him with dismay. "Depends on who you're expecting. I have answered to at least six names tonight. Part of the whole act, of course."

Liege Edith frowned at him, the line between her eyes deepening. Why did no one appreciate his genius?

"That is the most unconvincing wig I have ever seen," the gentlewitch said.

"It is *not* a wig." A wig would have been a better idea than rubbing his hair with charcoal ash.

Fintan appeared, wringing his hands. The poor fellow looked haggard. "It's been too long," he said to them both. "I wanted to give him space, but I'm afraid there is a point where we must intervene."

"I'll go," Liege Edith said quickly.

The guests were starting to leave. A crowd was still gathered around Petronilla Rookwood-Nourse, and it appeared Poppy was trying to extricate her with little assistance. Meanwhile, there was no sign of the Dowager Viscountess St. Albans. Which, for a reason he could not quite comprehend, made him feel anxious. Anxious?

He supposed they *were* related. Perhaps there was a modicum of familial affection still rooted somewhere deep inside his soul.

The gentlewitch took no time to get permission from Fintan—as if he could have stopped her, anyway—and Roland had to amble after her.

Strangely, it did not surprise him to find Silas was not there. If he dug down deep through the haze of drink to the core of him, that bloodthirsty animal chained inside, he'd have known he'd lost the scent of him at least half an hour ago. But he had ignored it.

Roland shivered as the evening breeze cooled the sweat from his brow.

Edith stood, holding a pair of leather gloves in her hands. Silas's gloves. Her mouth was open in shock, as if the gloves held some strange mystery only she could understand.

"Roland. Come here."

The command in the gentlewitch's voice made his spine tingle.

Fintan, who had already recognised Roland earlier in the evening, came forward as well so they could all examine the gloves. He was clearing his throat awkwardly, making a gagging sound that was not at all pleasant. No doubt the fellow was exhausted, but as soon as he was able, he truly should get to a doctor.

"These are the viscount's, yes?" the gentlewitch asked Fintan.

Fintan nodded, face strained still against whatever ailment had beset him.

Something soft at his foot grabbed his attention, and Roland reached down to find Silas's splendid topcoat, still damp with sweat from dancing. It had plainly been torn off him, though: some of the buttons were missing.

When the gentlewitch took hold of the garment, the ring on her finger flared red bright enough that Roland had to hold up his hands to shield his eyes. The light brought with it a palpable presence that reminded him of waking up late at night to find his mother at work in her study, the strange miasma of magic around her.

Now, Fintan was truly making a hideous noise, grasping at his neck.

"What the devils is wrong with him?" the Liege Rookwood asked.

"Maybe he had one of the snails," Roland said, but then had a true moment of clarity. Something caught in his mind, long covered with dust and decay, came free. "No—wait. I think I know."

Liege Rookwood tilted her head at him. "Please do tell, Roland. We haven't got all evening. The viscount is missing, and I fear his valet may choke to death on his own throat if we don't figure it out soon."

"It's a *geas*." Once, before Roland had given up any hope of a scholastic future, he had studied all magical schools in rather impressive detail. One that had captured his imagination, albeit briefly, was the world of fae magic and its connection to the powers of gentlewitches. His mother had a remarkable library on the subject and she rarely censored his reading.

"A what?" the gentlewitch asked. She had that irritated sort of tone very clever people often used when they were, somehow, outsmarted by people they believed quite inferior. It was a favourite of his, really.

"A *geas*. A kind of curse, typically done in a kind of bargain between fae and humans—or, sometimes, even among the fae themselves. It would prevent our good friend Fintan here from being able to divulge certain information, causing him rather severe pain," Roland said, gesturing to the valet.

Fintan nodded, taking a deep breath unimpeded by the *geas* at last.

"How would you know?" Liege Edith asked, not without her own share of bitterness.

"Just because I do not appear to have my mother's power or intellect, doesn't mean I left my childhood under her tutelage without *any* skill or knowledge. I promise, my profligate image is well-curated—much enjoyed, but wholly intentional," he said with a smile.

The gentlewitch turned her attention to Fintan. "You cannot answer questions or provide information regarding the whereabouts of the viscount, can you?"

Fintan gave a morose shake of his head, pale hair streaming into his face. "Not while I remain here."

He winced saying the words, but Roland had a sense perhaps the man was working around the *geas*. Language was always important to the fae, and especially in the wording of their curses. However, from what he remembered, there was almost always a way through them, somehow.

"And if you were not here?" Liege Rookwood asked.

Tears streaked down Fintan's face, his shoulders quaking.

It wasn't precisely an answer, but it was fairly clear to him that the gentlewitch had some kind of plan, or partial solution, to their most pressing problem.

Basil came blustering in through the threshold, cloak askew, looking far too handsome for the current situation. None of them could afford to be so terribly distracted by his fierce eyes and candlelit profile. "My liege. There is a situation."

"A few, it appears," said Roland, gesturing to the gentlewitch's glowing ring and the viscount's sartorial leavings. "Unless there is something more pressing than the viscount's sudden disappearance?"

Basil gasped, looking from face to face between those gathered. "Perhaps not more pressing, but altogether distressing. There is a pack of werewolves on the grounds. I have no idea how they slipped the wards we put together, but we're making sure everyone leaves as soon as possible. At the moment they are standing guard along the eastern border of the bluebell meadow. Molly has them at bay."

"What do they want?" Roland asked, even though he already knew.

"I think that's fairly obvious," Basil said, venom in his voice.

The werewolf scoffed. How could that wretched Warder be so impudent? Did Roland forget his last tonic? No, he couldn't have. "Are you accusing me of colluding with werewolves?"

"You said it, not me. Wards don't even seem to work around you, and I was wondering why. I think now I have worked it out," Basil continued. "I knew I should have kept a closer eye on you."

"Enough!" the gentlewitch's voice rose up. "Roland is not to blame."

Roland could not help his smug smile.

Before he could say more, however, the gentlewitch was back at her commands: "Basil, get every last person who isn't already being loaded into their carriage locked up in the house. No one is to come in or out."

Again, Roland shivered with the impact of her voice upon him, her command. He really disliked that sensation. And he didn't know what that implied about his relationship to gentlewitches in general.

"What about Silas?" Roland asked. "He could be out there—with the wolves."

"Wherever he is, Fintan is the key. And I can't get Fintan to talk until we are somewhere else," said the gentlewitch.

"I don't see what that—" Roland attempted.

"Will you stop speaking for *one confounded moment*, Roland?" Liege Rookwood said. "I need *you* to make sure Poppy is safe, and to tell her I'm terribly sorry." She paused, as if hesitating. Then added: "Again."

She withdrew a small, glowing object from her pocket— some sort of orb that was, perhaps, part of her witch's chatelaine—and then, before Roland could return another scathing riposte, she and Fintan were gone.

Their vanishing was not like the vampire sort, which included a black, shimmering mist, and the smell of dead roses. Instead, it was as if the red glow of her ring enveloped them both, burning like a cinder from top to bottom in the blink of an eye. "Never seen her do that before," Basil said, going over to where she had been standing to examine the ground. He drew his finger though the stone, bringing it to his nose. "Brimstone."

POPPY ARRIVED ON the balcony just as Edith vanished into a pillar of crimson, glowing light, and was gone. Viola was not there, either. And where was the viscount?

She was prepared to start demanding details from everyone remaining behind—thus far only Roland and Basil, who were looking at one another with barely simmering rage—when a sound rose up through the summer evening that set her skin to shivering.

Howling, high and mournful, eerie and almost human.

"You said they were keeping to the borders!" Roland shouted at Basil, in a most unnecessarily rude manner.

"I said Molly was. And she's just one person, you fool," Basil snapped back.

"Where has Edith gone to?" Poppy asked, searching the darkness for answers.

The howling rose up again, closer now.

"Get inside, Poppy," Basil said. She did not like the way he was addressing her, as if she was simply a wandering houseguest and not someone who had known him since their childhood. And certainly not a woman who had stared down the Boagane and lived.

"Where has Edith gone?" she demanded again.

"I think you know where she went," Basil said. "She had the celestial orb with her. She took Fintan."

"No. That can't be." Edith had promised. Despair sank its tines into Poppy's heart yet again. "Where is the viscount?"

"We don't know," Roland said woefully. "And for once in my life, I wish we had vampires with us, but they're gone, too. There has been altogether far too much appearing and disappearing this evening, thank you very much. Typically, such exits and entrances coincide with far better food and a considerably more extensive mix of alcohols."

Poppy might have been standing alongside Roland and Basil, but she felt the chasm of loneliness open up before her with alarming clarity. Viola had left her—had come to the ball and danced with the viscount and then *left her*—and then Edith had done the same. Within moments of each other.

Even their mother and Heath had left, over an hour ago, both despondent that Viola hadn't yet appeared. Poppy kept telling her sister that her family needed her, loved her, and wouldn't judge her for what she'd become. It didn't matter that she was a vampire.

But all those words were wasted. No matter how hard Poppy tried, she was never going to get Viola back. And she was never going to get Edith to stop breaking her promises. Because there was one thing Edith loved above Poppy, and it was her ambition.

Roland must have seen her expression, for in a moment he was at her side, putting his arm around her shoulder. "If it helps, Liege Rookwood did send her apologies."

"She said she was sorry, then added, 'again,'" Basil amended with a wince, his tone softening. "Clearly, she is going to have to face your ire sooner rather than later."

The dissonance of her anger and love for Edith made Poppy's head buzz. The feeling was overwhelming, embarrassing, and entirely unhelpful just at the moment. And worse, even, allowing herself to wallow in such emotion might result in terrible consequences for Netherford Hall itself, as it had a habit of reacting to her emotions.

She took a deep, measured breath, pushing away the need to shout and cry, and welcomed Roland's warm presence beside her.

"What are we going to do about the wolves?" Basil asked.

"Run away?" Roland offered, pathetically.

Basil made a strangled noise and balled his hands into fists. "You damned coward. What is the point of being a werewolf if you can't even help protect other people from them? I truly have no idea why Silas has bothered with you this long."

Poppy gasped at the Warder's most shocking language. Roland was not exactly a gentleman, but he certainly did outrank Basil.

Letting go of Poppy, Roland stalked over to Basil. He was only a few inches shorter than the Warder, but somehow Basil seemed miles taller, with his rigid poise.

"I am *not* a werewolf. I was poisoned with this affliction, not born to it," Roland snapped. "There is a marked difference. I will not allow myself to stoop to their levels of depravity so long as I am able."

She had to believe Edith didn't know about the werewolves before she'd vanished into the *liminalis*. Surely, she would never have put Poppy in harm's way intentionally. Even if she'd been so distant all night, shaking hands with people she'd never paid attention to before on the excuse of some fae-assigned bargain.

But perhaps there was no bargain. Perhaps it was all for her Parliamentary aspirations. Poppy hated feeling so naïve.

She tried to stop the argument, if only to wrest her mind from the ugly thoughts that plagued her. "Will you both stop it?" she asked, pushing them both back from one another with a firm palm to each of their chests.

"It isn't my fault he's so ill-informed," Basil said, throwing up his hands. "Clearly, everyone in his life has danced so delicately around the truth, sparing him whatever they could, that he's never realised it."

"What are you on about, Basil?" Roland sneered. "What would a Warder possibly know about my circumstance?"

"Plenty!" Basil shouted, his eyes blazing in anger. "Werewolves aren't *made*, you simpleton. They're *born*. Always. Lycanthropy isn't like vampirism. One can only be a werewolf if either of one's parents are. So, in plain terms, your mother tupped a werewolf, *et voila*!"

"Basil!" Poppy could scarcely believe he'd gone and done it. "You promised!"

It was the wrong thing to say. Roland stood still, his hair picked up in the gentle, warm wind, blinking rapidly. When his eyes met hers, hurt and blame in their expression, she felt the sting of it on her very soul. She had just revealed that they'd all known the truth.

"You knew?" Roland asked her. "How long?"

"Edith told me. She discussed it with Basil, and we agreed that, given everything, it would not make sense to add to your already weighty challenges," Poppy said.

"My mother would never have lied to me," Roland said, his voice trembling. "She—why would she? Why would everyone?"

"Perhaps she hoped she could find a cure, that keeping you innocent of the situation might offer you a hint of freedom from it," Poppy offered. "But we believe that's why the pack is pursuing you, Roland. Not because they turned you, but because they've always had a claim to you."

The wolves' cries were so much closer now. Poppy tore her gaze from Roland and out to the gardens below them. Just near the edge of where the light reached, she could see the hedges trembling as an unseen form made its way toward them.

"They shouldn't be here," Basil said, pacing back and forth along the balustrade. "I cannot conceive how they would have managed their way through the wards."

"Unless they didn't come in through the wards at all," came a voice from behind them.

Petronilla Rookwood-Nourse approached them, Auden Garcliffe by her side. She looked exhausted, as if she might have been crying. Poppy could not make sense of much of what had occurred in the last hour, but Petronilla did not seem like any kind of true victor in the fight for the viscount's hand.

"What do you mean?" Poppy asked. "Silas... He's gone."

"I know," Petronilla said, her voice laced with a longing sorrow Poppy certainly understood. "I felt it as soon as he left. There was a shiver of power—subtle and strange—that grabbed my attention, but I was so engulfed in the congratulatory choir inside I could not make it here."

"This is all madness," Roland said. "Silas wouldn't just wander off. Werewolves shouldn't just appear without alerting wards."

"No," Petronilla said, holding out her hand. On it was Silas's ring, a stunning garnet signet set in pale gold. "I didn't realise it until I put it on, but this ring is no common piece of jewellery. It is not unlike witch silver, in that it protects its wearer from powers—but in this case, it is the power of Faerie, not of other preternaturals."

At last, it made sense. Poppy fell backward a step, and Auden was there to catch her gently, as the realisation struck her.

Silas Drake was a fae foundling child. And he had been claimed. Edith had meant to find him, not knowing which young man he might be—she must have discovered the truth, and Fintan must have been connected with it all, somehow.

"Come out, come out, de Grateloup," came a sultry voice below them. "We can see you. We can smell you. It's time to come home."

Poppy remembered that voice from before, when their coach had been attacked. Glancing over the balustrade, she watched as a pale she-wolf emerged from the hedges, shaking her pelt. Her eyes shone blue, luminous and strange. Behind her, other pairs of eyes blinked into visibility.

Somehow, she knew they were hungry.

BRINGING SOMEONE ELSE into the *liminalis* was a calculated risk. If they were mortal, for instance, the shift might break them entirely, if not in mind, then in body. Edith had acted on impulse, but she needed information and fast. For everyone's sakes.

Silas was the changeling heir; she was quite certain of it. And Fintan was not a simple valet. She had known that since first meeting him, and she could not let it go. When she'd done some cursory research into the archives about Burkley and the Drakes, someone named Fintan had been in their employ for almost thirty years—at the time of his hiring, he was listed as forty years old. He did not look a day over forty now.

The *liminalis* trembled around them, the cool, welcoming blackness of the in-between stealing over their skin.

Edith held out the celestial orb and it illuminated, incandescent green, showering Fintan's face in light.

There it was. His true face.

Unmistakably, he looked like Fintan. Except the angles were all sharper: the edges of his eyes, the points of his teeth, the tops of his ears—and the tips of his silver horns. He was not the same kind of fae as Tailte, but certainly related.

"This is the *liminalis*," Edith said to Fintan, trying to calm him with a steady voice. "It is the place between Faerie and the mortal world, created—I now believe—unintentionally, when they were split."

Fintan nodded, pressing a hand—which was now delicately clawed—to his chest. "You guessed right, witchling. The *geas* does not plague me now." He glanced around, eyes flashing violet. "It smells strange here."

"Like old books and fresh water," Edith agreed. "I can tell you many details, but I am afraid time is not our ally this night. The celestial orb here helps me keep track, but we must be swift. Tell me then, is Silas Drake a changeling?"

"Of course he is," Fintan said, with a laugh.

"And you've been his protector."

"In a sense. More like his guardian. I am an *ellyll;* we are the courtiers of the Faerie Courts, and I serve Queen Tailte."

Queen Tailte. She should have guessed. "So Tailte is his real mother—not the woman that raised him. And his father?" If he wasn't truly the Viscount St. Albans, that might complicate things.

"Silas is truly a St. Albans, but Tailte is his mother, yes."

"But if the way to Faerie was closed, I don't understand how... something like that... could have happened." Edith felt her face flush, even as she tried to word her phrasing delicately.

Fintan's smile was only slightly condescending. "There is much you do not know, witchling. For there are days when the sun and the stars align, and mortals and fae can gather. That is when the most powerful bargains are made. That is when Silas was conceived."

"You seem to know so much, and yet you could not protect Silas just now."

"No. Not with all the witchling wards."

"But wards protect us," Edith said, trying to understand. The celestial orb thrummed—a warning. A half hour had already passed in the mortal lands.

Fintan frowned, as if he were disappointed in her answer. "They may help alert you and protect witchlings from each other. But when it comes to fae creatures, it can confound us. It made it more difficult for me to find Silas. His ring is intended to work as a beacon, but he gave it away to that fire witch, and they took him."

"Who took him, then?"

"Someone who seeks revenge against Queen Tailte, who was the force between the separation of our worlds."

"And they are in the mortal lands?"

"When our worlds were sundered from one another, some

of the fae were left behind. Some were put here on purpose; some were left cursed."

"Vampires, you mean."

"One among them was greater."

Edith gasped, remembering Tailte's lessons. "Moritasgus."

"Yes. King of the Vampires and eldest among them—a different being altogether, a pure fae turned vampire. He has lived for hundreds of years, waiting for when he could seek revenge against Tailte. He only needed leverage. And he has been feeding, so they tell us, upon tainted blood, growing stronger and madder by the day," Fintan shivered, looking down at his hands.

"The potion. *Azothine* ."

"Yes. If the rumours are true, he has been feeding his werewolves the same,"

"No wonder they have been so brazen," Edith said. "You gave up everything to protect Silas, but your power was limited."

"Yes. As a single act of power, Tailte tied my soul to the child's so I could protect him, but the *geas* would always prevent me from sharing the truth—for his protection. Her decision to help Silas's father was forbidden and would cost her. She did not anticipate what loving a child might do to her."

"Fae romances make ours look trifling," Edith said. "But it seems poor Silas is the true victim in all of this. How did Moritasgus find Silas now?"

"A good question. One I think I understand, though. I saw correspondence between Ophelia Byrne and a man named 'Maurice' in Bath. An old vampire. She told him about Viola, and the curious fact of her feeding upon the viscount and not killing him."

"Feeding? Oh, stars." Edith hardly knew what to think. What Poppy would say!

"Silas should have died when Viola fed from him—and without killing him, Viola should have turned revenant. The only reason she did not was because he is fae. When she took his blood, Maurice must have learned of his existence, as he is connected to them all."

It made sense, at last. "Poor Viola. Poor Silas. My heart breaks for them, Fintan. But why now? Why didn't Moritasgus—Maurice—get Silas sooner?"

"For centuries, Moritasgus was unable to travel, spending his time in his sprawling castle in Bath. He was injured gravely, his powers diminished, in a fight with Tailte; but I believe he has been using the werewolves to somehow fuel his domination. Feeding off them, likely. The pub portals have slowly chipped away at the line between Faerie and this realm, and he wants to return—without Virginia Cawley, that is a possibility. The *azothine* gives him, and his followers, truly staggering abilities, so they can kill their way through any circumstances; the pains of wards no longer bite so sharp, on their way through to Faerie."

"How horrid," Edith said. She wished, not for the first or last time, that Virginia Cawley had kept far less to herself.

Queen Tailte was manipulating Edith to get her son to safety and prevent Maurice from returning to Faerie. The High Witch might have known—had Tailte tried to convince her the way she had with Edith?

"It gets worse, I'm afraid. They—the werewolves and Maurice—have a common purpose: eradicating as many witches as possible. They are not unlike the Grey Moon, and have worked with them to this end."

"But why is that the case?"

"Navia the first, Rosmerta's daughter with a mortal man, is the progenitor of your ilk, and it was she who was queen of the werewolves. He blames her line for all his woes."

Edith's head spun with the implications of all Fintan revealed. "Navia. Is she still alive?"

"No, she died ages ago. But—"

The celestial orb flickered and guttered. Time to move, now. Every moment here put them at risk. As always, though, the peace of the *liminalis* made leaving so much more difficult.

"We have to go, Fintan. Take my hand."

With a great whoosh of air and heat on her face, Edith pulled Fintan back through the *liminalis* and back to Burkley House. The transition was nauseating, and she fell to her knees upon the balcony, shouting in pain. Fintan lost his footing entirely, weakened by the travel, and curled into a ball by her.

Why did it smell of fire?

THE HALLS OF Howarth Castle predated Burkley House by some four hundred years. Its oldest corridors were built in the thirteenth century by the now-extinct Lark family. Although Laertes could not recall the exact details, rumour was that their eldest daughter had fallen in love with a vampire. After a long and sordid affair, some general affront befell the fellow and eventually, everyone lay dead or undead.

The Byrnes took control of the house a century before, having left the streets of Edinburgh in search of a more refined getaway to winter in. Ophelia decided Kent would be the ideal place to settle given the proximity to London and the fact that nothing of true note ever seemed to happen there.

Their goal was assimilation. What a dream it was, too. They established voluntary thralls, attended operas and ballets, amassed a remarkable fortune, and nearly married into a well-to-do family once or twice. Over the decades, they'd seen people come and go in Netherford and the surrounds, involved themselves in the drollery of day-to-day living, and eventually felt, strangely, at home.

Now, as Laertes watched Viola at the window of her tower room, he wondered if all their work had been in vain. She hadn't spoken since they'd arrived. Nor had she tried to discourage Laertes and his sister from staying.

No amount of rumination could wrest him from the terrible truth of it all. He was going to lose Viola. She was going to die a true death at his hands. Well, Ophelia's hands. She always was the better killer of the two of them and, ever since this whole spawn business, she'd been the one with a slightly less sentimental attachment to the girl.

Oh, who was he kidding? Ophelia was just as utterly besotted with their spawn as he was; she was simply better at hiding it.

Ophelia sat a few feet away from him, picking at the cuff of her robe. She was slumped in the chair, dishevelled and exhausted. How were they going to manage?

"I suppose we have a few more days," Laertes said, his voice echoing in the high-ceilinged chamber. "I hope you find the room to your liking, Viola. We had some of the staff tidy it up a bit, wishing it might be a solace for you."

Viola remained silent.

"I do feel as if we'd see *something* by now," Ophelia said, voice low. "I don't sense any corruption in her. Just sadness."

"Perhaps the moon will be our final judge," Laertes said.

Ophelia glanced up from her anxious fidgeting. "Two days. Hardly enough time to do anything properly. It's no surprise Viola isn't interested in conversation."

"Love is a cruel and exacting mistress," Laertes said, wishing he could conjure up the viscount for her. Dead or alive. He didn't have a preference; both states had their use. "And, alas, so is familial duty."

THE LACK OF feeling was the worst part of being a vampire. Especially one who was going to be dying shortly. Viola sat before her sires at the other end of their long dining table at Howarth Castle, and wished she could feel anything other than the gulf of absolute emptiness inside of her. She'd eaten from one of the thralls earlier, and it made her feel worse. Sick to her stomach. As if drinking from Silas had ruined her altogether.

And perhaps it had. His blood tasted of life, deep forests, running rivers, and a bouquet of tuberoses just cut from the ground. The thralls were sustenance, that was all.

She could not stop seeing his face in her memories, his expression when she'd told him the lie that broke her heart: that she did not love him.

Ophelia had changed her gown three times before supper, finally settling on black taffeta with a green Spenser jacket. In the glow from the candelabra, she looked luminous, but her eyes were haunted despite the powder and her elaborate coiffure. They all knew she'd not been sleeping at all, instead trying to find some kind of solution to their impending problem.

Laertes looked miserable.

"You will both have to figure out what to do with yourselves once I'm gone," Viola said, not being able to manage one more minute of uncomfortable silence. "You lived without me for hundreds of years; you should be able to do so again."

Neither seemed to know what to say to that. One of the thralls, a surprisingly vivacious woman named Carmina— most of the thralls were named after shades of red—cleared her throat.

Licking his lips, Laertes sighed miserably. "You see, my darling, therein lies the problem. We'd never had a... a child before. *Spawn* seems too ugly of a word for what we feel for you. Perhaps it is biology, or perhaps a function of magic, but it has added a depth of love to our existence I do not think either of us were prepared for. Now we have had it, had *you*, going back to our lives as before seems rather perverse."

Ophelia was weeping, a rare and strange thing. Carmina was there immediately, presenting her with a scarlet handkerchief. "I wish we were crueller parents to you, Viola. We would insist you kill the viscount. For what use is a single man in our lifetimes? We have seen his line grow, diminish, and come back again. And for what? 'Tis folly to throw in with mortals, and yet we understand. We could never ask this of you, and I do not think you could do it, anyway."

"No, I could not." She reached into her pockets and procured the letters she'd been writing since the day before. She laid them on the table before her and pushed them gently toward Laertes. "I've made my peace. What I can salvage of it, I suppose. The longest one is for Poppy, of course. Then to Mama and Papa. I've written you both, as well, but I'd ask you not read it until..." She swallowed, trying to get the words out without her voice breaking. "Until it's over."

"Of course, of course, darling," Laertes said. "I only wish we could make your last few days more comfortable."

"I feel well. For someone who is shortly going to turn into a terrible monster, well, I hardly feel anything at all. Perhaps that is part of it. Perhaps I will empty myself of emotions entirely until there is nothing left, and what remains will be revenant."

"How vile," Ophelia said. "How utterly monstrous."

They fell into an uncomfortable silence again, the sounds of the castle intruding like errant punctuation.

Another late summer storm was sweeping over the valley, so when the castle beams shuddered and moaned, at first Viola thought it was just the wind. But then came a violent flash of blue-black light, blinding her momentarily.

Lightning? In the middle of the day. Shielding her eyes, she gasped as a pillar of smoke and energy crackled to life at the centre of the immense dining table.

A figure emerged from it, smelling of too-sweet gardenias, unfolding upwards as if growing from the centre.

It was a man in a long, lustrous cloak. He was handsome as men came, with angled cheekbones and slick spidersilk hair tied back in a neat plait. His form was strong, not grown soft like Laertes, the set of his shoulders like a warrior.

"Maurice!" Ophelia cried, rising to her feet. She did not seem at all excited about seeing him, Viola didn't think. Rather, her expression was somewhere between horrified and disgusted.

"My darlings. At last, I am renewed," he said, holding his hand to his chest as if he were a great king returning from a valiant crusade. His voice was resonant, beautiful. Viola had the strange desire to hear him sing. "In no small part due to you. And I come bringing the most joyous news."

Laertes looked even more concerned than his sister. He'd managed to quickly transport himself across the room and now stood in front of Viola, a protective arm across her body.

"You have not been invited," Laertes said with disdain.

"I need no invitation. At least, not any longer," Maurice said, brushing some ash from his jacket and then jumping down to the parquet floor with feline agility. "Do you not see how revived I am? How strong? Ophelia, gaze upon me and tell me you do not feel my power."

Ophelia gave Laertes and Viola a sidelong glance, then she straightened her posture and strode toward the vampire they called Maurice.

She moved with grace and beauty, her gestures fluid, as she examined the uninvited guest. "I feel your power. It is a strange thing. You've not been able to leave your home in centuries, Maurice. Something has changed, but I cannot tell what."

"Oh, everything has changed, my child. My shackles have been cast off. At last, I have all we need. I'd meant to come sooner, but we had to make arrangements. You will be so excited to hear what I have to say," Maurice said.

With a sharp turn of his head, Maurice took stock of Viola, his pale eyes glittering. Were other vampires this *angled?* His ears were pointed far more than Ophelia and Laertes', and his teeth were bordering on feral—not only his canines were sharp, but a few at the bottom were as well. Viola knew for certain that was not the case with her.

"And there she is. Viola Brightwell. Such an apt name, for you will bring light again to us," Maurice said. "In blood and in bond, it is time again for us to claim our due."

"Get out, Maurice," Laertes said, his cheeks flushing in rage. "You are unwelcome here."

Maurice scoffed. "I can go wherever I want now. That is the marvellous thing about this whole business. And to think, this whole time, the key to my freedom was in Netherford. Netherford!"

"Whatever plans you have, we will hear them at a later date," Ophelia said, taking a step closer to Maurice. "I will not ask you again."

"You know that tone is unacceptable. I'll tell you what. I will forgive you as soon as you all give me your obeisance. Bow, Ophelia. I know you do love that view," Maurice said.

"I will do no such thing," Ophelia said.

"Very well. We will begin with Viola. Come now, Miss Brightwell, show your sires how you treat your betters," the vampire lord crooned.

Perhaps, when she was mortal, she might have bowed to this man, acted as if she were less than he. But she was going to die a vampire, soon, and his presence made her uneasy, mistrusting, even if his demeanour was all gentility and charm. She could feel Laertes's anxiety and Ophelia's disgust, their emotions wafting over to her unbidden.

"You were not invited," Viola said tersely. "I may have only been a vampire for a short time, but I do know there are rules of decorum one must abide by. And to come into a house, fellow vampire or not, uninvited, is a dire insult. I will not bow before you or any man."

This made Maurice sneer. "Petulant little thing," he said, walking around Viola in a circle. She could feel his oily gaze on her. "Very well. I was hoping I wouldn't have to resort to an ostentatious display of power. But here we are."

Then Viola felt another strange sensation, this one highly unwelcome. The air thickened around her, and her breathing became curiously strained. That too-sweet scent of gardenias intensified, and she coughed, shuddering as Maurice's power continued to wash over her, over the table, over the room, over her sires.

"Ophelia, fetch me a thrall," Maurice said, waving his hand dismissively in her direction. "Now."

Viola felt the bolt of Maurice's magic crackle across the room and Ophelia went stiff as iron for a moment, before all connection with her ceased. All the music of her, the constant strain Viola had come to love and cherish, went dead.

Ophelia's eyes glazed, then flashed that same blue-black light Maurice's entrance had generated. And then she walked, without argument, toward Carmina. The thrall backed away, no longer the dimpled, smiling woman she had been moments before.

"Pitiful," Laertes said, scurrying between Ophelia and Carmina. "Come now, sister, you mustn't..."

His voice trailed off just as Maurice turned his attention to him. The ancient vampire quirked an impatient eyebrow and then cast another bolt of that profane magic, piercing Laertes in the chest. He twirled and fell unmoving to the ground, moaning. Then he reached into his pocket and took a sip from a little blue bottle, smacking his lips afterward.

Viola gasped but held herself back, the pain of losing her connection to Laertes sending daggers into her stomach.

She was alone, now. Truly.

Maurice sighed in indignation, shaking his head. "I honestly didn't think he'd be the harder one to subdue, but I suppose even the most pitiful vampires can surprise you now and again. Makes the centuries a little more tolerable, I say."

Ophelia proceeded toward Maurice, Carmina in tow, unseeing eyes cold and void of her acerbic and charming personality.

"Now, Viola, as I was saying," Maurice said, grasping Carmina by the arm and pulling her toward him. Her whole body jerked with the reaction, fear making her teeth chatter. "Or *trying* to say, before you so rudely spoke to me. You, my darling, have set in motion a most delightful chain of events leading me to your very doorstep this evening with a gift. Two gifts, in fact."

Viola stood very still, sweat beading on her forehead as she strained against Maurice's magic. She tried to connect her mind to her sires', but she might as well have been trying to hear the beat of a dead heart. Their powers, though formidable, were entirely eclipsed by this dread vampire's.

"I know better than to make a deal with someone willing to exert such power to control others," Viola said.

Maurice smirked, snapping Carmina toward him and sinking his teeth into her neck. The woman's face contorted in pain—no, agony—and something worse: betrayal. Even in her short time at Howarth Castle, she understood the thralls were here of their own volition. Laertes and Ophelia did not use the Allure on their thralls, unless requested; this was some complicated intimate circumstance Viola did not want to discuss.

The sounds Maurice was making made Viola feel ill, something between moaning and growling. Carmina was growing paler by the moment, her eyes beseeching Viola.

Maurice's magic was so strong, so heavy. What little Viola had learned about being a vampire was mostly limited to general care and feeding, nothing about her preternatural abilities. She'd wanted to repress that part of her, to avoid it. *When you truly accept who you are, you will gain your wings. Like a perfect angel of the night*, Laertes had told her.

But faced, now, with the prospect of Maurice draining this woman of her life right before her eyes, what point was there in avoiding it? Her vampire strength had given her time with Silas, had helped her stand up against the dowager viscountess.

She may have lived a woman, but she was willing to die a vampire.

A calm, shivering sensation trickled down her back and Viola moved, digging down into that well of power she'd been avoiding for months. Her sight shifted, blossoms of power erupting in her vision in colours beyond human perception. She gasped, thrilled, as she began to understand what she saw. It was magic: hers, Maurice's, and the residue of her sires'. It took a moment, figuring out how to move through Maurice's power, but she saw the pattern of it, like heat rising from the rocks at the horizon.

She thought of Silas, what he would think of her, allowing Carmina's senseless death. And thinking of him kindled something in her blood. A feeling like heroism.

In a flash, she was halfway across the room, Carmina in her arms—she'd barely had time to think of what she was going to do, and it was done.

"Shh," Viola said to Carmina. "You'll be fine. Just take deep breaths." Wetting her finger, Viola healed the puncture wounds at the thrall's neck, pushing back on a lingering, monstrous desire to finish the deed entirely.

"Empathy? How terribly banal," Maurice said as he strode toward them both. He wiped his bloody lips on his hand and then licked what remained there with relish. "We'll pull that out of you soon enough."

"Soon enough, I will be dead, so what does it matter?" Viola said, helping Carmina to stand. She turned to her, whispering: "Run, Carmina. Secure what thralls you can."

Trembling, barely steady on her feet, Carmina staggered out of the dining hall, leaving Viola alone with Maurice. Laertes still stirred now and again, moaning as if in a terrible nightmare; Ophelia stood still as stone, awaiting Maurice's next command.

She might as well die, now, fighting for her sires, for the thralls here. It was better, she thought, than dying at their hand.

Maurice laughed; a low, cruel noise that ended in a purr that made Viola's own power shiver. "Oh, the *dying*. Yes, I may have exaggerated a bit when it came to all of that."

"Exaggerated?" Viola brushed the dust from her gown and squared her shoulders. "It is perilously difficult to exaggerate beyond death."

"Well," Maurice drawled, twirling his finger in the air in a spiral, "I needed them to *think* you were dying." He indicated the Byrnes. "Ophelia is surprisingly industrious with her research; and indeed, the books I pointed to her would have supported the thesis I shared: had you consumed the blood of a mortal thrall and not taken their lives, you'd have become a revenant."

"But I did," Viola insisted. "I took plenty of his blood."

"After a fashion, but not in truth. Silas Drake is *not* a mortal."

Viola lost her grasp on words, language. She merely stared at Maurice.

"Turning revenant is a swift affair. The sickness falls upon a vampire almost immediately, and the desire to murder the poor mortal is a bone-deep impulse. There have only been a half dozen instances of a vampire managing to *not* kill their first thrall that I have documented, and those were typically killed by someone else in a time of war or conflict."

"I don't understand," Viola said, her mind a dizzying cacophony of emotion and reason. "Why would you lie to us?"

"I didn't lie. I omitted details to my benefit. If you live to be as old as I am, vicious darling, you will find you must carefully dole out information to those you must collaborate with."

"No one was collaborating with you. Ophelia was trying to save my life."

"Indeed. And look: she has. Shame she can't see it right now, or understand—but you will not die any time soon. Nor will you turn revenant. You've taken an unusual path, and in the meantime, given me the very thing I've been waiting for. You and the witches. It's too much, really," Maurice said, wiping a false tear. "And then the werewolves, falling right into place, giving me access to everything I needed to bolster my strength. The High Witch's blood—now *that* was a treat. Never mind that I've always fancied Howarth Castle, so you and I will now begin our life here."

"You took the High Witch," Viola accused.

"No. But I had access to her. You will understand all in due time, of course. I am willing to wait."

Viola swallowed on a very dry throat. "If Silas is not a mortal—what is he? How did he help you?"

"Oh, for that story you'll have to sit and enjoy more dinner with me. I am still quite famished."

CHAPTER SIXTEEN
THE FLOWERS FADE,
BUT ALL THE THORNS REMAIN

SILAS AWOKE TO the cloying smokiness of incense burning his nose, and cold stone biting into his face. His whole body felt at once too loose and too tight, as if he'd been thrown about and put back together in short order without concern for his person. The muscles all along the left side of his body ached, especially around his ribs, but he could not recall the cause of his injury.

One moment, he had been spiralling down narrow corridors of melancholy, contemplating his heartbreak upon the balcony outside the great hall at Burkley House, and suddenly he was in what could only be described as a medieval dungeon. A dungeon, perhaps, attached to an old house of worship, given the pervasive scent.

Blinking, eyes itching, he tried to bring his environment into clearer focus. Roughhewn stone met iron bars, and a sickly yellow light wavered in the distance. Echoes of dripping water made him shiver, and he looked around for a brief hint of comfort: a blanket, a cot, a jacket. He shouldn't have taken off his clothing earlier.

Someone had provided him with a rusty bucket for the necessities, but there was no food or water.

Viola. Brimstone! She had rejected him with swift, merciless precision. Had he dreamed her, then? No, if he closed his eyes, he could still feel the pressure of her delicate body in his arms, see the deep longing behind the silver mask. More than anything, he could feel the power of her, that utterly addictive mix of sensuality, wit, and vampiric charm.

By the Night Queen, he'd told Fintan to announce his engagement to Petronilla Rookwood-Nourse.

And now he'd been kidnapped. Well and truly.

The click of measured footfalls—booted, to be certain—drew his attention away from his self-flagellation. His heart began pounding in earnest, his muscles tightening in anticipation of a fight or, perhaps, an escape. Though there was little chance either would end well. He was no Sybille Voltairis.

A tall woman dressed in leather trousers emerged from the gloom, her features nearly indistinguishable as she approached. She certainly had the heroic look.

"So, the slumbering prince awakens," she said. Her voice had a smoky, velvety quality to it. If it was not for her mocking tone, Silas might have even liked it.

"No prince, I assure you. Merely a most confused viscount," Silas said. "And clearly in less-than-ideal lodgings, at the moment. May I inquire as to the nature of my offence?"

The woman tilted her head, a long, haphazard braid slipping out of her silhouette before swinging back behind her with the motion. The edges of her mouth were a sickly, mossy verdigris. "Your offence is, sadly, your mere existence. For that part, I cannot fault you. I would almost pity you if not for your politics."

Politics? Silas tried not to react to those words, his mind working to make whatever connections he could. He had the utterly deranged thought that perhaps he had fallen into madness, his mind trapping him in one of his adventure stories. For this was the sort of thing Sibylle often encountered. Often, however, those jailers were dim-witted and easily tricked by their wily charge. This woman did not seem dim in any sense.

"I've been rather unmoored in the political sphere for some time," Silas said, diplomatically as he could. "Perhaps you have me confused for my father who, indeed, was most dramatic in his political affiliations."

She said nothing in reply, but tossed a small loaf of bread into the cell. "Here. Eat. You'll need your strength for later."

"Mysteries upon more mysteries," Silas said, reaching for the bread. It was miles beyond stale, and he regretted not eating much at the ball. "Do you have a name? I'm afraid I've been too long among courteous folk, and it seems odd to accept food from someone I do not know how to address."

"Verenata," the woman said.

"An intriguing name," Silas observed. The bread was so hard he couldn't get his teeth through it. He would have to wait to gnaw it to pulp when she was gone. "Tell me, Verenata, do I have you to thank for these accommodations, or is something else at work?"

Verenata shifted, her boots creaking as she did so. "I suppose it's no harm telling you that no, I am not responsible for your *accommodations*. The master is upstairs, but the rest of us are keeping guard. I picked the short straw, so I brought you dinner."

"My thanks." Silas held up the bread. He did not wish to anger this woman. "And your master. Does he have plans for me?"

Shrugging, Verenata leaned against the bars, the light catching her eyes for just a moment. In that flash, Silas understood what she was: a werewolf. There were few tells about Roland if you didn't know him well enough—but just like a wolf, his eyes reflected light. Verenata's were green, though, where his cousin's were amber.

"He has plans for a lot of things," Verenata said.

"Is the rest of the pack involved?" asked Silas. "Werewolves typically roam about in groups, if I'm not mistaken."

"Observant." Verenata took a few steps away, peering down the smoky corridor. "Not at present. So far, you've proven far less of a challenge than we expected."

That was rude. Hero he was not, but there was no need to be so callous about it.

"Then I look forward to meeting your master and fellows, and hopefully proving I am not worth all this trouble," he offered. Though he also doubted that. Someone had gone to a tremendous amount of trouble to get him here.

Apparently, he was less than convincing, for Verenata simply walked back where she had come from.

It took an offensively long time to get the bread soft enough to chew, and with no method of dampening it other than his own parched mouth, Silas's lips were sore all over when he was done. And he was still hungry.

Above him, the ceiling trembled. It made his skin crawl. Where was he? How did he have no knowledge of getting here? Why on earth did they want him? And how had they gotten through the wards in the first place?

He had the sudden, terrible thought that his guests might have been mistreated in some way. And his aunt… She was a fragile old woman, despite her iron will and irascibility.

No, he had to believe that Liege Edith and Roland, the Hodes and the rest, had to be keeping them all safe.

A cold breeze blew into his cell, snapping him to attention. He must have fallen asleep, somehow, for it was brighter now and his neck ached from the awkward angle he'd adopted.

Silas spied windows across from him, the view almost

entirely obscured by vegetation. He thought he saw movement along the windowsill, but then his attention was drawn elsewhere.

It was a feeling, deep in his chest, as if the pressure of the place had shifted. His ears filled for a moment, began ringing, and he gritted his teeth against the sudden pain.

Then it was over.

Feeling a soft, wet sensation where his hands met the stone, Silas glanced down to see a circle of mushrooms had grown around him. They were crystal blue in colour, their gills so delicate they looked spun from lace. Tiny motes of shimmering spores gently rained down from them, illuminating the ground and giving him more light to see by.

His head felt gauzy, his eyelids a little heavy, as if he'd quaffed a snifter of brandy too quickly. Yet, through that curious sensation, he felt a sudden, welcome sense of clarity. The room itself came into far more focus, and his whole body felt renewed, as if that short sleep had somehow taken years of weariness from his soul.

Eat.

The voice came from nowhere and everywhere at once. Staggering to his feet, Silas carefully avoided the circle of mushrooms, looking to see if someone had called his name. The moment he stepped out of the circle, all the clarity he'd just experienced vanished.

With a slightly deranged laugh, Silas walked again into the circle of mushrooms.

Eat. You do not have much time.

That voice. He *knew* that voice. How did he know? The tone, deeply feminine and accented with a slight lilt, brought tears to his eyes.

"I am quite hungry, but they look too beautiful to eat," Silas said softly, not expecting a response.

They will nourish you and protect you where I cannot.

He had heard these words before! Stars, was it in a dream? Overcome with an emotion he could not place, tears coursed down his cheeks and, falling to his knees, Silas reached a trembling hand to one of the smaller mushrooms.

One thing was certain: he could use all the protection he could get. And this sensation, this voice, made him feel as loved and as safe as anything ever had in his life.

The sound of scraping iron screeching down the corridor broke the last of his resolve. With one smooth motion, summoning all the impulse he could and suppressing his doubts, he snapped off the mushroom and shoved it into his mouth.

Immediately, his hunger pangs stopped. The clarity sharpened; his muscles shivered, and icy tendrils slipped over his skin. It was euphoric, joyous, and again, familiar. Silas chuckled as the mushrooms shrank around him, but their effect remained. The feeling was like coming home, *truly* home, his face warm as if he had luxuriated in the sunshine for hours and tumbled through the grass as he once did in childhood.

The mushroom circle vanished at his feet, leaving not even a hint of the shimmering spores.

The door slammed shut at the end of the corridor, and Silas, for the first time in this place, did not feel afraid.

Not until he realised who was before him.

Laertes Byrne, his eyes transformed to blue-black voids, stared at him through the bars. The vampire's teeth were fully elongated, something Silas had never seen before, and the deathless power in him was overwhelming.

The voice that came from Mr. Byrne, however, was not his at all. Gone was the brogue and musicality; gone the snobbish air. Now, his voice was resonant, deep, and ancient, bereft of any hint of warmth.

"So, we meet at last. I apologise for the unusual

accommodations, but given the state of your affairs, it was best to be careful."

"Who am I addressing?" Silas asked. "Though you take the form of a friend, I do not think that is the case."

Laertes twitched, as if fighting the control of whatever spirit kept him in these strange throes. But again, the voice was not his. "*You have remained hidden from me these long years, and though I nearly pity you for your place in all this, you must know it isn't personal.*"

"You didn't answer my question," Silas said.

"*I have no desire to. Ultimately, you are as inconsequential to me as a fly upon the back of a great charger. A means to an end.*"

"Am I a house fly or a gadfly, though?"

"*Clever. In another time, perhaps, we might have worked together. But it is high time I left this place, and your blood is my salvation. A great lure.*"

"If Laertes is here, where is Viola? The last I saw, they were together."

Laertes shivered again. This time, Silas noticed the vampire's eyes guttered for a moment, returning again to the soulful expression he was familiar with. Then it was gone again. "*Yes, Viola. I thought long and hard about how best to do you in, viscount. And though I am merciless in some ways, I did decide to provide you a sweet exit from this mortal realm. You will see her presently. And it is she who will be the engine of your doom.*"

THE WEREWOLVES WERE crawling up the vines, making steady progress toward the balcony. Poppy tried to take measured breaths, to steady herself, but the threat of death—painful and lingering—made her blood run cold. Unlike most of those gathered here, she had no natural defences. If they'd been at Netherford Hall, she could use the house to her benefit, but in this marble mansion her powers were muted.

The flames had kept the werewolves at bay for a while, but they were relentless. Petronilla was a marvellously powerful gentlewitch, but sustaining a wall of fire that long was not only exhausting but impractical.

And Edith had abandoned her—all of them—yet again.

Basil drew Poppy closer, sweat dripping off the side of his face from the heat. "We will hold out for a little longer. I must believe Edith will be here soon."

They all started when someone burst forth from the doors again. Poppy was certain it had to be Edith, and her heart flipped in her chest. But it was not Edith: it was Molly Hode.

The Warder looked as if she had waded through a battlefield, her long braids a tangle, blood smeared across her face and her uniform torn right down the middle. Poppy could see Molly's exposed skin and the red, enflamed wound running from her collarbone to her breast. It looked like her stays might have prevented it from being a deadly blow.

"Molly!" Basil was by her side in a flash, but his sister was having none of it.

Molly raised her axes and dropped into a defensive stance before Roland and Poppy. In the glow of the fire, she looked like a demon incarnate, her eyes glittering with rage and pain. Poppy was relieved she was fighting for them, but she also felt completely useless.

Petronilla let out a cry and fell to her knees in exhaustion. The witchfire went out immediately, snuffed of its destructive power. She was muttering apologies, choking back sobs.

But there was no time for despair, not when three werewolves came rushing onto the balcony, leaping with inhuman strength. They all had white streaks down their backs, though their coats were varying hues.

"Roland, this would be a fantastic time for you to decide to embrace your wild side," Basil scolded. He typically fought with a staff, but unfortunately, he had not brought it with him.

Throughout the entire assault, Roland had been even more useless than Poppy, cowering in the corner behind a now charred statue of the High Witch. The irony was not lost on Poppy.

"I am no werewolf," Roland shouted in Basil's direction. "I told you!"

This got the werewolves chuckling. Or whatever term described the noise that slipped between their dagger teeth. This close, they were so much larger than Poppy remembered. From the coach, she'd had speed and distance on her side. Now, seeing the largest pad toward Molly, its head rising to her chin, she had a new appreciation for her companion preparing to fight them.

Edith. *Edith*. Stars and the speckled firmament, she'd better arrive soon, or she was going to come back to a very, very gruesome scene.

"There is our recalcitrant brother," said the werewolf. Once again, Poppy was taken by how human his voice sounded. His accent was akin to her cousin Jack's, who'd been raised most of his life around Bristol. "A great deal of fire and frenzy here, and all we need is Mr. de Grateloup."

"Mr. de Grateloup isn't going anywhere," Poppy asserted, the flame of protective courage kindling in her heart. She'd grown quite fond of the eccentric Frenchman. "At least, not anywhere he doesn't wish to go."

"And what are you going to do to prevent us from taking him, *ma cherie*?" That came from the rust-coloured werewolf behind the one who'd just spoken. He was missing an eye and had scarring webbed across his muzzle. His French accent was the heaviest of the lot.

Basil sighed, drawing up next to his sister. "You'll have to go through us," he said, with less enthusiasm than Poppy had hoped for.

"Do you hear that, Guy?" said the French werewolf. "We're being threatened by Warders. Warders who we've already outsmarted."

"You shouldn't have been able," Molly said, swinging her axe in a perfect arc. She looked ready to smash in any of their teeth if given a chance, even though she looked terrible. "Our wards were beyond complex."

Guy shook his pelt. "Oh, they were at first. I will admit, you had us slightly worried. But your guest—the one in the fancy coach—his Warders disarmed every last one on their way out, mistaking your work for some sort of charm or spell. The hubris of the Warders of St. James is forever an amusement. That, and we are stronger, now, than we have ever been."

Not good. Not good at all.

"So, truly," said the French werewolf, scraping his silver claws across the marble balcony tiles, "we can avoid any further disruption to your evening so long as you send Mr. de Grateloup to us."

"What do you want with me?" Roland half-shrieked. "I've *told* you, I have no desire to partake in your depraved activities. I am altogether uninterested in pack dynamics, transforming under the moon, or gallivanting around murdering innocent people. I much prefer the quiet life of a rake and libertine about town, thank you very much, all while on my own two legs."

Now the French werewolf was standing eerily still, staring directly at Roland. To Poppy's surprise, he did not look particularly malicious. If a werewolf could look thoughtful, he did; his one eye was wide, his tongue lolling.

"That is only because you have never truly tasted freedom," the creature said, his voice low. "You are family, Roland. Your freedom has been taken from you. The gentlewitches, as they so often do, have kept you twisted in to lies—like the lie you tell yourself. You have always been a werewolf. They are not made, they are born. And you were born… as my son."

ROLAND'S FIRST INCLINATION was to be sick upon the marble tiles, but he choked back on his bile and stared the big wolf down with the last shreds of his dignity. Basil had tried to tell him before that werewolves could not be *turned* in the way vampires did; at the time, he was sour at the revelation, but now he was glad he had some sort of preparation. Especially facing down this massive werewolf with one eye.

"Did you frame me for murder in Paris?" Roland asked, unable to respond to the larger questions brewing in his head. "Is this what it's all about? Because, frankly, if you're claiming blood ties but behaved in such an ungentlemanly way, I shall never forgive you."

"The last thing we care about is forgiveness," Guy said. "But no, not directly. The intent was to flush you out of that insidious corner of France, but our operative was slightly more enthusiastic than we expected."

"An innocent young man was killed because of you. And now I cannot live in peace," Roland protested, finding whatever shred of courage he had left in him kindling slowly.

"The hope was that you would come to us. I think you mean you cannot live a life free of consequences?" Guy asked. "Don't you think it's time to grow up a bit?"

"How dare you judge me!" Roland cried.

The older, one-eyed werewolf, was close enough for Roland to touch, now. Just being near him made Roland feel uncomfortable, strangely drawn to him. It was high time he had his next dose of tonic, but at the rate things were going, that was not likely to happen. He would have to transform in front of everyone. His worst nightmare, played out before the only people in the world he truly cared about.

"Have you ever even *let* yourself transform?" the French werewolf said. "The way your eyes are flashing, I don't believe you ever have."

"It is *beneath* me," Roland snapped.

"Listen to Roux," Guy said. Their other werewolf companion was keeping the others back while the conversation continued, growling and pacing before them. Molly was doing her best to keep everyone safe, but it was unlikely the stand-off would last.

"I've never listened to anyone in my entire life, and I certainly have no intention to start now," Roland said.

His stomach ached; his feet itched. He knew what it meant. He knew the danger lurking inside of him. How could he allow himself to fall into this trap? How could he change into a werewolf in front of the only people he'd truly considered friends in a very, very long time?

Roux laughed, raspy and ragged, tossing his head like an impatient schoolteacher.

"Petulant child," he said, sitting back down on his haunches. "You will learn, though."

It had begun to rain, though Roland swore there had been no indication of bad weather earlier. Now he had to add 'wet wolf reek' to the bouquet of things irritating him down to his nose hairs.

Roux tilted his head up and began howling, that same chilling sound that had terrorised them earlier. Fear sliced into Roland's chest, thinking he would be unleashed before all of them. For some reason, being revealed in his wolf form before Basil made him feel even more ashamed. And he truly did not want to think about that if he could help it.

Except, thankfully, Roland did not transform into his wolf form. Instead, Roux's body took on an alarming shade of red and twisted like an old dish rag, folding in on itself and then fanning up and out.

It happened so quickly, Roland could scarcely tell when Roux had ceased being a wolf and became a man.

A man with Roland's own brow and lips and the same slight gap in his front teeth. He did not share his pale hair, for that had come from his mother. And that would make this man...

"Yes, Roland. I am Jean-Pierre Roux, your father. And I have been looking for you for many years," said Roux. "Your esteemed mother, the great High Witch of England, held you in rather impressive protection—clearly not just from us, but from knowing who you truly are. Now that she is, shall we say, no longer a concern, we can speak, wolf to wolf."

The last shred of his control on his form snapped like a bowstring.

The change came so quickly, so sharply, that Roland did not have time to fight it. Despair, complete and unfathomable, sunk his fickle heart, and every shred of control he'd ever had over his form vanished. It was, he had to admit, exhilarating to give into it at last. Perhaps the fact he had no restraint in any other part of his life was simply because he spent so much time repressing the feral part of him, the part that longed for blood and freedom and death.

As his body shifted, so, too, did his senses. The colours, muted as they were in the night, dimmed further. Yet his vision became ten times crisper: Petronilla's body was limned in orange; the wolves in blue-black; Poppy, Molly, and Basil all in pink.

Roland could smell the late ripening blackberries half a mile away, the faint remains of Petronilla's lilac perfume that hadn't been burned away by the fire, and the sour sweat on his father's body. Worse—or better—he could smell Basil Hode, a comforting, honey-sweet scent with just a hint of bitter orange. He had the most alarming desire to roll around all over Basil and cover himself in it.

The pain of changing danced between agony and ecstasy, his body revelling in being able to finally do what he'd forbidden it for so long. Heat radiated down his spine, pulling apart his ribs to make space for bigger lungs; his face stretched, his teeth elongating and piercing through his gums.

He was howling. He was sobbing. He was laughing.

Poppy, unafraid, was at his side, her hands soothing and kind. "You're beautiful, Roland. You are so beautiful."

This appealed to his vanity, and he was glad it remained intact. His mother had told him, time and again, that turning into a werewolf would erode the parts of him that made him human, and that with time he would lose himself utterly to the beast.

Somehow, now, he doubted his mother had been even moderately honest about that, too.

Because being a werewolf felt *wonderful*. He glanced down at his paws, still trembling with pain: like his hair, they were pale as moonlight, the black claws curved and glinting.

"Get away from him, woman," Roux was saying.

His voice resonated twofold, a strange echoing, as if Roland could hear it in his mind before his ears picked it up.

"I will do no such thing," Poppy said, throwing her arms around him, and Roland loved her for it. He desperately wished he had half the courage she did, but already he felt his bones trembling before Roux.

After all the joy of transforming, once the initial rush passed, he felt *them*. The wolves. All of them. They were linked, as if by one great chain, their voices and scents and consciousnesses closing in on him, influencing him.

It would be so easy to let go, to turn on these soft mortals. Their only real protection had been the pyromancer gentlewitch, and even Roland could see just how far she'd exhausted herself. Yes, fire was a natural enemy of the wolves, but she had driven it too far and too fast, hoping the pack would retreat before she had properly drained her magic. Now she had burned her magic out so thoroughly that she would be useless for days.

Their bodies are weak, Roux's voice said, though this time there was no echo. Roland understood he was speaking mind to mind. *When have mortals ever been kind to you, accepted you? You've spent so long hiding yourself, ashamed, you have nearly lost your instincts entirely. But I see you as you are meant to be. A prince among wolves.*

A prince.

Roland had always wanted to be a prince. If he was honest, he'd suspected he'd had noble blood in him somewhere. His sartorial sense alone...

"Roland. Don't listen to them." Basil's voice. Loud and nearby, his body smelling of home and comfort and protection.

But Basil hated him. Basil would never accept him. He shook off Poppy's hold, stalking over toward the Warder.

Roland began growling, that reverberating reflex filling him with calm and satisfaction in a way nothing else ever had. No one had ever feared him before.

Now they would.

He felt the hackles on his back rise as he watched Basil

through his new lupine eyes. Yes, he wanted Basil; he had from the first moment he'd spied the amber-haired Warder. But perhaps it hadn't been simply a matter of lust. Perhaps it had been a matter of domination.

Killing Basil would not be difficult. Even Molly's axes seemed almost laughable now.

"You are better than this," Basil pleaded with him.

The wrong thing to say.

He was not better than this. He *was* this.

Giving in felt even sweeter this time, especially when he heard the screams—screams because of him. It made his heart thrum, his stomach swoop, and his throat thirst.

Roland pounced, vicious and free and alive.

When he bit down on Basil's forearm and fresh blood filled his mouth, Roland soared with a welcome joy, even as his father's laughter rang in his head.

"Roland de Grateloup! I command you to stop!"

Blinding light, deep violet with spinning golden motes, swirled into his head, making his head swim, his jaw immediately loosening and his muscles tensing.

Edith Rookwood had returned, and somehow, inexplicably, she had even more power over him than the pack. Every fibre of his body cowered to that voice; the whole length of his spine arched as if pushed down with an invisible hand.

Blood flecked his fur, dripping from his muzzle to the white marble tiles. Basil lay unconscious between Roland's great paws, Poppy was screaming, and the wolves were running away.

What... what had he done?

EDITH'S INITIAL THOUGHT was that she needed to get a better celestial orb, for hers had nearly cost her Basil's life.

The disorientation of coming back from the *liminalis* was never easy, but seeing the giant werewolf tearing into her Warder and friend had rent a primal part of her.

It was Roland. She did not know *how* she knew it was Roland, for he was now two-and-a-half yards long—and a wolf. She would have to think about it all later, for Basil was in grave condition, Poppy was screaming, and Molly was pursuing the fleeing wolves.

And Edith hadn't even pulled out her sword yet.

Fintan took off in a sprint toward the werewolves, making up the distance behind Molly with astonishing speed. No doubt he'd been keeping some of his fae abilities at bay.

"Edith..." Poppy was trembling from head to toe, her beautiful, embroidered gown covered in Basil's blood. "It happened so fast..."

Without concern for etiquette, Edith grabbed Poppy by the back of her neck and kissed her passionately. The sound of surprise her companion made at that sudden display of affection was reward enough, and Edith wished she could have whisked Poppy away in that moment and given her all the pleasure the apology she deserved called for.

Instead, she pulled away, breathless, and said: "I'm sorry. Again."

"I'm just so glad you're here," Poppy said, kissing Edith on the cheek again, tears staining her face.

"Tell me what happened," Edith said, throwing off her topcoat and rolling up her sleeves. She wished she were a better healer.

Petronilla, looking pale as milk, knelt on the other side of Basil. "I kept them at bay for a while, but I'm afraid I ran out of strength sooner than I hoped." She glanced at Roland, who was sitting like a well-trained dog, his ears back and head down, watching the proceedings. "We're fairly certain he was under their influence when he attacked Basil."

Basil, at the mention of his name, moaned, but did not open his eyes. His arm was bleeding profusely; Edith was going to have to staunch the flow soon. Thankfully, Poppy was already prepared, and she handed the gentlewitch her sash. Though Edith felt a pang of regret taking it for this purpose, she could not imagine a more noble use for Poppy's stitching. If Poppy could stitch her love into fabric, she could find a way to help Basil.

Edith began the gruesome work of assessing the damage of Basil's wounds. Thankfully, he had his satchel with him, and there was a wide variety of herbs, poultices, and a small wound kit, all pristinely organised, clean, and tidy.

She could do some rudimentary healing magic, but nothing on the level this sort of mauling would require. In a most frustrating slip of irony, the only person with the healing prowess needed was the very man bleeding before her.

"I do not know any spells or charms to fix this," Edith said, choking back her own tears.

"Time will fix it. And attention," Petronilla insisted to her cousin, laying her hand gently upon Edith's own. "Basil is strong." She cast a most venomous look over at Roland, who was still sulking in his wolf form.

"I don't understand why he's still listening to me," Edith muttered. "He never did when he was in his human form."

"I sincerely doubt that was personal, my love," Poppy said, her eyes still shining with tears.

A racket from the garden below caught their attention, and Edith, content for the moment that Basil was out of the worst of bleeding danger, left him to see what the problem was.

Uncle Auden was leaning over the balustrade, gesturing to the approaching figures. At first, Edith felt her whole body clench in dread—what new horrors could they endure this night? But then she recognised the familiar shapes of Molly Hode and Fintan, dragging a naked man between them. It was not, unfortunately, Roux, but presumably one of the other werewolves, given all the snarling.

"You'll keep your mouth tidily shut if you're wise," Molly was saying, her own voice ragged with the effort. She was sporting a new black eye.

Fintan turned his lavender gaze up toward the balcony. "We caught one."

The werewolf, a flaxen-haired man with a scar on his chest, caught Edith's gaze and started shrieking: "Cursed fiend! Damned devil! Navia's heir! Rosmerta's doom!" He had the strangest green discolouration around his eyes.

Molly silenced him with a fist to the face, but Edith couldn't help but shudder. No one had ever called her such a thing before.

The chaos only intensified when Molly reached the scene at the balcony. One look at her brother and Edith had to stand between Roland and the Warder to prevent yet another murder.

"You'd put that pathetic beast down for good, if you had any sense," Molly gritted through her teeth. "You're mad if you think he won't turn on the rest of us the first chance he gets."

Edith stilled her voice, focusing on keeping her expression neutral. "Roland is currently under my command. He was being manipulated by Roux. I don't entirely understand, but I promise you that I can feel his connection to me, his... subservience."

That was not the most agreeable word, perhaps, but it was as close as she could get to the sensation.

"Since when do you command werewolves?" Molly asked.

Edith most certainly did not appreciate the doubt from the Warder. "You'll mind your tone, Warder. I understand you're upset about Basil. As am I. But you have never struck me as the sort of person who would second-guess their gentlewitch in such dire matters as this, and I shall assume I am mistaken in interpreting you as doing so now."

To her credit, Molly bowed her head. She didn't say anything specific, no exact word of apology, but the silence was strong enough.

Roland was whining piteously, now, making Edith's head hurt even more than it already was. Edith needed to think.

"Navia's heir," she mused, looking at the werewolf captive. He looked as if he was about to wake up again.

Fintan was trying to speak to her, but again the *geas* had control of his faculties. He only gagged and shuddered and fell to his knees.

Mother of the werewolves, came a voice in her mind. Not just any voice: Roland's.

Edith whipped around, and the moment her gaze fell on Roland his ears pricked up. "Was that you?"

He walked in an adorable little circle, his fur fluffing out. *Yes. Yes, oh, thank the stars. Liege Rookwood, I am so terribly sorry—this is all quite terrible.*

Willing her mind still, she knelt to look Roland in the eyes. *You said 'mother of werewolves.' Someone told me a story about her recently. Why would that man call me Navia's Heir?*

Roland whined again, clearly incapable of speech as the other werewolves managed, and frustrated. Edith could sense his emotion roiling off of him. Shame, terror, and self-loathing. It was enough to bring tears to her eyes.

I only remember a bedtime story from my mother. Navia was the first witch, born of Rosmerta and a mortal man. She was the mother of werewolves and could command them. Ever since I met you, you've had an ability to... well, to make my spine straighten. It was stronger even than the call of the pack. Older. Entirely uncomfortable and rather embarrassing, but preferred to the alternative. It's no wonder he called you that.

Poppy came over beside her, putting her hand on Edith's shoulder. "My love? Are you speaking to Roland?"

Edith kissed her companion on the mouth, lingering just a moment. "You, as ever, are brilliant. Yes."

"Viola and the viscount..." Poppy wiped at her tear-stained face.

I can smell Silas on the werewolf, Roland said. *One benefit to this most inconvenient form. Come with me. I can take you to him.*

"Come with me, Poppy," Edith said. "Or stay here, with Basil. I leave it to you."

"Come with you?" Poppy asked.

"It's dangerous. And I cannot protect you. You are far from home, and we will be surrounded by vicious villains. But I cannot continue to leave you at the edges of this life, which has grown more dangerous and beautiful week by week," Edith said.

Poppy looked around, conflicted. "My sister... She didn't need me then. I don't think she needs me now."

"I doubt that's true, my love." Edith reached into her pocket and took out the small, blackened iron key shaped like an octopus. The Janus key. "If you change your mind, think of me. It will bring you to me."

"Edith, I'm sorry," Poppy said. "But I must stay here with Basil and Petronilla. I know it in my bones. I wish I could be in two places at the same time."

Edith took her companion by the hand and kissed her fingers, dirty as they were. "You are always with me, my love. Always."

CHAPTER SEVENTEEN
BEHOLD THE TYRANT'S AWFUL FORM

SHOULD ONE BELIEVE the Father of Vampires? Some mortals believed in devils, and perhaps even a Devil, but Viola had never put much stock in such things. The Brightwells' faith was common at best, a generally a good record of church attendance whilst keeping some of the house goddesses the rest of the week. But their faith did not define them in the way of some families.

Now, however, as she stared down Maurice, Viola began to wonder if their simple faith was folly.

He was beautiful, and beautifully cruel. A monster wrapped in the visage of a celestial being, wrought of power and magic and charm. Resisting it was a constant effort, and though Viola wished she could ascribe it to her resilience, she now suspected it had something to do with Silas, and his strange parentage, and the blood now in her veins.

Maurice sat in Laertes' favourite chair, swirling a glass of blood in one hand, and petting Ophelia's head with the other. She was entirely subordinate to him now, her eyes glassy and unseeing, glowing with that uncanny deep blue light. Worse even, Maurice's grasp on her was effortless. He almost appeared bored.

Wherever Laertes was, he was unable to help Viola.

"Silas Drake, Viscount St. Albans," Maurice chuckled to himself.

Viola sat across from him, her body rigid with the effort of restraint. She could smell the blood in Maurice's cup, and she wanted it desperately. Keeping his power at bay made her exhausted, her body burning through whatever gave her magic faster than she could summon it.

Still, she would not allow herself to show him her need, nor her strain. "That is his name," she said simply. "Do you find that amusing?"

Maurice sneered. "Amusing? Yes. Silas, the name, itself, comes from the Latin root *Silvanus*. A man of the wood. Faerie is, at its heart, a great wood. The irony is not lost on me."

"You say he is a fae. How can that be?" Viola asked. She was sweating, now, the beads of it trickling icy rivulets down her back.

"Foolish nobles among you made a deal with the fae. It happens more often than you think," Maurice said. "In this case, a bargain with no ordinary fae woman."

Viola doubted he knew of her own family's bargain, nearly twenty years ago, to keep Poppy's life. At the time she had not considered the Boagane as a fae creature, but given her power, it did make sense. "I assume Silas's father and mother could not conceive."

"Yes, you see the truth of it now. I must admit, I hadn't considered such a renowned family—known for their distaste of witches on the whole—would stoop to that level. But perhaps it was just that: Lord St. Albans would never have considered involving himself with gentlewitches, so the fae were the next best option."

"How would he have managed such a thing?" Viola needed Maurice to keep talking, and he seemed to love gloating. With every innocent question, he would relax a little more. "Faerie has been inaccessible for generations."

Maurice's knowing smirk was devastating, but also

terribly predictable. He revelled in being the oldest, wisest, and most accomplished in any given situation. With Viola, unremarkable save for her nascent vampirism, he perceived the advantage as significant.

"There have always been ways for us to get to the mortal realm, child," Maurice said. "Getting *back,* now... That has been the greatest challenge of them all. Precious few are capable, and none without limitations."

"I don't understand what Silas has to do with all this," Viola said, with real consternation.

She'd gone too far. Now her naivete was annoying him.

"You don't *need* to understand," Maurice hissed. "You were a means to an end. I suspect drinking Silas's blood has somehow mitigated my power over you, given his ancestry. Soon, it will wane, and you will be subjugated along with all the rest. But in the meantime, it allows for a rather fascinating experiment."

Resisting his magic was draining her, and his power to enchant the vampires seemed to have no end. Viola could sense it, currents moving through the room—he must be calling on vampires far and wide. And given his small cadre of werewolves, likely on them, too.

And she was alone. Utterly alone. She ought to have been relieved, knowing she would not need to kill Silas, but she was fairly certain Maurice planned to anyway. It had all gone so wrong, so fast. She wished she had her sister's optimistic determination, but in the moment she had naught but despair.

"You dislike Silas's parents, then. His fae sire," Viola volunteered, willing her hands still as the edges of her vision prickled with red spots. The cloying, dead gardenia scent of Maurice swelled around her, burning her nose and making her eyes water with blood.

"Queen Tailte herself. The very queen who banished me

from Faerie—mother of my wife, Rosmerta," Maurice said, glancing down into his now empty goblet. The way he said Rosmerta's name was a curse. "After a thousand years, I was beginning to think I was never going to leave the mortal realm. But slowly, I've felt the barriers come down. And now our peerless Queen Tailte has her due come at last; she knows I know."

"So, Silas is your hostage?" Viola asked. She was so, so hungry.

Maurice laughed, sharp and bitter as winter. "No, my child. He is my redemption."

"I will not allow it," she said through gritted teeth.

"Enough! I do not have time for your childish obstinance."

Maurice lunged at her so quickly, Viola had no time to scream. Every inch of her being was cloaked in his power, strangling and inescapable, deep as the bowels of the earth and as ancient as its foundations. Then, the taste of something wet and languid upon her lips.

Her head swum as blood filled her mouth, thick and sticky-sweet.

Maurice's blood. He plugged her nose with two merciless fingers as her body twitched and convulsed against the intrusion. The savage monster inside of her gulped it down, and the taste burned and flayed her from the inside, her hunger finally slaked. But it was tainted blood, bitter and dusty, profane.

A conflagration of rage rose up inside of her, desperation and fury mingled with regret. She never could have stood against him. What had she been *thinking?* Without her sires, she was nothing.

Violence. Viola. Violence. Viola.

Violence.

* * *

SILAS STARTED AWAKE from a fitful, filthy slumber in the corner of his cell, hitting his head.

A woman's shriek of agony echoed down the corridor, with enough pure, animalistic rage to make him void his bladder.

Some hero he made. The irony that his own heroine, Sibylle Voltairis, met her presumed doom at the hand of a pack of enchanted werewolves in his yet-to-be-published sequel to *The Lady of the Lost Kingdom* did not escape him. However, had he created a cell as dank and repugnant as this one, his publisher would have made him take it out.

Verenata flew across his field of view, her body arcing through the air before hitting the ground. She scrambled to her feet and, nails broken and bloody, fiddled with the lock on the cell.

"Verenata?" Silas croaked.

There was no time to explain. He heard a more distant door slam shut, iron and heavy oak barring the way with resounding finality.

More screaming down the corridor, and Verenata threw open the door to Silas's cell, then locked herself in with him, her hands shaking and her eyes wild.

"That vampire is out of his head," Verenata said, backing away from the bars to get as far as possible. "He threw me in here. As *bait*."

"Bait for what?" Silas did not what to think what kind of creature would make Verenata, a werewolf, tremble like a newfound lamb.

Verenata slid down the wall, shaking her head like a child trying to dismiss a night terror. "Don't let her near me."

Slowly, Silas walked toward the locked cell door. The already cold dungeon was draftier than ever, his nose chilling as he drew close to the source of Verenata's terror.

It was utterly silent save for the swishing of taffeta, and a measured patter of leather slippers across the stone floor.

Viola. But not the Viola he had left at Burkley House, the one who had shattered his heart into a thousand jagged pieces. No, this was Viola from before, in the weeks before Laertes had found his way to her. Before she had fed upon him—the monster in the dark. The one they'd had to keep chained for days at a time, for fear she might injure herself or others. But still, still, refusing food, refusing blood.

"Silaaaaaas..." drawled the creature who was once Viola Brightwell. Her voice was ragged from the screaming, lower, but unmistakably hers.

He still couldn't see her, no matter how he squinted and stretched his neck. And, stars, even though he knew she'd bring him his death, part of him wanted her to find him, to end him. It would be better this way, perhaps, to let the house of St. Albans fall into obscurity. Theirs was always a dynasty teetering on the edge. It would serve his father's legacy right that, even on the verge of a new age, his child would destroy its future.

"Viola," Silas said, even though his voice trembled. Since he'd eaten the mushrooms, he was no longer famished, but his body was worn from the ordeal, and he didn't know how much more he could endure. "Viola, come to me."

Smoke poured down the corridor in lavender clouds, the scent of oud and myrrh heavy in the air. It made Silas drowsy, but it made Verenata cough.

"Stop talking to it!" Verenata shrieked. "Are you trying to kill us?"

Maybe he was.

Viola slid into the watery light, an eerie glow limning her eyes—like shimmering starlight, but deathless and void of warmth or love. She had never looked so beautiful, nor so deadly. It took his breath away. Silas knew he ought to be terrified, and yet he still felt joy in seeing her again.

"There you are," Viola said, her eyes locking onto his.

She bared her teeth, and thousands of motes of blue-black light moved toward him, settling upon his skin and clothes like fathomless stars.

He had the sense he was supposed to feel something remarkable with this powerful show of magic. The Allure, he thought he recalled, when a vampire asserts their authority over a mortal, should be impossible to resist.

But it *tickled*. Almost ridiculously so. Each mote was as soft as feather down, moving as it reached his skin and prickled through his clothing.

It did not have the same effect on Verenata, who was screaming and moaning. Silas backed away slowly as Viola tore open the door of the cell with inhuman power, figuring he ought to at least give her the impression her power was working on him. Allure or no, he had no doubt Viola was extremely dangerous in the moment.

Verenata howled, her neck twisting as she tried to rally against Viola's power. Her body shifted, uncanny angles twisting as her skin erupted into soot black fur and her face elongated. All of Verenata's clothing melded into her skin, somehow absorbed by the transformation, and her hands— desperately clutching to the remnants of her humanity— became powerful, ivory white claws.

Viola sighed, her shoulders relaxing, as Verenata cowered, whimpering in the corner.

"Maim him," Viola said to the werewolf. "Leave him with enough blood so I may feed."

Verenata convulsed again, fighting the power just a moment before her eyes went an eerie azure blue, incandescent even in the thin morning light from the small windows.

"Viola, please," Silas said, trying to ignore the massive animal staggering to her feet, a look of devastating hunger in her eyes. "I know you decided you couldn't be with me, and I understand. Well, not entirely. You shattered my heart in a way I will likely never recover from."

Viola twitched, her eyes blinking rapidly. For a brief moment, Verenata slowed in her progression toward him, as if their connection faltered.

"Stop speaking," Viola said with a snarl. "I have had enough of you."

"I don't think you have," Silas said. For a moment, he wished Roland were there to hear. He'd always told Silas he was far too gallant with women, allowing them to proceed without any pressure. Not that he wasn't clear in his affections and his desires, but it always leaned toward the genteel. "You and I have long played a game of desire, and I have a feeling that story is still being written."

She strode toward him, halting Verenata with one hand. That power crackled through the room, and although it did not impact him, Silas felt the pressure of the magic, nonetheless. She had always been a powerful vampire in his presence, but this was another order entirely. Perhaps it was the strange mushrooms he'd eaten, or his curious environs, but he was quite certain her magic was intensifying.

"Perhaps I will take you between my legs before I bleed you dry," she said, a flicker of amusement in her expression. A brief spark of hope for Silas that the woman he loved still lived inside this creature. A creature he loved, regardless. A creature he would die for.

Stars help him.

Although it left a hollow feeling inside of him, echoing as a deep cavern, he would do anything to hold her once more, to feel her move around him, to lose himself in her darkness.

Silas tilted his neck to the side. He was filthy, exhausted, and far from the picture of noble poise. "Then let me feed you, Viola. Awake, and with my eyes open. I will willingly go to my end if it means sustaining you and, perhaps, giving you a chance at your own freedom."

"The master has told me to wound you," Viola said. She stepped closer, the bright scent of her unravelling like a storm: old incense, faded gardenias, and a dusty note he could not place. Not the smell of her magic, but something else. "But he did not say how quickly I had to do it. And he did not say I could not enjoy it."

"Do you remember how we came together upon the roof?" Silas asked, wicked love making him bold. "I remember the sounds you made as I touched you; I remember the words you barely managed as you slid down over me and took your pleasure."

"Yes…" Viola said, lashes fluttering again.

"How you arched your back, and I tasted the rain and the lightning from your skin, and you drank of me again, and the very skies seemed to tremble along with us. How I said I loved you."

Viola's eyes went wide—the eyes he knew, not the creature's eyes—and she gasped. By the Oath, he had never spoken such indelicate words to anyone before, but they resounded within him as if they were magical themselves.

"Silas." Viola's voice was quieter, still husky with desire, but tinged with confusion. "How did I get down here? How did you get here?"

Verenata let out a whimper and twitched, falling to her side as if stricken. Viola's hold slipped away, and the werewolf wasted no time running out of the cell and down, deeper into the dungeons.

Viola did not run into his arms as he had hoped, but she stood watching him for answers, occasionally looking around the room in confusion.

"We're in the dungeon of Howarth Castle," Silas said slowly, holding out his hands. He wanted to touch her—

needed to. His whole body throbbed with longing. "You were sent here, by Maurice, to kill me. I've been here for a while now. Since just after our last dance."

Viola ran her finger along her full, lush lips, her tongue peeking out for one, torturous moment. Silas's whole world narrowed to that tongue, and memories of its capabilities, and he had to hold back a shudder.

"You're a fae prince," Viola said, her eyes unfocused but still very much her own. "He's captured you here to lure out your mother."

"My mother is dead," Silas said, taken aback by her strange words. "She died when I was quite young. I've told you as much. Not long after my sister passed."

Reaching up to touch his cheek, Viola sighed deeply. "Yes. The woman you knew as your mother is dead. But your true mother is fae. A queen, from what I have heard. Your parents bargained with her, for an heir, when they struggled to conceive. And it is a very good thing, too, for it saved me."

The words hit him like a leaden shot to the chest. Those mushrooms earlier. The way he'd scrutinised paintings of his mother, trying desperately to find a trace of her in him and coming up, time and again, empty. The pervasive feeling that there was a world, just out of view, he could never quite reach. It was the very reason he'd begun writing, how he had found Sibylle. She could go where he could not, she could escape the cage of the mundane.

"And why is that a good thing?" Silas asked.

Viola twitched, looking behind her as if expecting to see someone lurking there. When no one was, she turned her attention back to Silas. "Good for me, terrible for you. Your blood is fae, and it prevented me from turning into a revenant. When I was made, Maurice—the King of Vampires—sensed your blood. It narrowed his focus;

and when Ophelia went to ask him for help, it seems he purposely sent them upon a false trail while he rallied his troops. For without the High Witch, the werewolves were free and awaiting his command. He's been feeding on the High Witch, and he keeps taking some strange potion I'm sure Basil would know the name of. I tasted some of it." She shuddered. "But I think your blood chased the effects away."

Silas's head throbbed. "So, you're not dying—and what you said, on the balcony..."

"I left you because I thought I had to kill you to avoid becoming a revenant," Viola said hurriedly. "But Maurice lied to us. And thanks to the gentlewitches breaking through the barrier between Faerie and here, he was able to claim vast amounts of power. My sires are completely under his control, and I fear I do not have much longer to resist."

Wrapping her in his arms, Silas drew her to him as close as he could, kissing her head. She no longer smelled quite so strongly of rotting gardenias; her own cold, rain-washed rose scent bloomed from her skin.

"You can fight this," he told her, though he did not know if she could.

"Perhaps if the High Witch were still around," Viola whispered. "But her protections are gone."

"You have me. And I have you. Even if we are both new to whatever we are. Perhaps, together, we can be more," Silas said, stroking a finger down her soft, cool cheek. "I don't feel particularly fae, but I did have some curious voices speaking to me as of late. And mushrooms."

Viola gazed up at him, and Silas forgot how to breathe. "I believe Maurice wants to unite preternaturals, somehow, or else use them to assist him in returning to Faerie. But he does not have power enough yet. The gift of your blood has given me strength, at least, to keep most of my mind."

"The werewolves I've seen do not look well," Silas added. "I think this whole business is making them sick."

"We will run away," Viola said hurriedly. "I would drink from you if I thought it was safe, but you need your energy. I'm certain there's a way out."

Silas often thought back to that day in his chambers at Burkley House. If he thought of it logically, the idea of offering his body and blood to a vicious monster was a terrible idea. Yet, in the moment, it had felt like the most important decision of his life. Perhaps, given this new information, it was a latent power inside of him, answering the call to her pain.

A fae prince.

He wondered if the dowager viscountess knew. Somehow, he wouldn't have been surprised to find she did. Given how much she loathed everyone with magical powers. And what had Silas's father done to bargain? And his mother, who he'd never known? Her middle name had been Sibylle.

"Yes, I'm certain there is," he said, kissing her fiercely. He did not want to let her go.

Viola went taut in his arms, at first he thought from passion, but then she cried out. He felt her muscles trembling, watched her neck twist and cord with the strain. Then he felt the weight of Maurice's power, suffocating and sweet and redolent of decay. Yet, he was nowhere near that Silas could see.

"Viola. Darling. Fight this," Silas pleaded, even as she shuddered and ripped out of his grasp with astonishing power.

Falling to her knees, Viola retched on the ground, black bile mixed with blood spewing from her mouth, her shoulders ripping through her dress like scythes.

No, not her shoulder blades. Her *wings*. They were black,

iridescent, limned with tiny feathers upon their smooth skin. Stunning. Deadly. Powerful.

Viola rose, her eyes incandescent orbs of cerulean death, and she sprang upon Silas. In a rush of wings and teeth, he saw no more.

GIVEN ROLAND'S GENERAL proclivities, he never would have thought he'd have enjoyed sprinting through the Kentish countryside as a werewolf with a gentlewitch on his back directing his every move, and yet he found it exhilarating. It wasn't domination in any sexual sense—for he'd been on both sides of such dynamics in his life and knew well that sensation—but instead a feeling of remarkable protection and connection. His magic, pushed to the very depths of his being for so long, sang in concert with the gentlewitch's, igniting his body from the roots of his pelt to the tips of his claws.

And he was, he had to admit, a most handsome werewolf. That was far from a surprise—he was a striking human— but it gave Roland some modicum of comfort to know that after years of repression, his form was not as monstrous as he'd thought. Not that he would be making a habit of it, if they survived the next few hours.

I am not certain how one gentlewitch and one most inexperienced werewolf are going to stand up to the King of Vampires, Roland said as they crossed the borders between Netherford and Valle Regis, the small town near Howarth Castle.

He could feel Edith's intelligence shimmer at the edge of his consciousness, a bit of amusement tempered with determination. So, he was not surprised when she said: *To be fair, we also have a Warder and a fae fellow under a geas... and two horses.*

Said fae gentleman, Fintan, was a short way behind them on one horse. Roland was more than a little smug on that count: he could easily outrun a horse in his current form. He'd never really thought of the applications of transformation. Granted, he still had remarkable physical prowess without turning, but if he'd let himself shift before, he might have gotten out of Paris more easily.

Alas, I am a wolf without a pack. That did hurt, surprisingly. Seeing his father, his hatred and his willingness to slink to the side of evil—as so many of the werewolves seemed to do—felt like worms crawling under his paws.

Edith gasped, and Roland sensed a frisson of fear go through her as she slowed them down near the edge of the castle grounds. A small sign, rotted with time, hung loosely, indicating that they were entering Byrnham Wood. Molly halted the small caravan, raising one of her scabbed hands.

Figures emerged from the treeline—lupine figures. He should have known Roux and his cronies would have been waiting for them. Panic began settling in, wariness in every pore of his being.

Except these werewolves didn't smell the same. His heightened nose picked up a low muskiness that should have been unpleasant but was more like a calling card. Then another; and another. Signatures in olfactory language.

"Roland de Grateloup," said the figure at the front, in a low man's voice, crisp perfection in his French pronunciation. "Liege Edith Rookwood. We are here to pledge our pack to your cause."

Edith straightened on Roland's back, her strong legs trembling with the effort of keeping calm. "And who do I have the pleasure of addressing, sir?" she asked. "We are headed into certain death against a foe of immeasurable strength, and last I checked, werewolf kind had thrown themselves to his side."

The wolf bowed his head. "Indeed, my brother Roux has long worked to appease the King of Vampires, seeding his spies in Parliament and beyond. But you have awakened, Heir of Navia, upon our lost kin. Our prophecies foretold this day."

More werewolves came from the trees, their pelts black as soot, and a few as pale as Roland himself. He counted at least sixteen of them and smelled a few more he couldn't see with his eyes.

Strangely, some of them smelled familiar.

"You did not answer the gentlewitch's question," Molly said, scowling. "For all the lovely words, we have very little time, and trust comes slowly these days."

The wolf inclined his head. "I am Lord Renard Philippe Roux, the exiled brother of Jean-Pierre Roux. Which makes me Roland's uncle, and eldest among our clan. These are my pack, most saved from the clutches of the King of Vampires, freed from the Grey Moon Brotherhood, or rehabilitated after the wars on the continent. We have long held the tale of Navia's Heir, she herself saying that we would know her by her taming of a wild werewolf, with a coat pale as snow."

Roland shivered, wishing he knew how to speak out loud again. It was tiring to have to think at someone rather than just using his tongue. *I'm far from wild*, he said.

Fintan went to say something but, as per usual, came up only with gurgling, courtesy of his *geas*. Apparently, the wolves and Roland were connected to Silas's own tales in some way not yet revealed.

Edith stroked Roland's shoulder. "He's only wild in the way of neglect. He has never been given the opportunity to run with his own pack. His mother, my mentor, must have had her reasons, but I admit I wonder. Like any prophetess, her ways are strange."

"They are, indeed, strange," said Renard. He was pure black save for a sweep of white across one eye. "But, if you will have us, we shall protect you and, should we all survive, teach Roland our ways."

Although I would like to spend time considering the merits of their argument, I must admit they simply smell *right. I feel as if I would know if they were lying. It's almost as if I can sense their motivations,* Roland said to Edith.

Renard's voice broke through Roland's own thoughts. *Then you are growing quickly in your abilities, nephew. As wolves, we can communicate in many ways, and it is difficult to deceive one another in this form.*

Renard's presence in his mind was comforting, welcome, unlike his father's. It stilled him, made him feel fortified. As if he had quaffed a particularly good vintage.

"Then I accept your assistance," Edith said, holding up her sword. It glinted and glowed in the late morning light, a beacon even in the sunshine at Roland's periphery. He had never felt so proud in his life.

"Are you certain, my liege?" Molly asked, always the sceptic.

Edith did not hesitate, even if the Warder was still far from convinced. "Entirely certain."

The wolves bounded out of the forest and encircled Edith, Roland, Fintan, and the horse. Sunlight turned their pelts brilliant, glittering, their eyes silver.

As one, the wolves howled, the sound rising around them like a mantle of power. Roland felt the magic of his pack imbue every hair on his pelt, tingling and welcome and filling up a part of his soul he'd been searching for his whole life. It ached as he listened, the tiny wisps on his ears shivering until he could hold back his howl no longer. Some essential, broken part of him became whole in that moment, and it connected him even further to Edith. And not just the two of them. They *all* felt more entwined, their power sharp and hopeful.

Then they ran as one, a small army of fierce warriors flying to the heart of Howarth Castle with purpose and destiny on their side.

VIOLA STOOD AT the centre of the Great Hall of Howarth Castle, flanked by her sires Ophelia and Laertes, as excruciating power flooded her veins. She was linked to them, and to the dozens of werewolves milling about the fortress, their power siphoning into Maurice, who channelled it into a single silver mirror up on the dais. It felt as if she were chained from the inside, her very being pulled apart and refashioned over and over again.

Alongside her own pain, she could feel that of her sires— their agony, their regret, their sorrow. But theirs was distant, like echoes of who they had once been, where before they had burned brilliantly. She knew, somehow, that the only reason she was conscious was because of Silas's gift to her, that tempered fae power. The Byrnes had been made vampires before they knew their own names. Maurice's own blood likely ran in their veins, too, though it did not boil as it did in hers.

It was taking Maurice a great deal of energy to keep her cowed, even though he did not show it.

The King of Vampires stood by the silver mirror, a crown of glittering blue stars across his fair brow, Silas sprawled at his feet. Beams of light fell from that crown onto the mirror's gleaming surface.

The mirror absorbed every drop of that power, the edges melting and shimmering like water under the moonlight. In a way, it was like sunlight coming through a magnifying glass, but rather turned the other way around. It smelled of raspberries and burnt toast and green things.

"Come out, come out, my dear queen," Maurice cooed into the mirror, pulling a long, wicked-looking blade from his waist.

Viola did not recognise the metal, but her blood did. It made her lungs quiver, her bones ache, just to gaze upon it. How he could even wield such a weapon without turning to vapour, she could not say. That was a weapon meant to slay vampires.

Her body was not her own. She had wings, beautiful and terrible, and they moved behind her in response to the conduit of energy cascading through her. Perhaps she ought to have hated those wings, as they represented all she had fought so long to repress, but she could not help but admire them, even if they were of no help. No matter her transformation, she was utterly helpless: all she wanted was to go to her sires, to go to Silas, but she could not. She was chained.

Silas stirred but did not wake, and guilt prickled at her again. Against her will, she had cut him down, wounded him, and presented him to Maurice, not before drinking as much of his blood as she could stomach. Viola hated herself for it. But resisting Maurice's power was a constant drain on her body, her mind. Her baser nature had won, and with it came that same, steely clarity as before.

Maurice waited at the mirror, impatient now, when nothing happened. Despite all the power flowing through him, the King of Vampires could not carry out his plan if his final guest did not appear: Silas's mother, the great fae queen.

The wolves began howling, and she could feel their pain. Maurice was bleeding them dry of their magic, desperate for a response. In his ancient magic, Viola glimpsed unfathomable power—the very touch of life and death—but knew he was limited in this realm. Whatever potion he continually took was changing him, too. Maurice's fingertips had gone a grey-green colour, along with patches under his eyes. Yes, it gave him power—but such power exacts a price.

"Wretched creatures," Maurice spat, kicking away one of the werewolves who had come closer to him, likely begging for mercy.

Viola felt two of their lives snuffed out, and the shiver across their collective bond made her heart ache and tears blur her vision in swirls of red.

Without warning, the mirror crackled, a bolt of lightning twisting out of it and landing just beside Silas's prostrate form. For a horrible moment, Viola thought Maurice had figured out some demented method for bringing more magic into himself, but that fear was short-lived.

With a crack like the heavens themselves breaking, every light in the hall went out, and the mirror dimmed to velvet blackness, frosted about the edges with a lacy filigree. Maurice still held to Viola's consciousness, but he was hesitating.

You're afraid, she dared to tell him.

Maurice ignored her, stomping over to the mirror to examine it. Viola's vampire vision gave her clarity despite the dark, but she saw nothing in the room to explain this strange turn of events.

"This is enough, Moritasgus," came a voice from the mirror, low and feminine. "You have gone to all this trouble to show me my son—now what do you *want* from me?"

At the sound of her voice, Silas's head rose. Viola wondered if he had been awake for some time, feigning a lack of consciousness to bide time. A naïve, human idea, but strangely endearing in that moment.

"There she is, at last," Maurice said, breathing heavily. Though he was indeed great, no-one could control such power for long. "I thought I was going to have to start indiscriminately murdering people for you to show up."

"You have my attention now, but my patience is limited," the woman said.

"Queen Tailte," Maurice said, performing a mocking bow. "You are the arbiter of the fae's very existence, the instrument of my continued exile. I no longer wish to live here, among the pitiable excuses for magical beings. Long ago, your line banished me, and now for over a thousand mortal years, I have languished here. Your protections are failing, however, and your child is not safe."

Viola watched as a pale figure, translucent and elegant, shimmered through the mirror's surface. The air in the room shifted, going cold and crisp as a deep winter's morning. And, strangely, she felt her own soul cry out in some kind of recognition to that new power. It was so much greater than Maurice's, so much older and more patient. He had boasted of a thousand years? Queen Tailte's power was *eternal*.

"You forget yourself, Moritasgus. My mother Demona did not banish you—you and Rosmerta chose to take what was not yours, and you fled. We merely closed the way to you," said Queen Tailte. Her measured, gentle demeanour was intoxicating, starkly different from Maurice's constant gnashing. "And we left you with gifts, you forget."

"These spawn are nothing compared to what my glory ought to have been. Rosmerta betrayed me," he said, gesturing to the wolves, then to the vampires. "This is a kingdom of fools."

"Then you are its most devoted king," Queen Tailte said. Her body was still incorporeal, and Viola sensed she did not want to risk setting foot in the mortal realm yet. "For you have torn a hole straight through Faerie with your ambitious scheming and poisoned your body."

"When I am in Faerie again, I will be healed."

"You are delusional. Surely, you know that."

"Delusional? You're the one who allowed the witchlings to tear holes in Faerie. And look where that has led us—has led me. They are weak, grown lazy on political intrigue and mortal concerns. If you hoped they would save you, look around you. No help comes. Your precious witches do not even know who you are."

"I am dealing with that," said the fae queen.

For the first time, Viola sensed a tremor in the queen's voice.

"Coward," Maurice shouted, jumping down to where Silas lay, grabbing him by his collar, and hoisting the viscount to his feet as easily as one might a straw scarecrow. "I wouldn't believe he was fae if I hadn't drunk of his blood."

"Moritasgus, leave the man alone. He is innocent in this."

"Innocent? *Innocent?*" Maurice asked. "No. His existence is a pestilence. I will make him fight. I will make him remember."

Viola thrashed against her mental shackles in a panic. A magical kenning gave her double vision for a moment, and she saw Maurice's violence before it happened: the vampire king raising his hand, crackling blue energy concentrating into a vicious orb, and then lodging itself into Silas's body like a cannonball.

She didn't need to know how excruciating the pain was as time sped up and her vision came to life. For even with the warning, she felt every bolt of agony alongside him.

YES, SILAS THOUGHT idly, it *was* the most terrible pain he'd ever experienced in his life. And, come to think on it, the measurement for such a thing was relatively limited. He'd lived a scant three decades, and the worst he could boast was a sprained ankle once and twisting his back so badly falling off his horse he'd been abed for a week.

This mad agony was pain on another level of existence. Made worse by Viola's scream, as if every tendril of magic Maurice forced into his body—for that appeared to be what he was doing, to Silas's utter horror—lashed at her as well.

And perhaps it did.

That voice in the mirror, then that strange apparition. Could it have truly been his mother?

It didn't matter so much now, not when death was hanging over him like a hungry vulture. He couldn't hold on much longer. And, perhaps, there was a measure of relief in that. One couldn't live forever, he didn't think, even if he was half a fae.

The absurdity of that thought cut through his pain, even for the briefest of moments.

And then the pain shifted. Maurice was not just torturing him, he was *changing* him. Or, rather, he was removing a part of him. A heaviness that he'd carried with him his whole life, a longing, that calling of a distant shore. That sense, whenever he looked in the mirror, that he didn't quite know the fellow on the other side.

Could a man be reborn? Silas felt his limbs strengthen, his jaw shift slightly. His ears began ringing, followed by a tingling sensation spreading down his spine, twisting and opening his lungs. The room sprang into colour, having been dampened in darkness just moments ago, and he could see a spectrum of light he'd never known before. Every velvet thread on Maurice's cloak shimmered in a thousand radiant hues; each noise every creature in the room made reverberated across his eardrums; and every smell assaulted his senses.

Especially Viola's. Her intoxicating fragrance enveloped him, welcoming him, calling to him.

With newfound strength, Silas grabbed Maurice's arm

with both of his hands and pushed back. Though the vampire king was still the stronger, Silas was far closer to his match. And he was taller—taller than he had been, and at a level with Maurice.

"There he is," Maurice said, letting go of Silas as if he were diseased. "Gaze into the mirror and behold your true self, Silas Drake."

Turning to look into that mirror—which moments ago held the apparition of his mother—Silas beheld his new form. He gasped, falling back, immediately touching the pointed ears and the sharper lines of his face. The face in the mirror was undoubtedly his—the same smooth, sable skin, the same hazel eyes, and the serious mouth. But the shapes had all shifted. Just moving made him dizzy, for he was broader of chest, now, and even the few inches of extra height were immensely disorienting.

Viola was no longer screaming. Whatever power Maurice had used to change Silas meant he could no longer keep the vampires in his thrall.

"Silas!" Viola ran toward him, her great wings half propelling her into his arms.

He could not embrace her. Not yet. But he needed to look at her, to ensure she was still whole.

"What is this I have become?" Silas asked.

The mirror crackled behind him, and the apparition of his mother reappeared, forming beside him, now. She brought with her the deep scent of resinous wood, fresh rainfall, and moonlight—he could not say how he knew the scent of moonlight, only that it exuded from her every pore.

Their eyes were the same shape, and she was of a height with him, draped in a raiment of silver floss and lace as delicate as spiderwebs, dewed with minute jewels. Her long hair, pin straight and purest white, fell all the way to her feet like a great silken cape behind her.

"I am sorry, my darling," she said, tears down her elegant cheeks. "I wish it had not come to this. I tried to protect you as long as I could."

"He seems far more likely to protect himself, now," came a familiar voice, once again his own: Laertes Byrne. He was cradling his sister, who looked unconscious, in his lap, smoothing her long, black curls. His skin was waxy, his hair plastered to his forehead. "But at what cost?"

Maurice continued grinning, and Silas struggled to keep him out of his eyeline. Viola, clearly confused he had not taken her in his arms, took a step back towards her sires.

"What am I?" Silas asked the fae queen. "I am told you are my mother. And now, I am transformed into a visage I see reflected in yours, so my eyes cannot deceive me." He touched his chest, which hurt, his skin pulled too tight, and winced. "Was this inside of me the whole time?"

Queen Tailte reached out to touch Silas, her fingers coming just within a breath before retreating. "I loved your father, but my love broke him in the end. He could not accept that he would grow old and die, while I would remain eternal."

"Was it not a bargain, then?" Viola asked. "You, who were quickened to a mortal's request."

The fae queen touched her stomach, as if in memory of holding Silas there. The gesture made his heart ache and his eyes sting with tears.

"I found the Viscount St. Albans upon a windswept hill, calling out across the land, desperate. There was a nearby channel, a passageway between our realms, and I, the fool, followed the sound of his cries. Perhaps we bargained, but we only bargained with our hearts," she said softly. "I tried to protect you. I sent you my most stalwart knight, Fintan of Overlee, though he was bound to secrecy." Her eyes turned toward Viola, and there was no hatred there, though her power crackled. "I should have known love would be your undoing, as it was mine."

"I don't understand," Silas said, emboldened now to take his mother by the hand. Her skin was cold, but buttery smooth.

"Of course you don't," Maurice scoffed, tossing his hair. "The queen and I have lived longer than you ever shall. But now that you are revealed, she is no longer protected."

The queen averted her eyes from Silas, taking her hand back as if he had wounded her, then she crumpled upon the ground. "What I did was forbidden. For a queen to do so... A sin of the greatest magnitude. Death, true death, is usually the penalty."

"And once she is dead, the way to Faerie will open, and I shall rebuild it in my image," Maurice said, striding toward the mirror. He rubbed his hands together, glancing over his shoulder to address the vampires. "You have one chance to follow me to a life of bliss and endless power, or else languish here in the land of the dead."

Never. That was Viola, the Byrnes, and most of the exhausted werewolves. Their joined voices were a chorus, a living thing in his mind.

"Very well. Remain here like the vermin you are," Maurice said, with casual dismissal. "You were all simply tools for this moment."

The vampire king pulled his brutal knife up to plunge it into the queen, and in Silas's sight it glowed a horrid, mottled green. It glittered with such malice that he wondered how Maurice could even hold it.

Queen Tailte did not even fight. She merely bowed her head, her long white hair streaming around her like pools of starlight, accepting her fate.

Then, the air in the room shifted again, as a high keening began.

Silas gasped, feeling a new power moving around the room, making his ears pop. He was certain his own doom loomed, but he could not leave his mother. Nor could he let her die. So he positioned himself between Maurice and Queen Tailte, even as Viola looked on, bloody tears streaking her face.

Then the wolves began howling. Dozens of them, haunting and strange and terrifying. Through Silas's new ears, he could understand parts of that unholy music—a calling, a challenge, a homecoming.

Maurice paused in his murderous stance, a look of genuine confusion in his features.

It was Ophelia who spoke, a low, raspy laugh proceeding her. "You did not expect another pack of wolves, did you, Maurice?" She looked a few breaths from death, barely more than a husk. "Perhaps, this time, you did not read your history well enough. Too busy looking for all the places that had your name. You drank their blood, their poisoned blood, and it pulled them to you."

What did she mean?

"We are the keepers of Howarth Castle," Laertes said, taking Viola's hand in his. "We are Rosmerta's true children, those whom she loved—Rosmerta, whom you murdered. And we welcome our guests."

"Guests?" Maurice looked around, sneering.

The great doors, which had been locked and shuttered, flew open on their hinges with such power Silas jumped back. For a moment, he could see nothing but the blackness of the corridor beyond. Then came another howl followed by the ghostly impression of a massive, white werewolf and its rider.

The rider was none other than Liege Edith Rookwood, and she raised her hand to brandish a mighty weapon, glowing vivid purple in her hands. And—brimstone!—the look on her face was pure determination, her eyes shining.

And then came more werewolves. Dozens falling into line behind her, spreading out through the room. Molly Hode rode upon one of them, her face splattered with blood, and Fintan upon another. Silas had never loved the old valet so much, seeing him resplendent upon a vicious werewolf, determination in his typically placid face. Fintan caught Silas's eye and nodded, appreciatively.

Maurice howled with rage, shaking his head back and forth as if in pain. "Get that away! Get that away!" he shrieked as the gentlewitch came closer, covering the length of the great hall in seconds.

Taking the moment's distraction, Silas grabbed Queen Tailte and pulled her out of harm's way, sparing a glance toward Viola. The look of love and relief on her face gave him such hope that he felt he might float across the room to her.

Edith cried out, "Maurice—Moritasgus—you are not welcome here: not at Howarth Castle, and not in my demesne."

"You pitiful wretch," Maurice said, staggering away from Edith's light. It was not clear to whom he spoke, so the insult was rather widely applied. "Wolves, to me!"

The handful of werewolves who had been part of Maurice's plan were too drained to be of any particular use. Silas watched them try and heed his call, but they only whimpered. Fintan quickly made his way over toward Queen Tailte and Silas, and they held one another a moment before turning their attention to the scene unfolding before them.

"They aren't listening to you, old chap," said the white werewolf Edith rode. "Not surprising, since you appear to have emptied them out."

By the heavens, that was Roland's voice! That was *Roland!*

Invigorated by the presence of his dearest friend, Silas bounded forward toward Maurice. Viola followed suit, flanking the vampire king between them, her eyes brimming with hatred. Silas had never seen her look so beautiful, her wondrous wings fanning out behind her, and her teeth elongated and ready for blood.

His blood sang to her. Her power sang to him.

"Navia's Heir is here to unite us," Ophelia said. Laertes still supported her to stand, but like Viola, she seemed propelled by vitriol. "As was foretold."

"Nonsense. That is all lies and myth," Maurice said, making a sorry attempt to look unconcerned as Silas and Viola closed in on him.

Edith had now dismounted, and she and Roland approached the dais where they slowly surrounded Maurice. A witch, a werewolf, a vampire, and a fae. All joined together, all connected as friends, as lovers, and as companions.

Their magic sang to one another: connected and projected by the remarkable weapon in Edith's hand.

Against all hope, they could do this.

Silas barrelled into Maurice, but he was too quick. The vampire king grabbed Viola by the throat, raising the wicked blade to her neck. "This is over."

As MAURICE BEGAN lifting Viola up into the air, his considerable magic raising them upward, she thought back to her most frightened moment after she'd finally began making peace with her vampire form. She had called a name, in that moment, and Laertes had come to save her. She had needed him with her whole heart, and he had heeded the call.

As she watched Silas scream below her, Viola knew there

was only one person who could help her in the moment, one soul capable of bringing her the strength she needed.

A crack resounded, searing white light bleaching the world of colour, and suddenly Poppy was in Viola's strong arms. Never easily rattled, her little sister had a look of pure determination on her face, and relief, as she held on for dear life.

"I'm here, Viola," she whispered. "I heard you call me."

"I love you, little sister," Viola said. "I have a vampire for you to deal with."

"What!" Maurice faltered in flight, his attention divided as he tried to wield his Allure against Poppy. His knife slipped slightly in his hand. "What are you doing?"

Viola flapped her wings to help keep them afloat, and then squeezed her sister tighter. "I can't hold on for too much longer," she said. Maurice's magic cascaded over her, clouding her mind, and she had to fight the desire to bite down on Poppy's neck.

But she would not. Let him drain himself in his pride.

"I can't be Allured, sir!" Poppy called up to the struggling vampire lord. "You'll just exhaust yourself if you keep trying."

"Impossible," Maurice snarled. "I am the first vampire."

Maurice twisted, but then he lost his grip upon the knife altogether, and Viola was able to swirl her sister away from him, her wings snapping into use.

"I *am* rather impossible. My companion tells me every day," Poppy shouted across, daintily brushing a curl from her forehead as if she were dancing across a floor and not swinging in midair.

They had managed to get quite high up, Viola realised, securing her grip under her sister's arms. She would just need to get them to a soft landing place.

Too late. Viola's hesitation cost her. Maurice leapt upon

her, tearing at her wing—that cruel knife slicing through the tendons.

"I can't hold on—I don't want to drop you," Viola cried.

"You can let me go," Poppy said. "I know what I'm meant to do."

She meant more than letting her go physically, and it was a balm to her soul, that permission.

Viola released her grip on her sister, willing her eyes open to see what would happen next.

The air smelled of springtime, of every flower Viola had ever planted at Burkley House all blooming at once: magnolias, freesia, roses, campion, honeysuckles, bluebells, fragrant grasses, all mingling in a haze of sparkling harmony. It smelled of Harrow House and Netherford Hall and love and magic. And oh, Viola understood.

Poppy was not just Netherford Hall. She was the land itself. And the land would rise to meet her. And the land would fight back.

As she fell, Viola watched the entirety of Howarth Castle explode into flowers, crawling upon every surface, and thicker than a mattress over the great table at the centre of the room. Poppy, indeed, had expressed her love in the most perfect language she knew. Roland was covered in narcissus and jasmine, Ophelia in datura and belladonna, Laertes a flourish of cornflowers and periwinkles, Molly twined with honeysuckle and iris, Edith crowned with ivy and bee orchids, and Silas wrapped in moonflowers and bluebells. Each a living pillar of floral admiration and love.

Just before she lost consciousness from the poison blade's effects, Viola watched as an enormous bower of thorns twisted around Maurice until he was no longer screaming, the gentlewitch approaching him with her own blade in hand to finish the deed.

CHAPTER EIGHTEEN
LIVE, AND BE HAPPY, AND MAKE OTHERS SO

"I CAN CHANGE your appearance back, if you prefer," said Queen Tailte, as they stood by the mirror. She was preparing to take Maurice back to Faerie, his body so completely ensconced in thorns he would be imprisoned for centuries. They hoped.

Reaching up to touch his pointed ears, Silas chuckled. "I appreciate your offer, but I do not think I will."

Roland, nearby, now returned to his own human form, overheard the conversation, and turned his head to listen.

This decision was, in no small part, for him as well.

"You will be the cause of much scandal," Queen Tailte warned. "And it will likely ruin you."

He glanced over to where Viola lay, upon a soft bed of moss, while her sires and sister doted over her. The queen had healed her swiftly, but she was still in and out of consciousness as the poison slowly left her body. It would take a long time for her wing to heal properly, and she'd likely have a scar all her days.

Roland was standing by them, now, confusion on his face. "I daresay she's right, Silas. You've worked for so much, to get to this point."

"What I am has been a lie," Silas said, and did not miss the stricken look on the queen's face. This had been in no small part due to her. "But it is my legacy. Yours, and my father's. If there are others like me, perhaps I will inspire them to live more authentically. I know how exhausting it is to live in a cage."

By now, Edith had made her way over to bid farewell to Queen Tailte. The gentlewitch looked grim, her face pale. There were still bee orchids in her hair.

"I've just received word that the witch portals are all... open," Edith said. "Sophronia Pemble ran all the way from the Holly and Sickle to deliver the news."

"Open?" Roland asked.

Queen Tailte inclined her head. "Moritasgus's spell tore open through the weaker spaces in the *liminalis*, all the way through to Faerie. Edith, you must go to London to meet with the Coven Council, and perhaps even with the Prince Regent, if he will hear you. I fear we will not be able to hold back the tides forever, and we must prepare."

"Hold back the tide?" Silas asked, feeling more than a little dim.

"Faerie, and its inhabitants, are free to roam," Edith said. "The pub portals, they were pinpricks in the *liminalis*. Now, they are gateways all the way through to Faerie."

"And what of my mother?" Roland asked.

Edith, eyes full of fire, approached the fae queen. Silas thought, for a moment, she might cast a spell on her, but she managed to bank her rage. "Yes. You promised me you would give me answers. I gave you back your son, after all. After a fashion."

Queen Tailte gestured over to the other side of the room where Renard Roux stood. "He has your answer. Edith, I'm sorry for you both. I do not think the answers you seek will make your lives any easier. But for now, Roland, you will have your father's confession of the murder of Henri de Roquelaure, and will live a free man. Or wolf. However you desire. You may not have your mother's protection, but you will have mine."

As SILAS FACED down his aunt yet again in the parlour of Burkley House, he wondered about inheritance, and the legacies of their progenitors. As a fae, he would live far longer than he ever anticipated. His story, it seemed, had barely begun after all, just as he thought it was coming to an end.

"Change yourself back this instant," the dowager viscountess demanded from across the room.

Silas sat on the divan, Viola on his right, their hands entwined. She was still weak from the attack, but sat as resplendent as a queen beside him, her back straight and expression imperious.

He'd never confronted Aunt May with someone else, let alone the woman who would be his wife. And he had balked at her blustering too long. Today, he would fight, and win.

He no longer cared if she was a vampire. He no longer cared if Aunt May disinherited him. If his body had been holding this secret all his life, then he had a great deal more to learn and a lot less to worry himself with.

"That is the strange thing about legacies," Silas said softly, squeezing Viola's hand. "One cannot escape them."

"Legacy? This is no legacy. This is *heresy*," Aunt May said.

Silas had spent hours in the aftermath of what had occurred at Howarth Castle, contemplating the end of this particular chapter of his life. As he'd stood, knee-deep in flowers, tending to Viola and speaking with his mother, the shape of it had come to him in an unexpected way.

"My father fell in love with a fae woman, Aunt May. I think you know this story." He looked at his hand, grown longer and more elegant than it had been before. The lines remained the same, the fingerprints, but it was still strange to see his body so changed. "I am their child. A child of two worlds. My friends and I helped prevent a great evil from coming into England, but in the process, there are now portals to Faerie open in pubs across the realm. My legacy, it seems, hinges on who I decide to be in this moment. And I do not wish to be pushed aside, time and again, by your prejudices."

The dowager viscountess said not a single word. But she did glance over at Fintan, who now wore his horns proudly. He was also no longer a valet but promoted to First Knight of Burkely House, though Queen Tailte said he would soon be called back to her service.

"As the heir to the Byrne fortune," Viola added, leaning forward, "I have ten thousand a year, in perpetuity. Such a uniting of our two houses would mean a comfortable life for you, and for both of my families, as well as the upkeep of Burkley House."

"You are a *vampire*," the dowager viscountess said, but with far less conviction. She tutted at Silas. "And you…!" She could not even complete the sentence.

"I am as I have always been. You just never saw past the guise," Silas said.

"You were a friend to me, once, my lady, and I helped you build this home," Viola said softly. Always the peacemaker. "And I am working tirelessly to help find your missing sister. And I love your nephew, Silas, with every thread of my being. Yes, I am also a vampire. As such, it is my duty to remind you that both Silas and I will outlive you considerably. You can, for now, prevent this union. But in time, it will no longer matter."

From anyone else, the words would have been cruel. Yet Viola managed to speak to the dowager viscountess with such smooth, matter-of-fact crispness, it was almost impossible to detect the low, burning ember of anger within it.

"Parliament will not accept a creature like yourself among its ranks," the dowager viscountess said, hiding her face from them both as if their mere presence caused her pain. Perhaps it did. A small part of Silas pitied her for that. "You know I speak true."

"No, but the Coven Council will," Viola said. She presented the dowager viscountess with the letter they'd received just that morning, signed by the Countess Rocksavage, Lady Claudia Cowes, and Lady Anne Redfern. "They've seats for both the viscount and Liege Edith Rookwood, on special dispensation in Silas's case, as an official emissary of the Exiled Fae. The world has changed, my lady, and we are its new guardians. Its new legacy. For whatever the future holds for Crown and Crescent."

THE FIRST HINT of autumn chill whispered in the air as Roland took his seat beside his uncle Renard. They had chosen the Holly and Sickle as their meeting place, and along with Edith and Poppy, they were meant to discuss the matter of the High Witch. Against his better judgement, Roland did quite like Renard. He was foppish and daring, and just a little chaotic, and he took considerable comfort in that. It was good to see a family resemblance, especially now.

Renard had also lived the last ten years as a spy, moving among the Grey Moon Brotherhood as one of them. He was a font of knowledge, but none of it was good.

As suspected, the werewolves of the Grey Moon were behind the High Witch's absence. But not in the way any of them had imagined.

"The Grey Moon Knights report directly to the Prince Regent," Renard said, leaning forward. He had rusty red hair, though it was greying at the temples, and freckles across most of his skin. "And I know by firsthand account that the High Witch is being held in a cell under Coldbath Fields Prison. Or she was. I suspect, now that they know my deceptions, she'll be moved. That is how Moritasgus was feeding upon her blood, mixing it to make *azothine*, fueling his followers and expanding his magic."

Roland's head swam with those implications. "And the Prince Regent was aware? Does that mean the Prince Regent had her committed directly?"

Renard nodded gravely, squeezing his hands together as if he could wring some sense out of it. "It seems so, though I have no absolute proof. I know her capture was approved by him. I have no idea how they're keeping her subdued, but I have my suspicions. Like other werewolves, we do take tonics to prevent the change from time to time. One of the primary ingredients has been extremely difficult to find since her disappearance."

"Silvered wormwood, I know," Roland mused. He only knew that detail from peeking at Basil's old notes while he was sleeping. Not that he was sneaking up on him during his convalescence or any such thing. That would be absurd. Basil had also been discussing growing his own patch to meet the demand. In high enough quantities, though, silvered wormwood could render a gentlewitch impotent.

"You would need a constant supply for a witch of her power," Edith said, quietly. "And now that we cannot be certain Faerie is secured, I fear for us without her assistance."

Renard favoured the gentlewitch with a glowing smile. "We have you, though. And that is a mighty comforting thought, my liege. I know you are yet learning what this means, but Navia's Heir walking among us is a beacon of hope for all of the wolves who remain." He looked at

Roland. "And you… Your return has given us reason to believe."

"If only my mother were here to explain herself. I have spent a lifetime avoiding my nature, and perhaps, in time, I will learn to live with it," Roland said. Still, he had gravely injured Basil in his fragile state. If he were to come up against the Grey Moon Brotherhood again, he could be susceptible to their powers for a second time. Would he stop at maiming? Could he murder outright? A frisson of warning, and a familiar self-hatred, sunk its teeth into Roland's mind.

No. He most certainly was not ready to live again as a werewolf.

Edith returned Renard's smile. Tired though she looked, Roland could not help but see the change in her. He could feel her power. In any other person, he might have been wary of her strength, the influence she had over him and over all the pack. Instead, it was a rightness. A welcome direction.

Poppy came by the table, at last, with a platter laden with fragrant cheese, compotes, biscuits, and dried meat. She was resplendent, her cheeks flushed, and a mischievous look in her eyes. Roland found he adored the woman more and more each day.

"Enough sombre discussion. Edith's due at Parliament tomorrow, and we must celebrate our last day of freedom," Poppy scolded. "Come, let us drink to the future, whatever it may hold, and peace between mortals and preternaturals, at last."

Viola sat on her favourite bench at Burkely House, enjoying the last rays of the sunset as they melted across the lawn. From her vantage point, she could see the last of the asters shivering in the breeze, their ragged heads bobbing back and forth as hectic bees danced from bloom to bloom. She never tired of looking at the bees. So single-minded, so utterly besotted with their work, covered in fragrant honey, their wings dazzling in the sunlight. She envied them their purpose, sometimes.

Silas's heartbeat had changed since his transformation, but she could still hear it from a good distance. He seemed to be more aware of her now, as well, seeking her out whenever possible, lips and hands ready to pull passion from her and whisper words of love.

It had been a week since they had defeated Maurice, and today the dowager viscountess was making her decision on Silas's future. They had tried to speak sense to the old woman, but she had remained resolute. The title did not matter to Viola, really, but this place... This place was everything to her. Losing Burkley House felt a terrible blow.

Sitting down beside her in the little bower of willow trees, Silas presented her with a bouquet of roses so deep red, they were almost black.

She gazed at Silas, her heart squeezing with the dearness of his features. As a mortal man, he had been remarkably handsome; in his fae form, he was devastating. The hazel of his eyes was so much more pronounced, green and gold spiralling into a kaleidoscope of hues more vivid than anything else Viola could see.

"I may not be able to see as many colours as before," she said to him, "but your eyes pierce me to my very soul, and I would have it no other way."

Silas smiled, scooting closer to her. "I didn't mean to disturb you out here, but I thought if I did, I ought to come with flowers."

"A bouquet of roses eases many ills, but I suppose you are here to discuss the dowager viscountess."

In the distance, the parish bells began ringing, and a fleet of doves took flight, the scent of harvest on the air.

After a long breath, Silas said: "The dowager viscountess is unmoved. She will not allow me to pass the title of Viscountess St. Albans to you. Not while she lives."

"Well, it was not the title I was after," Viola said, turning to drape a leg over his. The bower was especially nice for its privacy, and she did love the taste of his skin in the outdoors.

She placed a searing kiss upon his lips and felt him smile in response, knowing that devious dimple of his would be showing. But he pushed her away, gently, and handed her a small envelope.

"What's this?" she asked.

"Open it."

Viola's heart raced, reading the words of the highly official looking document twice over before understanding. Mostly. Disappointment descended upon her. It was the deed to Burkley House, but signed over to a name she did not recognise.

"D. B. Mansfield?" she asked. "Who on earth is that?"

"*I* am D. B. Mansfield," Silas laughed. "I told you; I write novels. And, as it turns out, once her venom was fully unleashed, the dowager viscountess had no desire to stay here and allowed me to broker the house through an acquaintance of mine. She cannot take *all* my fortune, after all. So, I have given her the legacy of Bellechamp House, along with her death's grip upon the St. Albans title, and D. B. Mansfield is signing this home to you."

She glanced up, fretfully trying to put the pieces together. "Burkley House?"

"It is more yours than it's ever been mine. And there's plenty of room for your whole family to live and visit. Both families, I mean. If they'd like," Silas said. "I'll start looking for a place in London for us while Parliament is in session,

344

but for now… I will remain the Viscount St. Albans, if only in name."

Viola squealed and threw herself into Silas's arms, crying and laughing. She felt so perfectly happy, so wonderfully calm, it seemed almost unfair on so many others in Netherford. With one of the most active portals to the fae, the whole town was in an uproar. But she would not allow herself to dampen the moment of joy; she and Silas had worked hard for this.

Pulling back to gaze into Silas's eyes, she just soaked in the beauty of him, the grace and the love in his expression. "I don't know how to reply, Silas. Only that I love you. And thank you."

He tilted his head and kissed her cheek, then her other cheek, then her forehead. When he pulled away again, he had produced a simple silver ring and held it out to her.

"Viola Brightwell, would you do me the honour of being my wife? I cannot yet give you the title you deserve, but you will be styled Lady Viola Drake, my beloved. Well, that last part I will keep to myself."

She did say yes, but it was quickly hushed as they began kissing in earnest, falling down to the soft, mossy bower ground, and revelling in one another's bodies until the sun sank below the horizon and the last fireflies danced.

BASIL HODE WAS in a foul mood, and the last person he wanted to see was Roland de Grateloup. He still dreamed of that attack on the balcony at Burkley House, the feeling of utter betrayal and terror waking him drenched in sweat, cradling his arm as pain ricocheted through his body. It had taken a week for him to get any feeling back into his fingers, and then another week be sure he wasn't going to lose the arm altogether after infection set in.

As it stood, he was still unable to do much with his dominant left arm. Which meant preparing highly unstable ingredients for tonics was an excruciating business—and with half a pack in and out of Netherford these days, he was both exhausted and resentful from their requests. And the wards were broken, perhaps irreparably so, leaving him feeling adrift. Molly was with the gentlewitch and Poppy in London, and he'd been assigned, yet again, to patrol Burkley House.

Roland, of course, looked healthier than ever. In the anticipation of autumn, he'd chosen a burnt orange frock coat and beautifully glossy boots, a bow slung across his shoulder. He practically shone.

"There you are, Basil," he said, as if he was surprised to find him in anywhere other than the Warder's cottage on the premises. It used to be the gardener's, but with Viola in residence, and Poppy visiting so often, there was no need for a full-time tender.

"Mr. de Grateloup." Basil did not look up from his work, which was time-consuming and precarious, even when he had use of both of his arms.

Roland watched Basil for a moment as the Warder worked the resin out of a long trench of wood. It had been imported all the way from Persia and had a wonderful smell to it: dark amber and smoke. Medicinally, it was excellent for a number of reasons, including alleviating pain. For now, however, it was for the gentlewitch's personal use.

"That scent is absolutely intoxicating," Roland said, creeping forward with anticipation. "It reminds me of a perfume I sampled in Paris once."

"Yes. It's been long used in such a capacity," Basil said, brushing at his upper lip. It still felt strange, not having a moustache, but as he couldn't tidy it himself any longer, he'd opted for a clean shave every morning. "But this sort is reserved primarily for the use of gentlewitches. Fae-touched, they say. Not to be pawed through by werewolves."

Roland snorted. "I do not 'paw through' things. I have an elegant touch."

"I'm sure," Basil said. He did not share that this wood, oud, also helped alleviate symptoms of melancholy, which had kept Basil in a nasty corner these last weeks.

"Well, I just wanted to drop by and invite you to come with us down to the dell. A flock of doves has just moved in, and I think they'd make an excellent dinner," Roland said, all in a rush. It was unlike him to be so.

Basil looked up at him. "I cannot pull a bow. If you recall, de Grateloup, you nearly ripped my arm from my body a few weeks ago."

Roland stared, mouth agape, red creeping up his cheeks. "Of course. I—my mistake. I mean, entirely. I should apologise. Again. Profusely. I was not myself. You're the *last* person I'd have wanted to hurt."

The phrasing on that last part was most peculiar. Basil finally glanced back up at Roland, who was making for the door. Had he been in wolf form, his tail would have been neatly tucked between his legs.

"Good day, de Grateloup," Basil called after him. Though he could not say why he hated saying those words, why part of him recoiled at the idea of speaking so harshly to the werewolf. But he deserved it.

He started when Roland spoke again. He'd thought him gone.

"I suppose you could start your own perfumery," said the werewolf. "If you needed something to do with a little less risk. It really does smell magnificent in here. And you seem to have all the ingredients you'd ever want—plus a neighbour who exudes flowers."

Roland plucked a little heliotrope from his breast pocket

and placed it next to Basil, its bright purple blooms brilliant against the copper table.

And indeed, the almond-bright scent of the flower mixed with the oud, and Basil let out a sigh of utter pleasure as he crushed the blooms between his resinous fingers. "Brimstone, but you're right, Roland."

Alas, the werewolf had already departed, and Basil was left alone to contemplate his future in perfumed silence.

Basil, Roland, and the rest will return in
The Game of Hearts.

ACKNOWLEDGEMENTS

USUALLY, I START books with characters. They show up, typically unprovoked, and just begin speaking. Sometimes, like Roland de Grateloup, they are incessant chatterers who take on a life of their own whether or not I had planned their existence, and before I know it they have entire points of view in my novels. Then there are the quieter ones, like Silas Drake, who linger in the margins of one story, only to have very curious inner lives and complexities I had not imagined.

Silas and Viola are not bold, brash characters like many of those in my fictional Kentish village, but when Viola walked into the Holly and Sickle in *Netherford Hall* and recognized Silas from his portrait, I knew they would be my next couple to tackle. There is something powerful in quiet love, and an unexpected sizzle when things truly kindle. Although they both deal with their own challenges in very different ways, their struggle is similar: both exist in spaces they did not necessarily want, but hold onto with a sense of duty. And in order for their love to work, they both must let go of something essential: Silas to his Parliament seat and reputation, and Viola to her old self.

Silas is patterned after Colonel Brandon in Austen's *Sense and Sensibility*, though a bit younger and eventually more bold—there is power in a man who becomes steadfast, a reformed rake who finds himself comfortable in the country and more than a little surprised by love. Roland teases him for being too serious, but Silas has had to carry the burden of his father's scandalous financial ruin on his own. Ultimately, it is not his status that saves him, but his hobby as a writer. A little fanciful liberty on my behalf, there.

Viola has echoes of Marianne Dashwood, though her overly emotional sensibility comes more from her change into a vampire than anything else. Like Marianne, her sickness is a pivotal part of her growth, but it is not just an illness of her body. Viola must confront her own inner demons, one way or another, and with little to no help for her very well meaning sires, Ophelia and Laertes. But ultimately, it is only Silas who can truly get through to her, with time and patience and attention.

Of course, it's a joy to continue Edith and Poppy's story as well, as their love grows, is challenged, and changes through the series. *The Game of Hearts* will answer many more questions about Navia's Heir, the consequences of Maurice's magic, and whether or not Basil finally admits his affections for Roland, and vice versa. The stakes get bigger, but love still wins.

Thank you to all my readers who have followed me to Netherford. This series has been such a joy to write.

To Brian Barrier for playing hours of *Baldur's Gate III* with me, but *only after I finished writing my words for the day*.

To the writers at Larian Games for creating Astarion, from the very same game, who in no small way inspired parts of Roland.

To my husband Michael, whose love is quiet and fierce.

To Jennifer, always.

To my sister Llana and the magic we shared as children.

To Dino Hicks, a hero among readers.

To my dog, Axel, who rested his head on my arms as I typed good portions of this book. Good boy.

To my *Worldbuilding for Masochists* co-hosts, Cass Morris and Marshall Ryan Maresca. What a joy and an honor it is to know you both.

Once again, gratitude to David Thomas Moore and the whole gang at Solaris.

Stacey Graham, my GOAT agent, who fell in love with Netherford first.

And to everyone brave enough to live their truth by their own terms.

December 2024

ABOUT THE AUTHOR

Natania Barron is an award-winning fantasy author long preoccupied with mythology, monsters, and magic. Her often historically-inspired novels are filled with lush description and vibrant characters. Publications include her 2011 debut, *Pilgrim of the Sky*, as well as *These Marvelous Beasts*, a collection of novellas.

In 2020, Barron's *Queen of None* was hailed as "a captivating look at the intriguing figures in King Arthur's golden realm" by *Kirkus*, and won the Manly Wade Wellman award the following year.

Her shorter works have appeared in *Weird Tales*, EscapePod, and various anthologies, RPG, and game settings. In addition, she's also known for #ThreadTalk, which dives deep into the unseen, and often forgotten, world of fashion history.

Barron lives in North Carolina, USA, with her family and two dogs. When she's not writing, you can find her wandering the woods, tending her garden, and collecting rocks.

🦋 @natania.bsky.social
🐦 @nataniabarron
📷 @nataniabarron
♪ @nataniabooks
🌐 www.nataniabarron.com

FIND US ONLINE!

www.rebellionpublishing.com

/solarisbooks   /solarisbks   /solarisbooks

SIGN UP TO OUR NEWSLETTER!

rebellionpublishing.com/newsletter

YOUR REVIEWS MATTER!

Enjoy this book? Got something to say?

Leave a review on Amazon, GoodReads or with your
favourite bookseller and let the world know!